Also by LK Hunsaker

Off The Moon (2009)
Protect The Heart (2010)
Moondrops & Thistles (2011)

The Rehearsal Series (2006-)

Rehearsal: A Different Drummer
Rehearsal: The Highest Aim
Rehearsal: Of Chaotic Currents

For Children

Stanley: A Raindrop's Story (2010)

The gallery

~~~

Finishing Touches & Final Strokes
in one edition

~~~

LK Hunsaker

The gallery. Copyright ©2013 LK Hunsaker. All rights reserved. No part of this book may be used or reproduced in any form or by any means without written permission from the publisher, except for brief quotes in reviews and scholarly works.

This is a work of fiction. Names, characters, places, and incidents either are the product of the author's imagination or are used fictitiously. Any resemblance to actual events or locales or persons, living or dead, is entirely coincidental.

ISBN 978-0-9825299-7-3

Finishing Touches
1st edition Infinity Publishing 2003 ISBN 0-7414-1647-6

Cover painting and design by LK Hunsaker
LKHunsaker.com

Elucidate Publishing
elucidatepublishing.net
PO Box 1262 Hermitage PA 16148

United States of America

Finishing Touches and *Final Strokes* also available in separate electronic editions.

*"To send light into the darkness of men's hearts
- such is the duty of the artist."*

Robert Schumann

Finishing Touches

One

Jenna inhaled deeply, allowing crisp fall air to invade her body. Feeling a nip of winter creep through the open window, she pulled the plush blanket higher around her baby's shoulders. Jenna loved the precious time spent rocking her child to sleep while he snuggled into her breast. During these moments, she felt the most connected to her only love. She also missed him the most vividly.

Running her fingertips over Aaron's tiny head, Jenna studied the perfect little features, so like his father's. Daniel had never tried to conceal the pride he felt whenever someone mentioned how much his son resembled him. He considered the child his greatest work of art, and his most important. Jenna's husband had been many things, but humble was never one of them. She couldn't help a grin at recalling his admission that he was a good-looking guy. And he really was, or had been. Even after he got sick and lost too much weight, his features were perfect and his eyes absolutely beautiful.

She snuggled her baby closer and returned her gaze to beyond the window. The view from their loft was breathtaking at this time of the year, with hundreds of maple trees along the banks of the Illinois River boasting their shades of red and yellow and green and brown. The Spirit of Peoria, a reproduction of the beloved old riverboats, often sailed by with passengers walking the decks or standing at the rails. Six years earlier, Jenna and Daniel watched the Julia Belle Swain together whenever they caught it floating along the river. Once, covered only with a sheet pulled from their bed, they had stood before the large window and talked of taking the short cruise on the old paddle-wheel. Some day.

"Some day" had never come. Neither had so many other days they planned. Their time together centered around his painting, but then, he told her to expect that. She hadn't argued when he refused to go out because he was working or when she had to go to bed alone. She had been warned and willingly accepted his terms. The naiveté of youth, Jenna mused. Now, there was no later for them. The Julia Belle and Daniel were both gone.

His baby stirred in her arms and Jenna coerced herself to rise slowly, moving across the loft to settle Aaron in his crib. Convinced he was still asleep, she wandered into the kitchen to pour a cup of mint tea, a habit she developed while carrying her first child. Daniel's mother suggested it might help settle her stomach and it seemed to work. Even well after the morning sickness was gone, Jenna continued the routine and joked with her husband that maybe he should try it as well, to calm his nerves. He didn't like mint tea. He didn't like boats either, except at a distance. Alan once said Daniel's work was the only interest they shared. Jenna quickly pointed out her advanced pregnancy proved him wrong. Her friend hadn't been amused.

Not sure what to do with herself while Aaron slept, Jenna returned to the beautifully carved oak rocking chair, a gift from her mother-in-law. Joan was nearly as excited as her son when he and Jenna were expecting their first child and she wasted no time making sure they had everything they needed. Jenna hadn't heard from Joan recently. She considered trying to call but she would have to talk to two or three other people just to get through and then most likely have to leave a message. She wasn't up to that. A fleeting thought of calling her own mother surfaced, then dissipated. She would only try again to invite Jenna to some social gathering. And Jenna's sister-in-law would insist on coming over and staying the day, with the kids. She wasn't up to that, either.

Alan. He would be at work, but she could talk to Cheryl for a few minutes until her twins interrupted. Jenna didn't want to talk to him, anyway. She only needed to feel the connection, to know he was there.

She dialed his number without stopping to think about it. She knew it better than her own. His voice startled her. After another prompt, she gathered herself enough to answer, grimacing at the shakiness of her voice.

"Jenna, what's wrong? Are you okay?"

She hesitated again. No, she wasn't, but she wouldn't tell him that. "Yeah, I'm fine."

"You don't sound fine."

With an attempt at composure, she fumbled for something to say now that he was on the phone. "I'm surprised you answered. I figured you'd be at work."

"We just finished a big job. I gave everyone the day off."

"Oh? How'd it go?"

"Another Nicklaus project."

Jenna grinned at the term. Nicklaus had been one of her friend's first clients, never satisfied and constantly insisting on changes. When she was been meeting Alan on Sundays for dessert and coffee, Jenna would hear about all of the complaints and revisions of the week and make jokes to put him in a better mood. It always worked.

"Jenna?" Alan's voice called her back.

"Sorry, I thought maybe you'd heard enough complaints recently and I should stay quiet."

"Do you want me to come over?"

Yes, she very much wanted him to come over. "No, I'm fine. I was just checking in to see how you guys are doing. Is Justin over the flu?"

"Jenna, that was two weeks ago."

She paused, holding her breath and wishing she hadn't called.

"I'm coming over."

"Alan, it's your day off. You should spend it with your family."

"My family is fine; you're not. I'll be right there." He didn't give her time to respond before she heard the click from his end.

Oh, hell. She wasn't ready for company. She hadn't gone out in nearly a week or showered in two days, and there were dishes in the sink and baby toys and blankets on the floor. Without time to shower and clean both, Jenna decided her own cleanliness would be more noticeable, so she checked on her sleeping son and jumped into the warm water.

The doorbell found her almost presentable as she slipped into one of Daniel's shirts, and she rolled the sleeves while heading to the door. A slow, deep breath prepared her for Alan's visit.

He glanced at her wet locks. "Hey, Jen. You didn't have to shower for me." He gave her a kiss on the cheek in his usual casual style.

"You didn't have to come over." She studied her friend. All the work he did outside was so good for him. He always had a beautiful tan and well-toned muscles. Daniel had been very pale-skinned and burned easily.

"It sounded like you need company. Has your sister-in-law been over recently?"

"No, her kids have been sick, too, and she didn't want to give it to us. I guess that's what I was thinking when I asked about Justin." She motioned for him to step in and closed the door softly. Aaron even slept as lightly as his father had.

Alan scanned the area as he strode easily to the small couch. Everything in the loft was small, except the space still reserved for Daniel's easels and canvases and large paint-stained work table.

Jenna followed her friend and wished she'd cleaned up earlier. "Do you want a drink? I think all I have is juice, but I can make tea."

"No, I'm fine. Come sit down."

Sitting alone with him was the last thing she wanted. She could hide her emotions from everyone else but could never keep anything from Alan. They had been friends since his family moved in across the street when Jenna was eleven, and she spent more of her teenage years with him and his family than with her parents.

As a distraction, she went to the sink and turned water on to part fill the metal basin. Alan moved to her side and took the dishes from her hands to dry, talking easily of his kids and his job. He never brought up his wife unless Jenna asked about her. She knew they got along well. They always had. Cheryl was a wonderful person, devoted to her family and especially to her husband. And she was a neat freak. Her house was always immaculate. How she did it with three kids, Jenna couldn't begin to imagine. But Cheryl completely adored Alan and he never did anything to upset her.

A quiet fuss from the opposite end of the room drew her out of her thoughts and she went to collect her baby from the crib which had claimed part of Daniel's studio space. Alan set to work putting the dishes away as she sat down to nurse Aaron. She knew it made her friend uncomfortable when she nursed in front of him, although she kept herself covered and Cheryl had nursed all three of their babies. But there was no such thing as privacy in the loft, unless she wanted to disappear behind the curtain that hid their bed ... her bed ... from the living area. And she didn't want to sit back there right now. She often slept curled up on the couch instead of going to Daniel's bed alone.

Her mother tried to convince her to move since Jenna had no further reason to live in an art studio, but she couldn't bring herself to sell it and couldn't move out and leave it empty. Maybe she would get around to redecorating some day, make it presentable for company. A useless idea, Jenna laughed to herself, since she was out of the habit of entertaining and was content to let it match her memory of the first time she stepped inside. She still thought of that moment as the rebirth into her new life – the life of her own choosing.

Her parents had worked everything out for her from the beginning. Their only child would graduate with honors from the school close to where they had carefully chosen to live, then attend the University of Illinois, as they both had. After getting to know Alan and his family well, her mother decided they would be the perfect match.

Alan was two years older than Jenna, a very good student, responsible, hard working and well-mannered. His parents weren't in the same social class as Jenna's parents, but Alan could get there with his career plans. He would also graduate from U of I and work on building a foundation for a family the following two years Jenna would need to finish school. Then they could marry and Jenna could start on her own career.

There were only two major problems with the plan. Alan had been intent on getting a job after earning his associates in horticulture from Illinois Central College and continuing school after building his bank account. And Jenna never had any interest in marrying Alan. He was her friend, nothing more.

Illinois Central. The junior college in East Peoria hadn't entered her mind in a long while. She wondered if any of its students could possibly have memories of the school that would come even close to equaling her own. Alan tried to talk her into going there after high school. He'd said it was the perfect place to decide what she wanted to do. She could take some basic classes as well as some that sounded interesting and would eventually find something to hold her easily-distracted attention. He even took her with him during spring break of her senior year to check it out. That was where she met Daniel.

She did like art, so Alan asked his art professor to let her sit in on his basic drawing class. Jenna could still see it clearly.

The students studied an elegant round vase that sat atop an old, weathered crate. The vase held a large handful of wildflowers. Jenna loved the mixture of old and new, of smooth and rough, of splintering grayness and soft pastels. And the flowers were fresh. Their scent mingled with the dampness of the basement classroom.

She felt out of place being the only person, other than the professor, not trying to capture the objects with charcoal and newsprint. The quiet was disarming, broken only by soft scratches made by budding artists and the occasional creak of metal stools or tapping of a nervous foot against the concrete floor.

The professor, a man who looked like he had been teaching a good many years, crept silently around the circle of art tables, stopping occasionally to study a student's technique but not interfering in his work. Until he came to an intense-looking male sitting directly across from Jenna. She had noticed the guy immediately upon entering, first because he was the only one with the initiative to begin working before class officially started, and then, because he seemed totally unaware of anyone else in the room. He had the darkest hair she had ever seen on someone so pale, and had strong, but small, features. She thought he had occasionally looked over at her while drawing the still life but scorned herself for even thinking that he would. She just happened to be behind the object he studied.

The professor stood over his shoulder. "Mr. Rhodes, you seem to have overshot the still life I so carefully set up this morning."

The young artist didn't bother to stop sketching. "I wasn't interested in drawing flowers, so I found something I was interested in."

Jenna waited for the reaction as a couple of others snickered. Surprisingly, the older man threw a crooked grin behind the artist's head and moved on to the next student. "This must be why Einstein received poor marks in school."

There was no response. The interruption hadn't stopped his work. Jenna had a hard time keeping her eyes from him. He still seemed to be watching her.

With twenty minutes left of the hour, it was time for critiques. The students, all in turn, set their drawings up on an easel and listened to comments from the others. The defiant, but good-natured, young man found something constructive to say about each and was the last to place his work up for review.

Jenna gasped. She sat for a moment staring at her own face with an increasing warmth in her cheeks. He had taken the liberty of drawing her shoulders uncovered, luckily not getting any farther than her shoulders, but the likeness was incredible. He received plenty of compliments from the class and the professor finally asked for her opinion.

"What?" She couldn't look at the artist who had made her blush.

"I think he should hear what you think of his work."

She felt Alan's eyes on her. He would not be happy about this. But the class was waiting. Jenna focused on the drawing. "It's ... better than real life." Catching a glimpse of the artist's grin, she looked away quickly. He packed his things and left the room.

"Jenna? What are you thinking so hard about?"

Alan's voice drew her from her memories, and she took a deep, quick breath. "College."

"Oh? Are you thinking about going?" He sat back against the couch, keeping his eyes away from the feeding baby.

"Going? Me?"

"Why not?"

"To do what?"

"Didn't you just say you were thinking about college?"

"Yes, but..." She stopped short, not about to admit where her thoughts had been.

He slowly stood and moved to the chair on the opposite side of the small end table. "Jen, I know the baby is still young enough you want to stay home with him, but you should at least start thinking about what you're going to do."

"The baby has a name. His name is Aaron, after his father, Daniel Aaron. I know you never liked him, but I loved him and I still love him and I can't even think about the future. All I can handle now is day to day and sometimes I'm not sure I can handle that." She lowered her voice as her baby objected and adjusted herself to raise him to her shoulder.

Rubbing his back helped her relax and she apologized to her friend. "Alan, you know I had no idea what I wanted before Daniel, and I sure as hell don't know what to do now."

"I know." He lowered his eyes while she refastened her nursing bra but now faced her directly. "Jenna, I never disliked Daniel."

"Then why did you stop coming over?"

"Because he didn't want me here."

"I wanted you here."

"You could have come to our place any time. Cheryl loves to visit with you. You didn't have to isolate yourself because Daniel wanted to be isolated."

"He didn't want to be isolated, he just..."

"Wanted to be left alone to work. I know, but he did isolate you. You always had a bunch of friends in school you never see anymore. Have you even talked with Karla recently?"

She shook her head. He was right. She missed running around with her cousin and chatting about anything and everything.

"I didn't dislike him; I just didn't like what he was doing to you."

"It was my choice and I loved being with him."

"But you lost yourself."

"No. Alan, I found myself with Daniel. I was lost before him and I'm even more lost without him now."

He began to argue but decided against it. "Jen, come spend the day with us."

With the happy couple and their three kids? "No, thank you. I don't really feel like going out."

"Maybe not, but you need to. There's a new art exhibition at Lakeview. Why don't we go see it?"

Art? "No."

"Jenna..."

"No. Alan, I can't."

"Okay, what about the zoo? The kids have been bugging us to take them again."

"Then you should do that. We're fine right here."

Her tone made it clear he wouldn't be able to change her mind and he gave in. "Well, I'm going to go. Cheryl didn't mind me coming, but I think she looked forward to having the day together, so..."

"So, you should spend time with your family, like I told you over the phone." She hadn't meant it as harshly as the look in his eyes said it sounded. Well, she couldn't help that. She asked him not to come.

Aaron started to fuss for the rest of his meal and Alan insisted she not get up to see him out. Jenna refused to watch him leave, but the click of the door nearly changed her mind. The rest of the day would be only her and her baby, again.

Cradling Aaron in the other arm, she appreciated the grateful expression he threw for letting him finish.

At least she had him. And he was strong and healthy. How could Alan have expected she would visit him and his pregnant wife after she lost Daniel's first child? Her friend wouldn't have had to stop coming over because Daniel didn't want to visit. She had wanted to see Alan, not his wife who reminded her of what she lost. Her husband hadn't isolated her. Losing his baby had isolated her. He wanted children. He had wanted children maybe even more than he wanted her. They were the link to the future he somehow knew he wouldn't have of his own. And she couldn't have handled walking around watching all of the families laughing and talking and making her feel like such a failure for not being able to carry her baby full-term.

But Daniel had loved her, even if she failed him.

The time he had given her always felt too limited, but it had been complete, and intense. Nothing distracted him from what he chose as his focus, and he focused on her often enough to keep her from feeling neglected, except for their bad time. She wouldn't let herself think about that. There was no point. Instead, she chose to remember how he picked her out from the crowds of girls around the campus.

After the art class, Alan left her sitting in the center area of the college. The main building of Illinois Central formed a nearly complete oval around a large open area paved with the same red brick. It reminded Jenna of an old amphitheater, the way the oval dropped into different levels. She could still clearly see the picnic tables scattered around the upper level, with students propped on their seats. A few were studying, but most chatted with others between classes. The narrow mid level was interrupted by short, wide columns of brick holding small trees, providing additional seats for loungers who wanted slight shade. The lowest level, only several inches from the highest, was free of obstacles and Jenna watched three males use it as a Frisbee court. She kept her eyes averted from the guy who had removed his shirt and shoes and was lying on a towel in his shorts with his head propped on his backpack. She thought it was still a little cool for tanning, but the sky was absolutely cloudless and the air was fresh following last night's spring shower.

She had chosen to sit just below the highest step and nearly against one of the tree columns. She didn't need it for support, preferring to sit with her legs crossed in front, but she didn't want to be too much in the open. Pulling her eyes from the Frisbee game, Jenna went back to her book.

"What are you reading?"

The voice was less startling than the face she found. It was the defiant young artist. He casually planted himself next to her, lifting the book enough to see the cover.

"The Agony and the Ecstasy? That's a good one. Have you read Lust for Life? Same author."

"No, not yet. I just finished Love Is Eternal."

"Irving Stone fan?"

"I'm becoming one." She stole glances of his face as he studied her overtly.

"So, where's your friend?"

Friend. Was he trying to find out more than he asked? "He's in botany."

"Botany? On purpose?"

Jenna couldn't help grinning at his expression, and she agreed with him. "He's studying to be a landscape engineer. He understands all that stuff."

He nodded, amused. "And you? What do you want to be?"

"I don't have the slightest idea."

His eyes pierced her skin as they ran down her arms, touched her fingers, and then returned to her face. "Have you ever considered being a model?"

Was he joking? He didn't look like he was. So, he was either hitting on her or crazy. "I know you can't be serious." Jenna knew she wasn't model material. She wasn't built badly but was constantly fighting five or ten pounds she didn't want and her features were too masculine for her taste. She had always wanted her jaw line to be less square and her eyes to be less narrow. Her mother had taught her tricks with carefully applied makeup to round out her jaw and widen her eyes, and she had pulled her long hair into a loose bun, leaving a couple of wisps to curl at the sides of her face. But she still wasn't model material.

"I'm very serious." The intense eyes continued to study her. "I thought you were being modest earlier, but you honestly have no idea how beautiful you are."

Jenna again felt her cheeks get warm and pulled her eyes away to watch the Frisbee players.

"I'm sorry, I didn't mean to embarrass you. I have a terrible habit of saying what I think. But I always tell the truth, and I don't waste my time drawing or *painting anything I don't want to see again."*

Her son pulled away, letting her know his tummy was sufficiently filled for the time being.

Jenna studied his round cheeks and square jaw. Aaron had inherited some of her appearance, though he looked much more like Daniel. Five and a half months old already. Maybe it was time to give him cereal. Wasn't that what the pediatrician had suggested? She would have to go out to get it since she hadn't thought that far ahead. She supposed she could. It wasn't like she had any other plans, but she would likely run into someone who would insist on offering condolences again. Jenna didn't want to deal with that today. Maybe she should have accepted Alan's offer. He was good at running interference whenever the subject arose, and she missed talking to him.

With Aaron propped against her left side, she reached over to pick up the receiver, started dialing, then set it down again. She hadn't been very nice after he had gone to the trouble of coming over. He would understand, though. He always had. But the zoo? Did she really want to go there?

Jenna pushed herself off the couch and walked over to the sketches still hanging along the corkboard strip which ran the length of the studio wall. Finding the one in her mind, she sat in front of it, holding Daniel's son close against her heart, and studied the image she could still feel. Her mother asked every time she came over, which thankfully wasn't often, when she intended to pack Daniel's things and try to sell the sketches. Jenna didn't intend to do either. The loft was their home and it would stay their home.

But maybe Aaron could use some fresh air. Aaron Matthew, after Daniel Aaron and Alan Matthew. She took a long, deep breath, then made herself get up.

She again found the voice she wasn't looking for at the other end of the telephone. "Cheryl, hi, is Alan there?"

"*Hi,* Jenna. He's outside; we were just leaving. Did you want to change your mind and come with?"

He told her she refused. He surely didn't say how rude she'd been.

"Did you need to talk to him personally?"

"Oh, no. Just ... are you sure you wouldn't mind the intrusion?"

"Of *course* not." She sounded genuinely happy. "Should we come by and pick you up?"

"No, the baby seat's already in my car. I'll meet you there."

Two

She ambled, nearly scuffing her feet, toward the entrance and stopped in front of a large stone slab bearing the words Glen Oak Zoo. The sign from which a security guard tried to kick her off until Daniel showed him the sketch in progress. The sketch that became the first of several Daniel made as zoo advertisements to help pay for her engagement ring. The only one he turned into a painting. He didn't care much for drawing animals, but he enjoyed capturing images of children as they pointed excitedly or pulled back nervously, and he often talked about bringing his own child to sketch with the goats in the petting area, when he had a child.

With a sigh, Jenna unhooked the buckle and pulled Aaron from the small navy stroller that looked like paint had been thrown all over it. That was how Denise explained her choice of patterns when she gave it to them. Jenna remarked that the multi-colored splotches were too neat. The manufacturers should have looked at Daniel's jeans if they were trying to achieve an actual paint-splashed look. The colors needed to overlap and be different shapes, with finger-size streaks here and there. Daniel had laughed and suggested his wife join his mother's fashion design company to create a painter's line.

Aaron gasped as the light breeze hit his mouth and Jenna turned his head into her shoulder, running a hand over his shiny dark hair. She stepped closer to the sign, touching her fingers to the coolness of the stone. The sensation triggered memories of her bare legs resting on top of the granite while Daniel carefully but quickly captured the scene with his charcoal stick. He always sketched in charcoal. He said he could get more life in a charcoal sketch than in a pencil sketch.

The leg lying against the stone took a while to get warm again; the other was propped up so only the bottom of her foot was cold. Daniel asked her to remove her sandals because it was more natural and fitting for a zoo sign. He was the one to convince her that true art was more felt than learned. It had to come from deep within the soul.

"Are you coming in?"

Startled by a voice, she calmed her son while recognition alighted. Jenna turned to face her friend. "Yeah, I was just..."

"There's nowhere in the city you can go without thinking of him, is there?" Alan set a hand on her shoulder. "It really is a beautiful painting, the one of you sitting here. It's always been one of my favorites."

"Mom keeps saying I should sell it, but it's special to me, too."

"Jen, ignore her. She never understood."

"Did you?" Jenna looked at him.

"I have always understood you, more than you could know." He pulled his hand away. "Come on, the kids are probably driving Cheryl crazy waiting to go in."

Jenna didn't protest when he took control of the stroller, but she kept her baby in her arms. And Alan didn't argue when someone remarked what a beautiful baby they had. When his own children ran to his side, however, he had to give up helping her to become father and professor, doing his best to answer questions. She reluctantly set her son back in his seat and strolled along next to Cheryl.

Alan's wife was a willing companion, always glad to have other adults around with whom she could share her daily events. Justin, her oldest, was barely four and his biggest thrill was doing anything with his father. He had Alan's medium brown hair and greenish brown eyes along with his grandmother's small build, and his metal-framed glasses constantly slipped down his tiny nose. Jenna couldn't help a special affection for the child. Tranquil and serious, Justin had a real kindness about him. Animals were his passion.

Alex and Rae, the twins, were nearly three and larger-boned like their parents. Cheryl talked about them constantly, how they were more accomplices than siblings. There was never a time when only one was mischievous, and they couldn't sit still for a minute. Their brother had been content, since birth, playing quietly with his own things, but the twins were constantly into something, and always in it together.

Jenna half-listened to their most recent adventures as she watched Alan with his kids. Justin was more like Jenna than like his father, but Alan seemed to also have a special affinity with his eldest. Of course, Jenna and Alan had always gotten along well, too. For a while, a little too well. But that was before his marriage.

She could still feel his lips. His kiss had been more intense than she could have imagined, but she'd pulled away. Knowing how much Alan wanted to be with her during the time Daniel barely noticed she was there, and after the huge fight about Jenna refusing to go to one of Daniel's shows after her miscarriage, Jenna let her guard down enough to let Alan kiss her. She didn't want Alan, though, not like that. She wanted to be needed, but she wanted to be needed by her husband, not her friend. So she pushed Alan away and he proposed to Cheryl, who didn't want anyone but him. Jenna wondered if Alan ever told his wife about their brief encounter. He most likely hadn't.

Wandering away from his dad, and from the twins who were taking too much of Alan's attention, Justin came over to talk to the baby. He touched Aaron's fingers softly and talked to him as though her son understood every word. Cheryl complained that he was too dirty to play with Aaron, but Jenna said he was fine and gave him a disposable cloth to wash his fingers.

Aaron grabbed it away and put it in his mouth, scrunching his face about the taste. Justin laughed.

"Honey, don't let him chew on that. It has soap on it." Cheryl coaxed the cloth out of Aaron's chubby fingers and pulled her son away to clean his hands.

"I can do it."

"I want all the germs off. Hold still a minute."

Jenna started to argue. She didn't want Justin to be afraid to play with Aaron, and her son fussed for his companion to come back. But it wasn't her place to interfere. She did notice Alan's glance. He agreed with Jenna but wouldn't interfere with his wife, either. He never had when it came to the kids.

They stopped at the petting area at the end of their visit to feed the goats. Aaron wanted nothing to do with the noisy animals, which was fine with Jenna. She didn't either. Once, a long time ago, she had fed them and was disgusted by the slimy saliva their tongues left, along with the food pellets they couldn't pick up. Alan didn't care much for it, either. He joined her and Aaron on a nearby bench, commenting on Cheryl's habit of hauling her camera everywhere.

Alan hated having his picture taken. Jenna didn't especially like it but didn't complain the way her friend did. She watched Cheryl get a close shot of Justin feeding a very small goat with one arm propped around the animal's neck. Jenna supposed she would have to think more about carrying a camera, to get a record of Aaron growing, but she never thought far enough ahead. Maybe Cheryl would give her a copy of that one; it would make a beautiful painting.

"What are you thinking about?"

She glanced at her friend. He was sitting closer than necessary, leaned back against the wood-slat bench, one leg propped over the other. Jenna always felt rigid in public, never able to let go of her mother's over-emphasized lessons on posture. Alan's always relaxed attitude was one thing that attracted her. He made her feel at ease by being so at ease himself. "You know, Justin is really good with animals. You should get him one."

"A goat?"

Jenna grinned. "Well, maybe not a goat. But he'd love a puppy and it would give him his own playmate while the twins play together."

"He does get left out, doesn't he?" Alan sighed. "I'm always afraid he'll be too much of a loner."

"You worry too much. He's just fine, and he has a great role model." She met his eyes for a moment, then pulled hers away to focus on her own son. He was sitting happily in his stroller, watching Justin. What would he do for a male role model? Jenna had never even met Daniel's father, her own father wasn't the kind of example she wanted her son to follow, and she didn't intend to ever get married again.

Alan touched her arm. "I have a feeling Justin and Aaron will get along well. Maybe they'll hang out together as they get older."

"That would be nice." She gave him a grin. It was an offer to help with her son. She knew it for what it was.

A flash of light hit them and Cheryl laughed at catching them by surprise. Alan stood and called to his children that it was time to go. Jenna wondering if she would get a copy of that picture, also. Cheryl had taken several pictures of Jenna and Alan together over the years and Jenna had most of them. Many of the snapshots Cheryl gave her were stored carelessly in a shoebox, but the ones of her and Alan were placed in her keepsake journal. And she had a beautiful picture of Alan and Justin on her refrigerator, beside one of Cheryl with the newborn twins she kept there only to curb suspicion. Actually, both pictures had only been put up recently. She would never have done it while Daniel was still there.

Cheryl wouldn't let her refuse when Alan invited her over for a barbecue. And Jenna was glad for the offer.

Kicked back on a woven folding chair, eyes closed, she listened to the crickets chirp in the twilight. Cheryl had taken the kids up for their baths and Aaron was sleeping soundly in her arms. Alan was quiet, as he often was when they spent time together. Jenna enjoyed the silences with her friend as much as the conversations. She read or heard once that people who were truly comfortable with each other were never uncomfortable with the silence between them. She supposed that was true.

Shivering at a cool gust of air, she opened her eyes and checked to make sure Aaron's blanket was still pulled up around his head.

Her movement pulled her friend's attention from whatever he was thinking as he studied his yard, his constant habit. "Should we go in?"

"No, the air is wonderful tonight." She loved the crispness of fall, even though it was beckoning winter to come in its place.

He chuckled. "I still think you should come work for me, as much as you love to be outside."

"I don't know, that much togetherness might not be good for us." She grinned, then grew serious. "I'm sorry I was so rude earlier."

He didn't bother acting surprised at her apology. "It's all right. I know I was pushing, but I worry about you, Jen."

"I'm not much fun to be around anymore, am I?"

He sat motionless for a few seconds before pulling his chair close enough she could nearly feel the warmth of his breath. "Jenna, you need to start letting yourself live. It's not good for you to be alone so much, and it's not good for Aaron. You saw how happy he was today. He needs to be around other people. And so do you, whether you want to be or not."

She stared at her best friend, the only one in the neighborhood who had seen her for who she was. To him, she wasn't just the daughter of the revered hospital administrator who pushed her into being a socialite and the distant and discerning business editor who made more playing the stock market than at his job at the Journal Star. Alan didn't care about that. "If I get testy with you, ignore me. I don't mean it against you. And I know you're right. It's just hard."

"Think about what you're going to do, Jen. I'll help you any way I can. And Cheryl will babysit if you want to go back to school."

"And do what?"

"You like art and you're good at it. You'd be a great teacher."

"Art was Daniel's thing, not mine."

"It was yours before you met him. You have a lot of talent and a real love for it. Don't let him take that from you, too." He didn't give her time to respond before he moved his chair back to its original position. "It's getting late. I'll follow you home and walk you in."

"You don't need to do that."

"Don't bother to argue. Just let me tell Cheryl."

After Jenna settled Aaron in his crib, Alan gave her a quick kiss on the cheek and thanked her for spending the day with them.

The loft was mostly dark and seemed emptier than it had before. She stood in the hot shower longer than usual, then sat with a cup of mint tea and thought about Alan's comment. *Don't let him take that from you, too.*

Setting her cup down, she wandered over to the art table, pulled her journal from a drawer, and flipped the pages to find her favorite photo. With one of Daniel's unused sketchbooks and a charcoal pencil, she sat at his table and began a rough outline of two figures.

Three

"Jenna, I could give you more than this. I would give you more of myself than he gives you."

"Alan, don't. Don't do this to me. We're just having problems right now…"

"Because he's completely ignoring your needs. He's not being fair to you. Jen…"

She felt his chest against hers, his hands on her arms, pulling her in. The words got lost. She knew what he wanted, but … he stopped talking as he felt her giving in, accepting the closeness she so desperately needed. The warmth of his lips made her pulse quicken; the passion was so much more than she would have expected from this man she had known for years. The man who knew her better than anyone, better than her own husband knew her. Her husband…

She pulled away. "Alan."

The intensity and longing in his face nearly drew her back. It had been so long since she felt wanted, needed. But it was the wrong face. "I can't do this." Her voice was low, shaky. Her lungs filled quickly and she turned away. "I can't do this. I'm married."

"So leave him, Jenna. I'll wait for you."

Leave him? How could he think she would ever leave Daniel? He was what she waited for all those years her parents had tried to shape her into a debutante. He took her away from that. He gave her the kind of life she had longed for. Well, for a while, anyway. But they would get it back again. They were both trying to adjust to his new success. He had a lot of pressure to perform for the public, to keep creating better and more beautiful paintings. He didn't have the energy.

She missed him, though. She missed being held and being the most important thing in someone's life. Well, she had never been the most important. His work had always come first. But she had been a central motivator for him ever since they'd met, until recently, until…

She felt Alan's gentle touch and didn't fight him when his arms moved around her waist from behind. He didn't think she was a failure. He was still attracted to her. But then, it wasn't his child she lost.

He snuggled his face against her hair and planted a kiss on her head. Closing her eyes against the pain and the longing, Jenna felt a tear tickle down her cheek.

Alan turned her to face him "Jen." He wiped the moisture away. "I can't stand to see you so unhappy. He's not good for you. Leave him to his art. Leave him, Jenna, and come to me."

The tears fell faster and she leaned into her friend. "I can't." Involuntary lung *spasms interrupted until she calmed herself enough to stutter the words she had to say. "I ... can't, Alan. He's my husband. I love him. I can't... I don't want to fail at this, too. I don't want to fail at my marriage."*

His arms tightened around her back and a hand moved up to hold her head in against his shoulder. The soft Celtic music she used for relaxation caught her attention and she forced herself to focus on the soothing strains. Eventually, her breathing slowed and the tears stopped and she held still in his arms.

"I'm sorry. I didn't mean to upset you more. I just... It's so hard for me to watch him ignore you when I would love to be the one you wanted, when I would love to be able to give you what you want from him. I love you, Jenna."

The tears started again and she pulled away. "I can't see you again, Alan. I can't do this. I'm having enough trouble trying to hold my marriage together and this isn't helping anything."

"Jen..."

"No, please, just go. I can't see you anymore."

He stepped closer again, trying to bridge the gap. "You don't mean that. You can't push me away."

"I'm not leaving him. I love him and I'm going to make it work."

"And what about us? All the years between us? You're going to let him take that away from you?"

"Alan, you're just my friend. I don't love you." She immediately regretted the way that it had come out, but she couldn't take it back.

He lowered his head, then grabbed his coat and went to the door.

"Alan." She caught up and took his arm. "I'm sorry, I meant..."

"No, Jenna, you don't have any reason to be sorry. You've been trying to tell me that for years and I wouldn't listen. I'll leave you alone."

"Don't ... not like this."

He refused to even look at her. "Goodbye, Jen." Pulling out of her grasp, he fled through the door without closing it.

She lay awake staring at the ceiling. The charcoal drawing still sat on Daniel's table. Maybe she would try to paint it, but she could never do it justice the way Daniel could. And so what if she couldn't? No one had to see it. It could be something to occupy her time. Eventually she would have to think about earning a living since the royalties and money from his sales wouldn't last forever. But for now, all she needed was a distraction.

The sky was beginning to lighten and Aaron would soon force her to start the day. Maybe she could get an hour or two of sleep first. She could show Alan her work. He wouldn't be critical. And he would see that she did actually listen to him, occasionally.

"No baby, not already." She couldn't remember falling asleep, but she must have. What time was it? She turned her head to no avail. The alarm clock blinked twelve-seventeen. The power must have gone off.

A loud clap of thunder made Aaron's cry more insistent and Jenna rolled out of bed to find him. The cold floor surged a chill through her veins. Pulling her old sweatshirt over the long T-shirt she wore to bed, she gathered her son and took him back to cuddle in the blankets with her. He quieted immediately and began searching for her breast.

"Okay, hold on." She pulled the garment out of his way as rain pelted the large windows and a nearby tree danced fitfully. The strange yellow cast of the sky made her wonder whether she should find lower ground. But where would she go? She didn't know the people who lived below her since Daniel always made it clear he didn't want to be bothered. And she wasn't about to take her baby out in this weather.

The lightning startled Aaron again and her thoughts turned to keeping him calm. He hated loud noises, but he loved music. Searching her brain for a soothing melody, she sang quietly, one of her favorites.

"Follow your heart when I'm not by your side, I'll take you wherever I go..."

His innocent, trusting eyes peered into hers. This was what it was about. This baby they both wanted so badly. A new life they purposely created, knowing the likelihood she would end up a single mother, although Jenna never allowed herself to believe it would happen.

"You'll dance in my dreams and lie in my thoughts; I'll sing you to sleep though we're miles apart; So rock-a-bye baby, good night; Rock-a-bye baby, it's all right."

She watched his perfect little face as his tummy filled and his eyelids began to flutter. When he finished, or became too tired to eat, she laid him beside her and they both ignored the rain.

His fussing stirred her again. The clock now flashed four-thirty-two and the sun was trying to peak through gray clouds. Lifting Aaron, she set a soft kiss on his head and set him in his crib. He protested at being put down, and she quickly took care of her needs and splashed cool water on her face before she returned to calm him.

Jenna wondered where Alan was working now. She hoped the job would be easier than the last one and wished she could be there for the initial planning stage. He was so good at seeing a tree- and shrub-filled landscape where most people saw only grass and dirt patches. It had been ages since she wandered with him while he planned exactly what kind of foliage to use and just where it should be planted. Maybe it would be too wet today, though. She chuckled at herself. Even if it was still raining, Alan would be at the location, thinking and planning.

She could find out where he was. Cheryl would know. But then Jenna would have to explain why she was asking and she wasn't sure she could. She should call Karla. It would be safer than letting herself get too close to Alan again. Maybe safe wasn't the right word. After all, he wouldn't hit on her now that he was married. And she had really enjoyed talking with him again.

Instead of calling either friend, Jenna picked up the sketch she finished late the night before and studied the figures. Very amateurish. But it had been a while and she was out of practice. She could try it in paint instead. Were there any blank canvases left? She hadn't been able to go through Daniel's things other than to look at the sketches. Aaron found his plastic mirror she had placed on his blanket, so he would be fine for a while.

Lifting some partly done canvases out of the way, she found one her husband had used and covered again with gesso, unhappy with the results of his work. She could do the same. Setting it on an empty easel, Jenna rifled through his oils to find the right colors. Choosing browns and yellows, with a red for some accent, Jenna set to work. She thought of her husband, and didn't attempt to imitate his style, but listened to his voice describe his approach to art.

Jenna wandered around the studio side of the loft, studying the paintings, some in progress and some completed. She stopped in front of one she recognized as the sketch he had done of her at the zoo. It was now in full color on a large canvas. Her fingers ran lightly over the blades of grass, feeling not the paint, but the sharpness of the edges. And the stone reflected the sun so well she could feel the warmth from it.

"Daniel, this is beautiful. How do you make the sunlight look so real?"

He crept close enough she could feel his breath on the back of her neck. "I paint it the way I see it."

"Do you always see things better than they are? I mean, that's not me, it's…"

"I never see anything better than it is. I simply look beyond the external to find the full beauty."

She caught her breath when his skilled fingers brushed her neck. She had again wrapped her long hair into a bun, leaving only a few wisps to fall in waves. When he didn't get resistance, Daniel slid an arm around her waist and his fingers found the pins holding her hair. It took him no time to release them, dropping them onto the floor, and he smoothed her auburn hair, then turned her to face him.

"You are beautiful, Jenna. Will you be my inspiration?"

She couldn't respond. She was having enough trouble breathing. And she couldn't pull back as he moved closer. His intensity was overwhelming and his kiss made her want more. But she couldn't. She was seventeen and her parents would have him locked up if they found out. His lips moved to her neck. How would they find out? She was supposed to be with Karla. Her cousin would cover for her like she had for other dates. But this wasn't a date ... this was...

He leaned down and took her into his arms, carrying her across the floor and to the other side of the room. She tried to ask him to stop, but the words wouldn't come, and he set her on his bed, leaning down to kiss her again. She didn't want him to stop. He wanted her, and he needed her, and she had wanted to be needed for so long. Finally, someone was willing to give her complete attention, and he walked away from his work to be with her.

"Daniel, I..."

"Jenna, I know. It's all right." He brushed her hair back again.

"I've never..."

"I know." He sat up enough to pull his shirt over his head.

She cautiously raised a hand to touch his bare chest. "I've wanted to be yours from the moment we met."

"I know."

At day's end, she had completed her first painting and started a sketch for another. Her style was nothing like Daniel's. He was a realist, with the touch of an impressionist. She was ... well, kind of expressionist and kind of surreal. And not anywhere near as talented. She wasn't going to show this to Alan, but maybe she wouldn't paint over it, either. She would need to get more canvas. She had seen a new art supply store the other day, one she and Daniel hadn't been to, so maybe she wouldn't be recognized there.

Four

She stepped back for a better perspective, then trudged over to answer the phone. Jenna would have ignored it, but it was most likely Alan since she hadn't talked to him in three days. He left a message on her machine a couple of times, once when she had been at the art store and once when she was letting the hot shower try to wash away the caked-on paint. She hadn't called him back. Thoughts of the past kept invading and she wanted to be left alone to work.

"Jenna, it's about time you answered. I've left several messages. Are you all right?"

Oh, hell. She should have let the machine pick up. "Hello, Mom. I'm fine."

"You sound tired. Are you sleeping?"

"Not at the moment."

"Jenna, I meant..."

"I know what you meant. What's up?" She looked over at the crib. The phone must have bothered Aaron, too.

"Don't refuse before you hear me out. There's a social at..."

"No."

"Jenna..."

"Mom, I don't want to socialize."

"There's a very nice young doctor who is not much older than you, a surgeon; he's specializing in..."

Jenna held the phone away from her ear. Not again. Daniel had only been gone four months and this was at least her mother's fifth attempt at a blind date. Of course, they were all professional men: doctors, brokers, anyone who would pull her back into the right world. But it wasn't going to happen.

Aaron started the soft cry that warned her he was about to get upset. She put the phone back to her ear. "Mom, the baby's awake. I have to go."

"At least consider it. I don't need an answer now. He's a very nice man and I've checked out his record."

"I'm sure they're all nice, but I'm just not interested."

"Jenna..."

"I have to go. I'll call you later." Barely giving her time to respond,

Jenna severed the connection. The call would probably be returned quite a while later. Although, her mom wasn't likely to be home if she did try to reach her. She never was, and she never had been.

It wasn't time for Aaron to be awake, so she found his pacifier and stroked his hair until he fell asleep again. She still had trouble believing she was the mom now and he would look to her for whatever he needed. And she would be at his school events, whether or not it was something that actually held an interest for her. She would be there.

With a deep breath, Jenna sauntered over to put a cup of water in the microwave. She needed mint tea. Actually, she needed a friendly voice. Why was it that every time she talked to her mother, she ended up calling Alan? Because he knew what she put up with, maybe. Or because she'd been running to him to complain since she was eleven.

At the beep, Jenna retrieved the cup, dropped in a tea bag, and tugged the string while staring into the steaming liquid. The moisture warmed her fingers. A young doctor, specializing in ... heart surgery? Maybe he could replace hers so she could start over. Okay, she didn't really want that. She didn't want to lose what she did still have. But she sure didn't want to be set up, either. Especially by her mother. What on earth would make her parents think she would want her child to grow up that way? With neither parent ever around to take part in his life, any part of his life?

She walked back to the art table where she had scribbled on a piece of newsprint. Alan's house: her escape. The perspective of the porch swing wasn't quite right, but perspective had never been her strong point except when actually looking at the object she was drawing. Still, she could see it clearly. The two-story, Victorian-style house had slightly peeling white paint, a short railing around the front porch, and shrubs and trees of every kind. Alan's mom was nearly an expert on flowers and could grow anything. Jenna guessed that was where he inherited his love of nature. Being the only boy, Alan was given the duty of lawn care and helped his mom plant trees and trim the bushes and kept her company while she was weeding or watering.

The lilacs had begun to bloom a few days ago and their scent filled the air around the friendly home. Jenna's spirits raised as she tapped on the screen door and went in. She never bothered to wait for someone to answer if the large front door was open. The Taylors made her feel like family from the time she walked over to welcome them to the neighborhood.

Janice Taylor greeted her with a smile and asked if she wanted a warm cookie. She was always baking; it was her third love, after her family and her flower gardens. Jenna sat at the table, waiting for information on her friend. She never had to wait long.

"I'm not sure when Alan will be here. His finals are next week and he's staying to study at the library." She set a glass of milk in front of her, just as Jenna had seen in the old movies she enjoyed watching.

"I knew his car wasn't here. I just thought I'd wait, if it's okay."

"Of course it's okay, honey. If you don't want to sit here with me and be bored, the girls are in their room. They're supposed to be studying, but I'm sure they're not. Go on up. I'll tell Alan you're here when he comes in."

Jenna grinned as she headed up the gold-carpeted stairs. Janice Taylor was anything but boring, but she knew when Jenna wanted to visit and when she only wanted to see her friend.

Amber and Carrie looked up from the magazine lying on top of their school books. Carrie, the soft-spoken fourteen-year-old, flashed a guilty look. Amber, however, jumped up, grabbed the magazine, and rushed over to show Jenna their newest treasure. A smiling face headlined the front of her Tiger Beat. "Isn't he just adorable? I saved my allowance and got it today! There's a big article about him. Do you think he'll ever come to Peoria? I just have to see him in real life!"

"I think he needs a haircut, but I like his voice." Jenna watched the girl's mouth drop open.

"A haircut? He's perfect just the way he is! I thought you liked Donny?"

"I do, but he needs a haircut. And aren't you supposed to be studying?"

Amber yanked her possession away. "Are you in a bad mood again? Alan isn't home. Wait and take it out on him. He doesn't mind." The girl flopped down on the ruffle-trimmed bedspread and flipped through the magazine.

Jenna crossed the small room and claimed the wire-backed chair with matching cushion. "Sorry, I was teasing." But Amber wasn't listening anymore. She was so sensitive. A year older than her sister, her name was well suited. Her hair was a straight brownish-blonde and just like the dictionary definition, she was "quickly electrified with friction." Carrie, on the other hand, was easy-going and had nearly the same shade as Alan's light brown hair.

Jenna decided to let Amber sulk. "Carrie, what are you studying?"

"I'm helping Amber with her French. She doesn't like it much, though."

"It's a waste of time. I don't know why we need to know a foreign language."

So Amber was talking to her already. She never stayed mad long. "What if you want to go to France some day?"

"Why would I do that?"

"To see all the beautiful things: the Eiffel Tower, the Louvre..."

"If I get to travel, I'll go to California, and they talk English there."

"They speak English there." A male voice interrupted. "Maybe you should *study your English grammar, as well."*

Jenna smiled at her friend. It wasn't as irritating when he corrected his sisters' grammar as when he corrected hers. Although, she didn't really mind. He always sounded intelligent and graceful. It would be nice if people felt that way about her.

"Mom said you were here. She also said the girls are supposed to be studying. Amber?"

"Okay, okay." Amber closed the magazine and went back to sulking in her textbook.

Jenna tried not to grin as she stood. They never argued with him. She always heard of brothers and sisters fighting constantly, but it didn't happen here. Amber and Carrie bickered with each other fairly often but never crossed their brother. Maybe because he was so much older.

Alan was almost twenty, the son of his mother's first husband. The girls were technically his half-sisters, but no one ever mentioned that. And Lee Taylor had taken him in as his own son. Alan got along with his adoptive father so well that as soon as he had a choice, he stopped going for the once-a-year two week visits with his biological father.

"Do you want to walk down to the store with me? Mom needs eggs and it's beautiful today. I could use fresh air."

"Sure." Jenna passed Alan into the hall. He always waited to let her go through the doorway first and always opened doors for her, though she often told him it wasn't necessary. It was his nature. He was a true gentleman, not only taught, but inborn.

Stepping out into the sunshine, Jenna lost the urge to talk. She noticed little things that were missed during everyday distractions: iris beginning to push their purple skirts through green shields, bright yellow dandelions overtaking spikes of deep green grass that needed mowing, clumps of violas growing around bushes (she loved violas and would have a yard-full when she had her own house), bits of sparkling gravel beside the road. Crossing the road and climbing the three cracked steps up to the sidewalk that led to town, she focused on the grooved dirt along the side. She remembered having helped create the little path by riding her bicycle down the small hill onto the road, as many of the town kids often did. She hadn't done so herself since her mom had caught and admonished her.

"So, what's up?"

Ignoring the intrusion of her thoughts, Jenna watched ants scurry to move away from her feet. As if they had anything to worry about. She would never purposely step on any living creature. The thought of unnecessarily ending their lives seemed inhumane. Not that she had any particular fondness for them, but as long as they didn't bother her, she saw no reason to bother them.

"Jenna?"

She gave in as she watched the ants. "I can't go on my senior trip."

"Why not?"

"Because Brian will be there."

"And?"

"And Mom doesn't think we'll be chaperoned well enough." Silence again came between them until she stopped at the little bridge to pick up a small stick and drop it into the trickling creek below, pushing a strand of hair away from her face.

"Jenna, it's not that serious, is it? You and Brian?"

"Of course not. I'm seventeen. I don't have any interest in that." She moved to the other side and held the rusty metal rail to watch the stick bounce along, getting caught for a short time before the movement of the clear water set it free. "It's an excuse. She wants to keep me under her thumb forever."

"She worries about you. You know, if you didn't rebel against everything she says, maybe she wouldn't worry so much."

Her eyes shot to his. "You're taking her side? Alan, I'm a straight A student because she insists on it and I'm on the volleyball team because she was captain of hers. I hate volleyball. And all I do is that and chorus. It's not like I sneak out to party like some of my friends do. I don't do anything exciting. What does she have to worry about?"

Alan set a hand on her arm. "Jen, you know I'm not taking her side, but don't you think she can see you don't want the life she wants you to have? She knows she's running out of time to change your mind."

"Why should I have to live that way just 'cause she wants me to? It's my life."

"Yes, it is, and you're nearly eighteen."

"And then I can live by my own rules and go where I want."

His eyes cast a warning. "Don't do something stupid just to get back at your parents. You'll end up hurting yourself more than you hurt them. It is your life. You have to decide what you really want."

"You have to decide what you really want."

Picking up a clean sheet of paper, Jenna began to sketch the bridge.

Five

The water under the bridge became more a focal point than the old bridge itself. Though she could see it clearly in her mind, painting the clarity and translucence was another story. Not to mention the movement. And the movement was important. Water under the bridge, washing the old leaves and sticks away until they were out of sight. But were they less important or real because they were no longer in her vision?

Mixing gray into brown sienna, Jenna used her small putty knife to etch a rough line onto the canvas, added shadow until it became elliptical, then splashed a bit of white water over the side. Moving away to study her work, she realized the stick was the most realistic object in the painting. Well, she supposed that was appropriate. Water, like time, was fleeting, but the objects, or events, it washed away were still as real as if they were in plain view.

Satisfied enough to continue, Jenna found a stiff brush and dipped it into the barely mixed grayish-white. She wanted the sidewalk to stand out, as well. First, the basic outline, then the details – shadows, highlights where the sun hit, separations and cracks, and grass pushing over the edge. The two steps back to again get a more distant view turned her attention to a slight ache in her feet and a heaviness in her arm. Ignoring the present, she concentrated on the painted scene and the following day's events. It carried her back to her parents' home.

She made her way to her mother's room. Another social event, or socialite event, as Jenna liked to call them, had come up at the last minute. So again, her mom would miss her chorus concert. At least Alan and his family were going so she wouldn't be there alone.

Louise Givens was wearing something Jenna hadn't seen. Like everything her mom owned, it was meticulously fit and elegant and the black pearl necklace and earrings matched exactly.

At the doorway, she grew tired of waiting to be noticed. "You look nice. Is that new?"

"Oh, Jenna, you startled me. I didn't see you there."

Of course she hadn't. "I know you're busy, but Alan asked me to go to I.C.C. with him over Easter break to look around the campus. I wanted to answer him tonight at the concert."

"Concert?"

Jenna sighed. "My chorus concert. It's tonight."

Spritzing perfume on her wrists, she glanced at her daughter through the dresser mirror. "Oh, yes. Alan's going with you?"

"Yes. At least someone's interested."

Finally turning, her mom acted apologetic. "Jenna, you know I'm interested. But this is very important."

"Of course it is. They always are." She changed her tone. Her mom wasn't about to agree if she got rude. "Is Dad going with you?"

"No, he couldn't get off, but he won't be late tonight. Why don't you order something from the little Italian restaurant?"

"The Taylors are taking me out after the concert."

"You mean Alan's taking you out?"

Jenna took a deep breath, keeping control of her voice. "No Mom, his family is. So, can I go to I.C.C. with him?"

Her mother sat genteelly on her silk bedspread to push four-inch heels onto her feet. "Jenna, I thought you applied to U of I."

"I did, but only because you wanted me to."

"It's an excellent college. Your father and I both went there and look how well we've done. Don't you want to be successful in life?"

"I'd rather be happy. And I don't want to move so far away."

"You can't be happy without being successful. And I imagine if you go there, Alan will change his mind and go with you."

Jenna ignored the first comment. "He doesn't want to get his bachelor's right now. He wants to work first."

"He'll make more money with a better degree. You would do him a favor if you talk him into going. And when he graduates in another two years, he can start a career while you're finishing. That way you'll have a solid basis to begin a family." She stood, testing the heels, then crossed back to the mirror.

"Mother, he's just my friend. You know I'm dating Brian."

"Yes, but he's only temporary. Jenna, he's a nice boy, but he'll never do any more with his life than his father did. You need a husband who will be able to keep you in the right society."

"I'm seventeen. I'm not ready to think about marriage. And it's bad enough you won't let me go on my class trip. At least let me do something half-way interesting over break. I'll be with Alan, and that's what you want."

Louise Givens paused only for a moment. "All right. You can go with Alan to Illinois Central if you'll agree to check out U of I before deciding which one to choose. We'll make a run up to Chicago after graduation."

Jenna approached her painting again warily, then backed away and dropped her brush into the solvent. What was the point? All the painting she did wouldn't change anything and wasn't getting her anywhere. It wasn't even her palette knife; the brushes lying around weren't hers, and neither was the paint. Well, some of it was. She found a few colors at the art store she couldn't resist and the canvas she was now using she bought there. But mostly, it was Daniel's.

Warming another cup of water, she dropped in the same tea bag she used the last time. Daniel had fussed about her reusing a tea bag, saying they could afford for her to use a new one each time. But it seemed wasteful. She had never stopped doing so, though she thought every time about his objection. Many of his comments stayed in her mind and presented themselves on different occasions. She wondered whether that would ever change.

Wandering over to the window and the big oak chair, she set the cup on a small plant stand she'd been using as a table ever since the plant died. A sudden chill raised goosebumps on her bare arms and she stood again to grab the old frayed sweatshirt she wore only in her apartment. It had a couple of small holes from where the seams had finally given and a touch of paint here and there, mostly from when she dared to bother her husband while he worked. Sometimes it had been okay and he responded warmly. Jenna quickly learned to judge when she could interrupt and when she needed to keep her distance ... until he became sick, and then his painting hadn't seemed as important anymore.

She still felt guilty for enjoying the extra time he spent with her then, knowing the only reason was because he didn't have the strength to work so many hours after the cancer took control. And because he knew their time together would be severely limited.

Was it too cold in the apartment? Crossing over to the crib, she pulled the blanket higher on her sleeping son and touched his cheek. He felt warm enough. Jenna felt his slight movement when she cupped her hand over his tiny head. She was bothering him. He hated to be bothered while he slept, but the touch warmed her and her baby decided to ignore it. He was so like his father. What would he do with his life? Would he be interested in art? Maybe he would surprise her and do something completely different. Whatever he chose, it would be his decision. It wasn't her place to interfere.

Her tea was cool by the time she returned to the rocking chair and she set it down again. She didn't like cold tea. There wasn't much she liked cold. She never put ice in her water and generally kept her soda in the pantry rather than in the refrigerator. Daniel always shook his head when he picked up her glass by mistake.

Jenna watched her husband approach. His chest muscles contracted and expanded in reply to the stretching of his arms, first overhead, then behind his back. He had been working for hours. She made lunch, which he hadn't bothered to stop for, flipped through a magazine at the table alone, cleaned the dishes and counters, took a load of laundry down to the machines in the basement, and was sitting with her most recent novel from the library while waiting for the dryer to finish.

Daniel set a hand on her shoulder as he grabbed a glass from the stand.

Her eyes traced his arm, fell to his stomach. She loved warm days when he didn't bother with a shirt.

"Hm, wrong one." He returned it to the stand and grabbed the other, which was still colder than Jenna's although the ice had melted. "How can you drink it that way?"

Jenna shrugged. "That's how I like it."

He grinned, took a couple of swallows, and returned to his easel.

She watched him for a moment as he sank back into his own world. This painting was going well and he was in a good mood. Maybe she could risk an interruption before he was too lost.

Setting her book down, she moved up from behind and set a hand on his back, as though checking his progress. If he ignored her, she would back away again.

"So, what do you think so far?"

He wasn't ignoring her this time. She moved in closer and ran the other arm around his stomach, still as flat and hard as ever, though his sister had teased him about gaining weight after he was married. Jenna didn't know how he could possibly gain weight when he rarely took time to eat.

"Are you afraid to answer? Is it that bad?" He turned, holding his brush.

"You know it's brilliant. That's why you're in such a good mood." She grinned into his eyes and let a hand wander on his chest.

"I'm covered in paint."

"Do I ever care?" She kissed the side of his neck, in the place hair didn't grow. He often fussed about the unevenness of the beard he always shaved anyway because it was an imperfection he didn't like. But she loved the soft places that didn't scratch her lips in the evenings when it started to grow back in. When she was allowed to get that close.

"Jenna..."

"I know. You're working. But I need you." She moved her lips to his bare shoulder and felt him begin to give in.

"I guess I have been busy recently."

She took the brush from his hand and dropped it carefully into the turpentine.

Aaron's cry pierced her reverie. She took a deep, ragged breath and pushed away tears. Starting toward the crib, Jenna noticed the time. It was nearly six; Alan should be home by now.

Cuddling her baby in one arm, she watched him nurse for a few minutes, then reached for the phone. After waiting through four rings, Jenna paused at the voice. Wrong one.

The greeting came again before she responded. "Hi, Cheryl. Is Alan home yet?"

"Jenna! Are you okay? He's been trying to reach you all week. He even stopped by the apartment a couple of days ago and no one was there. Is everything all right?"

He came over? "Yes, we're fine."

"Good, I'm so glad to hear from you! Just a minute, let me get him. He's been so worried!"

She listened to silence while waiting for her friend. The loft was so very empty tonight.

"Jenna? Where've you been? I've left four messages."

"I know. I'm sorry. I just... I didn't feel like talking."

"Are you okay?"

"Yeah, I'm fine."

"And Aaron's okay?"

She couldn't help grinning. He hadn't said *the baby* this time. "Yes."

"I stopped by."

"I know. Cheryl told me. I had to go to the store."

Silence again.

"Alan?"

"I'm here."

"I've been painting this week."

"That's great, Jen. How's it going?" He sounded cautious. Jenna assumed Cheryl had stayed within hearing distance.

"Um, I'm not sure. I..." She swallowed to try to keep the emotion from her voice. "I was thinking about..." She stopped again, unable to suppress the tears this time.

"Do you want me to come over?"

"Yes, but you shouldn't." Her baby was startled by a drop on his cheek, and she had to prop the phone between her neck and shoulder to adjust herself and raise him to the other side. She barely heard Alan say he would be right there.

Though Aaron's tummy filled before the doorbell rang, Jenna was still holding him, letting him comfort her. He complained when she interrupted his restful state but a kiss and a few soft words calmed him by the time she opened the door.

Alan had brought his son. Jenna wondered whether it had been his idea or Cheryl's. "Justin wanted to see Aaron and I thought he could entertain him for a while. I hope you don't mind."

"Of course I don't. Come on in." She returned the boy's shy grin and led them to the living area, setting her baby on his blanket on the floor. Jenna refrained from wrapping Justin in a tight hug when he flopped beside Aaron. The cowlick at his nape had grown back enough to form an untamable half-moon that drew emphasis to his perfect little-boy neck. There was something especially beautiful about the soft skin and ridges just below a child's hair line.

"Come show me what you've done." Alan stared at her with a softness Jenna didn't see often. He had been worried.

Standing, she pushed a fallen strand of hair behind her ear. The ponytail was messy and her old T-shirt had a spot or two of baby food, but he still gazed at her as if she were in a little black dress, perfectly made up. He always had.

"Jen?"

She pushed at the strand again, though it hadn't fallen. The last time he came over to see her work, while Daniel was in Chicago at a show, Alan kissed her, and she nearly gave in to him. She quit painting after that. She didn't want to quit again.

The boys laughed at some private joke and Jenna relented. Alan was married now and had his son with him. There was no danger. With a nod, she moved into the studio.

Alan's arm brushed against hers as he studied the painting on the easel. "I have always loved your style, Jen. I don't always understand your art, but I always enjoy it."

She looked up at his strong chin, and at his gaze focused not on her but on her work. "You don't understand this one?"

He grinned and turned to find her eyes. "Oh, yes. This one I get. And I love the water. It's so alive. It's so ... you."

Six

"Well hello, Jenna. How is my favorite daughter-in-law?"

"Hi Joan. I'm fine. How's business?" Jenna pulled the phone cord from her son's reaching fingers, propped the receiver between her ear and shoulder, and grabbed his rattle.

"Oh, you know, the same. More to do than I have time for."

"And you wouldn't change that if you could." She sighed when he dropped the toy and again reached for the cord.

"You know me too well, dear. And how is my precious baby doing? Growing fast, I suppose? I need to steal time to come see you both again. When would be good for you? I may be able to get a couple of days ... maybe ... next Thursday. No, I have a meeting Friday morning. How is..."

"Any time you can get here is fine." Jenna tried bouncing him in her arm while she paced as far as the cord would reach.

"I wouldn't want to interrupt any plans."

"I don't have plans. Please, come any time. He isn't growing real fast, but I'm sure he'd love to see you again." She grabbed his teether and brushed it against his mouth when he fussed.

"He's okay?"

"Yes, he's fine. The doctor says he's very healthy; he's just not going to be very tall."

"Like his father."

Jenna's heart skipped a beat. No, not like his father. Daniel had been small because of his illness. Aaron took after her side of the family. He was simply not meant to be tall.

"Jenna, honey, I didn't mean... Is that my baby I hear?"

"Yes, I think he's cutting a tooth. He's been fussy since last night." She kissed his little cheek while she listened to Joan throw out suggestions for easing the baby's irritation, all of which she already heard from Cheryl. None of it worked well. Her own improvisation of putting her finger in his mouth to chew on worked best, but her fingers were getting sore.

About to thank Joan for the well-meant advice, Jenna heard a soft knock. It had to be Alan. He always knocked quietly so he wouldn't disturb Aaron if he happened to be asleep. But why was he there? It was the middle of the work day.

"Joan, can you hold on a second?" She lay the receiver on the table and went to the door, hoping Alan would keep his voice low enough her mother-in-law wouldn't hear him.

"Hey Jen, throw clothes on and come out to the site with me. It's a perfect day."

"I'm on the phone." She kept her own voice quiet as though she could lower his that way.

"I'll wait. Want me to take him?" He reached for Aaron before she answered and the distraction calmed the baby for a moment.

"Thanks. I'll just be a minute."

"Take your time."

He was in a good mood; his job was apparently going well. But Joan had surely heard him. Jenna braced herself for the inquiry she expected from the other end of the line. "Sorry, I'm back."

"If you have company, dear, I'll let you go."

"Um, no, I turned the television up instead of down, and Aaron was getting hard to hold with one arm." Luckily, Joan was interrupted and promised to call back.

"Was that your mom?" Alan gave in to Aaron's little arms shoving toward Jenna and returned him.

"You're in a good mood today. What's up?"

"Jenna?"

"It was Joan."

"Why did you tell her I was the television?"

"I don't know. It just seemed..." She turned away from his curious stare. "Why are you here?"

His silence said he didn't appreciate her being so evasive, but he relented and settled on her couch. "As I said, I thought you might want to go out to the site with me. It's beautiful today."

"Why aren't you taking Cheryl out?"

He paused again. "You know she's not an outdoor person. She still finds my work boring. And I thought you and the baby ... sorry, you and Aaron, could use some fresh air."

She pivoted back to him. "Alan, when I jumped on you about that the other day, about you saying 'the baby,' I ... you don't have to..."

"You just needed to vent. I know. And I'm just tripping your trigger. One of my worst faults, remember?"

She grinned. "Yeah, only one of your many irritating qualities. And you think I wanna spend the day with you?"

He shrugged. "Wouldn't be the first time."

"The baby's fussy."

"I'm plenty used to fussy babies. Go get dressed."

Jenna gave in, the lure of fresh air and Alan planning a site too hard to resist. Watching him work alongside his men – well, there were a couple of girls, too, but he didn't have the same kind of camaraderie with them – was stimulating. She appreciated the respect they gave her, not because her best friend was the boss, but because they respected him as a person. And they were all as tan as Alan, several as muscular and none afraid to model their build as they hauled plants, earth, and stone.

She lectured herself silently as she changed into jeans and a snug-fitting blouse. Those thoughts were unnecessary and she felt traitorous to Daniel. His light brown eyes peered at her from the photo on her dresser. Lifting it closer, Jenna touched her fingers to the glass. Maybe she shouldn't go. Would her husband understand how she could need Alan's company so much so shortly after losing him? Would it look bad to anyone who saw them together? It didn't matter what people thought of her. She'd never cared much about that. But she wouldn't want to reflect badly on her husband, as though his death didn't matter enough. Anyone who knew them couldn't think that. But then, most people didn't know them well.

Jenna pulled the blouse back over her head and replaced it with one of her husband's shirts, rolling the sleeves above her wrists. She hadn't worn it yet. She could still smell him.

Alan didn't see her right away as she stepped out from behind the curtain. Aaron was chewing on one of his knuckles. So, that was where the idea had come from. She had forgotten. "You know, maybe..."

"I think this tooth is in. Feels like a tiny knife in there."

She put aside her previous thought and moved close beside them. "Really? It wasn't. I looked just before you came over." She pressed a finger into her son's mouth and felt the sharp edge press into her skin. "His first tooth. I can't believe he's that old already."

"Goes fast, doesn't it? I already miss the baby stage."

"So you can help me. You're a great dad." Jenna felt his stare and pulled back. She shouldn't have...

He set a hand on her arm. "I'd love to help you with Aaron; any time, Jen."

"Thank you. I hate that he won't have a dad around." Jenna took her son and kissed his cheek.

"I'm sure you'll find someone else to be part of your family at some point, but, until then…"

"No." She looked directly into her friend's eyes. "I'm not getting married again, ever."

"You can't know that now. Of course it's too soon."

"Yes, I can. I promised Daniel forever. That's what I meant." She didn't give him time to respond. "Maybe we shouldn't go today. I'm sorry I wasted your time here, but…"

"Jen, don't do this. Don't pull away from me again."

"I don't want people to think…"

"Think what? That you have a friend? Well, Heaven forbid you should have a friend. You know, you had a lot of them before. Why shouldn't you have one now? Is that why you lied to Joan? Because you don't want her to think you might possibly be able to go on with your life without her son? Jenna, she has, and Denise has. Why shouldn't you?"

"It's not the same."

"Why isn't it?"

"He was my husband."

"Yes, your husband, not your Siamese twin. Your life didn't end because his did."

"I *know* that." At Aaron's fuss, she lowered her voice. "Alan, I know. That's why I'm painting again. I did listen to you. I am doing something. Maybe nothing constructive, but something."

"Then why don't you want to go today? You used to love it, or at least you acted like you did."

"Of course I did, and I do want to. I love being out there with you. I always have, but…"

He moved closer to her and stroked Aaron's head. "But what?"

How could she tell him she was afraid of getting too close, that he would get too close? She didn't dare insult him like that, but the way he kept moving in beside her, and touching her…

"Jen, it's different now. I'm married and I'm not about to leave my family, so if you're afraid of me proposing again, you can relax."

She stared into his eyes. He was never afraid to say what he was thinking. She loved that about him.

"I'm right, aren't I? Because of what happened before?"

"I don't want that to happen again."

"Next time, talk to me. Don't make me guess." He ran his fingers along her face. "You're right. I still love you as much as ever, and if I wasn't married, in time... But I am, and I don't intend to do anything to change that. I made Cheryl a promise, too, and she's a wonderful person and a great mom, and we do well together. But Jenna, she doesn't share my interests the way you do. She supports my career because I love it, but she won't go to a site with me and she doesn't want to hear about it because it bores her. I've missed having someone who is interested. And I've missed having a best friend."

"So have I." Her voice was nearly a whisper. Hearing he still loved her came as a shock, though she supposed it shouldn't. She could tell. That's what scared her. But she never guessed he would say it openly.

"So? Now what?"

Good question. He stood silently, waiting to see whether or not he still had his best friend. "Let me feed Aaron before we go."

The cool late September air had both rejuvenated and exhausted Jenna by the time she pulled her sleeping baby from the car seat. She shivered while Alan moved the seat from his truck back to her car. He of course walked them upstairs.

"Do you want a cup of tea? Or I can make coffee."

"No, thank you. Cheryl will have supper ready. I need to go." He kissed her cheek. "Thanks for coming."

Jenna shifted Aaron to one side and gave her friend a hug. "Thank you." She relaxed against his shoulder and enjoyed the feel of his arm around her, and the scent of aftershave remnants mixed with pollen and dirt and a touch of now-dry sweat.

He held her for some time before he left. Aaron stirred when she pulled his jacket off but remained mostly asleep, so she laid him in his crib and went to put a cup of water in the microwave. It was after six; she couldn't let him sleep long but she needed a few minutes of quiet.

Staring into the steaming tea, she saw Alan's site. He and his crew had planted shrubs around the large brick house, newly built, and Jenna and Alan talked with the owners about different ideas for the rest of the landscaping. Well, Alan had talked about landscaping. Jenna mostly listened and chatted with the elderly woman who lived there with her daughter and son-in-law. The woman insisted Jenna and Aaron go inside to sit with her a while and didn't think anything of Jenna nursing in the kitchen while they had tea.

She asked them to return the following day to keep her company. Alan hadn't mentioned that he wanted Jenna there again.

Seven

Mrs. Goddard poured steaming tea into a delicate china cup and set it in front of Jenna.

She was glad Alan stopped by again in the morning, even though she'd had to answer the door in a towel with her hair dripping water all over the floor. But sitting in a real kitchen accented with lush, green houseplants after walking around outside with her friend was far nicer than sitting in her plain loft nearly alone. Maybe she needed plants. Except Jenna wasn't good with them. She had tried once, right after she and Daniel were married. They had either been over-watered, or under-watered, or something. Only one remained and it looked sorely neglected. She felt too guilty about killing them to want to try again.

"Are they real?" Jenna noted Mrs. Goddard's confusion. "The plants. They're beautiful."

"Thank you. And yes, everything my son and daughter-in-law have is real. They never settle for anything but the best." She returned the teapot to the stove and eased into the chair opposite Jenna. "That's why they chose your husband. Believe me, they did plenty of checking before they hired him. I would imagine your house is just living with greenery."

Husband? She meant Alan. "Oh, we're not married."

Mrs. Goddard glanced at the baby with a weak attempt at hiding her disappointment.

"I mean, Alan's married, and yes, his house is beautiful. Aaron isn't his." She felt compelled to explain. "I'm recently widowed and Alan makes me get out of the house now and then. We've been friends since we were kids." The woman didn't look convinced. "He has three of his own, including twins."

Mrs. Goddard stirred a teaspoon of sugar into her tea. "I am sorry. But the two of you remind me of myself and my late husband. It's a shame. You would be a good couple. There is real love there." She paused only a moment. "Forgive my bluntness. When you get my age, time gets too short to wait for the right time to speak your mind."

Jenna lowered her eyes. Maybe there was real love between them, but shouldn't there be in friendship? Why did everyone see something that wasn't there, or more than what was there?

"Please, tell me about your husband."

Jenna hesitated. Tell her about Daniel? She didn't talk about him. Not to anyone who hadn't known him.

Taking a cautious sip of the strong tea, she said he was an artist, a very talented artist, and they married young because her parents didn't approve and wouldn't let her see him. She turned eighteen just after graduating and they were married within two weeks. Her father still barely spoke to her because of it. Not that it mattered since he'd barely spoken to her before then, anyway.

"You married to get away from home?"

"No. I got married because I was in love."

"You were in a hurry for a young girl. Eighteen is still a child."

Yes. Maybe that was true. But she hadn't had a choice.

The Chicago branch of the University of Illinois was a beautiful college, and Jenna could almost see herself spending a few years there, away from her family. But she would be away from Daniel, too, unless he was willing to move. That could be the answer. His mother was close to there, anyway, and they could see each other freely without her parents knowing. She liked his mom, and his mom seemed to like her, so maybe Joan would be an ally. If he still wanted her to move in with him, they could get a small apartment near campus and she wouldn't have to live in the dorms. Jenna didn't want to share a room with other girls and have to use the community bathrooms and showers. Of course, her mom said they would pay for a private room, but still, she would rather be able to wake up with Daniel every morning. He could paint while she went to school, and she could get a part-time job if she needed to. They could make it work.

"Jenna, are you listening to me?"

"What?"

Her mother rolled her eyes. "I do wish you would learn to pay attention when someone is speaking to you. I said the president seemed very interested in having you attend in the fall, didn't he? He knows high quality students when he sees them."

She turned again to stare out the car window. "Of course he did. You send enough money every year."

"And you don't appreciate anything we do for you. We have been sending money every year in order to help secure your place here. Of course, your grades will help, but there are a lot of students with good grades. We wanted to give you a better opportunity."

Jenna stopped listening. She'd heard it before. Instead, she studied the city buildings, wondering how far they were from the art gallery where Daniel's work would be exhibited in the morning. She had barely managed to time her trip to Chicago so it would coincide with his opening. But how would she get there? She had Joan's phone number, where he was staying...

"By the way, your father and I have some business to attend tomorrow. Will you be okay in the hotel alone? I promise we'll do some sightseeing on Sunday morning, although we do need to be home by early evening. If you're uncomfortable with that, you can come with us, but I think you would be bored."

"That's fine, Mom." She tried not to sound as relieved as she was. *Was it really going to be that easy?*

"Are you sure? We'll be all day, possibly late."

"I'll be fine."

"If you're sure. You can look over the materials Mr. Jakes gave you today. See what you might be interested in as a major. There's a lovely pool in the hotel. Order room service as you need."

Or she could sneak off to see Daniel. How would she do that? A bus, maybe. She could ask at the front desk, but they may report her to her parents. She would call Joan tonight after her parents were asleep so they wouldn't hear her talking from the next room.

"Have I offended you?"

Mrs. Goddard's voice pulled her back. "No. I'm sorry, I got lost in my thoughts." Aaron fussed and squirmed in her arm.

"If you would like to lay him down, I would be glad to keep an eye on him. My old legs don't handle a lot of walking anymore, but maybe you would rather be out with your friend."

She stroked her baby's head. "Thank you, but I don't leave him." She did want to be outside. "If you don't mind, though, I think I will walk with him. He seems to like the fresh air." Jenna hoped she hadn't offended the friendly woman as she thanked her for the tea and excused herself.

Stepping back into the sunlight, she squinted. The sun was directly above, spilling warmth through a light breeze. She wished she'd worn a tank top so she could feel the direct heat on her shoulders. She didn't want it on Aaron's face, however, and pulled his receiving blanket into a curve around his head.

Finding her way to the back of the house, Jenna felt like she was sneaking around again. But that was crazy. There was nothing wrong with her being there with Alan. So, then, why did she feel guilty?

She stopped as she came into view of the landscapers moving small trees around the yard. Alan watched, checking the entire scene, then walked over to a leafy maple bound in a burlap ball. He easily picked it up, though it was nearly twice his height, and moved it close to an elm. A good decision. He had a natural artistic eye, and Jenna did enjoy watching him work.

Deciding to stay out of the way, Jenna lowered onto the grass, under shade of a small tree planted the day before. The sod was still damp around the trunk, so she was careful to stay on the outer edge. Aaron had fallen asleep before they had turned the first corner and she was able to sit quietly and study the landscape, and the men working it. She loved trees. She loved the smell of grass and freshly turned dirt. She loved the light breeze playing with her hair and the warm sun penetrating her skin. She loved... Alan called to one of his employees. His voice filled the air. She loved being there with Alan. She loved ... Alan. No. She didn't. She couldn't. She had been in love. It wasn't the same. With Daniel, she hated every minute she was away from him. She had needed to be closer. She hadn't had a second thought about giving herself to him. Well, maybe a second thought, but it didn't last long, and it was only because of her age. He was everything. She didn't feel that way about Alan. She enjoyed being with him and loved that he enjoyed being with her.

He turned and spotted her. Obviously in the middle of giving instructions, he turned back, pointing at the horizon, and walked away from his work. He headed toward her. She also loved how he always stopped what he was doing to pay attention to her, even if only for a minute or two.

Alan strode the distance easily and nearly brushed her arm as he sat, his arms loosely wrapped around his knees. "Did you have a nice chat with Mrs. Goddard? I know she enjoys you and Aaron."

"She thought we were married."

He raised his eyebrows.

"She said her son and daughter-in-law only accept the best – that's why they hired my husband."

The corners of his mouth turned up. "Well, that's nice to hear."

She waited for him to realize how it sounded to her.

"Jenna, I mean... I'm sorry. I guess I should have made it more clear so you didn't have to..."

"You let them think I was your wife?"

"No. I didn't tell them that. I mentioned I was married. I suppose they assumed..."

"That it would be your wife you would take to work with you. You know what Mrs. Goddard is thinking now, don't you? I told her we were only friends, but I don't think she believes me."

He glanced toward his workers, then shifted to face her more directly. "Why wouldn't she?"

"Because she thinks..." Why had he glanced back just then? "Have you told Cheryl I'm out here with you?"

"It hasn't come up."

Jenna felt a knot in her stomach and turned her face away.

"Jen, I thought our talk yesterday cleared things up. Why are you making a big deal out of this?"

"Why didn't you tell Cheryl?" Silence. "Alan, what if something gets said? Okay, I know and you know there is nothing going on, but people talk and if she hears something second-hand..."

"Okay, you're right. I'll tell her tonight that you came out with me. But Jenna, she won't care. She never listens when I talk about my job. That's why I don't say anything. It's a waste of time."

"She loves you. Hell, she nearly worships you."

He shifted again, farther from her. "I guess I expected her to be as involved in my career as you were in Daniel's. I would love her to want to come out here with me, to let the kids play in the grass where I could see them, and be with them more, but it's not going to happen. I was so jealous of what Daniel had and he didn't even appreciate it."

"You think he didn't appreciate me? How can you say that to me?" She jumped up, startling the baby. How dare he? Of course Daniel appreciated her. He was only busy.

"Jenna." He grasped her arm.

She jerked it away and kept going. But where would she go? He had picked them up. He was her only way home.

"Jenna, I'm sorry."

She whirled to face him. "Are you? Are you trying to tell me he wasn't as perfect as I think he was just because you don't have exactly what you want? What is wrong with you? Cheryl is pretty, and smart, and a wonderful mother, and she takes care of everything so you have nothing but your job to think about, and you're not satisfied? Just what do you expect? So she doesn't like trees. So what? She loves you, and she is completely devoted to you."

"And we never argue. We never fight. We never even disagree. Maybe there's something wrong with me, but I need excitement now and then. I guess that's why I bait you. I like to see sparks."

As if she needed that now? Peace and contentment would be a good thing. How could he need more than that?

"Jen, I miss having the real fire that you and Daniel had. Is it wrong to want that?"

She closed her eyes. She missed it too. And she couldn't imagine never having it. Finally, she took a deep breath. "Then you need to make it, with your wife."

He nodded. "I can run you home if you want."

Jenna pulled her cup from the microwave and dropped in the tea bag. Aaron would sleep well after two long days of fresh air. She hadn't let Alan take them home early. It would have been more than an hour's drive round trip, and she didn't have anything to be home for, anyway. He stopped and picked up a sandwich for her so she wouldn't have to make supper, then went home to Cheryl and his kids.

She tugged at the string, focused on the swirls of brown leaking fragrant flavor into the water. How could Alan not be content with what he had? At least he had them. He had no idea… But then, she couldn't imagine not having the fire inside from wanting with every part of your being to be closer to the one you love. To not be willing to give everything and anything to make it happen.

Pulling out the bag and adding a touch of sugar, she moved to her rocker, her cup in both hands. The late afternoon air had become chilly as the sun descended and she was still a little too cool. Her hands were, anyway. The rest of her was plenty warm. She had felt that way when Joan had picked her up outside the hotel that Saturday morning. From nerves, she supposed. She told the hotel doorman she was going for a walk when he stopped her to ask. Her mother apparently asked them to look out for her. It hadn't taken her long to find Joan's car a block down the street.

Daniel's mother was in a talkative mood, but Jenna didn't mind. She loved hearing how Joan set up Daniel's first real show, how much publicity she had managed, without telling anyone he was her son. She wanted his work to stand on its own, not to be purchased for the sole means of buttering up to the influential fashion designer and art benefactor. They would think he was another of her "finds." After he was established, she would brag.

They pulled up in front of the gallery and Jenna wrung her hands together. They were cold, but her face felt flushed. Why was she so nervous about seeing him? Maybe because they had been apart for a couple of weeks. She had been so busy with end of the school year activities and with her final term paper and senior project that she hadn't been anywhere except school, the library, and her room. Well, and at Alan's now and then just to wind down. But he wasn't there much. He was graduating next Saturday and had finals on Monday and Tuesday.

"Are you coming in or should I send him out here?"

Jenna apologized and forced herself out of the car. Heat reflecting from the sidewalk burned into her skin. Still, her hands were cold.

The gallery was small, barely noticeable, but there were a few people straggling in already. Jenna watched them, fascinated by the whole scene.

"The early birds." Joan took her arm as though expecting Jenna to bolt. "They always come early to get the first peek at a new artist, then stand back and watch other people's reactions. Spies, I like to call them."

"Journalists or art critics?"

"Oh, neither. You have much to learn about the art world, child. Journalists are obvious — always with a notebook in hand and usually with a cameraman in tow. Critics come fashionably late. They like to make an entrance, although they always appear to be trying to hide who they are. Rubbish. The important ones know they're recognized. The others are sure to make their presence known."

Jenna let Daniel's mother pull her toward the door. Joan would make a good critic. She was well-dressed, but not extravagantly. And everyone either made a point to say hello to her by name, or glanced sideways at her, jealous of the attention she received. Jenna wondered if she should have dressed better. She'd worn her nice pants and her favorite blouse, but it didn't compare to the women in dresses and suits and salon hairdos. She had left her own hair down, with one small barrette holding the right side back. She looked childish compared to all of the city women. Would she embarrass Daniel? What would he be wearing?

He probably wouldn't have time for her, anyway. His mom would keep him too busy showing him off and he would have to chat with the art patrons. Maybe she shouldn't have come. What would she do while they were busy? She hated standing by herself and looking as though she didn't belong.

Jenna tried to be friendly and sound intelligent to everyone she met. Joan introduced her as a friend of the artist's, which seemed to bring her some respect. She really should have dressed better.

Inside the gallery, she stopped. Daniel's art was everywhere. It was wonderful. The soft light cast upon each painting by the fixture above brought out the highlights in his work. They were alive in this sterile, beige room. Forgetting about the people around her, she wandered off to be closer to his paintings. The first one that caught her eye was the scene below his studio, from the window. And the window was there. She felt as though she was standing inside his loft now, wrapped in the sheet with his arms around her. She hadn't seen this one before. She loved it. She loved everything he did. And she missed him.

"This is his newest piece. He said you were the inspiration, although he wouldn't explain why. Would you have any idea?"

She nodded but kept her gaze on the painting. She missed him.

"Joan, darling! You must introduce me to the artist. These are magnificent!"

Jenna turned to see a heavy-set woman burdened with too much jewelry smiling broadly at Daniel's mother.

"They are rather good, aren't they?" Joan played the benefactor part well, maintaining a professional distance from her son. It was a good thing she had kept her maiden name, or took it back again. Jenna wasn't sure.

"Good? My dear, you're being too modest. You have such an eye for finding quality. Where in Heaven's name did you find him?"

"In a small city I visited recently. I decided he should have a wider audience."

"Oh, without a doubt! He is here, isn't he? I do so want to meet him."

Joan smiled. "Of course. We were on our way to find him. You are welcome to come with." She turned to Jenna. "Edna, this is Jenna Givens, a friend of Daniel's. She came up to the city in order to be at his first opening. Jenna, Edna Covington."

"Ahhh, the girl in the paintings! I can see why he chose you. He didn't have to do any touch-ups to make you look paintable."

Paintable? Was that a word? In the paintings? She thought he changed his mind about the student series she posed for. Joan hadn't told her...

"Come now, let's go find him." Joan avoided her glance and took her arm again, talking with Mrs. Covington as they drifted through and among small groups of people.

Jenna studied the paintings visible from the main path while listening to any comments she could grasp from those around. Most of the artwork she recognized, some she didn't. All were amazing. She wished Joan would release her so she could wander on her own. She wouldn't be alone there. She was very much at home standing in front of any of Daniel's pieces.

"There he is, trying to act like he doesn't belong here."

Jenna looked in the direction Joan nodded. Her breathing stopped for a few seconds. She had missed him so.

Joan released her arm and took her other companion to introduce to her son. Jenna hung back. She didn't want to be in the way. Okay, she wanted to get herself under control so she would be able to act like a friend. And he hadn't seen her yet.

He smiled politely at Mrs. Covington and accepted her hand and obviously some compliments. He was wearing jeans and a T-shirt with a blazer thrown over the top. She watched him nod slightly and treat his mother as an acquaintance, then Joan turned her head toward Jenna, and he did the same.

He walked away from the women. Jenna wondered if she should meet him part way but couldn't seem to move her feet. In no time, he was in front of her grasping her fingers. "I was afraid you wouldn't come. Your parents brought you?"

"We came to look at the college. They don't know I'm here. Daniel, this is *wonderful. You should hear what everyone is saying. They love your work."*

"I've missed you, Jenna." He set a hand on her arm and leaned in to touch his lips to her cheek. "How long are you staying?"

"I have all day. They have business."

"And tomorrow?"

She shook her head. "They're taking me sight-seeing. They want me to get to know the city for when I start school here."

He backed away slightly. "You're going to U of I?"

"They want me to. I don't know."

"I would never get to see you."

"Unless you move here."

"You're asking me to move back to Chicago?"

"No. I just thought ... your mom's here, and your work..."

"Jenna, I can't live in a big city. Peoria's big enough and I like it there. I may have to visit for shows, but..."

"Then I'll go to I.C.C.; I like it better, anyway."

He studied her face. "I feel like I should argue, but I don't want you so far away. As soon as you're eighteen, I want us to tell your parents we're dating so we don't have to hide it, so I can see you more often."

"Daniel." Joan announced her presence before getting close enough to hear the conversation. She had someone else who wanted to meet him.

Tell her parents? They would never have it.

The telephone's ring startled her and tea splashed onto her jeans. She set the cup down and grabbed the receiver before it woke Aaron.

"Jenna, I got a reprieve from the meeting. I'll be at Denise's first thing in the morning. Can I come tomorrow afternoon to see you and the baby? Actually, let me take you all to lunch. Should we pick you up or would you rather meet us?"

Joan? Tomorrow? Well, Jenna had told her any time. "Sure. I'll meet you there. When and where?" As if she had to ask. Joan always took them to Jumers. The castle-shaped restaurant really was beautiful, but too elegant for Jenna's taste although she got used to dealing with that whenever necessary.

Luckily, Joan didn't hold her long and she went to grab a towel to soak the tea from her jeans. Forget it. She was too tired. Beginning to strip them off, she headed to the shower she hoped would help her sleep. She would need the extra rest in order to be with Daniel's family the following day.

Eight

Jenna pulled onto Western Avenue and searched Jumers parking lot for an empty space. She hoped it wouldn't rain. Dark clouds threatened and the temperature had plummeted overnight. Was that why Alan didn't ask if she wanted to go with him again? Or did Cheryl object? She couldn't have gone anyway, but she would like to know why he hadn't asked.

Finding a space close to the door, she eased the Mustang in. It wasn't a practical family car; the van would have to replace it as Aaron grew. But she preferred to drive her red sixty-six Ford, a gift from Daniel after his first big success.

She sighed. She didn't want to go in. They would be there already. Joan was always early and Jenna always tended to run a few minutes late. She was so different than her mother-in-law. She never felt together enough, or smart enough, or interesting enough around Joan and Denise. Daniel's sister was a lot like his mom: tall and thin and always dressed perfectly, even when home tending her children. Jenna liked sweats and big T-shirts to cover her extra weight.

Her son began to fuss. "Okay, baby. Just a second."

She climbed out, careful not to hit the Cadillac beside her, and pushed her seat forward. Gathering Aaron and his bag in one arm, she rubbed his head and grinned about the dark hair slightly curling in front of his ears. In response, he raised a tiny hand to her face and pushed his head against her neck.

"There is so much of your daddy in you. He would be so proud to take you everywhere and show you off." She kissed his cheek and noticed a couple staring. Jenna ignored them. It used to bother her that Daniel's notoriety for being rude kept people from speaking to her, but now she considered it a blessing to be mostly left alone. Though occasionally, she wished his public image hadn't been so negative. People had no idea how wrong they were about him.

Giving Joan's name to the maitre d', Jenna followed the man through the dining room. She studied the sparkling chandeliers that echoed crystal candle holders on each table, enjoyed the scent of exquisitely-prepared entrees and focused attention on the classical music emanating from all around her. Anything to avoid stares from strangers at surrounding tables. Most were in business clothes. She still didn't dress well enough for Joan's crowd.

"Jenna, dear."

If Joan was bothered by her attire, she didn't let it show. Her mother-in-law performed the social touch of the arm and peck on the cheek. Denise gave Jenna a warm, sisterly hug and claimed Aaron.

"I'm sorry I'm late. He slept longer than I expected and he gets grouchy if I wake him up too soon."

"Nonsense, you're fine. Denise and I were just saying we should do this more often. We do miss seeing you both." Joan tugged Aaron's sweater from his arms. "I swear he gets more handsome every time I see him. You do look like your father, don't you, my love? Jenna, please sit. We've ordered drinks. Get whatever you like."

The maitre d' had waited and Jenna thanked him for pulling her chair out, then requested an iced tea, without the ice, from the young waiter who had come over immediately.

She fidgeted with her silverware while Denise entertained her son. She would have preferred to keep him to give her hands something to do. Joan asked how they were and what the five-and-a-half month old was doing by now. Denise chatted about her own children and related how much she loved working part-time just to be out of the house.

The waiter returned with the tea but forgot to leave out the ice. She wouldn't send it back as Daniel would. She hated doing that.

"Excuse me, but she specifically asked for no ice."

"Joan, that's okay."

"Now, Jenna dear, I may not see you often, but I do know you don't like anything too cold. Please bring her another glass."

Jenna wished Joan hadn't noticed.

"You know, Daniel always laughed about that. He thought it was the funniest thing to order iced tea without ice or to keep cola in the pantry so it wouldn't be cold. I'll never forget his look when he first realized... Jenna?"

She looked up at Denise.

"I'm sorry. I wasn't laughing at you."

"No. I know you weren't."

"Are you all right, dear?"

Joan's hand on her arm didn't help. She breathed deeper to calm herself. She didn't want to sit there pretending everything was okay.

"Maybe we should order." Joan pulled back and picked up her menu, as though she didn't already know what she would have. Jenna's mother-in-law had a specialty in every restaurant she frequented.

Not especially hungry, and uncomfortable with the surroundings, she searched for something simple and easy to eat. Finally deciding on tortellini – no cutting or crunching – Jenna returned the menu to the waiter and tried to stay conscious of her posture. Her mother nagged endlessly about her "lazy shoulders," convinced it was a sign of low class. Jenna had often been convinced the hospital sent her home with the wrong parents. Except that she looked too similar to her father, which also gave her mother fits. High-class ladies were supposed to have fine, delicate features. Like Joan, and Denise.

Aaron began to fuss and Jenna was glad to take him.

Following the conversation proved difficult between the baby squirming and glances and whispers coming from nearby tables. She picked at her meal and accepted the offer of a box for the remainder. And she let Joan talk her into dessert. Aaron finally relented and sat in the high chair with a teething biscuit.

"So Jenna, I saw the Russells the other day and they asked me about you. They want to know when you're coming up to Chicago. They would dearly love to see you and the baby again. Aaron was just a tiny thing when they saw him at..." Joan sipped her coffee, avoiding talk of the funeral. "And they aren't the only ones. I'm asked about you quite often." She set her cup down. "I wondered if you were up to a visit. Next weekend there's an opening by a young man who has potential. We could do some shopping and throw a little gathering for a few friends and attend the show."

"I don't do art shows anymore." Jenna hadn't meant to sound so unfriendly, but she didn't want to be around those people. She didn't want to walk into a gallery and know it should be Daniel's work there.

"Dear, it won't go away because you run from it. I know. I've tried."

"I can't do it. Not yet."

Joan touched her arm again. "Come back to Chicago. We don't have to attend the show, but you should get away and I want to spoil my grandson."

Jenna averted her eyes. Joan always had a bunch of people around her. She wasn't ready for that.

"We'll talk. You will come over to Denise's with us?"

"It's going to storm soon. I don't want to have to take him back out in the rain."

"Of course not. It's been too long since I had a little one. We'll go back to the loft with you."

Back to the loft? Jenna hadn't counted on that. She cleaned that morning, but her paintings were still on the easels. And she didn't intend to share them with anyone, except Alan. "Okay, just give me a minute when we get there. I wasn't expecting company."

Joan smiled. "Dear, we're not concerned about a dish or two in the sink. You have your hands full right now and I do wish you would let me hire someone to help you."

"Thank you. I don't need help, I..."

"Jenna."

She turned her head. Her mother. What was she doing there?

"I tried to call to ask you to lunch. I can see I was too late." Louise Givens semi-politely forced herself to greet Joan and Denise.

"We were just finishing." Jenna glanced at the woman and younger man beside her mother.

"Yes, well, Jenna, since you're here, I'd like to introduce you to Mrs. Martin and her son, Robert."

Jenna groaned to herself. Not again. She stood on command and took their hands. The woman who looked slightly older than her mother was wearing a double strand of pearls around the folds of her neck and large pearl clip-on earrings. They weighed her ears down too much, though she was a stout woman. She studied Jenna as she would a piece of meat in the supermarket. The son was in a light gray shirt and darker gray suit pants, most likely custom-tailored, with an exactly matching tie. He wasn't tall, but his shoulders were quite large and his chest tapered into a slim waistline. If he studied her the way his mother had, Jenna didn't bother to notice.

"It's very nice to meet you." He smiled. His handshake was weak. She didn't like that in a man. "Your mother speaks very highly of you."

Of course she did. She was trying to auction her off again. "Thank you." She pulled her hand away. "This is my mother-in-law, Joan, and my sister, Denise."

The strangers said hello, with a curious glance.

"She's no longer married. I keep trying to convince her to come home again so she won't be alone."

Jenna bristled. "I'm not alone. I have Aaron." She went to pull her baby from his chair. "And I'm not dating, so stop trying to set me up."

Her mother fumed but held her tongue.

Jenna didn't care. She'd had enough. "Joan, thank you for lunch. I'm going to take him home. Come by if you want. I'll be there."

She said goodbye to Denise and gathered her belongings as her mother explained with an apology of how she wasn't herself yet.

"Jenna, I'll call you later. We can talk."

The woman had to get the last word in. But Jenna didn't feel like answering, and she most likely wouldn't pick up the phone later.

~~~

She sat nursing her baby. It started to rain just before they reached the loft, and she stared out at the drenched leaves. Well, there weren't many leaves anymore. Most had fallen off and had been trampled or blown away, or washed down the river. The trees were still beautiful to her. She loved the pattern they made against the sky, even when clouds made them hazy. If she could paint well enough to do them justice, Jenna would never stop painting them.

Daniel had been more into people, but his painting of their window had been an eye-catcher at his first show. He had several offers on it but refused them all. She was glad he hadn't sold it. It was theirs. She didn't want it to belong to anyone else, although Mrs. Covington offered quite a lot for it.

Jenna could see it hanging in the gallery. The likeness was so great she was convinced she would be able to feel the warmth of the glass if she'd let herself touch it.

She stood quietly by Daniel's side, trying not to let the crowd around them bother her. A group of girls about her age were watching him, hoping to catch his attention.

"I don't normally make such an outlandish offer for new artists, but there is something about this one. I would love to have it over my fireplace. Can you see that? A window over the mantel?" The constantly happy lady turned her eyes back to the painting.

Joan glanced at her son, questioning him again.

He shook his head.

His mother gave in. "I am sorry, Edna, but the ones meant for sale are marked. This one isn't. Maybe you could take another look at some of the others?"

Jenna knew her eyes had to be larger than usual. She couldn't believe he wasn't accepting her offer. Five thousand dollars was an incredible amount for a painting by an unknown, although the lady insisted he would not stay unknown for long.

Mrs. Covington ignored Joan and faced Daniel. "Well, I may have to settle for another one for today. But if you change your mind, you will give me the first chance to buy it?"

Daniel grinned. "Of course, and thank you." He set a hand on Jenna's back
~~~

and addressed his mother. "I'm taking Jenna to lunch. She was nice enough to come all this way, I guess I shouldn't let her starve."

"We have a buffet arriving shortly. I assure you, it's the best quality."

"I'm sure it is, but it's hard to talk here. And I want to hear her opinions." He didn't wait for more arguments.

She walked calmly alongside him, though they were stopped several times before they escaped through the heavy front door. He led her down the busy sidewalk, helping her dodge the fast-walking business people and trudging younger people. As they moved away from the gallery, his hand found hers and he flagged a taxi.

Daniel opened the back door, then slid in next to her and threw an address at the driver. The lurch of the car pulled her closer against him, or was it the arm he'd wrapped around her shoulder? Either way, she didn't fight it. His scent mingled with the mustiness of the old taxi. His warmth invaded her. She wanted to tell him so much — how she had missed him, how proud she was of him, how... His fingers brushed against her face and, gently, he raised it to his own. He searched her eyes and she tilted her head just enough...

The touch of his lips burned into her memory. His fingers entwined with her hair, locking her head into his possession.

Sliding her hand down his arm, Jenna drew the courage to go farther. Her fingers slipped underneath his blazer, around his waist. His skin was tight under his T-shirt, allowing her to feel his ribs move with his breaths. She drew closer. And he kissed her more deeply then backed away, enough to search her eyes. Jenna knew the driver was watching in the rear view mirror and she was slightly embarrassed at the thought. But it had been so long. And she wanted to be closer.

"Daniel..." Her voice came out as a whisper.

"Sh, don't talk. We'll be alone soon." His lips returned to hers and she delighted in his touch, his taste. When he again released her, Jenna leaned her head against his neck and shoulder, still caressing his back through the soft material. Alone. They weren't going to a restaurant. She closed her eyes, waiting for the taxi to stop moving, basking in the feel of his hand running through her hair.

The movement stopped and she pulled back to let him pay the driver and slide out of the car. She followed closely and brushed against him while he held the door. They didn't talk as he grasped her hand and led her up the steps of a large red brick building. The row of townhouses was well-kept, with pink and white blooms sparsely decorating the small patches of grass between the many sets of stairs. Jenna assumed it was Joan's house. Would she care that they were there alone?

Daniel released her hand to pull keys from his pocket. He unlatched the regular lock with one and the deadbolt with another, then stepped inside.

She moved barely past him so he could close the door, again locking it. It gave her a funny feeling. Jenna's parents never had the door locked when they were home *and didn't always remember when they went out. Their back door was never locked.*

"I hope you don't mind not staying for the buffet. There isn't much here, but we can find something." He removed his jacket and tossed it onto the cherry-wood coat stand.

"I'm not hungry."

"No?"

She shook her head slightly.

"Neither am I." He studied her face, and let his eyes fall. "You look good."

"I was worried it wouldn't be dressy enough. Everyone else..."

"Is too pretentious. I like how you dress." Daniel caressed her shoulder and slid his fingers slowly down her arm. "Do you want to see the rest of the house?"

She nodded and pretended to be interested in the furnishings and paintings and collectibles Joan had carefully displayed. He didn't say much about them and didn't linger in any one room very long. She followed him up the carpeted stairs and into a room with more paintings, but also sketches, framed and unframed. And a bed stuck back in the corner to make room for a large art table.

"Your room?"

"Whenever I'm here. I keep telling Joan to convert it to a guest room, but she refuses. There is one spare room, though. So if you ever need a place to stay in Chicago..."

Jenna moved in and wrapped her arms around him. She loved being where he had grown up, with all of his beginning work.

"Or you could share my room." He pulled her closer. "Just one thing. Joan knows you're not eighteen yet. She strongly advised me to wait until you're legal. She doesn't know..."

Jenna reached up to kiss him. She wouldn't tell Joan anything. And she would soon be old enough no one could stop them.

Contrary to his own words, he stepped back enough to reach the small buttons on her blouse.

The doorbell made her jump. There had been no interruptions then and she wanted to stay in her memory, but Aaron objected to the distraction as well and complained. She put herself together and tried to calm him, and herself, as she answered. Luckily, Jenna had taken the time to put her own paintings out of sight.

"I dropped Denise off. She thought you and I might like to talk alone." Joan touched the Aaron's cheek and pulled the suede coat off her shoulders.

"Would you like tea? I was about to make more."

"That sounds wonderful. Let me take my grandson."

Joan wandered the studio with Aaron while Jenna put water on to heat. She stopped in front of the zoo painting, and turned. "You know you were very important to him, though I doubt he showed it well enough, except in his work."

Jenna didn't answer. Why would Joan think she didn't know she was important to her husband?

"It was my fault, I suppose. I was never much for showing affection. I do hope he was better about that with you." She paused, waiting for a response she didn't get. "I have always liked you, Jenna. I was so happy he found you. I was afraid he would spend what he had of his life alone because of his passion for painting, for creating something that would last." She looked down at Aaron. "I think knowing he was leaving a son made it easier for him, but this hasn't been fair to you. He should have told you..."

"It wouldn't have mattered." She turned away to place the tea bags into two cups, then watched the pot. What was the saying? A watched pot never boiled? Well, it did. Eventually.

Joan came up behind her when Aaron whimpered. "I think he wants his mom."

"He was eating before you came. I guess he's not done."

"Let me finish the tea. I'm not much of a cook, as you know, but I can manage that."

Jenna couldn't help a slight grin. She knew better.

Aaron grew more insistent so she accepted Joan's offer and took him to her favorite armchair. Nursing in front of her mother-in-law didn't bother her. Joan had nursed both of her children until they were nearly a year old, unlike Jenna's mother, who used a bottle because researchers said it was better for the baby. Jenna didn't believe for a minute her mother thought that was true. But it worked as an excuse.

Joan set Jenna's cup on the table and sat across from her. She didn't look at home there; it was much too casual for her style. To her credit, she tried to act comfortable. "Your mother is trying to set you up already?"

"I can't imagine why she would think I'd be ready."

"Because she never accepted your marriage. She refuses to believe it was real."

"And now that he's gone, she thinks I'm just going to write the last six years off and suddenly start doing what she wants."

"You won't let her do that to you?"

Jenna looked up. "Of course not. He will always be a part of my life. And he taught me that it's okay to be who I am."

Joan grinned. "Have you started painting yet?"

Painting? Joan didn't know...

"Daniel told me. When he knew he wouldn't make it. He wanted me to support you the way I supported him all those years when he was starting out. He said you have real talent with nature."

She shook her head. "No. I'm not a painter. That was his thing. I... I dabble now and then. It's nothing."

"You're doubting he knew talent when he saw it?"

"No, but..."

"I'd love to see something you've done. And if you haven't yet, think about it. Unless you have other plans."

Jenna looked away. She didn't have any plans, but painting was Daniel's thing. She wouldn't interfere with that.

"What do you do with your time, Jenna? Other than the baby, I mean."

How could she answer? She wasn't going to tell Joan she had been spending a lot of time with Alan, or that she was doodling, and sometimes painting. Otherwise, she sat around daydreaming about the past. But she didn't suppose Joan would want to hear that, either.

"You know, depression is a sneaky thing. It attacks while you're not looking, and I know the signs." She studied Jenna's face. "I want you to come for a visit. It's too hard to make yourself get out when you're alone. And you know how pushy I can be." She smiled.

Jenna felt a tear run down her cheek and reached up to brush it off. Depression? Was that what was wrong with her?

Aaron had fallen asleep. She refastened her bra, trying not to move more than necessary.

"Dear, you are a wonderful mother, but you have to take care of yourself, too. It isn't good for your baby for you to be so unhappy, and I promised Daniel I would look after both of you."

Her tear multiplied and Joan took Aaron, managing not to wake him. "Come. Lie down a while and I'll make some phone calls.

Nine

Joan placed the call to Jenna's mother.

Jenna had stalled as long as possible. Her nerves were frayed. She couldn't deal with the arguing and questioning, and worse, the lecture she would have received. Her mother-in-law, on the other hand, had no qualms about telling Louise Givens she was taking her daughter to Chicago. Jenna thought Joan was a bit too happy to do so.

They spent the day before with Denise and her kids, shopping and lunching. And they had supper at her house, with her husband. Jenna liked Terry. He was nothing like Daniel, very quiet and relaxed, but with a sharp wit. She supposed his calm nature was necessary for a veterinarian. He loved animals, sometimes to a fault, and would have had a house full if his wife hadn't overruled him. They did have two cats that loved to rub against Jenna's ankles. She liked cats okay but had to keep Aaron in her arms, or in someone else's, so they would stay away from him.

Exhausted by the time Joan dropped them off after the visit, Jenna had gone to bed early. She'd meant to call Alan. He had to know she would be away for a while. How long, she wasn't sure. But after stumbling through the day, Jenna was unable to force a phone call to her best friend.

Now she was packed and Joan was waiting on her to finish feeding Aaron so they could leave for the city. Denise would keep on eye on the loft and Jenna told her downstairs neighbor they would be gone. She had to call Alan.

"Is there anything else you need me to do before we leave?" Joan hovered nearby, completely unused to waiting on anyone.

"No, I'm ready as soon as he is."

"Don't rush him. It's a long ride for a little one. Maybe he'll sleep most of the way if his tummy is full. You do have a juice bottle, in case?"

"Yes. It's in his bag."

Joan wandered over to the studio, again studying Daniel's artwork. How was Jenna going to call Alan? She should have made herself do it the night before, or in the morning before Joan came. Her mother-in-law arrived early, though, before Jenna had even showered. It was an excuse. She didn't want to make that call, either.

Aaron pulled away. She had to think of something. "If you want to take him down and put him in his seat, I'll be right behind you." She would have to check the car seat latch before they left if she didn't put him in herself, but it worked. Joan gathered Aaron and asked if he was ready to go. He gave her a big smile in return.

When the door closed, Jenna took a deep breath and picked up the phone. It rang four times. Five. Maybe they had gone out. Well, she could call from Chicago...

"Hello?"

He sounded hurried. "Alan? Is everything okay?"

"Jen, I was on my way over. You didn't return my call yesterday and didn't answer again this morning and I was worried."

"Yesterday? You didn't leave a message." She hadn't thought to check last night, but the light wasn't blinking.

"Yes, I did. You didn't listen to it before you deleted it?"

"I didn't... You must have dialed the wrong number."

"Jen, I know your voice when I hear it." He paused. "What's going on? Where were you?"

"I, um, Joan's here. We went out."

"She's there now and you called me?"

"She's outside. Waiting." Did he hear the tremor in her voice?

"What's going on, Jen?"

"We're going to Chicago. I called to let you know so you wouldn't worry. She wants to spend time with Aaron."

"For how long? Do you need me to pick you up next weekend?"

Next weekend. No, she imagined it would be longer than that. "Thank you, but I'm not sure how long. I just... Joan thinks I should get away for a while."

He was silent again. What was he thinking?

"Can you wait ten minutes? I'll be right there."

"No. She's already waited longer than she wanted to, and I really need to go. I just..."

"Jenna."

She waited. Why was this bothering him?

"I'm not sure this is a good idea. I want you to wait till I get there so I can talk to Joan. Have you told your mom yet?"

Her mom? "I saw her a couple of days ago. She tried to set me up again."

"I know. She wants me to talk to you."

"She what?"

"She came over yesterday, to ask me to encourage you to date."

Jenna felt her jaw clench. How dare she?

"I told her it was too soon for that and she needs to back off. She's pretty ticked at me now."

"Thank you, but it won't work.. I have to get away from her..."

"Are you sure it's her you're trying to get away from?"

She held her breath. She knew what he was asking.

"Jenna, you know..."

"Alan, don't. I have to go."

"Jen."

"I'll call when we get back."

Silence. Just for a moment. "Call me when you get there. I'll be home. And Jenna, I know where Joan lives."

~~~

She stared through the car window at Lake Michigan, past the walkers and joggers. Jenna loved the part of the drive where she could see small boats anchored in the cove and those a little farther out with their sails wide open. It was chilly, the last day of September, and had to be even more so on the lake. But she wouldn't have minded being out there with them.

"You do like the water, don't you, dear?"

"Yes. I always wished..." She stopped. She would never complain about Daniel to his mom.

"That Daniel shared that love with you?"

She glanced at Joan. The bumper-to-bumper traffic didn't faze her. And neither did talking about her son. Maybe nothing did.

Joan swung from one lane to the other, dodging slower cars. "He was always afraid of water. I even had a hard time getting him to take baths when he was little. I'm not sure why."

Jenna turned back to the lake. "The same reason Cheryl doesn't like being outside, I guess."

"What?"

"Nothing. I guess some people aren't into nature." She shouldn't have mentioned Cheryl, but maybe Joan wouldn't recognize the name. Anyway, she let it go.

Jenna glanced behind her to check on Aaron. He was still asleep. His little head was tilted to one side, resting against the soft material of his car seat, his mouth open slightly. He stayed awake for nearly an
~~~

hour, which was unusual, but maybe because they were in Joan's car instead. He was always more comfortable in familiar surroundings. She hoped being away from home wouldn't be too hard on him.

The scenic drive gave way to city buildings crowding each other and pedestrians darting between the slowing or stopped cars. Jenna couldn't imagine stepping out in front of a moving vehicle. Peoria's traffic wasn't nearly as heavy, but she always waited on the traffic light to tell her it was safe to cross.

Joan pulled into a parking garage. "I do need to run into the office. You can come in and say hello."

Jenna took a deep breath. It was starting already: the socializing. Maybe she shouldn't have come.

Taking her usual space, Joan switched the engine off.

"Aaron's asleep. I'll keep him here so he doesn't get grouchy."

He fussed and Joan smiled. "Well, now you don't have an excuse."

~~~

She awoke to a light tapping at the door. Who was there so early? Her eyes parted against their will and took in her surroundings, forcing the realization that she wasn't home. And the knock came again.

Aaron was still asleep in the crib on the other side of the room, so she pushed herself out of bed and shuffled to the door, peering out into the brightly lit hallway.

Her mother-in-law was adorned in a straight skirt and matching jacket, carrying her heeled shoes by their straps. "Jenna, I'm sorry to wake you, but I have to get to the office. There are eggs and bread. Help yourself to whatever you can find. I'll be back to pick you up for lunch. We'll go to The Zodiac Room. I'm not sure what time I'll be free. I'll call." Joan took a breath. "Did you sleep well?"

Jenna nodded, more asleep than awake. She must have slept hard after the long period of tossing and turning.

"My number's by the phone if you need anything."

She waited until Joan started down the stairs and shut the door again. Aaron moved a bit but wasn't ready to get up, so she went back to the Queen Anne bed and slithered underneath the covers, allowing her head to sink into the deep pillow. She had decided to stay in the guest room rather than be in Daniel's room, without him.

But she couldn't sleep.

Instead, memories of the first time she'd been to Joan's apartment invaded. Jenna was certain she and Daniel conceived their first child
~~~

that day, the daughter who would have been six years old now. Jenna missed her, too. She got up again. Taking the few steps down the hall to her husband's room, she brushed tears from her eyes. And she stopped at the door.

Daniel's room looked the same. His sketches adorned the walls. His art table took up much of the space. And his bed was still pushed back against the far wall, out of the way. She stood a long while, feeling him there, feeling herself with him there. But she didn't go in.

Time slipped past until Aaron began to fuss, forcing her return to the present.

The Zodiac Room, on the fourth floor of the Neiman-Marcus building, was one of Joan's favorite places to lunch. It reflected her personality. Just off Lake Shore Drive on Michigan Avenue, the elite restaurant boasted valet service and old-fashioned elegance. The bar held no interest for the well-known designer, but she had a set table in the art deco room.

Jenna didn't like any of it. It was too showy, too...

"Joan, darling. I have been trying to call you for the last week. You are the hardest person to reach."

Aaron fussed at Mrs. Covington's grating voice and Jenna used the excuse to back away in hopes of disappearing into the furniture, behind her mother-in-law.

"You know what they say, Edna: no rest for the wicked." Joan turned and grasped the arm not holding the baby, pulling her up to her side. "You do remember my Daniel's Jenna?"

Was she always going to introduce her that way? She hoped the day before at the office had been a slip.

"Why, of course! Jenna, darling, you look *wonderful*. How are you?"

"Fine, thank you. How are you, Mrs. Covington?"

"Oh, I'm always wonderful. I have found a treasure, an absolute treasure. Joan has been helping to convince the gallery to show his work and we finally have a date. You simply must come see this young man's work." She stopped. "Oh, darling, I'm sorry. I shouldn't discuss this in front of you. Joan, do call me. We'll talk later."

Mrs. Covington attracted attention, as usual, and Jenna focused on her son, trying to ignore the looks and whispers. The woman didn't quit. "What a *beautiful* little boy. I'm afraid I don't remember what you named him."

Fighting to remember her manners well enough not to embarrass her mother-in-law, Jenna forced an answer. "Aaron, after his father, and it's fine. I think it's wonderful Joan is still supporting art. There are a lot of young artists who deserve the recognition."

"You were always the sweet one. You should come with Joan to see him, then. He is a modern artist, nothing like Daniel, but I enjoy his work. It's bright and makes me happy. Will you come?"

Jenna hesitated. After what she had said...

Joan rubbed her arm. "Jenna and the baby just arrived yesterday. We haven't talked yet about our schedule."

"Will this be a lengthy visit, then?"

"That depends on Jenna. She's welcome to stay as long as she likes, and you are welcome to come over this evening, if you would like. Jim and Lois will be there, and a few of my co-workers. But if you'll excuse us now, I don't believe the child has eaten yet today."

"Oh, of course. I'm keeping you from your lunch and my male friend is most likely wondering what's become of me. I am sorry. I will see you tonight, then?"

Joan agreed politely, then signaled to the maitre d'. He nodded and led the way to the back of the room, to a private spot next to the windows, and beckoned to a waiter who appeared immediately.

Joan was right. Jenna hadn't bothered with breakfast and the scent wafting from a filet mignon at an adjacent table surged a hunger pang. Daniel's favorite meal. She ordered her customary tea without ice, which didn't even faze the man, then looked through the menu while holding Aaron on her lap. Until he reached for the tablecloth, and she shifted him to her shoulder and let him pull on her hair instead. He loved pulling on everything recently. Good thing she didn't have a sensitive scalp.

"We must find someone who will sit for you while you're here. A mother needs her time away."

"Oh, I don't leave him yet."

"Never? You can't be serious? He's nearly six months."

"I have no need to leave him."

Her mother-in-law would have argued if the waiter hadn't come back with their drinks. This one had remembered to leave out the ice.

She decided on the restaurant's classic tuna pecan sandwich and thanked the waiter, noticing glances from the filet mignon table. The whispers around the room made her self-conscious. Maybe they weren't talking about her, but then, why did she keep feeling their glances? Joan pretended not to notice. She was horribly good at it.

While her own mother made a point to talk to everyone she even vaguely recognized, Joan was the opposite. Most of the patrons knew her, or at least knew who she was, but she acted as though she and Jenna were alone in the room. She said a few years before that her unavailability made people more interested than if she were friendly to just anyone. But if Jenna hadn't known her better, she would have thought Joan a real snob.

"I hope you don't mind that I've invited a few people to the house tonight. Only close associates and a few friends. Nothing fancy."

Jenna pried Aaron's fingers off her ear. "What should I wear?"

"Anything you like. As I said, it's nothing but a little get-together."

Maybe she would wear her old sweats. Joan did say "anything." She supposed she wouldn't. Remembering Joan very often had people over, Jenna brought many of her nice clothes. In fact, she only had two of what she called house outfits, one to wear while the other was washing. She basically lived in the same old clothes day after day, anyway, only pulling out something decent to leave the apartment. Unlike Joan, who stayed in her work clothes until after her evening shower, when she replaced the meticulous garments with a long robe. Jenna simply slipped into clean sweats until changing into a long T-shirt for bed.

Lunch conversation centered around Joan's work and troubles with her newest client. Jenna only half-listened as she tried to keep Aaron happy by giving him pieces of bread from her sandwich since he preferred her food over his teething crackers. Once, they were interrupted by someone Jenna vaguely remembered meeting at one of Daniel's shows. The lady wanted to see his son, and of course, told her how much he looked like Daniel and said she was so sorry for her loss, and the loss to the art world. Jenna thanked her politely and wished she would go away. Why did she care about the loss to the art world? It would keep going just fine without him, with some new kid taking his place. Maybe Mrs. Covington's "treasure."

But, she made it through lunch and looked forward to getting back and being alone. It seemed funny to think about slipping back into her sweats while walking through the polished marble foyer and out into the main building.

"I have to put in a little more time in at the office today. You can come visit while I finish." She saw Jenna consider an objection. "I'll pull the curtains closed when the baby gets hungry so you'll have privacy. It won't be more than an hour or two."

Behind Joan, who was outpacing her, Jenna grimaced. She always had trouble keeping up with her mother-in-law. Whenever Daniel had been with them, he'd walked more slowly for her and asked Joan to do the same. Being five-eight and mostly legs, Joan didn't realize how hard it was for someone three inches shorter and not all legs to walk as fast, especially with a baby on her hip because he didn't want to be in his stroller.

Finally, Joan turned. "Oh, Jenna dear, I'm sorry. Here, let me take him. You must be getting tired."

She didn't argue. He was getting too heavy to carry around and Jenna hadn't made herself lose the extra pregnancy weight. The additional six or eight pounds were enough to make a difference in how she felt. She supposed she should think about getting rid of it. But, for what reason?

As they approached the elevator, Jenna caught the face of a man who stepped out of their way. Tall and sturdy, but thin, he had a classic look, highlighted with a speckled tan sweater and brown twill pants. He glanced over while chatting with a companion, then returned his gaze to hers and smiled. She turned away. He wouldn't have looked twice if she still had the baby in her arms. But still, it was nice. Maybe she didn't look all that bad.

Ten

Jenna found herself thinking of him as she prepped for Joan's second soiree in two days. The guy at Neiman-Marcus. Why did his smile still haunt her?

He was cute, in an adult way. Young, but not boyish, and appeared ... well, normal. There was nothing different about him. His gold-brown hair was in medium layers, perfectly combed, and he wore wire-rimmed glasses that were barely noticeable, blending in with his natural coloring. So what made him stand out so much in her mind?

His smile. It was genuine, sincere. And he appeared comfortable with himself while leaving out conceit. How did he get that way? What was he doing with his life that made him so content? And why had she been so rude?

Jenna studied herself in the standing mirror. The Victorian frame didn't match the image the glass reflected. She hadn't bothered to change after finally getting back to the apartment and was still in her soft cotton-polyester pants and long sweater. The outfit hid her shape well. She could just as well have been wearing a sack. But, it had been good enough for the guy at Neiman-Marcus. It was good enough for Joan's ... whatever they were. She didn't have to impress them.

With a spritz of soft musk on her wrists, Jenna collected her son from the little crib that held his father as a baby. Aaron politely fussed at her while she freshened and combed her hair. He held himself up with a grip on the wooden rails and reached a hand out when she got close. "Okay, baby. Come here." He thanked her for the rescue by pressing his mouth against her cheek.

Wiping the baby drool, Jenna returned his kiss. "And why would I want to leave you with a sitter? You're the one who gets me through the days." She stroked his soft hair and grimaced at his chubby hand yanking her not-so-soft locks. "Ouch!"

He laughed.

"That's not funny. That hurts."

He looked at her face and gave her hair another pull.

"Aaron." Despite knowing she should discourage him, she found his laugh too uplifting and kissed his head. "Okay, let's get you changed. They'll be here soon."

He didn't want to be down long enough for a diaper change but tolerated it since she stayed right there and talked to him. She didn't bother to change his clothes. He was fine the way he was.

Jenna sat on the bed and held him a while, enjoying their private talk, until a deep breath gave her courage to start the evening. The second of many long ones, she assumed.

The doorbell rang as she reached the bottom of the staircase. She and Joan nearly collided in the entry. "Oh, there you are, dear. I set up the playpen so you wouldn't have your hands full all night. Go ahead and find yourself a drink while I get the door." She didn't wait for an answer before turning to greet her company.

The first few intrusions weren't bad: an associate from the office whom Jenna had met already, and three people she faintly recognized from the gallery. They were talking business, mostly leaving her out of it. She hadn't put Aaron down. She wanted his company and he was happier that way. One of the women tried to take him but he refused outright, as only a young child was allowed to do. Jenna apologized perfunctorily while thinking adults could learn something from babies.

As dark set in, Jenna hoped she would be able to sneak away since she had made an appearance, and edged toward the hall in the guise of making Aaron happy. Her escape nearly complete, she got to the stairs.

The doorbell rang. Jenna sighed. Again? How many were coming? "I'll get it." She propped Aaron on her hip and turned the antique, gold-finished knob. Mrs. Covington, and...

"Hello again, Jenna! And how is the young Mr. Rhodes tonight?" She touched Aaron's chubby calf and he pulled away.

"Shy, as usual. How are you?" Jenna glanced at the man hanging just behind. Most likely the "treasure."

"Oh, wonderful as always!" The bubbly woman swept past Jenna into the hallway, pulling her guest along.

Jenna closed the door and started to ask them to go on in.

"I must introduce you to this brilliant young man. I mentioned him briefly at lunch yesterday, if you remember, and thought I'd bring him along. Jenna Rhodes, this is Trevor Dade."

He took her hand. "Jenna Rhodes? You're not *the* Jenna Rhodes?"

She raised her eyebrows at the guy. He was roughly her age and obviously trying to make a statement with the long blond bangs hanging partly in his eyes, and long, loose black clothing accentuating his overdone thinness. "I'm sure there are several. Rhodes is a fairly common name."

"You weren't married to Daniel Rhodes, the painter?"

Her stomach tightened. She should have known anyone in Joan's circle would recognize her name.

"Well, of course!" Mrs. Covington beamed. "I did say you simply *had* to come tonight." She protectively held his arm. "Trevor is not much into the socializing arena. I had quite a time convincing him he wanted to be here. Much better than going to some bar, now, isn't it?"

He paid no attention to the woman clinging to him. "You still live in Chicago?"

Jenna fidgeted with Aaron as a distraction. He was sitting calmly in her arm, watching the conversation. She would have loved for him to interrupt. "No, I'm visiting Joan."

"Oh? Why did you move away?"

Move away? "We never lived in Chicago. Daniel moved before I met him. We just came up a lot for his shows."

He nodded with a piercing stare directed mostly at her eyes. "I heard rumors he had a kid, though most say it's just a rumor. I guess they were wrong."

A rumor? They had kept track of every detail of Daniel's life while he was still painting, and his son was just a rumor?

"Jenna, dear, are you going to invite them in or keep them in the foyer?" Joan took Jenna's side but spoke to her guests. "Edna, I'm glad you could make it. And this must be Mr. Dade."

Jenna watched the introductions, and the way Trevor Dade was using a rehearsed politeness that didn't fit him. And he refused to go along to the main room with Joan until Jenna went first.

He used the same politeness with the other women and grabbed every opportunity to find his way to Jenna, though she tried to keep her distance. Of course he only wanted to get inside details of Daniel's life. She was used to that. Her only purpose in his world, as most people had seen it, had been to play the supportive wife and feed information to the curious. Although, she hadn't been just playing supportive as she'd been accused of more than once, and she never told anyone anything about their personal lives. It was none of their business. But she didn't feel like dodging questions tonight.

"You dig modern art?"

Jenna turned. How had he come up behind her without notice?

"I know your other half was a realist, but I'm kinda curious about what you like."

She paused. Had anyone asked her art opinion before? "I'm not really into modern art, no offense intended."

"None taken." The grin didn't appear fake. "What are you into?"

Was that a come on? He was standing closer than necessary and she didn't have Aaron to serve as a buffer since Joan had insisted on taking him. She stepped back. "I've always liked expressionists, and some of the surrealists."

"Let me guess. Van Gogh and DuChamp?"

"Well, yes, I like Van Gogh best of the expressionists even if they call him impressionist, but my favorite surrealist is Marie Cerminova."

"For real? She's not one of the better known names."

"And you're surprised I know anything except Daniel's work."

"No. I think you probably know a lot. And you think I only want to talk to you because of your old man."

"Yes, that's what I think. And don't call him that."

"My apologies. I meant no offense." He grinned. It was crooked and accented his city speech. "Well, Edna talked a gallery into showing my work, which you just said you have no interest in, but you could drop by, for kicks."

"I'm not sure Aaron would have much fun there. But good luck." She turned away before giving him time to object.

Staying close to Joan until her son began to fuss for his supper, Jenna managed to avoid any further conversation with him. There was really no reason for the avoidance. He was polite enough. And he seemed honestly interested in her opinions, which was nice, although it could be an act. Either way, she didn't want to find out.

She relished her escape from the small crowd and went upstairs and into the guest room with her son, then stopped. It wasn't where she wanted to be. Grabbing a receiving blanket, she found her way back to the hallway and to Daniel's door. She hadn't been able to make herself actually walk into the room since they'd arrived, and hesitated. The bedroom reverberated with his presence. Jenna could almost feel his fingers running through her hair and his breath on her skin. But she didn't retreat this time. She wanted more.

Jenna slipped out of her shoes and folded a leg in front of her on his bed, using it to help support his son while Aaron ate. The silence, broken only by occasional suckling sounds, only heightened her sense that Daniel was there with her. Would her baby be able to feel it? His innocent round eyes peered at hers, communicating the best way he knew. Did he miss his father?

Pushing the thought from her head, she concentrated on the

drawings of strange faces and studies of the masters. His version of the Mona Lisa could easily rival Da Vinci's, though it was in charcoal instead of paint. He'd told her he had done it in oil but wasn't happy with the results, so he painted over it. She wished he hadn't. More than once while they were together, she insisted on keeping a painting or sketch he wasn't happy with. He never understood why she'd wanted them, but now, she was obsessive about keeping everything and was glad she argued with him.

Well, they hadn't actually argued. She'd only had to promise to keep them to herself. No one had seen them still, and she liked having a part of him no one else had. They could study his public paintings all they wanted. His private sketches were hers.

She had teased him about how the staunch critics would react if they had seen any of his private work. The sketches he had done only for himself. The ones she had done of him, as a joke, while he was asleep. And while relaxing in the Jacuzzi. That had to be her favorite. On their third anniversary.

"Fine way to spend your anniversary. Are you wishing you could be somewhere more secluded?"

Jenna smiled at Marilyn Russell. "Not at all. I love seeing him enjoy his work so much. It's a wonderful turn-out."

"Well, of course it is. He is quite a name in Chicago. We all keep wondering when you'll give in and move here."

Jenna studied her husband across the room. These events were becoming so much easier for him than they had been in the beginning. Still, he was always ready to leave. "I would be very willing to do that, but Daniel says there's less to distract him in Peoria."

"He does still hate crowds, doesn't he?"

"I guess, but not so much." She caught his eye. He was radiant tonight. Maybe not the right word for a man, but he really was. His stylish suit jacket and contrasting shirt and tie over nicely-fitting blue jeans truly emphasized his personality, and his build.

She watched as he broke off conversation with potential buyers and made his way through the crowd. Stopped briefly a few times, he didn't allow himself to be detained long. Jenna was glad to be his destination.

Daniel slid an arm around her, speaking to Mrs. Russell out of courtesy until Rosalyn excused herself to find her own husband.

"I'm sorry we had to spend the evening this way."

"I'm not. This is what you do and I'm happy to be here to share it."

His other hand brushed her face. "We won't stay long. Joan booked us a room at the Regency, her anniversary gift, the wedding suite, with a Jacuzzi."

He had been true to his word.

They left early, ordered room service with wine and candles, and drifted between the bed and Jacuzzi. Daniel finally pulled his sketchbook from the bag he carried as religiously as his wallet and captured her relaxing in the warm bubbles with a glass of wine. Using only one half of the page, he asked her to finish it. With some persuasion, and maybe too much wine, Jenna dared to mess up his drawing by sketching her husband beside her.

The difference in quality and style were unmistakable, but he loved it.

Every show since that one ended the same: in a posh hotel room where Daniel made up for the time he had spent getting there.

Eleven

Jenna closed her book. Five days in Chicago hadn't helped her feel at all better. But five days wasn't very long; her mom would tell her she was being too impatient. And maybe she was. Jenna supposed there could have been some truth to at least parts of her mother's lectures, although she hated to accept the admission, even in her own mind.

Aaron played contentedly with the safety mirror on his blanket, pawing at the blurred baby in its reflection, then chewing on the frame holding it. She watched him for a moment, took a deep sighing breath, then moved to a small window and brushed the lace curtain away. It wasn't dark yet, only threatening darkness. Still, there was nothing to see. Joan's living room ran the length of the apartment, with windows at each end, one facing the street, the other overlooking a bit of grass interrupted by another row of townhouses. An under-grown sapling with few yellowed leaves stood in between the buildings. Jenna imagined it didn't get much light, or attention. She missed the lush, stately trees outside her own window.

Letting the curtain fall back into place, she returned to the couch and picked up her book. She didn't bother to open it. Used to the smell of paint as a backdrop as she read, she found it nearly impossible to concentrate on the story in Joan's potpourri-scented apartment.

Her eyes drifted to the phone. She hadn't talked to Alan since the night she arrived, and then just briefly. She supposed she could check in to let him know everything was fine.

The receiver grew warm in her hand. What if Cheryl answered? Well, then she would talk to her instead and try to sound as though that was what she wanted.

She dialed quickly before she changed her mind. An imperceptible sigh of relief escaped when she heard his voice. "Alan? Hi, I wasn't sure you'd be home yet."

"Jenna, I hoped to hear from you tonight. I just walked in."

"Oh, then Cheryl probably wants you to clean up for dinner."

"No. She's not home. PTA meeting."

Good timing. Should she have known that?

"Are you home? I can pick you up and we can find something..."

"No. I'm still in Chicago."

The silence seemed longer to her than it must have to him.

"You know when you're coming back yet?"

"I don't know."

Another pause. "Is Joan close by? Is that why you're so quiet?"

Quiet? "Um, no, she's out. You can't hear me?"

"I hear you fine when you talk. What's up? What have you been doing?"

"Oh. Well, nothing much. I don't even know why I called. I just wanted to let you know everything's okay."

"You've been in Chicago for a week and haven't done anything? Wasn't the point of you going so you could get out of the house?"

Was it? "Well, we've had lunch a few times, and Joan had some people over the first two nights. She's helping some new abstractionist. That's where she is now, at his opening."

"And you didn't want to go."

"I don't like abstract art."

"And if it had been surrealist? You still wouldn't have gone."

No, she still wouldn't have gone.

"Jenna, I know you don't want to be there. Just tell Joan. She'll understand."

"No, I don't want to be here. But I don't want to be home alone, either. And I have nowhere else to go." She held her breath until she could speak calmly again. "So tell me what I should be doing."

"You know I can't tell you that." His voice softened. "If you want a path, Jenna, you have to make one. It's your life. It's up to you."

"I don't know how." She brushed a tear off her cheek and wiped the wetness from the receiver.

"Come home, Jen. Running away isn't helping you."

Aaron scooted closer and tugged at her leg.

"I have to go. The baby's hungry."

"How's he doing there?"

"Not sleeping well. I usually have to put him in bed with me, and then I don't sleep."

"Careful. He'll get used to that and you won't sleep until he's four."

She chuckled, remembering how long it took Alan's oldest to start sleeping on his own. But Justin had colic as a newborn. Anything that stopped his crying had been worth doing.

Aaron started to complain. "Well, I'll call again ... sometime. Give the kids hugs for me. They're okay, right?"

"They're fine, and I will. Take care of yourself, Jen."

She nodded. Futile, since he couldn't see her, but it was the best she could do. "You too." Replacing the receiver, she pushed away more tears and went to find a tissue. She needed to calm herself before trying to nurse. Aaron would feel her tension otherwise.

After blowing her nose and running cold water over her face, she stared at her reflection. She detested crying. She detested the weakness she felt in herself recently. And she detested feeling helpless to stop it.

The tears strengthened and Jenna grabbed more tissue. It had to stop. She had to take control again. Her emotions hadn't been so tight in years, not since the few months after her miscarriage. At least then she'd been able to blame her hormones. The doctor said it was natural. But Daniel pulling away hadn't helped either. Maybe it had been her imagination, as he said. Maybe it was purely coincidental that demand for his art had increased and he'd had to do so many shows. And maybe she should have objected to him going to Chicago without her.

It wouldn't have happened then. Alan wouldn't have moved in the way he had if she hadn't cried in front of him. If she hadn't been so sick of being left alone that she had gone to his apartment...

"Jen, you need to do something of your own. Stop being so dependent on him that it kills you when he's away."

"It's not that." She flopped onto his couch, pulling a leg in front of her.

"Then what is it? Why are you so upset?"

Jenna wiped a tear. "He's been so distant since ... he's always so busy, even when he's home. I miss him."

"Because you are too wrapped up in his life. You need more than that." Alan moved closer, towering above. "Jenna, you have a right to live your own life instead of only following someone else's."

"I am living my life. This is what I wanted."

"No, it's not." Crouching in front of her, he set a hand on her exposed ankle. "This isn't what you wanted. You expected more from him. You expected him to always pay as much attention to you as he did before you were married."

"I was young. That's not realistic. He has so much work to do."

"That's an excuse, Jen. He could alter his schedule if he decided. But you don't push him. You have to tell him what you want."

"I can't. I don't want to change him."

"Why the hell not? He's changed you."

Her eyes jumped to his. Alan didn't swear, ever. He was mad, either at her or Daniel. She wasn't sure which.

"I'm sorry. I shouldn't talk to you that way. But he didn't have the right to

change you." Alan's hand drifted to her face. He touched her gently. "Jenna, you are perfect the way you are. Either insist he leave you that way ... or leave him."

The brush of his fingers against her cheek, and her hair, and the closeness, mental as well as physical, lowered her defenses. A very slight move toward him was all it took for Alan to slide his hand behind her neck and pull her closer. And he kissed her.

He was warm, and inviting, and she clung to him while he kissed her more deeply. She had to stop him, to push him away. But Daniel hadn't even touched her in over a week, maybe two. She wanted to be wanted like this, like nothing else in the world had any meaning.

Alan pulled her down to the floor, still owning her mouth. Her knee slid between his legs. One hand thrust against the cold wood floor, barely holding her body above his. The other cradled on his shoulder, feeling his strength.

His fingers crept under her shirt, ran slowly up her spine.

She shoved against him, breaking the kiss. "No!"

"Jenna..."

"No. Alan, I'm married, and you're dating..."

"So we'll leave them. I would be better to you. We could do everything together. You can help me set up the business, help me run it, and still have time for your painting, and..."

She shook her head, wrenching away. "No. Alan, no. I can't. I don't want to leave him. He's what I want." Hoping her shaky legs would hold, Jenna stood amd quickly gathered her things. She was to his apartment door before he caught up, grabbing her arm.

"Don't go."

Without looking at him, she jerked away and ran down the hall.

An insistent cry pierced her thoughts. She'd left him too long.

Splashing her face again quickly, Jenna yanked several tissues from the box and went to find him, cuddling him close, letting him calm her as she calmed him. The memories were too strong. She wasn't ready to go home.

<center>~~~</center>

"Good morning, Jenna." Looking up from her newspaper, Joan eyed her too long. "The coffee's fresh and it looks like you need it. Didn't you sleep well last night?"

"No, I... How'd the opening go?" She poured herself a cup while listening to Joan's account of the gathering. It hadn't gone as well as Daniel's, of course, but then, few openings had.

Jenna sat across from her, enjoying the morning peace before her son awoke. "I'm glad it went okay."

"Yes, he does have talent that could become something. I'm not sure I care much for him personally, however."

"Oh? Why not?" She stirred more than necessary. The cream was well mixed in by now, but it kept her fingers busy.

"A bit arrogant, I think. And quite the ladies' man, constantly paying more attention to the young women than to those who might actually provide his income. He will have to have some lessons in decorum if he expects to get anywhere."

Jenna didn't answer. Maybe he wouldn't get as far as Joan's son, who had been taught decorum all his life and had done well with patrons and critics. The girl who ended up with the abstractionist would most likely get more attention, though.

"Oh, the Russells stopped in. They didn't stay long since you weren't there as they'd hoped. I asked them to come by tonight and Edna overheard so she may be here, as well. I hope that's all right."

"Sure." As if she had any choice. Charlie and Marilyn Russell were quiet and unobtrusive. Mrs. Covington was exhausting. But at least Joan hadn't mentioned the abstractionist. And she would have the rest of the day...

"I thought we might go down to the Loop today and wander a bit. The fresh air will do you and Aaron some good. You are rather pale for having just come through the summer."

"Actually..."

"Don't even try to argue with me. Run get yourself together while Baby is still asleep and we'll stop for a croissant." She paused to finally look at her daughter-in-law, laying the paper on the table. "Jenna, dear, I realize I sound a bit pushy, but I do want you to get on with your life and be happy again. Daniel would expect me to help you do that. So go get ready and we'll have some fun."

Jenna found herself enjoying the meander through the antique and art stores. She listened, amused, to the Chicago accents, some stronger than others. Daniel's had been barely detectable, though more obvious than Joan's. Trevor's was strong.

Pushing the last thought from her head, she picked up a vase. It had an unusual curve and distorted color – green, which generally didn't appeal to her, but this one she wouldn't mind having in the loft.

"Oh, Jenna, you do have an eye. A beautiful piece. You simply must have it for your home."

She turned it over to check the price tag. Incredible. "Not at this price. That's outrageous."

"Nothing is outrageous if it suits your needs well enough. That vase was made for you." Joan stopped the salesman and took the prize from Jenna's hands to hand it to the attentive middle-aged man. "Hold this for us, if you would."

Of course he would. Joan wasn't asking.

"Joan, really, it's too much. I have no real need for it."

"Need? Dear, sometimes it is very unclear what our needs are. You seem to box your needs into only the basics of living. It's such a shame. You have a superlative creative energy waiting impatiently to be let out. I saw it in Daniel, and I see it in you. You must learn to open the box now and then, Jenna. Come now, there is another store I want to browse before lunch."

Open the box? After the years of her parents forcing her to close it? She'd fought quietly against keeping it closed while still at home, and now she had the freedom, but somewhere she had lost the nerve.

"Edna, do come in. Charlie and Marilyn are entertaining Jenna and the baby. Oh, and you brought Mr. Dade."

Jenna jerked her head toward the door. She'd been heading upstairs when Joan responded to the doorbell, hoping to make her escape to nurse Aaron without much notice. But Trevor's slight grin said he'd seen her reaction to his name. Why was he there again?

"Yes, I do hope you don't mind. I should have telephoned."

"Not at all, Edna. It's nice to see you again, Mr. Dade."

Jenna noticed the fakeness of Joan's greeting, but most likely the visitor wouldn't. She was too practiced at the art.

"It's just Trevor. I don't go in for all that formal stuff. Hey, Jenna. I missed you at my opening."

She didn't speak. What did he mean, he missed her? And what was that grin about?

Joan turned to notice she was there, with a questioning look, then recovered to fill in for her lack of an appropriate response. "I'm afraid Jenna no longer attends art shows, but I hope it is temporary. And I must apologize. I nearly wore the girl out dragging her and the baby all over the Loop today." She motioned for her guests to enter as she spoke, and Mrs. Covington gave Jenna a too-long hug as she passed.

"And did you find any treasures in that part of town? I cannot for the life of me understand what Joan sees in that section. She should have taken you uptown."

"Now Edna, the Loop is swarming with potential from the art world and Jenna did find a wonderful piece for her loft. Come, let me show you. I believe she will be busy for a moment attending to her son. Mr. Dade, I think you may remember..."

Jenna watched her mother-in-law pull them into the apartment, allowing her to continue upstairs. She hated that she would have to return to socialize with the abstractionist.

She sat in Daniel's room far too long after Aaron finished. Maybe she could stay a while and move out of the guest room into her husband's room. They always stayed in Daniel's room together during business trips to the city and Joan tried to give it to her this time.

Aaron pushed against her. He was ready to move again.

"Okay, sweetie." Making sure she was put together, Jenna forced her legs to take them back to the living room.

Trevor stood to meet her but spoke to her son. A familiar scent caught her attention and she wondered where she'd smelled it before as she started to apologize for Aaron pulling away. Except he didn't pull away. He smiled at the stranger. Mrs. Covington remarked how babies were great judges of character and the abstractionist grinned.

"If Aaron isn't afraid of me, maybe you shouldn't be either." Then he pushed the bangs back from his eyes and offered her a drink.

"I should be asking you, since you're company."

"But I make a hell of a piña colada and Joan is being hospitable about my using her bar." His eyes sparkled.

"I don't drink."

"Never?"

"Not as long as I'm nursing. I don't think babies need alcohol."

"Ah well, a virgin colada, then. I wouldn't want to contribute to the delinquency of a minor."

His sly grin and his accent on the words "virgin" and "minor" stiffened her back. Did he know..? Of course he didn't. No one knew. Joan and her parents had been very careful to conceal the fact that her first pregnancy began before she was eighteen. For different reasons, of course. Joan didn't want it to interfere with Daniel's integrity as a professional artist. Jenna's parents didn't want it to interfere with their own social status. She didn't care, herself. And Daniel insisted he didn't, although Jenna was never sure he hadn't been trying to spare her feelings. The way he'd reacted when he'd found out...

"Jenna, dear, come sit down. I'll take the little one." Joan didn't give her time to object.

Obediently taking her place, she pushed Daniel's reaction from her conscious thought and did her best to join the discussion. They were talking about designers, though, and she paid little attention to the fashion world. She supposed she should take more interest in her mother-in-law's work. But the thought of rich women trying to outdo each other with their selection of extravagant clothing held no appeal for her. She didn't even have a clue whose name was on the outfit she was now wearing.

"You know, Daniel told me Jenna is quite the artist herself. She has yet to show me any of her work, however."

Her eyes widened and she felt a warmth push into her cheeks. Mrs. Covington and the Russells cast curious glances and questions at her. Trevor stared while handing her the drink.

"I ... no, I just dabble." Why would Joan do this?

"Don't be so modest, dear. My Daniel would never compliment an artist who wasn't quite good. He was nearly as particular about everyone else's work as he was about his own."

Jenna thought of the comments Daniel had made about the other artwork at their first meeting. "Well, he's a diplomat. He always found something good to say about everyone's work, even if most of it was not very good. The first day we met..." She stopped. Every eye in the room was focused on her, and she suddenly couldn't speak. She never talked about their past.

"How did you meet?"

She looked at Trevor. He wasn't being facetious. He wanted to know. But she couldn't tell him.

"They were attending the same art class." Joan set Aaron in the playpen, then recited the rehearsed story. "Daniel had an old art teacher he befriended, and even after he graduated, he dropped in on his classes occasionally. He met Jenna there and asked her to model for him."

"You were the model?" Trevor's thoughts were too apparent.

"No. It was a still-life. I was just in the classroom and he decided to draw me instead."

"She was quite an inspiration to him, and I still have that first drawing." Joan disappeared into the den and came out holding an elegantly framed charcoal sketch.

Jenna's cheeks warmed again. Trevor stared at her portrait, which looked as though she was uncovered.

"Darling, it's beautiful. And just why have you been hiding this away? It should be shown with the rest of his work."

"No. I don't want it shown." Jenna stood and collected her son, ignoring Mrs. Covington's further questions. "I'm going to try to get him to sleep." She also refused to answer Joan's apology and fled up the stairs to the guest room.

Twelve

"Can I come in?"

Jenna glanced up at the voice, nodded, then returned her stare to the bit of dark sky she could see from the bed. She assumed her mother-in-law's guests had retreated, leaving the two women to nurse their wounds privately. Joan, of course, would have brushed it off, with an apology for chasing Jenna from the room and continuing to be the perfect hostess. Jenna had changed her baby and held him until he let his eyes droop. Placing him in the crib, she settled onto the bed, crossing her legs in front, and had been sitting, staring out the window at nothing for however long it had been.

"Jenna, honey, I am sorry if I embarrassed you. That wasn't my intention. I simply thought if you had a slight push, you might open up a bit and let us see some of your work."

She shifted her eyes to the floor. "It's really not that good. I'm not the artist. Daniel was."

Joan sat close and wrapped an arm around Jenna's shoulders. "Having talent of your own won't change anything Daniel did, or was. There is no reason for you to hide your own gifts."

"I don't want to try to be what he was. I could never even get close. There isn't any point." She jumped up, with the ruse of needing to check on her son, and stood at his crib trying to escape Joan's questioning.

"How long have you been creating art? How old were you when you began?"

Jenna took a deep breath. Her mother-in-law wasn't going to let up this time. How old? She turned slowly. "I don't know. I can't remember not doing it. It just..."

"It's a part of you, a part you shouldn't bury with your husband."

Jenna blinked back tears trying to push their way through. "I don't know how to do this. I don't know how to let go and move on. Move on to what?"

Joan paused before speaking. "To whatever it is you need to do for yourself. Not for me. Not for your parents. And not for Daniel. For yourself, Jenna. What is it that you want?"

"I really don't know. I've been doing some art again because Alan pushed me into it, but it's not good and it's not what I want to do for a living or anything. I don't want to get so wrapped up in it that I neglect my son."

"The way Daniel neglected you for his art."

"I didn't mean that."

"Yes, you did. Maybe you didn't mean to say it to me, but you did mean it. And I know he did. I talked with him about it. He assured me he would make time, and he was so sorry, after..."

"I don't want to hear this. It was fine. He gave me everything he could. He gave me his son, even though he knew..." She wiped the wetness from her cheeks and let Joan move in to hold her.

"It wasn't fair to you, honey, but I'm glad you stayed with him. He was truly much happier after finding you, and he never would have gone as far without you. But he would never want to hold you back."

She couldn't sleep. At least Aaron was.

Pushing her feet into her slippers, she grabbed the baby monitor and went into Daniel's room. She could smell him, or imagined she could. Joan was right; she would let him down by withdrawing and doing nothing. But she wasn't qualified for anything.

She sat on the old stool by her husband's drawing table and looked out the window into the blackness. October had descended quietly. So far, it was still fairly warm. By the time the end of the month arrived, winter would announce its impending onslaught. Jenna never looked forward to winter. She could never get warm enough. She did love the turning of the seasons, though: the day she would step outside and feel Halloween was near, the sudden crispness signaling childhood trips with Alan's family to select the roundest, most perfect pumpkin to shape into a jack-o-lantern. Even after she married, Jenna refused to let go of the tradition, hauling Daniel out to the patch and ignoring his raised eyebrows. One of the few things she had absolutely insisted he do with her.

For the children who would come trick-or-treating, she had said. He knew the kids were only half the reason. But each year, Daniel had become more involved, talking to the little ones who ran up to the door of their building, proudly dressed as superheroes or goblins or princesses. He even sketched a few.

The kids. Whatever Jenna decided to do with her future, she was sure it would involve children.

A flash of an old idea returned. She could go back to I.C.C. and get a teaching certificate. Teaching art wouldn't require her to paint like a professional. She simply had to know the techniques and learn how to describe them. Working with children would be easy for her, and no one could say she was trying to fill her husband's shoes.

Even in the brief moment that she could see herself using her art in a productive way, with the satisfaction of having some control over her life, Jenna realized a bit of inner peace. Rising again, she went to the bed in the corner, drew back the covers, slid out of her slippers, and curled up with her husband's presence supporting her new thoughts.

~~~

She woke to her baby's muffled cry. It was late. He rarely woke before she did anymore.

A deep yawn as she rose accentuated her more relaxed air. Her slippers were left behind. She wanted to feel the soft carpet gently tickling her bare feet. It reminded her of fresh spring grass through which she loved to walk.

The light cry for attention quieted as she approached her son. He held his arms out, waiting for her to comfort him.

"Morning, sweetie." Jenna kissed his head and sat to nurse him. What would they do today? Maybe tell Joan she was ready to go home this coming weekend. She wanted to be back in her loft, surrounded by her things. She wanted to tell Alan her thoughts about going back to school. He would be proud of her, and he'd said Cheryl would babysit. Aaron was six months now. There was no reason she couldn't leave him for just a little while now and then. She wouldn't go full time, but a class or two she could handle. It would take some time, but that was okay. It was a start.

When her baby was sufficiently full, she went to find Joan.

The apartment was dark. Jenna twisted the black knob of the nearest living room lamp to cast a soft glow into the room. The grayness of the sky didn't help. She pushed the curtain aside. Joan had already left for the day. Well, she supposed she could wait to tell her when she came home. While she stood, staring out at the apartments across the street, the mist gave way to small drops of rain. She watched a while longer as the drops grew in size and determination, until Aaron yanked at the lace in her hand.

"Oh no, honey. Grandma wouldn't like that. Let go now." She carefully pried the tiny, plump fingers from the curtain and moved
~~~

away. There was no point in irritating him by continuing the struggle. He settled for his squishy bright yellow plastic book of farm animals and Jenna set him in his playpen and returned to the window. So, it was fall now, already into the school year, but she could begin with the January term when Aaron would be closer to a year old. Would she start with art classes, in which she had the most interest, or get the basics out of the way first? Maybe one of each. She could do her language or math homework first, then do her art as dessert.

Dessert. That sounded good. With a glance at Aaron, she went to the kitchen, searching first the cabinets then the refrigerator. Nothing much. There was plenty of fruit and she usually settled for that, but it wasn't what she wanted at the moment. She supposed she should have a normal breakfast instead of the chocolate cookies she generally had at home. Giving up and deciding it wasn't quite worth taking a taxi in the rain, Jenna returned to check on her son. He was fine, still making the little book squeak from the pressure of his palm.

Flopping down on the end of the couch, she picked up the phone. He was likely at work already.

Cheryl answered, as Jenna expected. "Hey, Jenna! Alan said you called the other day. Is everything okay? He said you sounded upset."

"Oh, you know, off and on, but I'm okay. I just wanted to let you know that I'm going to try to be home this weekend, if Joan can get the time off."

"Wonderful! I'm sure he'll be glad to hear it. Just a sec, let me get him before he leaves."

Get him? He should have been at work. She waited, wishing she had held out a few more minutes. Why didn't she want to talk to him? She was ready to go home, to tell him...

"You're coming home this weekend?"

She froze a moment. She wasn't ready. What was wrong with her?

"Jenna?"

"Sorry. Um, maybe, if Joan can get the time."

"If she can't, let me know and I'll come get you."

No. She didn't want that. "Alan, no, that's okay. I can wait until next weekend if it works better for her."

"Jenna, it's no problem."

"Please, I'd rather."

He was silent, likely making it more than it was. Honestly, she didn't think Joan would appreciate her arranging her own ride back. It would look ungrateful.

"Okay, but let us know one way or another."

"I will, and thanks for the offer."

"Any time." He was holding back. She could hear it.

She answered the normal questions then hung up and took a deep breath. Maybe she should have talked to Joan first. Well, it was done; she was committed.

The doorbell startled her. No one ever came over while Joan was away. She glanced at her son and went to peer out the peephole.

The abstractionist. Why?

After a slight hesitation, she unlocked the deadbolt and opened the door just enough.

He grinned. "It's wet out here. Are you gonna let me in?"

"Joan isn't here."

"Now, you don't think I came to see Joan?"

"Then why did you come?"

"I brought lunch. You like Chinese?" He held up a brown bag spattered with rain spots and a slight grease stain.

"Lunch? It's only ten."

"Yeah, well. I don't do the breakfast thing, so I do lunch early. Are you still full from bacon and eggs?"

"No. I haven't eaten, but..."

"Great. So open the door just a couple more inches, why don't you, and we can eat together."

She hesitated. She didn't want him there, not while Joan was away.

"I'm not gonna bite, unless you want me to." He winked.

Why did this guy think he was so funny? He was much too full of himself. Arrogant, as Joan said. But it was raining harder and he was already wet, and he'd gone to so much trouble. But was he safe?

"That was a joke. Don't look at me like I'm Jack the Ripper. I'm completely harmless. Well, not completely, but close enough." He seemed to never stop grinning, but his eyes were kind and Aaron had accepted him fairly well the night before. "Take your shoes off. I'll get a towel."

"Wow, you sound like my aunt. Must be an adult thing I haven't learned yet."

Jenna didn't bother to answer. She went quickly to the linen pantry and grabbed as close as she could find to an old towel. He thanked her when she handed it to him, again with a grin. He gave her the brown bag. It did smell good, grease and all. Trying to be a polite hostess, she waited as he dried his head and rubbed the towel up and down his arms. And they traded the towel for the bag.

He followed her to the kitchen and asked where to find plates. Pointing to the cabinet, she dropped the damp towel in the hamper and went to check on Aaron. Her son was standing, holding on to the edge of the playpen, and smiled as he saw her. He wouldn't be hungry yet, but she didn't want to leave him alone in the living room so took him in her arms and returned to their visitor. The abstractionist had found the silverware and set everything up by the time she strapped Aaron into his high chair.

"I didn't know what you liked, so I got some of this and some of that." Trevor greeted the baby by rubbing his head and opened boxes as he chatted, acting as if he and Jenna were old friends who normally ate lunch together. She was uncomfortable, not frightened of him, but wary of his intentions.

Aaron gave her a distraction, though, and she tended to him even when he didn't need it. He was quite content gnawing on his biscuit and intermittently picking at the rice she put on his tray. She never bothered with the plastic dish she had for him since he always dumped it over first thing.

"Do you plan to have more?"

Jenna looked at the man across from her, waiting for clarification.

"More children. You're good with him."

Her jaw clenched. He had no right...

"Was that a bad question? You know, I don't have any manners. I just say whatever comes to mind."

Which was refreshing, in a way. "No. But that's not something I can do on my own, so pretty irrelevant, I would think."

He chuckled. "Well, I didn't mean now. I meant when you get married again. Do you want another kid?"

"I'm not getting married again."

"Never?"

"No."

They ate in silence for longer than was comfortable. Eventually, her manners took over. "This is very good, thank you."

The abstractionist grinned. "Well, good. I was afraid you were only eating it so you wouldn't offend me. That is what your clique does, right? Me? If I don't like something, I flat don't eat it. No offense meant, but what's the point?"

Her clique? And just what did he mean by her clique?

"And I offended you again. Wow, that's easy to do, isn't it?"

"I'm just wondering what you meant by 'my clique'." If he liked directness, he might as well get it from her.

"The uppity class, of course. Isn't that where you come from? I know it is; I can see it in your actions and your speech. Not that that's a bad thing. You don't seem quite as uppity as most of them. But still, it's there."

"If you think I'm uppity, why are you here?"

"If you're so bothered by me, why did you let me in?"

"It's raining. I may be uppity, but I'm not cruel."

"No. I know you're not. And I don't think you like being uppity. Thought you'd like to try something else for a change."

The glint in his eyes gave more meaning to his words than what he'd said. For a moment, only a split second, she was intrigued. Try something else? No, not what he had in mind. She didn't want that, not from Alan, not from the abstractionist ... not from anyone. She pulled her eyes away. Hopefully, he hadn't read her first thought.

He made idle chatter, with her and with Aaron, as they finished and insisted on helping with dishes, though she tried to dissuade him. He wasn't one to be easily dissuaded and she wasn't used to that. She had always been able to stop Daniel with a word, and she could with Alan. Maybe she shouldn't have let him in.

He worked close to her, occasionally running his arm into hers. She didn't believe for a minute that it wasn't on purpose, either. Two or three times she backed off but gave up because he kept following. And it was slightly comforting, in a way.

She pulled back. "Don't you have to get to work?"

"Work?"

"You don't have a job? Other than painting, I mean."

"I work nights so I'm free all day."

"Nights? What, security or something?"

He laughed. "Hell, do I look like a security guard?"

No, he didn't. He was too scrawny.

"I'm a bartender, at a shabby little club I'm sure you would never lower yourself to be seen in. But it suits me and it gives me great ideas for paintings." He shoved the bangs out of his eyes and they fell immediately back in place. "Guess I just made you even less interested, didn't I?"

He wanted her approval. Why?, she couldn't imagine. He seemed to have everything together and was living the way he wanted. What could her approval, or opinion, matter to him? Jenna took advantage of his openness. "Why do you care what I think?"

He stepped closer. "Because I'm willing to admit I'd like to try something different." He touched her fingertips, briefly, then told Aaron goodbye with a soft shake of his hand. Heading toward the door leading to the hall, he paused. "I'll be back another day, and I hope you'll let me in again."

Thirteen

Jenna lay in Daniel's arms, her head propped against his chest and shoulder. She debated whether it was the right moment to tell him. Or, she could wait a while. It wouldn't be obvious for several weeks. And the longer she waited, the closer she would be to eighteen. Would he change his mind about wanting her to move in? He still wanted to tell her parents they were dating, to face them and let them know he was in love with her. Of course, he agreed they maybe shouldn't tell them the full extent of their relationship. Not yet. But Jenna couldn't even agree to let Daniel meet them. They would object, strongly. And she didn't want him insulted.

"What is it, Jenna?"

She pivoted her head to meet his eyes. "What?"

He grinned. "You can't hide your thoughts from me. There's something bothering you."

"Oh, am I that transparent?"

"To me you are." He stroked her hair and kissed her forehead. "What is it?"

She cuddled closer against his bare skin. She didn't want to ruin the moment. They were too few. "I was just thinking of my parents. I think they're starting to get suspicious."

"We need to tell them."

"No. Daniel..."

"Jenna, this is bothering you too much. I don't like for you to have to sneak around behind their backs. If I had known before..."

She tensed, tears suddenly pushing to her eyes. If he had known ... if she hadn't deceived him ... they wouldn't be here together now. "You do regret it."

He pulled away enough to raise her face to his. "That's not what I meant."

A tear refused to be held back any longer. She turned her eyes away.

"Oh Jenna, I'm sorry. I didn't mean..."

"Yes, you did. I should have told you, and now you regret it, and I can't change it."

He forced her chin up until he found her eyes. "Jenna, no. I only meant that it's too hard on you." He wiped a few more tears from her face. "Would we be here like this now if I regretted being with you? Do you think you're forcing me to make love to you?"

She couldn't answer. He didn't act like he was being forced, but the way he reacted when she'd told him she was seventeen... How would he react knowing she was carrying his child?

"I love you, Jenna. And I don't regret anything. I just don't want you to have to hide from your parents for another month. We need to tell them we're dating. I'll talk to them, make them see…"

Her tears strengthened. It was too much. They couldn't tell her parents. She wouldn't be able to see him again, not until she was eighteen. By then, he would find someone else, someone older, and she'd have to do it alone.

He pulled her against him. "Sh, honey, don't cry."

"We can't. We can't tell them. You don't know them. They'll…"

"Okay. Okay, Jen. If it bothers you that much, we'll stop talking about it. It's only another month. We can wait. But you will move in with me then. You do still want to?"

She nodded, rubbing her head against his chest.

"Okay. Calm down now. Everything will be all right."

She clung to him and concentrated on his breathing, the rise and fall of his chest. She couldn't believe everything would be all right, but it was for the moment.

A loud clap of thunder made her jump. Her senses crept in and she realized it was Daniel's pillow she clung to, not Daniel. The image of him had been so clear in her mind that waking without him stabbed pains of longing into her heart. She silently cursed the thunder for taking him away.

The monitor on the stand next to their bed told her the storm had also bothered her son. But she didn't want to leave Daniel's bed. She waited. Maybe he would go back to sleep. The pillow still in her arms, Jenna sank her head into it and tried to return to where she had been. It didn't work.

Forcing her feet to the floor, she pushed herself to stand. Then she stopped. Aaron was quiet; maybe he had been too tired to let the storm continue to bother him. He should have been, as long as it took to get him to sleep. She usually didn't mind rocking him for as long as he wanted before he gave in, but the night before it irritated her. Exhausted, she sat down again. His sudden quietness was too eerie.

Nearly to the door, she paused when it opened. Joan had him. "I'm sorry he woke you. I thought he might go back to sleep."

"I guess he doesn't take after his father in every way. Daniel always slept best during storms." Joan caressed the baby's head.

"He doesn't like noise."

"No, neither did his father, but for some reason he liked storms. He was always a bit odd." She grinned.

"I'll take him so you can go back to sleep."

"Are you okay, honey?"

"Yes, just tired, but moms are supposed to be, right?" She knew Joan wasn't buying it. "Actually, if you're free this weekend, I think I need to be home."

Her mother-in-law nodded. "Well, I was hoping you would stay longer, but I'll take you. You'll be all right there?"

Jenna claimed her son. "We'll be fine."

Unwilling to leave her husband's room, Jenna cuddled Aaron in next to her on the bed. She wouldn't sleep now, anyway. The dream had taken her home, too far home. Her parents had been furious. And Jenna had been furious with Alan for helping them find Daniel's loft, even if he had been worried about her.

With the threat of her father pressing charges against Daniel, Jenna had finally blown. She hadn't even told Daniel yet that she was pregnant. But in the middle of the yelling, with Alan barely preventing her father from attacking Daniel when he looked like he wanted to himself, she told them all. She admitted she was pregnant, almost four weeks pregnant, and that everyone would know and she didn't care. She would wait for him if he went to jail and take care of her child on her own until he was free. Or do it completely alone, if she had to.

Her parents, after beginning to breathe again, argued between themselves about how to handle her "situation." She ignored them. She ignored Alan's stare.

Daniel moved closer. Jenna waited nervously. Her parents were too busy arguing to keep them apart. Finally, he reached a hand to her face and slid his fingers into her hair. "You won't be alone, Jen. I'll be here. Marry me."

With a sigh, Jenna gazed at her sleeping son. She wished they'd had him earlier. Daniel would have been a wonderful father, for even a few years.

<p style="text-align:center">~~~</p>

Thinking she would be lucky enough to get away before Mr. Dade honored his word about coming back, Jenna packed while her son slept. With not much to pack and three days left, it wasn't necessary, but she was restless. She hadn't called Alan back to let him know, as he'd asked, but there was time for that. And she'd been busy. Joan insisted on taking her to lunch twice during the week so far, and the Russells had come over the night before. She hoped that would be the end of company. Entertaining wasn't her thing. It was exhausting.

As Jenna stood in her room, deciding which clothes could be returned to the suitcase, she was startled by the doorbell and hurried down the stairs before it rang again and woke Aaron.

Trevor grinned. "Told you I'd be back. Have plans today?"

Yes. She was packing, but she didn't tell him that. "Why?"

"Thought you might keep me company. There's something I've been wanting to do but I don't know anyone else who'd be interested."

"In what?"

He chuckled. "Are you going to let me in?"

"I don't know. It's not raining, so I wouldn't be cruel not to, would I?"

"It would be more cruel not to, since it's not raining. I wouldn't want to think we were only bad weather friends. Or do I need to go get more Chinese food to coax the door open?"

She grinned, unwillingly, and only for a moment. "No. I just ate."

He passed her more slowly this time when she moved back. She smelled the cologne again, still unable to place the familiarity.

"So where's the little guy?"

"Asleep."

"Does he sleep long?"

"Why?"

"Well, so we can go, of course. Unless you have a sitter you call for last minute interruptions by crazy men who want to take you out."

She stared until her bearings returned. "I don't use sitters and he may be a while, so maybe you should find someone else."

"Jenna, I don't want to do this with someone else. I want to do it with you." His face suddenly lost the momentary seriousness and regained its grin. "And I won't bite, unless you want me to."

"Shouldn't you spend time on your painting? I know they'll want to do more shows."

"They can wait. I paint because I enjoy it. I'm not about to let it rule me, not for anyone. It isn't art if you do that. It's work, and then what's the point?"

Of course. That was how she felt, too. It had been one thing she hadn't understood about Daniel, until he became sick. Then she knew why he'd been so driven; he wanted to leave as much of himself behind as he could. But the abstractionist couldn't see that far into the future. He was probably about Daniel's age chronologically, but he was so much younger. And his exuberance was contagious.

She didn't want him to leave. "Do you want something to drink?"

"Sorry, that's my line. Sit down and I'll see what I can find."

"You're not at work here. I'm supposed to be the hostess."

He grinned. "That role doesn't suit you. I'm more comfortable with it." With a wink, he passed her and headed to the kitchen.

She sat, pulling a knee up in front, wrapped by her arms. What was he trying to accomplish? She wasn't encouraging him in any way, and with his looks, he could easily find someone without complications. Why was he wasting his time?

Handing her a can of soda, the abstractionist sat a little too close. He chatted with her as comfortably as he had the day before. Luckily, he never seemed to run out of things to say, so she didn't have to answer much. Jenna used the opportunity to study him, doing her best to try to figure what he wanted. Secret information about her husband was a possibility, though he hadn't mentioned him again. And what would be the purpose? Daniel was an artist. Everything people needed to know about him, they could see in his work.

"So you've never shown your art to anyone except your husband?"

She paused. Nothing had come of Joan's remark until now. How much should she tell him?

"Okay, so I take your silence as a negative, but why is it such a big secret? Are you embarrassed to be an artist?"

"I'm not an artist. I only dabble now and then."

"So then why does it matter if someone sees it? Let me guess. You're actually better than the great Daniel Rhodes and you don't want to show him up."

"Not anywhere near."

"Then why has no one seen it?"

"Someone has."

"Oh? You mean your parents and you think they just say they like it because they're your parents."

"My parents had no interest in anything but my grades." She felt warmth in her cheeks. Too much information. "I have a cousin who has, and a friend. Like I said, it's not good enough to show."

Trevor eyed her with a light tilt of his head. "Then why would your husband have told Joan it was?"

Why? She had no idea.

"I'd like to see some of your work."

"I don't have any with me."

A soft cry broke off the response she didn't want to hear anyway. Was she paranoid, or were his eyes following her, tracking her path to the stairs? A deep breath accompanied her escape. How would she get out of going with him to wherever he wanted to go today? Maybe she could say Aaron wasn't feeling well, or was too grouchy.

Turning into their room, she doubted he would believe that. The baby smiled at her sight, reaching out happily, waiting to be held. He didn't look anywhere near sick or grouchy. He would be hungry, though, and she wasn't about to nurse in front of the abstractionist, but could she stay upstairs that long without telling him? Maybe she could get him to leave by saying she had to feed him and that he needed a bath. Anything.

Gathering Aaron into her arms, she did stop and change him first. Then she braved the downstairs again, and the living room. Trevor was perusing Joan's book collection, most of which her mother-in-law hadn't read. They were for show, but they provided Jenna with entertainment whenever she was in town.

Aaron's babble turned the artist's head and brought him over. "Hey, partner. Wanna go sight-seeing?" He offered his hand. Her son smiled and grasped the strong fingers.

"See? He wants to go. I'll take him while you put something warmer on. It may be chilly."

"I don't know..."

"Don't even argue. I've been sitting here waiting for the little one and you're not turning me down now that I'm revved up for it."

"But he needs to eat ... and..."

"So fix a bottle and bring it along."

"He doesn't use a bottle."

"That's right. You said you nurse. Hey, that's cool. So it can't take long as small as his stomach is. I'll wait."

Too befuddled to argue, she nodded and went back upstairs.

Jenna hated cabs. They always scared her, zipping in and out of traffic. Luckily, they had a fairly short ride before he helped her out onto the sidewalk beside a boat dock.

"It's an architecture cruise of Chicago's most interesting buildings. I've wanted to do this for a while, but like I said, didn't have anyone else who wanted to go, and I hate doing stuff alone. Figured you wouldn't mind, seeing as you're into art." He read the hesitation on her face. "Unless you don't like boats. Damn, I hadn't thought of that. Can you handle boats?"

"Yes." She kept her gaze on the dock.

"Cool. Then let's go."

"No, I..." She didn't want to go on a boat with him. She'd wanted to go with Daniel.

"What?" He moved in front of her to get her attention.

Aaron pulled at the hair beside her face. When she grimaced, Trevor took the baby's hand away, allowing his fingers a slight brush of her cheek.

She met his eyes. They were still waiting for her answer. Patient. Calm. And Aaron liked him. "Nothing. Okay."

His grin was more gentle, reassuring.

Jenna soon found a pride at being there with him, listening to his comments about certain aspects of the tour. He had studied architecture, and he knew art. He knew the different styles, techniques, thoughts that went into each structure. He knew pieces of art within some of the buildings, pieces he thought she should see. And she found herself wanting Trevor to show them to her.

He spent quite a bit of time helping with Aaron, talking to him, holding him, grinning at people who cooed at the baby. He acted more a father than even Alan had.

Alan. She hadn't called him yet. Maybe she'd been too hasty. There were a lot of things in Chicago she always wanted to see but hadn't found the time. She could stay another week, now that she had someone willing to show her things she had interest in. After all the time she spent following someone else's interests...

"Jenna?"

She let his eyes touch hers.

"Are you listening to me at all, or have I been talking too much and boring you?"

"Oh, no. I'm listening. I just got lost in my thoughts a moment. I'm sorry."

"No problem. I tend to get too wrapped up in my own voice."

"No, really. I'm enjoying this. Keep talking."

He searched her face. "Are you? I don't want you to do or say anything just to make me feel good. Be honest."

She was being honest, and somehow, she knew she could be with him. "So are we touring the insides of the buildings tomorrow? Or do you have other plans?"

The abstractionist was taken aback, then he grinned. "No, I have no other plans tomorrow. Is the same time good for you?"

"Yes."

Fourteen

She let Joan carry the conversation during dinner as her thoughts turned over the events of the last three days. The abstractionist had surprisingly become a pleasant companion. He didn't remind her of the past and didn't pry and didn't ask anything more than to spend time with her.

Jenna and Aaron were scheduled to go back to Peoria the day after next, but she hadn't told him. She hadn't called Alan yet, either. Thinking seriously about staying another week, Jenna struggled to find an excuse. She hadn't told her mother-in-law about Trevor. Joan knew nothing about the two days of sight-seeing trips, although the way she kept studying Jenna implied she knew something.

And why was Jenna hiding it? She and Trevor were becoming friends. There was nothing wrong with that. He had been very much a gentlemen, and other than the slight brush of her cheek, he hadn't even set a hand on her. It kept their relationship comfortable. Her thoughts of Daniel remained, of course, but they hadn't haunted her as badly since the architecture tour. Maybe she would be able to get back into the art world in this roundabout way. Ease into it by focusing on different mediums. The building styles had been fascinating. She wouldn't mind taking a sketch book and recreating the angles and shadows and lines...

"Jenna?"

She looked up at Joan. "Yes?"

"What on earth is keeping you so deep in thought?"

"Architecture." It slipped out before she could stop it.

Joan raised her eyebrows. "Architecture?"

"Well, buildings." She replayed the partial truth started earlier. "While Aaron and I were out walking, I was looking at buildings. The differences. Thinking about how old some had to be compared to others. The lines they made against the sky, and..."

"And I thought you were more into nature than architecture. Isn't that why you hang out with that friend of yours? Alan, isn't it? The one who does the gardening?"

"He's a landscape designer." She pushed her remaining vegetables with a fork. It was always a struggle to make herself eat them.

"Yes. Well. I thought it was your love of nature that drew you to him. I've never heard you talk about being interested in buildings."

Because she had never thought about it before. "Well, there isn't much to see in Peoria, as far as architecture. Most of it is pretty plain, so I guess I didn't have a reason to think about it before."

Joan waited, knowing there was more, fishing for information about her relationship with Alan. But there was nothing more to say about it. They were friends. He was a landscape designer. What more was there? Nothing she would admit to Joan.

"There isn't a lot around this neighborhood worth seeing, either." She threw Jenna a pointed glance. "Now, if you go into the middle of the city, or along the shoreline, you'll find buildings worth your concentration. Maybe I can take the afternoon off tomorrow before you leave, and we can drive around to find them. I can pick you up early and we'll have lunch. What do you think?"

Trevor was supposed to be over again, but she couldn't tell Joan that, either. He knew a mostly unknown art gallery, sporting unknown artists, and talked her into going. She most definitely couldn't admit she was going to a gallery. "I was thinking I might stay a little longer, if you wouldn't mind. You're already cutting your schedule back for me, and I know you're busy right now. So maybe next weekend would be better for you? And maybe sometime before then we could sight-see?"

"That would be wonderful, honey, if you want to stay. But don't feel like you're putting me out. If you need to get back..."

"No. I don't. I guess I was having a bad day when I said that."

"And you're feeling better?"

"I guess so."

Joan perused her face. "I'm glad. I hoped a different atmosphere would help. For a time, I was afraid it was making it worse."

"Maybe it did, at first. But I've always liked being here."

Daniel's mother smiled. "I was always sure you did. I kept trying to talk Daniel into moving, for his sake and yours." She leaned back a bit from the table. "Now that you are free to do as you choose, Jenna, you might think about it. I can help you find a place."

Move? Permanently? No, she didn't think she could. The loft was her home, their home. She didn't want to leave it. "Thank you, Joan, but I can't. Not now."

The "gallery" was well-disguised. Smoke burned into her nostrils upon passing Trevor through the entrance, a heavy burnt-wood door with cross beams separating from it. She hoped the abstractionist wouldn't end up with slivers in his fingers.

He motioned for her to proceed, but she waited. Jenna had no interest in leading the way. She could barely see after the brightness of the noon sun. Covering Aaron's head with his thin blanket, protecting him from the nicotine-laden air and from anything else floating around, she stayed close behind her companion. She didn't notice any artwork. She saw bookshelves, dusty and untouched, small grimy tables with somewhat matching chairs, a few slovenly dressed patrons slumping over a counter that separated them from dusty glass bottles on warped wooden shelving, and a girl with piercings in places that made Jenna cringe. This couldn't be called a gallery in any sense of the word.

Trevor greeted a couple of guys who acknowledged his presence. They stared at her like she was a leper. He didn't seem to notice. "This is a friend of mine. She's into art."

One nodded, the other continued to stare. He pulled her past them, around a corner. Slight strains of acoustic guitar playing a blues number – Jenna had no idea which one – became louder, pulling her eyes to one of the large circular tables. She turned away when a broad-shouldered man with a gray-sprinkled beard noticed them. He sat alone, a cigar burning on the table within his reach.

"Hey, D-Day, what ya got there wi' tcha?"

Trevor grinned. "Only the prettiest thing you'll ever set eyes on."

"Yeah, yeah, you been feedin' those lines again, ain't ya? Don't listen to a word he says, darlin'. Run while you got the chance."

Jenna glanced at her companion. He was still grinning. With a slight pressure of his fingers against her back, he indicated for her to sit and pulled out a chair. She hesitated.

"I don't bite, darlin', not hard anyways, with these pretend teeth."

She looked back at him. That was Trevor's line, or a variation of it. Which one had taken it from the other? Aaron woke when she sat down and yanked at the blanket.

Trevor reached over to snuff out the cigar. "Sorry, you'll have to let it burn away after we're gone. Don't think his mom wants him to pick up that habit yet."

"You got a babe with a babe? D-day, don'cha tell me you're handling another brother's woman. I'll kick your ass right out o' here."

"Now, how long have you known me?" He rubbed a hand over Aaron's head. "This is Daniel Rhodes's kid, and his widow, Jenna."

"Well, I'll be. You're pullin' my old leg. No one like that would be hangin' round wi'chyou."

She looked from one to the other. So she'd been right. His only interest in her was her husband. Did he think she could help his career by people knowing they were..?

"Tell me the truth, now, darlin'. You ain't the painter's ole lady. He's just settin' me up for a laugh."

Jenna considered lying, telling the man she wasn't who Trevor claimed as a way to get even. But she could never deny her husband. "Yes. I'm Jenna Rhodes."

"The painter's lady?"

The painter's lady. That pretty much described her. Daniel's wife. His son's mother. She took a deep breath, raising her chin just a bit. "Yes, Daniel was my husband."

"Well, I'll be." He squinted at her. "There's a lot of sadness in your eyes. He was a good man, was he?"

Her steadiness faltered as Trevor watched her. So he wanted to know what she thought of Daniel? Fine. He should know. "He was a very good man. Caring, kind, obsessed with whatever he was doing." She stroked her baby's hair. "He very much wanted to be a father, and he loved holding him while he could." Emotions got in the way and she stopped.

Trevor lay a hand on her shoulder. "So what do you think of the gallery?" He was changing the subject, and she was grateful. "You haven't looked at the paintings yet. C'mon." He stood and pulled her chair out.

Following, she realized he was referring to the framed artwork, if it could be called that, encircling the room. It was abstract and made no sense to her. One, she could tell, was supposed to be a nude: male or female, she wasn't sure. Picasso-style, but not as sharp. The rest looked like Daniel's palettes, where he mixed the paint he used on his work. Except for the ones with sharp lines. She didn't get it.

"You're not impressed."

"Well, I just... I guess I'm not as trained in art as I should be. I don't see what you're seeing."

"You're not supposed to see what I see. That's the idea. It should be personal. You can take away whatever you want from it."

He moved closer, pointing out a particular piece with blue and green shades and tints. "What about that one? How does it make you feel?"

Jenna studied the painting, following the lines and changes of hue and trying to find a pattern, something that would give her a clue as to what it was supposed to be about. And trying to ignore his scent. Finally, she sighed. "I don't know. It doesn't make me feel any way that I can tell."

"You're keeping your mind too closed."

"I'm sorry. I can't help that. It's the way I was raised." Her tone was too sarcastic and she turned from him, embarrassed, as soft guitar wails filled the air. "Can we go? This isn't a place for a baby." Her eyes burned, from the smoke, she told herself.

Jenna bathed Aaron and showered quickly after the abstractionist left. Everything they'd been wearing was thrown into the washer. Joan would notice the smell on their clothes otherwise.

With her son in one arm, she ran water into a cup and pushed it into the microwave. While it warmed, she set Aaron in his high chair and handed him a hard biscuit. He munched it gratefully. Hopefully, he hadn't inhaled enough smoke to do him any harm. Jenna tried to cover his face again as they left, but he wouldn't have it. He kept pulling it off and smiling at her. But they hadn't been there long.

The beeping drew her attention and she went to drop a tea bag into the cup and carried it back to the table. She tugged the string. As the steaming water darkened, it reminded her of the watercolors she had worked with for a while.

She'd enjoyed trying it and turned out some relatively decent work, but her hand was too tight, so Daniel said. He told her to loosen her grip and let her feelings about her subject take over. When she tried, the results were even worse. He'd said her feelings must have been too intense. She was too uptight. His "messing around with it" had turned out wonderfully, absolutely beautiful. She gave up on watercolors.

But she did love them. The variations in intensity and clarity that could be achieved were unlike oil. There was a softness to it... It didn't matter. She didn't have the skill it needed.

After mixing a touch of sugar into her cup, Jenna picked up the pencil and pad of graph paper. Joan had notepads or graph paper everywhere so her ideas could be immediately saved no matter where she was. And there were always drawing pencils nearby. Maybe that helped prompt Daniel into his art – watching his mother constantly doodle dress designs. Denise, however, had no artistic interest, other than in following, and actively supporting, her brother's career.

A figure of a lady began to emerge from the page: a Victorian lady. Jenna worked on the details of her robust gown. Delicate lacework, pearls and flowers, a plunging neckline with not much to support it. Gathers on the front, at the bottom, pulling the hem up to reveal sleek, toned shins. More flowers to tie the gathering. Then shoes ... no, no shoes. She was barefoot ... barefoot ... walking on a cobbled path. The stones were smooth, but round, with crevices that would catch a spiked heel. On either side was grass, wiry and bent. The girl's only choices were to stay on the hard, stone path or swerve off into the prickly half-dead grass.

Jenna set the pencil down and studied her work. It reminded her of the drawings she had done in high school, the ones she gave Alan. She wondered if he still had them. He should have thrown them out years ago, after she finally let him know there would never be anything more between them than friendship. He had to have claimed to like them only to spare her feelings. He said they were her. Her thoughts and emotions. They were only quick sketches, nothing more. But she gave him the whole stack when he'd asked, to save them from the garbage.

Aaron coughed, choking.

She bolted out of the chair and grabbed him. He coughed a couple more times, then stopped, breathing normally, and chewed the rest of the crumbs in his mouth. She had to force herself to breathe again.

"*Don't* do that to me."

He laughed and grabbed the finger she pointed at his tummy. He wasn't even bothered. Of course he wasn't; he had no idea yet about the fragility of life. How quickly you could lose someone. How it could shatter your world.

She held him close, ignoring the soggy bread slobber he was rubbing on her shirt. A click from the hallway told her Joan was home. Jenna stepped out to meet her.

"Jenna, what's wrong?"

"Oh, nothing. He was choking on his biscuit. It scared me."

Joan set her briefcase beside the coat rack, then shrugged off her suede jacket, hanging it above. "It gets less scary after a while, when you start to realize it's a common baby thing to do." She rubbed Aaron's head. "You're getting your mommy all messy."

He smiled at her and reached for her face.

She backed away and took his chubby arm in her hand. "Oh, no, I've done that enough already. I'll take you when you're cleaned up."

Jenna followed her into the living room. She must have driven her kids crazy with her obsessive cleanliness. Or maybe she hadn't always been. How could you be with constant baby drool and diaper changes and toys around and food spilling over the high chair?

"So did you do anything interesting today?" Joan slipped out of her shoes and picked through the mail on her side table.

Interesting? "No, not really."

"Are you getting bored being in the house alone?"

"I'm not alone. I'm happy with Aaron as company." Again, she wasn't lying, only circling the truth.

"Well, I have half of tomorrow free. We can take a drive through the older part of the city. I'm not sure you've been there before. There are some very pretty old houses on certain streets. At times I've longed to buy one, but I have no need for such extravagance. And I certainly wouldn't want to intrude in the wrong circle." She said all of this without so much as looking up. Her sarcasm wasn't well hidden. Although Joan was successful and had more money than she could ever want to spend, she was new money and unmarried after three unsuccessful attempts. The women in the "wrong circle" preferred to suffer silently in horrible marriages than face the humiliation of failure. Jenna thought they were crazy. Why would being stupid enough to stay miserable be less a failure than daring to find something to make themselves happy?

Her stomach twitched. What right did she have to judge? She enjoyed Trevor's company but was shielding herself from him. It was different, though. She was merely protecting herself from more pain.

"Jenna?"

She looked up, erasing her thoughts from her face.

"Does that sound all right?"

"Oh. Sure. I don't have plans."

No lie, not even circling. Trevor asked again, about her running somewhere with him the next day. She'd refused. She still hadn't told him she would be around an extra week. He would stop coming by, thinking she was gone. And she still hadn't called Alan.

Fifteen

"This is nice. Did you do it today?"

Jenna glanced toward the kitchen door where Joan was holding her sketch. "Oh. Yeah, I was just doodling. I forgot I left it there."

"I'm glad you did. Daniel was right, you do have real talent."

"No. It's..."

"You?"

She let Aaron slip down to the floor. He immediately crept back toward the trinkets on the bookshelf. "I don't know. I wasn't thinking about it. I just tend to pick up a pencil when there's one beside me."

"I'd love to see this in paint, on canvas."

Jenna went to get him. "Aaron, no honey. They're not toys." He fussed. "I think he's getting hungry. I'll be back." She didn't wait for Joan's answer. Her mother-in-law had suggested once that she could stay downstairs instead of hiding, a receiving blanket would work fine. And she had, in her own loft. For some reason, she couldn't do it in Joan's living room. People dropped in at Joan's, unlike at home.

Of course she'd nursed in front of Daniel. It was a bittersweet memory, how he would gingerly touch his son's fingers as she sat on the bed beside him. On the days he'd had more energy, he let his own fingers roam, teasing her.

She stirred inside, then took a quick, deep breath. She missed his touch, the way his eyes took her in, caressing her even when he wasn't able to do more than that. Forcing her thoughts elsewhere, Jenna replayed Joan's comment about her drawing. *You do have real talent.* The Victorian girl emerged from somewhere in her subconscious. Had she sketched her own image? She could, at times, picture herself long ago, dressed as a lady, mingling in a large ballroom. Except she didn't like dresses. She hated hose and heels. There was nothing practical in that. In jeans, she could sit in the soft, cool grass when she pleased, or on old dusty park benches, or ... on a granite zoo sign. Off which side of the stone should she step? The Victorian girl would have a rough time with either path – continuing over the hard cobblestones or veering off into the sharp browned grass. Was there a better choice? Was there any choice?

When Aaron pulled away, Jenna rubbed his back and let her eyes drift around Daniel's room. It was an artist's room, careful decorating cast aside to make space for things more important. She always had to keep her room the way her mother wanted it: perfectly matched and spotless, and much too pink. She didn't care for pink. How would she do Aaron's room, if he had one? That was another thought. He would eventually have to have a room, not just a space in the corner. Maybe she could do a partition. It would cut down too much on the studio space, though, and there would be no soundproofing. They would have to move when he got older.

He released the air in his tummy, then hinted he was ready to finish his meal. He had eaten his carrots well earlier. She was surprised he was still as hungry as usual. But he was growing, already wearing size nine month clothes although he hadn't reached seven months. He grinned from one side of his mouth when she stroked his cheek. He especially looked like his father when he grinned.

Jenna lingered after Aaron finished, walking with him around the bedroom, touching, caressing, Daniel's sculpture in the corner. It was an abstract done as a class requirement. He never said what it was supposed to represent and she couldn't begin to tell, but she did like the lines. They were smooth and flowing, unhurried and uninterrupted, the way he'd always worked. Of course. It represented his personality. Funny she had never thought about it before.

Abstract. A genre he said he'd never understood. The sculpture in his room was the only one he kept. The rest was garbage. She had a hard time believing it was possible for Daniel to have created garbage.

The half day of touring old houses with Joan turned into a day-long marathon, including lunch with two of her work friends and the rest of the afternoon in the office. They tried to include Jenna in some of the design discussions, then tried to hide their surprise about how little fashion knowledge she had. Not to mention her disinterest, which she had trouble hiding.

It didn't seem to bother Joan. She smiled patiently and showed her some of what they talked about in fashion terminology. The buildings had been more interesting.

Aaron was restless by the time they returned to the townhouse. He was tired, and tired of being contained all day. Jenna had a hard time keeping up with his exploring and fussing and finally took him upstairs to see if he would settle in early. Laying beside him in the guest room, she refused to make herself get up again after he fell asleep.

~~~

On Monday morning, she called Alan. Luckily, she reached Cheryl instead and explained that next weekend would be better for Joan to drive them home. Alan had tried to call the loft, then Joan's house. Her mother-in-law hadn't said anything. Jenna apologized for worrying them and promised to call as soon as she got home.

Flipping through the television channels in an attempt to occupy her restless mind, Jenna paused at a man leaning over his garden. She listened to his advice on weed prevention with organic methods as he pulled perfect red tomatoes from the lush greenery. Maybe she should try gardening. Alan would help her, she was sure. But she had nowhere to put a garden. Besides, she had trouble keeping indoor plants alive. She switched the channel.

By the time Joan arrived home, Jenna had finished the novel she started the week before, spent considerable time playing with Aaron, and watched an old romantic comedy. She was ready for her mother-in-law's company.

The following days were mostly the same and she found herself wondering whether she should let Trevor know she was still in town. No, she'd ended that and had no use getting it started again.

Thursday morning, she found a sketch pad and drawing pencils lying on the kitchen table. A hint from Joan, obviously. She wasn't going to give into that, either. Until Aaron was napping later in the day and she went into the kitchen to make herself a cup of mint tea. The pull of the art supplies was too hard to resist, possibly because she was bored. With no conscious idea about what to make of the blank page, she let her hand guide her. An old table emerged, with smoke rings rising from it, and the briefest hints of artwork in the space behind. The old musician holding his guitar intercepted the empty space in between. It wasn't a very good likeness, but the idea was there. She could nearly smell his cigar.

Jenna grabbed her cup and went back to the living room. Trying to sit, her thoughts of calling Trevor bothered her and she went to the window. Sunny, with no breeze she could see. All was still except for cars moving in both directions people strolling the sidewalks, some in shorts, others in light jackets. A nice day for sight-seeing.

The lace fell back between her and the outside world. Shouldn't Aaron be be awake?

She jumped at the ring of the phone. Hesitating, Jenna let it ring
~~~

once more, then raised it to her ear, warily greeting the caller.

"So you are still here."

Trevor. How did he know?

"If you didn't want to see me again, you could have said so. Remember? I like directness."

"I didn't lie. I planned to leave last weekend. I just ... we changed our plans."

"And you didn't keep my number?" He sounded hurt.

"Yes. I have it." She needed to find a good excuse. There was no reason to leave him with bad feelings. Nothing came out.

"Well, if you're ever in town again and feel like looking me up ... but I guess you won't. Safe trip, Jenna. I enjoyed your company. Thanks for indulging me."

The click at the other end stopped her protest. She held the receiver still for a moment as her bridge painting came to mind. She was sure burning hers.

Setting the receiver down, she took a deep breath. It was for the best. She would be home soon. He wouldn't follow.

<div align="center">~~~</div>

Joan carried Aaron into the loft, leaving Jenna free to set her bags down and return for his car seat. Denise had taken care of the one plant Jenna had been told couldn't be killed, an ivy with broad leaves. It looked better than when she left, and the windows had been opened occasionally so the loft smelled fresh. But it was different. Her home felt emptier than it had three weeks before.

She closed the door and made her way to the kitchen while Joan settled Aaron into his playpen. "Do you want some tea?"

"Thank you, dear, but I think I'll run over and see Denise and the kids while you settle in. Is there anything you need from the market?"

Jenna turned after setting the microwave to warm her water. "Oh, I'll have to go pick some things up, but I'm okay for today. Tell Denise hello for me, and thanks. I'll give her a call later."

"I'll do that."

Her mother-in-law headed to the door and Jenna wandered into the studio. The door clicked open, then shut, and she reached out to touch one of Daniel's paintings that had been left on an easel. The zoo sign. She could still see him putting the final touches on the canvas before turning to take her in his arms for the first time. Their first time, only a few weeks after they met. Her eyes closed, she could feel him again, caressing her hair, loosening the pins that held it in a bun and helping it fall to her shoulders. Moving closer against her...

"Jenna?"

She jumped.

Joan apologized. "Are you all right?"

"Yes, I ... I thought you left." She tried to push the image from a moment ago out of her head.

"You were quiet on the way back, and you seem... Will you be all right here alone?"

"I'm not alone. He's still here."

Joan came closer. "I don't think I should leave you. Why don't you pack up a few more things and we'll go back to Chicago tomorrow."

Jenna was tempted. She could handle living in Chicago, but she couldn't leave. "No. This is my home. I think ... I might go back to I.C.C. to go into teaching."

"Teaching art?"

She nodded and a slight smile replaced Joan's look of concern. "I can see you as an art teacher. Let me know if you need anything. Of course, you can do that in Chicago, or transfer there."

"Maybe, eventually."

"Well, you will call me at Denise's if you decide you need anything tonight? The baby is tired from the trip. You should keep him in and let him get readjusted." With a rare hug, Joan left.

"Well, sweetie, just you and me again." Answering Aaron's call to be picked up, she hugged him with a kiss. "Guess we should check the machine."

The light blinked too many times in a row for Jenna to bother counting how many there were, so she hit play to wade through. There were several from her mother and a couple from Alan. He sounded worried. Her mother sounded annoyed.

There was also a message from Karla. Jenna hadn't heard from her in quite a while, since the funeral. She and her husband had moved to the East just after they got married and Jenna missed her. The message was short, with a number attached. Starting to dial, she paused and decided to see if anything else was pressing.

Just Alan. The newest message was strained. Maybe he was mad, but there was something else. It disturbed her too much to ignore it.

With determination not to let his anger provoke her, Jenna dialed his number. He had several messages waiting for him, too. When the beeps stopped, she let him know she was home safe, then hesitated, and told him to stop by when he had time.

Something was definitely not right. They never left the machine unchecked for so long. She could go over, but there wouldn't be any point if they weren't home. She'd have to wait until he called back.

No. His mom. She would know if anything was wrong, and Jenna hadn't talked to her in a very long time, either. Again, she dialed. This time it was answered quickly.

"Mrs. Taylor?"

"Yes?" A slight pause. "Jenna? Sweetie, how are you? I've been asking Alan about you and he never says much. You know how he is. He did say you went to Chicago. Are you still there?"

"No, we just got back. I tried to call Alan and got the machine. Is everything okay? His last message..."

"You haven't heard, then. They're in St. Louis. Cheryl's mother is not doing well and you know how close they are. I tend to think she's making more of it than it is, just to have Cheryl home with her, but I could be wrong."

"What happened?"

"She hasn't taken care of her diabetes; you know she never did. But I'm sure she'll come out of it, as usual. I would imagine she's still trying to convince them to move down there."

"Alan won't move."

"No, I don't think so, though it might be better for him if he did. Not that I want him farther away, you understand, but it does tend to strain their marriage. Oh, I'm not supposed to know that, so you won't say anything?"

"Of course not." Strain their marriage? She couldn't imagine. Alan and Cheryl were so close.

"Enough of that. How was your trip?"

"Oh. It was interesting."

"Yes, I'm sure it was. Joan is such a fascinating person. And how is the baby?"

"Wonderful, still easy. And growing fast."

"You'll have to bring him over and we'll sit and chat."

Jenna grinned. "I'd like that." She agreed on Sunday afternoon.

Leaning back into her rocking chair, tea cup in hand, Jenna felt a bit of peace. An afternoon with the Taylors was long overdue. It would only miss Alan. *Strain their marriage.* Had her friend hid it from her on purpose? Or maybe she had been too caught up in herself to notice. That couldn't go on. He was still her best friend.

Sixteen

Glancing at her parents' house, Jenna pushed it from her thoughts and turned her car into the driveway across the street. She pulled in behind their silver Ford, leaving the space to the side for Alan's car. Silly, she supposed, since he wouldn't be there. But it had been his spot for so long, she didn't feel the need to intrude.

The wind chilled her as she opened the car door. Fighting gusts, she pushed hair back out of her face and took a moment to again admire the old house. She had always loved it, not only because of its occupants, but because it was charming. The spaces were well-proportioned and looked as though they had been planned for both friendliness and privacy, whichever was needed. The girls complained about it looking too old and being too drafty. To Jenna, it simply looked like a real home.

A stir at the window caught her attention. Not more than two seconds later, Carrie bounded from the front door. She didn't have time to pull Aaron out before being descended upon. "Jenna! Mom said you were coming, but I didn't quite dare believe it! It's been so long! Oh, let me take him!"

Handing Aaron to the little girl who had grown enough to tower over her, Jenna grabbed the diaper bag and pushed the door closed. "Yes, it really has been too long. How's school going?"

"Oh, college is so much better than high school! Jenna, he's just precious. You have to let me babysit for you sometimes."

"Careful, I might take you up on that." She grinned and followed Alan's sister to the door.

The sudden converging of people frightened her son and Jenna reclaimed him. He clung to her neck through their welcomes and hugs.

The aroma of baked chicken forced the realization that she hadn't bothered with breakfast or lunch and she was famished. Possibly, it was mental; the thought of Janice Taylor's cooking would give anyone hunger pangs.

Settling into the living room, Jenna studied the group. The girls had switched roles from when they were children. Carrie talked incessantly, interrupted occasionally by her parents. Amber had grown into a very mature young woman. The light freckles she'd hated had all but disappeared and her straight hair fell most of the way down her back. The man she introduced as her fiancé was also quiet, though friendly. A banker. Jenna never would have guessed Amber would find her match in a banker.

They met in a theatre class two years before. He wrote plays. Interesting combination. Amber graduated, not exactly with honors, but with determination. She had no interest in acting, though her fiancé credited her at having the talent for it. She wanted to start with backstage production and move up to directing and producing. Jenna decided she wouldn't be at all surprised to see Amber's name on a film sometime in the future.

Time flew, dinner was wonderful, and the descending dusk caught her unaware. Aaron finally relaxed and spent quite a bit of time with Carrie holding or playing with him as he crawled around the carpeted floor. Amber didn't have as much luck.

With her son occupied, Jenna stole away to find the restroom. Coming out, she stopped at Alan's old room, which had been turned into a den, and crept inside. His ownership was still present, with a few pictures and a couple of small trophies he left behind that had never been taken down not quite matching the room's generally soft feel. There was also a large box on one of the shelves marked with his name. Apparently, more keepsakes he left.

She checked back to see if she was missed yet, then wandered deeper into where she shouldn't have been. The lid of the box was loose, not taped down. She wondered what he'd thought okay to leave behind that his mom couldn't part with. Brushing off a slight trepidation, Jenna pulled the box onto the desk and raised the lid. She had to know, right or not.

Most was school stuff, certificates, special papers and projects, some memorabilia from baseball games and vacations ... and a large manila folder. It was familiar. Pulling it up out of the jumble, she looked inside. Her drawings.

He hadn't thrown them out, but he also didn't take them.

Jenna perused each one and still didn't understand why he wanted them in the first place. Realizing too much time had passed, she slipped them back into the box and returned it to the shelf. Somehow, it satisfied her that he couldn't throw them away.

Shivering, she cuddled Aaron into her for warmth and hurried to the door of her building. It felt like snow, though it was only October.

The Taylors had invited her to join them for Thanksgiving if she didn't have other plans. She didn't have, although Denise would likely invite her as she did every year. It would be hard to go without her husband.

Watching the steps around her wrapped-up baby was difficult in the dimly lit stairwell. She wasn't out after dark often. It was too quiet.

Nearly to the top, she stopped at the sound of feet and a presence.

"I got your message. I didn't figure you'd be out so late."

"Alan. You scared me." Breathing again, she continued past him to her door, digging for her keys.

"How was Chicago?"

What was wrong with her? He had obviously just come from his in-laws and she hadn't even asked about it. "Oh." She turned the key, then faced him. "How's Cheryl's mom? Is she okay?"

"Nothing serious. How did you know?"

"Your mom. When I got your message then called and didn't find you, I called her. Is everything all right?"

He took a deep breath, studying her eyes. "Maybe we should go in. It's too cold out here for Aaron."

Jenna led him into her loft, hoping to keep the conversation on Cheryl and her mom. She set Aaron in his playpen, assured him she would be right back at his fuss, and pulled his coat off. "Do you want something to drink? I can make coffee."

"That sounds good. I'll help you make it."

"No, I got it. Have a seat. I'll be right there. Oh Aaron, you're fine. Give me a few minutes."

Alan came to her side soon enough to reach the coffee she would have had to stand on her toes to grasp. She didn't drink it very often, but Alan did. And he looked like he could use it.

After silently working together, they stood in the kitchen to wait. Jenna did like the smell of it, more than the taste. Aaron had found his yellow animal book and filled the loft with squeaks.

"So her mom's okay, then? And Cheryl isn't too worried?"

"As okay as ever. And no, I don't think she is. But she stayed in St. Louis with the kids."

"She what?"

"That's where she wants to be and this was an excuse to get there. I'm in the middle of a large contract and she kept complaining about me being gone so often, and suddenly her mom was very sick."

"She lied? That doesn't sound like her."

"No. My guess is her mom gave her an excuse. She does tend to choose convenient times to not feel well." He leaned back into the counter, palms against the edge, elbows bent behind him. "I told her I had to get back, that we'd return soon and stay longer when I could afford the time away."

"And she refused to leave?"

"No. She would have come back if I'd pushed it, but I didn't want that kind of tension."

"But Alan, you couldn't have stayed? Just a couple more days? If she's been missing you, you don't want to be away from her now."

"Jen..." He caught himself. "So how was Chicago? You haven't told me much." He was done talking about himself. It was more than he had in a long time.

She checked the coffee. The machine was much too slow.

"Did you go to any shows?"

She raised her eyebrows. He knew better. "No. I'm not interested in shows anymore."

"Jen, I meant theatre. Doesn't Joan usually take you to one?"

"Oh. No, we didn't. She didn't even bring it up. Because I said I wouldn't leave Aaron with a sitter, I suppose."

"So what did you do?"

Jenna avoided his eyes. "Nothing much, really. I stayed in a lot, had lunch with Joan a few times and sat through some of her office work, did some reading, wandered the Loop. Nothing much."

"Why did you stay the extra week?"

"This weekend was better for Joan to take off from work. I told Cheryl that over the phone."

"Yes, she told me what you said. I want to know the real reason."

"What do you mean?"

"Jen, I talked to you, remember? You were ready to leave. What changed your mind?"

She turned again. It was close enough to ready. Grabbing two cups from the cabinet, she added sugar and cream into one. Dark liquid still dripped slowly into the decanter. She grasped the handle and waited. The heat felt good next to her cold fingers.

Aaron stopped sqeaking the book and complained.

Alan set a hand over hers. "I'll get the coffee."

She had to give in. Aaron was hungry. Settling into the sofa, she thanked her friend when he brought her cup.

"Did he ever start sleeping there?"

Maybe Alan was dropping the earlier subject. She hoped. "Yeah, fairly well. But I think he's glad to be home."

"Are you?"

She grinned. "Yeah. I missed you, even with your questions."

He chuckled. "Guess I am doing the third degree thing again. I just want to make sure you're okay."

"Well, can I tell you something?"

"Anything."

"I did something I shouldn't have."

"You? I can't imagine." His eyes sparkled.

"Funny." She helped her son readjust under his blanket. "I had dinner with your family today. That's where I was."

"Did you? I'm sure they enjoyed that. Why shouldn't you have?"

"Oh, it's something I did while I was there. I ... snooped."

Alan laughed. "Like there's anything you haven't already seen?"

"You kept my drawings. Why?"

His face softened, thoughtful. "You went through my box. Why?"

How could she answer? She really had no idea why. "I don't know. I've just been thinking about the past, about how you wouldn't let me get rid of them. I've never really known why it mattered so much. I guess I just wanted to know what was important enough to you to be worth keeping, but not important enough to take with you."

His head lowered, dropping toward the half empty cup he held in both hands between his knees. "It's not that they weren't important enough to take with me, Jen. That box is full of things I had in my apartment that I didn't want to get rid of but didn't want to share when I got married. So I took them back home for safe-keeping." He looked at her again. "The drawings especially. They remind me of how we used to be when you did them. Best friends, with my hopes still intact about us eventually being more than that. No, they aren't your best work, but they are you."

She held his gaze, fixed on his beautiful round soft gentle eyes. On his sincerity, his openness. "I should have fallen in love with you, Alan. It would have made things so much easier."

"You can't help that you didn't."

She leaned up just enough to grasp her cup and took a sip. Not sweet enough, but it didn't matter. She didn't really want it.

"I should go."

She nodded, but he didn't move. Aaron did. Jenna fixed herself and raised him to rub his back.

"Do you mind if I don't go?"

"I hoped you wouldn't. This place is so quiet after he goes to bed." She hadn't meant to be suggestive and knew she should ask him to leave. This was too dangerous, with Cheryl out of town and Alan disappointed in how things were between them. And Jenna wanted company. She wanted him to stay and talk to her.

They chatted about old times while Aaron finished eating. He fell asleep as soon as he was full, or at least Jenna hoped he was full so he wouldn't wake during the night to finish. She went to change him and laid him in his crib. As she turned, Alan was behind her.

Very softly, he touched her hair, her shoulder. Her eyes followed, but she didn't object. She did miss...

"I have to go now." He stepped back, moving to reclaim his coat and head to the door.

"Alan?"

He turned as the doorknob twisted in his fingers. "I have to go out to a site tomorrow. I know it's cold, but..."

"I'd love to go."

He gave her a time and told her good night.

She went to her rocking chair. Few stars penetrated the blackness; clouds she couldn't see blocked all but the brightest from her sight. Alan. What was she going to do about him? From the time she realized he was interested, she'd done her best to discourage it, despite her mother pushing him at her. It seemed to work, mostly. Until Daniel. Until Alan could see she was serious about someone else. He hadn't given up easily. He tried to convince her she was too young, that Daniel wasn't right for her. It only made her keep more distance from her friend. Jenna didn't want Alan to object. Her parents made enough trouble about it. Alan was supposed to stand beside her, support her, against her parents. She never expected him to take their side.

Especially when she found she was pregnant. At seventeen.

The shock had worn off, replaced by uncertainty, fear. The news was easier on Daniel than it had been on her. He bravely stood up to her parents and insisted they were getting married. Her parents didn't press charges because they didn't want the publicity but also wouldn't give permission for marriage before eighteen. So they waited only until she was eighteen and she had lived with the Taylors until then.

Now and then it bothered her that Daniel assumed she would marry him. It had been a demand, not an offer. But what other options did she have? Her parents would never let her stay there, unmarried with a child. And she didn't want to be a single parent. Besides, she loved Daniel. She wanted to be with him. He had to have known she would want him to marry her, to help her take care of their child.

Living in Alan's home during that time was near torture.

"Jenna, you don't have to do this."

"Alan..."

"Before you say anything more, I have to tell you ... I kept hoping you would see..." He moved closer, taking her hand. They were in his room, sitting on his bed. The door was open, barely.

"Jen, do you honestly not know how I feel about you? I haven't pushed because I know your mom drives you crazy with the idea of us being together, but that is what I want. This ... artist ... you don't owe him anything just because... I hate that you've been with him, Jen. I'm not going to lie. But I can get over it. You don't have to marry him. I have job offers already. I'll take the best-paying and we can get a small apartment until I can do better."

"No. Alan, don't."

"Marry me, Jen. Not because you think you have to get married, because you want to. I've always loved you. We're best friends. We understand each other..."

"No." She bolted.

He caught up and took her arm.

"Alan, I'm sorry. I know how you feel. I have for a while. But I don't... I can't. I'm sorry. I love Daniel. We already planned to move in together..."

"You can't." Alan touched her hair, her shoulder. "You can't love him. You hardly know him."

"That's not true. All the times I've said I was with Karla recently, I've..."

He backed up suddenly, like she was a disease.

"I'm sorry. I didn't want to lie to you, but ... Alan, it was the only way. They wouldn't have let me see him."

"And they would have been right. Look what he's done to you. He's completely messed up your life. This isn't you, Jen. You don't sneak around. You don't lie. You don't..."

"Sleep with someone I love?"

He shook his head. "You only think you love him because he wants you, because he gives you attention. That's not enough. You're not old enough..."

"Stop it! You're only doing this because you're jealous! I am going to marry him because I do love him. And I don't need you to act like my parents!" She hurried from his room and didn't stop to answer his mom. He could tell her if he wanted. She could think whatever she wanted to think. It wouldn't change anything. Nothing would change anything now. Her path was set.

Seventeen

"Joan called while you were in the shower."

"You didn't answer it?" Jenna picked up her son and turned at her friend's silence. "Alan?"

"Does it matter?"

Yes, it mattered. He knew it did. "What did you tell her?"

"Why does it matter, Jen?"

She stared. Was he purposely annoying her?

"You know, we've spent the last three days together and you still haven't told me about Chicago." Alan followed her movements as she settled in her chair. With a leg propped over the other, he looked entirely too comfortable in her home. "What's going on?"

Three days. Of casual friendship, as it should be. Why was he bringing this up again? "There's nothing going on. I don't know what you want to hear." She gently fought her son off trying to eat. It was time for him to start weaning off her.

"Trevor stopped by her place and asked for your phone number. She wanted to know if she should give it to him. So, you made a new friend? Or is he an old acquaintance?"

Suddenly, she resented his attitude. What the hell business did he have giving her the third degree about... Trevor. He wanted her phone number? She hid her face by going to the kitchen for a bottle. Aaron didn't take it well yet, but it was a good time to try again.

Alan followed. "He's why you stayed an extra week. Is that what the silence has been about?"

"It's not like that." Jenna fumbled with mixing the formula with the baby squirming and fussing.

Alan took him. "What is it like? Why didn't you say anything?"

"There's nothing to say." She shook the bottle and set it in the microwave. The stove took too long.

"Then why does he want your number? And why didn't you give it to him while you were there?"

"I don't know. And he didn't ask for it."

"Jen?"

"Alan, I really don't want to do this with you, okay? Can you leave it alone?" The beeping gave her an excuse to avoid the hurt look, and she replaced the top, shaking the bottle gently and testing it on her wrist. Her son reached for it.

She took him from her friend and returned to her chair.

Alan stayed still a moment before heading to the door. "I told Joan I was babysitting while you were in the shower and you'd call her back. See you later, Jen."

She didn't try to stop him. Let him pout if he wanted; it wasn't her concern. She had the right to see anyone she wanted to see. She was free now, it wasn't wrong to...

Free. Was she honestly starting to feel free?

Obviously not, or she wouldn't try to hide Trevor from Alan, and Alan from Joan. Why did she care? Her parents hadn't stopped her. Why should anyone else?

He wanted her number. Why? Hadn't she ticked him off enough to discourage him? A flicker of a thought said she didn't want him discouraged. She wanted Joan to give him her number. Maybe he would see her again the next time she was in Chicago.

~~~

Alan didn't stop by the following day. And Trevor didn't call. She had yet to find the nerve to return Joan's call and have to explain why he wanted her number. How much had he told her?

She spent her free time doodling, and painting. Damn. She left her sketches in the book at Joan's, including the one of Trevor's gallery, as he called it, and some quick drawings of the buildings they saw on the architecture tour. If her mother-in-law found it, she would have a lot of questions. Well, it didn't matter. Jenna could think of something when the time came.

She started to sketch the gallery onto a large canvas: the knotted table, the old musician with smoke curling around him: the artwork in the background. Her fingers took over, remembering the scene vividly. Jenna refused to let herself think. Thinking messed her up. Her mind's eye led her, searching for details. Then she stopped.

Dropping her brush into the turpentine, Jenna walked over to the window. She didn't see empty tree branches. She saw water ... and buildings. Beautiful structures, with her tour guide's voice emphasizing lines and styles. With seagulls calling out, and fingers brushing her cheek. She should have called him that last week. They could have seen more, done more, talked about ... anything. He hadn't done more than touch her lightly, casually. Somehow, it was more intriguing to her
~~~

than if he had attempted a kiss. That was why she hadn't called. He scared her.

~~~

Searching the pantry, Jenna decided she would have to go out. The only candy left over from Halloween was baby lollypops with hooped handles. She needed cookies, or chocolate ... something. Maybe some real food to go with it.

Aaron had loved the excitement of children running up to ask for candy. Jenna set up in front of their apartment building again, which she and Daniel had always done to keep kids from having to walk up the stairs. Rain threatened but luckily had given all of the trick-or-treaters a break and held off until later in the night. Jenna even chatted with one of the downstairs neighbors who sat outside with them a while. An elderly man, he said he appreciated how quiet she kept her apartment. They never heard anything from their ceiling. He was a retired factory worker who had no idea who her husband was or why they kept to themselves. He offered her assistance if she ever needed it before escaping the chill of the wet breeze.

Mid-November already. She hadn't talked to her neighbor again since but hadn't been out much. No visits from Alan, although he called a few times to check in. Cheryl and the kid were home from St. Louis. Jenna hoped they were all doing well. Alan didn't say.

She rubbed a hand through her hair. It would have to be washed before she could go out. Pushing the playpen close to the bathroom door, she gave Aaron his favorite toys and asked him to give her five minutes. He smiled wide and tapped on her stomach. She never would have imagined a baby being so easy.

With the door partly open, she could hear him babbling to himself. It would be harder to find five minutes for a shower as he got older without someone to keep him out of trouble. The playpen wouldn't hold him forever.

Drying, she was surprised by a knock on the door. Jenna slipped into her robe and rubbed her son's head, in no rush. It was probably a salesman and she could ignore him.

The peephole disfigured Alan's face. She supposed he had finally forgiven her. Pulling the garment tighter, she opened the door.

"Hey, Jen. I wanted to let you know I'm on my way out of town."

"Going back to St. Louis?"

"Yes, andd we'll be there through Thanksgiving. Mom says you're
~~~

welcome to spend the day with them, or any other day."

"Denise wants us there again."

"I figured, but I said I'd let you know. And you know they're still there for you if you need. Don't be afraid to call and invite yourself."

"I'll try. Alan, everything okay?"

"I suppose it will be, but I need to get out of here." He started to leave and turned back. "If you need to talk, leave a message with Mom and she'll let me know. You're going to be okay at Denise's?"

"I suppose I will be." She grinned at echoing him. And she gave in. "He's a painter. Trevor, who wanted my number. We spent a few days sight-seeing. I started to enjoy the art world again and it was uncomfortable. I didn't want to talk about it."

He studied her face. "Has he called?"

"I never gave Joan the okay. I couldn't even call her."

"Jen, if you like him, you need to face that, regardless of what the rest of us think. It's your life." He leaned in to kiss her cheek. "Have a nice Thanksgiving. I'll call when I get back."

She returned the sentiment, told him to drive carefully, and closed the door. Aaron's fuss said he wanted out.

"Okay, baby." Crossing the room, she was increasingly confused by Alan's remarks. *If you like him, you need to face that.* Have to face it? The rest of us? He mentioned his mom. Had he talked to her about it? He really didn't know anything. So she'd met a painter. What was new about that? There were always artists in Joan's circle. Is that why he'd been so hesitant about her going to Chicago in the first place?

She took her son out of his crib. He wanted down. That was fine. He could explore while she made some mint tea.

You need to face that. Why was he making it a big deal? It wasn't. She and Trevor were only friends, not even friends, just acquaintances, fellow art lovers, nothing. She pulled the cup from the microwave, dropped in the tea bag, and wandered over to her painting. It wasn't quite finished. The artwork in the background had only a hint of shape. They needed to be brought to life, to be completed.

Picking up a tube of paint, she rolled it between her fingers and set it back down. Not today. She couldn't finish it today.

Going back to pull the bag from the cup and stir in a touch of sugar, she watched her son. Trevor was great with him. Alan rarely acknowledged his presence. She supposed he reminded him of Daniel, and no matter what he said, her friend had not liked her husband. He wouldn't like Trevor, either. He was even more the artist type – living on his own schedule, making his own rules, obligated to no one. And he sure looked more the part, with his baggy shirts and long hair. She yanked herself away from her thoughts.

The radio distracted her for a moment, taking her to a faraway beach where young people were running around playing volleyball and walking through the waves. She still loved the Beach Boys. Her mom called it too simple. Maybe it was. But it was fun and light-hearted. She needed that. She always had.

Aaron looked up at her and smiled when she sang along. He liked the fun music, too.

Back in the studio, Jenna looked through her recent scribbles. The ship caught her eye. It wasn't the *Spirit of Peoria*. It was the architecture tour boat, still docked. She wondered if she could put it in paint well enough to be worth a canvas. If not, she could always gesso over it.

Moving Trevor's gallery from her easel, she chose her colors and began to wash in the blue background of the sky, a light airy color in the middle of the canvas that deepened as the brush rose higher. She wasn't sure whether there had been clouds that day but she wanted a few wisps for variation. With a technique she saw Daniel use, Jenna daubed the white and brushed it in. Yes, they looked like clouds. Cumulous.

She didn't stop until her son interrupted.

Her tea was cold, mostly untouched, and her feet ached when she sat to cuddle Aaron and hold his bottle. He'd entertained himself for a long time. She had a good outline and quite a bit of detail on the ship. It was blurry detail, a bit surreal. But so far, she didn't think she would have to gesso over it.

The next several days brought more paintings into being: buildings she had seen and some she created in her head, shoreline images with white sails of all sizes, and a view of her studio with the large window in the background. None were finished. She wasn't sure why she kept stopping before they were done. But other ideas floated around in her head and took over before the previous thoughts could take full shape. That was likely why she had never really gotten anywhere. She'd never been able to keep her concentration still long enough.

Joan called to check on them and Jenna did admit to painting but downplayed how much. It worked well enough. Her mother-in-law sounded relieved, and maybe ... well, Jenna wasn't going to become one of her artists put on display. It was only a hobby, not for show.

She needed to go to I.C.C. and check on classes starting in January.

The thought of teaching appealed more through the days of painting. Hopefully, she would be able to make herself stick with it long enough to get her degree.

~~~

Denise not only invited them for Thanksgiving; she insisted. Jenna delayed getting ready as she worked on one of the paintings. She didn't want to go. Joan would be there, and Terry's parents: the same crowd as the last several years, except without Daniel. She didn't want to do Thanksgiving without her husband. But she couldn't refuse Denise.

A few minutes after eleven and the last to arrive, Jenna apologized.

"Oh, no, it's fine. We're just sitting around talking. Here, let me take him." Denise took Aaron, though he tried to refuse. "Take your coat off and make yourself at home. It's cold today, isn't it?"

"Yeah, it feels like it might snow."

"Feels like. You're so funny. Oh, Aaron, stop your fussing at me. You know who I am." Assuming Jenna would follow, Denise led the way into her living room and announced their arrival.

Aaron willingly went to Joan and Jenna accepted the traditional welcoming glass of egg nog from her brother-in-law. She assured him she was doing fine and sat next to Joan.

Conversation was forced, the omission of a family member too vivid. Jenna answered when spoken to and avoided talk of her art, even with Joan trying to approach the subject. She was glad to go help Denise finish dinner, leaving Aaron with his cousins and uncle.

With the family gathered around the large table, her thoughts of escape heightened. It was too much too soon. Joan set a hand on her back and asked how she was doing, and Jenna fled from the table into the nearest bathroom.

"Jenna? Can I come in?"

She wiped at her eyes, trying to compose herself before turning the knob. "Sorry, I'm fine."

"It's all right, dear. Holidays are hard for a while. Come back and sit down. No one blames you for being upset."

"I don't want to mess dinner up for everyone. Maybe I should go. I almost didn't come."

"Of course you're not leaving." Joan wrapped an arm around her. "You can't be alone today, and you're not messing anything up. We all miss him, but he seems closer when you and Aaron are here with us."

She gave in and made herself get through dinner and talk a little
~~~

while afterward, until she told them she'd promised to stop by her mom's. She didn't want to do that, either, but for Aaron's sake, she would. He should know his other grandmother, she supposed.

Aaron was an excuse, of course. Jenna knew her mother didn't have much interest in her grandson. Why would she? She had never had much interest in her daughter, either, especially since Jenna had married "out of her class." A promise, though, was still a promise.

Pulling into the drive, she noted the difference between the one extra car beside her and the overflowing driveway across the street. Alan's aunts, uncles, and cousins were there, laughing and hugging, truly enjoying each others' company. Jenna sat a moment to draw up the courage to enter her parents' house.

She didn't stay long. The extra car meant another single, wealthy young man, along with his parents. It proved impossible to avoid him, as her mother kept pushing them together. Aaron didn't even deter him. The guy with the obviously fake snob accent had grown up in private schools, away from home, and believed it was the best way to raise children.

Jenna asked what the point of having children was if you were just going to give them away, then lied and said she'd accepted the Taylors' invitation. Her mother threw a fit, as usual. Her father didn't bother to acknowledge that she was leaving. He'd barely spoken to her. Worse, he had barely looked at his grandson.

It didn't matter anymore.

She scurried across the street, cuddling Aaron close, and the warmth of the Taylor house flowed through her even before Jenna alighted the stairs and became sheltered within. Aaron, tired from the day's commotion, drooped against her until Mrs. Taylor set a thick blanket in the library where Jenna could see him through the glass doors. He stirred when she laid him down but didn't object.

Gratefully accepting a slice of re-warmed pumpkin pie and a cup of hot tea, Jenna claimed a space at the casually-set table. Wooden bowls filled with mixed nuts still in their shells and whole ripe fruits were scattered among pies. They'd already had dessert. The remaining pans were at best half-empty, with cherries and filling spilling out from under the crust, and cheesecake beginning to sag from the room's heat. The pumpkin pie, with only her piece and one other taken from it, was always the least popular. Mrs. Taylor made it for sake of tradition only, since she, Jenna, and Alan were the only ones who would eat it..

With most of the men absorbed in a loud football game at the far end of the room and the youngsters upstairs with their books and toys, the women reveled in semi-private conversation at the table. Amber's beau remained beside her, alternately grasping her hand and rubbing her back. A comment he threw out, breaching the no-politics-in-socializing rule, incensed Carrie and her mother had to jump in to save a quarrel.

Mr. Taylor, passing by, stopped and took a seat as his wife asked Jenna how her day had been.

She would rather have listened to a political argument than to relive her day, but she surrendered. Telling them how Daniel's family had avoided talking about him and how she left the table, embarrassing herself, how she had been hit on for the ten minutes she was at her parents' house, she felt her neck muscles tense.

Her hand shook when she sipped her tea.

Mr. Taylor left again. The noise of the football game took over. On return, Lee Taylor set a glass of wine beside her only-nibbled-at pie. Jenna started to object. She hadn't had so much as a sip of alcohol since she knew Aaron was on his way.

"It's only enough to help you relax, then you can go back to your tea." He gave her a wink and set another glass in front of his wife.

She relented. Aaron could have a bottle tonight.

Carrie coaxed her dad to let her have a small amount of wine also, and took over the conversation by bantering with her sister. Jenna chuckled, glad some things never changed. With the alcohol's numbing effect, she loosened enough to admit she had been painting. Talking of her trip to Chicago, omitting Trevor, she began to miss the whole adventure when a noise at the doorway caught her attention.

Carrie bounded to the hall and nearly knocked her brother over with a big hug. "What are you doing here? Where's your family?"

Jenna watched Alan's avoidance while he pulled out of his coat. He used the snow as an excuse, the prediction of five to seven inches overnight and more in the following days. With an occasional glance at Jenna, he said he had an important meeting on Saturday he couldn't afford to miss. Cheryl decided to stay with her family.

He excused himself to use the kitchen phone to let her know he made it. Returning in about two minutes, Alan again looked at her.

His mom offered pie and coffee and the group watching the game used a commercial to welcome him. Finally, he sank into the chair Carrie temporarily abandoned beside Jenna, forcing his sister to move down a space when she followed.

"I thought you would be at Denise's." He thanked his mom for the dessert she set in front of him.

"I was." Jenna took another swallow of her wine, now two-thirds empty. She noticed him look over his coffee cup. "I also went over to Mom's for a few minutes. That was all I could handle. She tried to fix me up again so since I was out here, I stopped in."

"You plan to stay a while?" He glanced again at her wine glass.

"I really shouldn't if it's going to snow."

"Where's Aaron?"

She nodded toward the library.

Mention of the baby started Carrie off again and Jenna fell silent. Listening to the surrounding chatter, her brain blurred. She had barely eaten and the wine added a heavy, unseen weight to her limbs. Alan watched her in between talking with his family. She could feel his stare but didn't let it bother her. She would let nothing bother her tonight.

Lee Taylor refilled her glass. Jenna objected but took a couple more sips. The relaxation it gave her became addicting as she listened to surrounding chatter. Alan's eyes pierced her skin, and he took the glass from her hand. She gazed at him, found a resoluteness in his face, and didn't argue.

"Why don't you two stay here tonight? You're both tired and it's getting late. Jenna, we'll pull out the bed in the library for you and Alan can take the couch."

"I need to get home." Jenna heard herself argue with Alan's mom but wasn't sure why she was so insistent. She continued to refuse against the Taylors' objections.

"I'll take her." Alan's voice buzzed beside her ear. "Give me your keys and I'll grab his seat. We'll come back for your car tomorrow." He took a sip from her wine glass.

Jenna stared at him ... too long. She couldn't refuse. She was in no shape to drive. But...

"Jen? Where are your keys?"

Snapping out of a haze, she rose, unsteadily, to find the diaper bag. The keys... She grasped the chair for balance. Maybe it would be better to stay. But she didn't want to stay. She wanted to be home, in her own bed ... in... Forcing the thought from her mind, Jenna plodded to the front hall, retrieved the keys and took them back to Alan, glad most of his relatives had left earlier.

He held her hand longer than was necessary. "Are you okay?"

"I'm fine. Tired." Maybe she was holding his too long.

"Jenna, come wrap up whatever you'll eat. We'll never finish this ourselves. Alan, go warm the truck for the baby."

Jenna followed Mrs. Taylor into the kitchen, expecting some kind of question about Alan's touch, or about the way he'd looked at her all night. She said nothing, but pulling Jenna away was intentional.

Alan met them at the front door and took the dish while Jenna bundled herself and Aaron.

Carrie hugged her too long. "Bring your paintings when you come tomorrow. I want to see."

"Paintings?" Alan raised his eyebrows.

"She said she's been painting again. Make her bring something so we can see."

Jenna ignored his look and didn't answer Carrie. She hoped they would all forget.

Eighteen

Jenna watched illuminated snowflakes fly toward the windshield then dash out of the way. Some made it; others were swept off the glass by ruthless wipers. They were beautiful, as long as they weren't threatening her. She was glad Alan offered to take her home. He had even gone over to her parents' house to let them know Jenna would be back for the Mustang so they wouldn't worry that it was parked in the drive. Jenna could hear her mother's brain twirl about Alan taking her home until she blocked it out.

The roads became persistently more snow-packed as they headed down I-89 to Peoria. Jenna wondered if the driving conditions kept him silent, though it wasn't likely. Maybe he was afraid she would mention Cheryl. Maybe he hadn't appreciated her being at his family's home, catching him in the act of leaving his wife and kids. Or maybe he didn't like that she had been drinking. But she wasn't drunk. Jenna had never in her life been drunk. She had always remained in control, unable to imagine not doing so.

Alan finally parked in front of her two-story building. Jenna hoped the draining tension wasn't obvious when she nearly leapt from the front seat to pull her son from the back. If her friend noticed, he didn't mention it. He grabbed the food from behind his own seat and came around to close the door.

They would have looked like a family to a casual observer, walking side-by-side to the apartment, Aaron drowsing against his mom and Alan holding the door for her. She wasn't too proud to accept his help. It made him feel better whenever he could, whenever she would let him. Leading through the dark stairwell, she supposed sometimes she was too proud for her own good. Why else would she insist on living alone, taking care of things mostly by herself, when so many were standing by waiting to help?

At the top of the stairs, Alan unlocked her door and Jenna brushed past him into her loft. "Do you want to come in? Or do you want to get home before the roads get worse?"

"I want to see your paintings."

She stared at him as he stood just outside her door. Her Chicago paintings were inside, not hidden. The gallery was propped against the wall. He would want the story behind it. This time, she welcomed the intrusion of her personal space. "Just let me get Aaron in bed."

She stepped out of her shoes. Her frozen toes and the cold wood beneath her feet sent her quickly to the sitting area, where she had suggested adding a large rug as soon as she moved in. Daniel brought one home the next day. The few paint splotches now decorating it only added to its warmth.

Aaron whined half-asleep as she pulled him out of his coat. "It's okay, baby. We're home." Laying the garment over the couch to take care of later, Jenna took him to the changing table and slipped out of her own jacket, hooking it onto one corner. He whined again when she laid him down. "I know, sweetie. Just give me a minute. I'll hurry."

He peered at her while she changed him and wrapped his arms around her neck when she picked him up again to go fix a bottle. As she returned to the couch, Alan picked up both jackets and took them to the coat rack. No wonder he married a neat freak.

"Can I go look?" He glanced toward the studio.

"If you have to."

The corners of his mouth twitched upward, and he wandered into the studio, switching on another light.

He first checked the easel, a view from Joan's window with the sapling pulling the eye. It was barely started and he didn't linger there. Meandering along the stream of canvases propped along the wall, he didn't speak and didn't stop at any one ... until he found the gallery. He bent to study it and then stood, grasping each side. With a large rise and fall of his shoulders, Alan turned. "This was in Chicago."

"Yes."

His eyes fell back to the canvas for some time before he returned it and left the studio to lower into the chair across from her. "So you were collecting inspiration while you were there."

Not intentionally, but it seemed to work that way. She shrugged. "I've always loved the lake and the boats."

"The buildings are a new thing for you."

"Yeah. We went on an architecture cruise. It was..."

"You and Joan?"

She caught herself. But she wanted to talk to him, to have one person she didn't have to hide anything from. "No. Trevor took me."

Her friend listened silently, no judgment apparent in his face.

"He knew Daniel's work and just wanted to hang around with his wife, I would guess. The guy in the painting is one of his friends. The painter's wife, he called me. It's supposed to be a gallery, with his work hanging in the background. Trevor's work."

"A gallery? It looks like a bar."

"Yeah, it is, but they call it the gallery."

"Is he good?" He continued at her hesitation. "Trevor's artwork."

"Oh. Well, it's abstract. I don't really get it. Maybe that's why I'm having trouble finishing the painting. It's hard to imitate something you don't understand."

Alan glanced back into the studio. "And the others? Why are none of them done?"

"I don't know." Her son released the bottle. He'd fallen asleep. Instead of waking him to finish, Jenna took him to his crib and pulled the blanket up over his shoulders. She shivered and went to push the thermostat up. Saving a few dollars wasn't worth Aaron being cold.

Alan had returned to the studio and was bent before the gallery painting.

Jenna moved up beside him. "You don't like it."

"Well, it's dark, different than the rest. But it's good, Jen. It's quality work." He noticed her doubt. "Honestly. It's ... more mature. There's a new level there I haven't seen before."

His opinion mattered more than she wanted to admit. And she thought about telling him to leave before the roads were blocked. "Should I make coffee?"

He stood, too close. "Do you want me to stay, or are you changing the subject?" He was teasing, but Jenna didn't want to answer either question. "Jen, this – you and I – have nothing to do with Cheryl staying in St. Louis."

"Doesn't it?"

"No more than your trip to Chicago had anything to do with us."

Her eyes touched his. "Do you think it didn't?"

Alan watched her, waiting.

Jenna didn't pull away and didn't back down. She felt him get closer, lower his face, brush a hand into her hair. She stayed still, wondering how long it would take before he stopped himself, before he realized he didn't want this. He pushed in closer and her heart beat faster. Jenna knew she should pull back but she needed him to stop it this time. He had to...

His lips met hers, gently, probing to see how far she was willing to let him go. Her eyes closed involuntarily. His warmth invaded. With the wine affecting her judgment, she returned the kiss. He would stop, remember his vows and... He moved away, barely.

"Jen?" His voice was a whisper. She could feel it on her cheek. "Why are you not pushing me away?"

"Because you have to. This time, you're the one who's married. I knew you wouldn't... You would never..."

"Don't be too sure." He pressed back in.

She let him. She gave in to the kiss, accepted his affection, his attention, enjoying the soft caress of his strong arms holding her.

No, she couldn't. He was married. If he wasn't, maybe...

She broke the connection. "Go."

He held still.

"Alan, go home." Taking advantage of his loosened grip, Jenna pushed her hands against his chest and backed toward the door. "You have to go now. Go back to St. Louis and get your family. Or stay there with them. But you can't be here."

"Jen..."

"Don't. Please. I... I have looked up to you for so long. The thing before, while Daniel was in Chicago ... I thought that was just ... because I was so upset and you... You would have actually taken me away from him?"

"Yes. If I could have." There was no tone of regret or guilt in his voice. "I love you, Jen. You know that."

"Then why don't you want what's best for me? Why are you constantly pushing me? You keep urging me to paint, and I do, but ... I can't finish anything with you, Alan. I told you that years ago and it's not going to change."

He inched toward her, slowly, as though she wouldn't notice. "Then why do you keep letting me get so close?"

"Because I need you. You're the only friend I still have. I let everyone else go because I had you. Even Karla stopped hanging around because she warned me and I wouldn't believe her. Daniel's the only one you couldn't chase away, though you sure tried hard enough."

"You think I don't want what's best for you? Jen, you're a painter, but you won't let yourself be one. You should be free to stay home and paint, or wander, or travel. Whatever you want to do. Daniel wasn't going to give you that. Even after he could afford to, he was too involved with his work. I could give that to you. My job is flexible, since I make the rules..."

"Then why is Cheryl in St. Louis alone?" She had him. His cover was blown, leaving him unable to answer. Jenna had to get him out, before he could see how much it hurt her to uncover what she had never wanted to know. This wasn't her best friend. She couldn't accept it. It was just...

"I wanted to marry you."

"You wanted to own me, the way you own Cheryl. But that's not me, Alan. You have what you need. Why can't you see that?"

He shook his head, moving within arm's reach. "What I need... Maybe I do have what I need, but I don't have what I want."

"Get out."

He didn't stir.

"Please. I need you to leave now."

With a slight hesitation, Alan swerved around her to grab his coat. She held still, her back to him. The latch turned.

"Goodnight, Jen."

She didn't answer. Her voice would have broken.

"You should finish the paintings."

In a movie, she could see the heroine throwing a wine glass at the door as it closed. Maybe she would if she had a wine glass handy. But it would wake Aaron.

Instead, she stood where she was, not wanting to acknowledge what had just happened. Not wanting to feel like her last supporting leg had just been yanked from underneath. Minutes passed, enough for the cold in her feet to rise and consume her body. A shiver stirred her from the self-induced hypnosis and unblocked the dam holding her tears. With a slight tremble slowing her path, Jenna found her bed and collapsed on top.

She woke to Aaron's cry.

Fighting the urge to ignore the child and stay in bed, still atop her blankets, her conscience took over. He must have been awake for several minutes, since he generally called to her softly before he got so insistent.

Tense muscles pulled when she moved. She was cold. Fussing at herself for being too stupid to even crawl underneath the covers, Jenna ran a hand through her hair to push it from her face and rubbed at her eyes. There were probably bags underneath. So she wouldn't go out today. What did it matter?

While feeding Aaron with the afghan around her shoulders, Jenna looked at her paintings. Chicago. It had been an inspiration. Maybe

Joan was right that she needed to move there, but leaving Daniel's loft was still out of the question.

As she wiped away occasional tears, she thought more about the architecture tour and Trevor's voice sharing his love and knowledge. She felt his fingers brush her cheek and wanted to see him again, to chat and walk together. He could be a good friend if he would settle for that. Maybe he could even help her understand abstract art. But he would push for more, too. She needed a female friend, no more males.

Carrie would come over, she assumed. Alan's sister? No. Jenna wouldn't be able to talk candidly to her. Karla was too far away. Who did that leave? No one, as she had told Alan, there was no one else.

Aaron occupied most of her day and was patient enough to let her cling to him too often, smiling as if he knew she needed to feel better. The radio helped entertain them both. During his nap, she searched for a book she hadn't read. It didn't take long with so little storage room in the loft. She generally picked novels up from the library instead of buying them. This one she'd had for years and hadn't bothered to read. A romance. Vaguely remembering she had saved it in case the mood struck, Jenna took it over to the oak rocking chair with a cup of tea.

Night descended quietly. She set Aaron in his crib, stood watching him for several minutes, then wandered into the studio. Standing before her most current canvas, Jenna shook her head. She couldn't pick up the brush. Alan's voice echoed in her head. *You should finish the paintings.* The hell with him.

Gathering the canvases along the wall, she pushed them into the supply closet, in the back corner. She wanted no more to do with art. Too tired to pack everything else away, Jenna ignored it and went back to her book.

~~~

The next morning, while waiting on her coffee, Jenna threw all of the art supplies into a box, stuck it onto one of the shelves, pushed the drawing table against the wall and contemplated how to best use the open space. Possibly a tall divider that would create a temporary nursery, or two or three together. She could buy colorful patterned sheets to tack to the inside, giving Aaron a more cheerful atmosphere, or paint a colorful scene on them. No, the sheets would work better and be easier to remove to use elsewhere at a later time.

Since there was no real line to separate the space, only the backs of
~~~

the chairs and the rug marked the living area, she could extend it, push it closer to the large windows.

Finding the perfect sheets on one of their rare days out, Jenna stopped to look at curtains. The loft would look more like a home with some kind of a window treatment. Lace, to soften it without cutting out the light. A salesman was happy to point out that the set she was considering had a tablecloth to match, completely washable sturdy lace that could cover a plain-colored cloth or stand alone to show the beauty of the wood.

"Thanks, but I don't have a dining table."

He raised his eyebrows. "You're just starting out then, I take it."

She contemplated his question as he focused on Aaron, judging her. "No. Just starting again."

He nodded. She didn't care what he thought. It was odd not to have a dining table, she supposed. And she did like the pattern of the lace. She figured quickly. Six valances would cover the top of the three large windows with plenty of folds, then meet one panel at each end to frame the sides. "I need six valances and two panels."

"And the tablecloth?"

"Yes. I suppose I'll be able to find a table to go with it."

"Very well. Can I show you anything else?"

Jenna chuckled. "No, I'm taking baby steps for now."

Nineteen

"You know he wants to be more than your friend."

Jenna raised her eyes to Daniel's.

"The landscape engineer. He wants more from you than friendship."

Risking another slight rebuff about moving, she turned her head to see him better. Maybe getting the two men together hadn't been such a good idea. Jenna convinced Alan to go with her to the art show at Illinois Central two days earlier. Daniel was showing his work there and invited her, but she hadn't told Alan that. Her friend had no idea they had seen each other more than the one time in his art class.

She was glad Daniel hadn't mentioned the invitation, or that she had modeled for him several times, always in public places, or that she'd had lunch with him more than once. Alan caught the way the other man smiled at her when they bumped into each other at the show. It made him suspicious of Daniel's intents, but he so far knew nothing of Jenna's. She wondered how long she would be able to hide it. She didn't want to deal with the argument that would come with her refusal to stop seeing him. The modeling didn't matter. Being with Daniel mattered.

Perched atop a picnic table in Glen Oak Park, arms around her knees, Jenna watched him set his charcoal and newsprint pad down and walk up to her.

"You already know he wants more than friendship?"

"Yes."

His eyes lowered a moment. A breath brought them back to hers. "Are you involved with him?"

During all their time together, Jenna had watched carefully for a sign, anything that might tell her Daniel could be interested in her as more than a model. She had hoped. She had even stayed up at night wondering. "He's my friend. I don't want it to be more than that."

"He does."

"I know. I haven't... I avoid that subject. He has to know I don't."

"You're sure you don't?"

"Yes. I never have."

A slight grin highlighted the sparkle in his eyes. "Good. I don't get involved with anyone even partly attached."

Involved?

Jenna had to force her breaths when he slid up onto the table, his leg brushing hers, facing the opposite direction so he stared into her eyes. The breeze played with a few wisps of his hair. She wished it were her fingers instead of the breeze. Involved. How involved did he intend to get?

"And what about me?" Daniel studied her face as though still caught up in the sketch, trying to capture every detail. "Do I have a chance of being more than your friend?"

"You want more?"

"Yes, Jenna. I want more." He raised a hand to her face, studying it now with his fingers. They brushed back through her hair, and he cupped her head into his warm palm.

His kiss sent a shiver down through her body to her toes. Still, she didn't move. She felt frozen, with a flame running through the middle, melting her from within. Parting her lips, Jenna accepted him.

Young voices were in the distance. children swinging or sliding ... something. Their parents would likely object to them making out on the picnic table. Jenna didn't care. He wanted more. How much more wasn't a concern at the moment.

Losing the touch of his lips, Jenna opened her eyes. She wanted to see his. They were still closed. Daniel's chest expanded, and relaxed.

When his eyelids parted, they revealed the soul her world now wrapped around. His fingers returned to her face, touching her skin like a blind man trying to see her in a light most people never would. They rested on her lips for just a moment before sliding underneath her chin. "You are what I've been waiting for." The words were breathy, full. They clutched her heart.

Jenna broke out of the sketch pose and threw both arms around his shoulders, clinging, afraid to fall. She pushed her mouth back against his, hoping her aggression wouldn't turn him away. Her actions startled herself. Never had she been so openly affectionate in public. To be honest, she had never been so openly affectionate anywhere, with anyone. He had shattered her natural defenses, allowing her to connect more with herself than she ever had before.

Judging from his gaze when their eyes met again, Jenna couldn't see that Daniel was at all bothered by her response. He stroked her skin as skillfully as he did his paintings. It made her long to be alone with him, if only for a few minutes.

"I suppose we should finish the sketch so you can get home."

Squeezing her eyelids to block out the memory, Jenna pulled back from the window. The grayness blanketing the sky sank into her spirit, thwarting the work of the last week. It was nearly December now and the loft was beginning to look like a home – more hers, less Daniel's. Aaron had spent much of his energy trying to push the screens over as he pawed at the red and blue sailboats and yellow ducks, until Jenna tied them together and angled them so they couldn't move. She was pleased with the windows now highlighted with lace, though a few words she didn't want her son to learn escaped while she'd been hammering the brackets to the wall. But overall, she felt good about the whole thing.

The wood floor desperately needed to be refinished. That, she wouldn't attempt alone. Though maybe a coat of paint would work as well. Off-white, to create a more open feel. And a deep purple throw rug under her living room furniture. The paint-spattered light brown one could go in the studio area. Their dark green couch would fit in well and patterned slip covers over the chairs would add some interest. A pansy print maybe. Purple and green on an off-white background. She'd always loved pansies.

Jenna jumped at the phone's ring. Irritated at the intrusion, she didn't rush to answer. The machine took over.

Cheryl's voice made Jenna pause. Alan had apparently gone to get his family. His wife wanted her to come for dinner.

Setting a hand on the receiver, she changed her mind. She didn't want to talk to Cheryl now. And she most definitely didn't want to have dinner with them. Jenna walked away and returned to stare out the window at the over-flowing river banks. Most of the snow had melted, leaving only traces of ice. Bare trees cast an intricate design, breaking the open space. The darkness of wet branches amid the gray sky and muddy brown water created a wonderful color scheme. She wondered how well she could imitate it. Or maybe abstract it. Use the colors more than the actual objects...

Capture the emotions the colors and lines conveyed. That's what Trevor did. He painted emotions. Daniel had provoked emotions, bending them with his brush. Trevor captured them.

She pulled the gallery painting out of the closet. Aaron had gone to sleep more than three hours before and Jenna needed to do the same, but Trevor's voice haunted her, telling her to think outside the lines. She had been so rude and he was right. Her parents had no further control and neither did Alan. It was her choice. They couldn't keep standing in her way if she refused to allow it.

Trevor would be at work, in the bar. And she had the number.

Setting the painting on the table, Jenna wandered to the phone, picked up the receiver and sat, contemplating. He wouldn't want to talk to her after she refused to let Joan give him her number. He was probably flirting with some girl who was more his type. But she could at least apologize.

The telephone rang five, six times. Maybe it was too late. How long did bars stay open?

"Hullo, you've got the Rocky Oyster."

It wasn't Trevor. Did she dare ask for him?

"Don't let the name scare you off. We're all friendly here."

"Oh, I'm sorry. I was just looking for..."

"Lady, I can barely hear you over all this racket."

Jenna nearly hung up. The bar obviously wasn't closed. She could hear laughing and music in the background, the hum of voices and occasional clink of a glass.

"Hullo?"

"Is Trevor working tonight?" She held her breath and ignored a slight throb in her skull.

"Trevor? You mean D-day?"

"Um, yeah, I'm sorry. Is he there tonight?"

"Honey, he's always here. Hold on." The deep voice laughingly called the artist over to the phone and teased about the caller being too lady-like to ask for him. She nearly hung up again.

"Yeah?"

Her stomach knotted. Stupid idea, calling him at work.

"What? Was this a joke?" His voice had moved away from the receiver.

"Nah, she don't talk loud enough. Tell her to yell."

A pause. "Hello?"

"Trevor, I'm sorry. I really shouldn't have called you at work."

"Jenna?"

"Yes. Do you want me to call back tomorrow, at home?"

"No. Hold on. Don't go anywhere."

She heard more laughter and Trevor telling them to shut up, then the noise lightened.

"Okay, maybe I can hear you now. What's up? It's after midnight. Is everything okay?"

"Well, I was just... I called to apologize." She wrapped the cord around her fingers, entwining it into a knot.

"For what?"

Was he kidding? "I wasn't... I didn't mean to be so rude ... at the gallery when ... well, in general. It wasn't meant to be directed at you..."

"I know. Forget it. Are you back in Chicago yet? I tried to get your number from Joan, but she wouldn't give it to me. I guess she didn't know we'd been sight-seeing together."

"She told me. I asked her not to give it to you."

Silence.

"And I'm sorry. I just needed time to think. I'm still at home, but only part of me is. I keep thinking ... the next time I'm in Chicago maybe we could..."

"Do more sight-seeing?"

"Yeah, or something."

Another pause. "Something ... less touristy and more intimate?"

Intimate. Her stomach fluttered. The idea wasn't completely out of the question ... or undesirable.

"Guess that's not what you meant." His voice was searching.

"I don't know." Her grip on the phone cord tightened. "Maybe." She would never be able to fix it. "I'd like to see more of your work. I didn't really give you a fair chance. Maybe..."

"Come back to Chicago. I'll pick up Chinese food and we can take it to my place. I have a bunch of stuff lying around there."

"I won't be back for a while. The weather is too risky to have Aaron on the roads and maybe get stuck."

"And that would be bad? Being stuck here?"

"No, I just mean... I'm in the middle of fixing up the loft. When I get into something, I have a hard time pulling myself away."

"Okay. You need more time. I got it."

She wasn't sure she appreciated how well he understood her.

"Can I have your number? Or is that still off-limits?"

Jenna couldn't very well not give it to him, since she'd been bold enough to call him at the bar. Trevor asked what time Aaron usually slept so he wouldn't wake him and said he had to get back to work. A friendly, casual goodbye left her wanting to talk longer. There was something soothing about speaking to him.

~~~

Waking to tight neck muscles, Jenna stretched her head back and forth. She would have to stop sleeping on the couch. It made no sense.

Light filtered into the room. It was too early, as late as she'd been awake, but there was no going back to sleep. Bad habit. Once she was up, rarely could she drift off again. She yawned and forced herself from the couch to heat her cup of water. Setting it on the microwave tray, she changed her mind. Coffee sounded better.

A strong richness soon drifted from the carafe. Biding her time, Jenna wandered into the studio. She stopped at the gallery painting she
~~~

left on the table. Her fingers brushed the beginning outlines of the artwork. It needed to be finished.

She backed away again.

Returning to the couch, she flipped through channels and stopped at a home decorating show. It looked so easy. With unlimited money and trained designers, it would be. She glanced around her own home. A great candidate for a room makeover, even without professionals. Maybe this was one project she could complete.

The rumble of the old coffee pot at the end of its brewing cycle pulled her back to the kitchen. Jenna poured in sugar and creamer and stood waiting for the slow drip to cease. The green vase Joan bought for her sat unceremoniously on the counter. While redecorating, she would have to force it to work with the pale lavender curtains and find a setting more suitable for its elegance.

The pouring motion stirred the coffee and she went back to the couch. Much too hot, the mug was set on the end table, nearly forgotten as soon as she pulled her legs up onto the cushions and covered them with the afghan. Her head dropped against the pillow-soft back. Dozing to the light hum of the television, she grimaced at the unwelcome ring of the phone.

Jenna sipped from her cup and waited for the message. Aaron started to stir.

"Jenna? Pick up the phone."

She ignored him.

"I know you're up by now and I'll keep calling until you answer." He paused. "Jenna. This is crazy. Answer the phone."

"Damn." She bolted, splashing the now-lukewarm coffee as she banged it down on the table and yanked the receiver to her ear. "*What?*"

"Hello."

She seethed at his calm. "You woke Aaron. What do you want?"

"Isn't he usually awake by now?"

"No."

"I'm sorry, but you don't return my calls if I leave a message."

She heard no actual regret in Alan's voice. "Because I don't want to talk to you." A surge of power swelled. Aaron cried for her.

"Okay, you're still mad. That's fine, but at least answer the phone so I know you're okay."

That's fine? As if she needed his permission to be mad? "Alan, I can take care of myself. Stop treating me like a child."

"Jenna, what is wrong with you? Did you just talk to your mom and decide to take it out on me again?"

She again saw herself throwing a glass of wine at him, or on him. "I have to go. Aaron wants out now that he's awake."

"Jen..."

"I don't want to talk to you right now. I'll call you when I feel like I can. Go take care of your wife and leave me alone. Please."

A pause on the other end nearly made her reconsider. Alan was her friend...

"I'm coming over. We need to talk about this."

"No."

"I can't leave it this way. You know that."

"I won't let you in. Please, just give me space." Another pause. "Goodbye, Alan." She dropped the receiver before he could answer.

Aaron's demand for her attention was a nice distraction. She didn't care that he was awake, only that Alan hadn't cared and hadn't thought about it before calling so early. They would have to go out. She couldn't handle sitting in the loft wondering if he would actually come by, or call back. Maybe she would go buy paint for the floor. Denise would watch Aaron so she could get it done without him painting his hands and knees.

Elbow-deep in off-white semi-gloss, Jenna stood and stretched. She hadn't realized how tiring it would be to paint a floor. Of course, she hadn't been satisfied to do it the easiest way, all one color with a sprayer. She found a dark green she was sure would match the vase and decided to accent the indentations with it before rolling over the top with the lighter color. Stroking in the green all along each crease with a fairly small brush was nearly more tedious than she could stand, but nearly one third of the loft was done by the time she had to stop. Denise insisted she and Aaron stay at her house until the floor was finished. Jenna couldn't argue. It would make the job easier and she wouldn't have to move furniture back to keep it safe for her son.

The loft started to remind her of an old country home. It hadn't been her aim. Actually, she didn't have any direction in mind. Deciding on one thing at a time likely wasn't the best decorating approach, but it worked so far. Something would have to be done with the walls, as well. It would come to her eventually.

She pushed the lid back onto the paint can and tapped the edges with the hammer. Heading to the kitchen to wash out the brush, she paused when the phone rang. Alan again, she imagined. He called twice during the day and had been ignored both times.

With a deep breath, she picked it up.

"Jenna, I hoped you would answer this time. I'd like you to come for dinner tonight."

Worse than Alan. "Mom, I really can't."

"We've barely seen you. I have your favorites in the oven so it will save you from having to cook."

"I have plans."

"Oh? Someone we know?"

"It's not a date so don't get excited. I'm going over to Denise's."

"Can't you do that another night? I'm sure she will understand."

"No, I can't. She's babysitting for me while I'm painting and we're staying with her until it's done."

"Painting? I thought you had given up on that frivolity by now. You should think of your future, Jenna. Come over tonight."

"I can't. My brush is drying and Denise will have to hold supper if I don't hurry and shower. But thank you, maybe another night." A quick goodbye wasn't too soon. *That frivolity.* Her mom would have felt better if Jenna had told her what she was painting, but she had no need to try to make her feel better.

The next ring was Alan. She picked it up, told him she was busy and to stop calling her, and hung up on him for emphasis.

With the brush cleaned, she headed to the shower and barely got undressed before the phone rang again. Cursing, she wrapped herself in a towel, stomped back to the phone, and grabbed it before the machine could answer. "*Stop calling me!* I don't *want* to talk to you!" Starting to slam it down again, she decided to tell him she would change her number if needed and raised it back to her ear. A voice was there, but not Alan's.

"Jenna? Hello?"

Trevor. Damn.

"*Jenna.*"

"Hi. I'm sorry. I thought it was..."

"Who? Someone's bothering you? Have you called the police?"

"No, it's nothing, really."

"It can't be nothing if you're that upset. What's going on?"

She attempted to normalize her voice with a deep breath. It did the opposite, allowing frustrations to surface, restricting her throat.

He called out to her, asking simply for her to respond. But it was more. It was a beacon that pulled her mind back to Chicago, to the architecture tour, the easy conversations...

"Jenna? Talk to me. About something else if you'd rather, but talk to me."

She wanted to be with him, walking along the pier or the city streets or anywhere.

"Hey. Come on. Say so if you don't want to talk now, but let me know you're okay, at least."

She forced an answer. "Yeah. I am. Sorry. How's work?"

He told her how he'd been teased about her phone call.

"I'm sorry. I won't call there again."

"No, call whenever you want. They have to have something to laugh about, right? Isn't that why they go to a bar?"

She wouldn't know, but she didn't want to admit she didn't. She hoped he would keep talking, about anything. Clenching the towel tighter in her hand, Jenna settled onto the edge of the chair. Her legs felt weak.

"I didn't wake Aaron, did I?"

"He's at Denise's. I was getting ready to go over and get him." Her voice approached normal.

"You're leaving him with a sitter now?"

"I'm painting the floor and didn't want him to crawl over it."

He chuckled. "Painting the floor? Did you run out of canvas?"

Jenna felt her tension drain as she told him about her decorating. He listened patiently, whether or not he was actually interested, and said her eclectic style would make for an interesting home. She invited him to come see if she had been successful with it when she was finished, casually, not expecting he would have any reason to come to Peoria. He didn't scoff at the idea.

They talked long enough for Jenna to start shivering. A mutual pause gave her the chance to tell him she needed to get off the phone, to shower and dress, but she didn't. Instead, she sat, holding the towel and listening to the silence on the other end.

"Well, I should let you go. I didn't mean to hold you so long. Are you going to be late now?"

"It's okay."

"You could've kicked me off, you know."

"I guess, but..."

"You were being polite. Jenna, just tell me if I call at the wrong time."

"No. Really. I was... I'm glad you called."

"Are you okay? Can you tell me now what that was about?"

A part of her wanted to tell him. But she felt like too much of an idiot to admit. "I just had an argument with someone. Nothing worth talking about."

"You're okay there alone?"

"Yes, it's nothing like that. And I'll be at Denise's overnight."

"You'll be home tomorrow?"

"I'll be here painting."

"Mind if I call again? I can make it earlier."

"Sure. Maybe an hour earlier?"

"Sounds good. Have a good rest of the night, okay?"

Jenna was reluctant to let him go. She held the phone a while after their goodbyes and rose slowly to continue her evening.

Twenty

A light sprinkle of snow sparkling in the darkness beyond the loft's windows perfected the ambience of the evening. With her favorite holiday music in the background, Jenna added black olives to a small dish in the center of the cold cuts and cheese platter and took it over to her table. The buffet-style platters, flaunting an array of breads and cut vegetables and chips, weren't as elaborate as her sister-in-law's dinner would be the following day, but Jenna didn't have much host experience, or interest. She did have soft sugar cookies decorated and two cinnamon sticks simmering on the stove to scent the air. Her guests should feel the holiday spirit, whether or not she could.

She looked around her home. The floor had turned out well. Her overstuffed chair had its pansy cover – not as hard to find as she'd been afraid. And she'd purchased a coordinating runner for her old coffee table, which still needed to be stripped and given new varnish. But that could be overlooked, she supposed.

After considering the matter of a dining table, she found one unfinished at a price she could afford and painted it the same dark green as the floor accent. The lavender lace tablecloth added a softness and pulled the eye from the curtains. Deep red silk poinsettias and bits of real mistletoe propped inside the green vase served as a centerpiece. The vase and leaves accented the color that peeked through the lavender. She hadn't bothered with a tree since she didn't want to fight Aaron to keep it standing, but she found him a stocking and a baby's first Christmas ornament. The ornament, with the few others she had, hung from the curtain rods and floated just under the lace. His stocking was hooked on the front door knob. The gifts were stacked on the drawing table, intentionally to keep them out of reach of the nine-month-old, unintentionally adding to the décor.

Jenna checked the clock, looked around to be sure she was ready for her guests, visited with Aaron to pass time and calm her nerves, and finally set him back in his playpen to light three gold-colored taper candles beside the vase. She was ready when the doorbell rang.

She wasn't ready to find Trevor with Joan.

Her mother-in-law gave her a quick hug and a bottle of wine. "Something smells wonderful. I hope you don't mind that I brought an extra guest. He had no plans and I couldn't see him spending the holiday alone. Oh, Jenna, is this the same apartment?" Joan dropped her coat onto the stand and wandered in farther.

Jenna didn't mean to ignore the question but she caught herself staring at the man in the doorway. How did Joan know he didn't have plans? How much had they talked? He looked nice.

"Is it okay that I'm here?" Trevor's bright green eyes shone.

Collecting herself, not quickly enough, she managed to answer. "Of course. Come in." She waited while he scuffed the snow off his shoes and removed his coat, then stepped closer to take it from him. The warmth from the lining penetrated her fingers.

"You didn't do all of this yourself?"

Joan's voice pulled Jenna away. She'd drifted closer to him than necessary. "Yes. It filled a lot of hours. And Denise kept Aaron now and then so it wouldn't be impossible."

Joan stood next to the playpen and stroked her grandson's head. "It's very nice, dear. Much more comfortable for you, I'm sure."

"Daniel wouldn't like it much."

"Oh, honey, I don't think he'd even notice. It was only a work space to him. I kept thinking you would do something to make it livable."

"I meant to, but he liked it the way it was." She led Trevor into the apartment. Why had she brought Daniel up in front of him? "I have coffee made, and tea, and there's cider in the fridge. Can I get you something?"

Joan agreed to coffee while she gave in to Aaron's reaching arms. Trevor followed to help with drinks.

He was just as at home in her kitchen as he had been in Joan's. They worked well together, only slightly brushing arms once. Again, she didn't believe it was an accident. It was nice to have him there, though Daniel would probably not like that, either.

They had talked several times over the past two weeks, about decorating and his job, his art and how sometimes he wanted to paint and sometimes he didn't. How he never forced it, to the chagrin of Mrs. Covington who wanted him to produce faster. How she was nearly ready to stop backing him blaming what she thought was lack of drive. Jenna refused to give her opinion. It didn't matter what she thought. He had to do what was best for him.

She poured Joan's coffee while he poured cider for her and for himself. He wasn't a coffee drinker any more than she was. Unable to think of anything to say, Jenna turned to leave the kitchen area and stopped when he touched her hand.

"You look great." Trevor's voice was barely audible.

"Oh. Thank you." She pulled back and took the coffee to Joan. It had struck her while getting ready that there wasn't much point in worrying about her appearance just for her ... for Daniel's family. They had seen her at her worst. But it was Christmas Eve and her first hosted party. Her hair was in a bun, as it had been when she'd met her husband, with a few loose strands slightly curling around her face. The shiny navy and green vest over her navy pants and turtleneck made her look thinner than she was – a trick she'd learned from her mother to hide her flaws. Dark plain colors are more flattering on round figures. Not that hers was bad, just not as perfect as her mom wished.

"You can put him down. I'm sure he's ready to wander again." Jenna pulled the steaming cup away from Aaron's reaching fingers and waited until he was off in search of trouble before she handed the coffee to her mother-in-law. She gestured for them to have a seat.

Trevor handed Jenna her glass, set his on the end table, and went to join Aaron on the floor, patiently accepting one offered toy after another. He was great with the baby. And Aaron enjoyed his company. He babbled happily as though Trevor understood him.

The doorbell drew her attention just as Trevor looked up to see her watching. She grinned at him and went to welcome Denise and her family.

Opening the door, her stomach knotted. Alan. No, not now.

"Hey, Jen. I just came by to drop off a peace offering. I know I was very out of line the other night but I..."

"I have company." She cut him off and hoped his voice hadn't carried into the room.

"Oh?" He glanced into the loft. "You fixed up the place."

"Working on it. Can we maybe do this later?"

"Alan, isn't it?" Joan came up behind her. "I didn't realize you had invited more company, Jenna. Maybe I shouldn't have."

He glanced from one to the other. "No, I'm not staying. Nice to see you again. I'm sorry to interrupt."

"No apology necessary. Jenna has gone all out to decorate. I'm sure she won't mind showing the place off more. Or maybe you've already seen it."

They both knew she was fishing, but Alan acted innocent. "No, I haven't. It's been a month since I've been here, I think."

"Well, do come see what the child has done, and by herself." Joan took Alan's arm and pulled him inside.

Jenna wished she could crawl behind her bed curtain and stay there until everyone left again. She remained close to the door as Joan bragged about her decorating skill and introduced the two men. Trevor stood when he saw Alan. He was holding Aaron, possessively unless she was imagining things. Jenna still hung back. She wanted nothing to do with this exchange. They were civil, one more than the other, the differences in each glaringly obvious.

Alan excused himself with a mention of his family and stopped in front of Jenna to hand her a small package.

She didn't want it, whatever it was. "You shouldn't have."

"It's nothing, Jen. Just something that looked like you."

Only because of the eyes on them, she accepted and started to pull at the light blue paper covered with baby angels.

"No, wait till tomorrow. Have a nice Christmas." Alan touched a hand to her arm, gave her a quick peck on the cheek, and left with a rushed goodbye to the others.

She took it to the drawing table to get it out of her hands. And she lingered there.

"Peace offering?"

Jenna turned to face Joan. "We had an argument. Guess he figures I'm still mad since I haven't answered his calls."

"Are you?"

She thought a moment. "No. I'm just ... not interested in getting gifts from him right now."

"It must have been serious to separate good friends for a month."

"Yeah, it was kind of big, and I'd rather not go into it."

Joan set a hand aside her head. "I guess this isn't the time, but if you ever need to talk, you know I'm here for you. You will always be my daughter, Jenna. And I have a lot of experience with men." She winked and went to answer the doorbell.

The smudge Alan rubbed into the evening dissipated as Jenna became immersed in her guests and playing hostess. Aaron, content to be entertained by his older cousins, and by Trevor, allowed Jenna to talk with her in-laws. Joan again suggested a move to Chicago. Terry jokingly told his mother-in-law to quit harassing his sister. Denise raved about the change in the loft and chatted freely with Trevor whenever she could pull his attention away from the children.

Jenna mostly avoided Trevor, though the rest of the family treated him like ... family. She wondered if he had become a substitute, but it was hard for her to see him that way. Yes, he was an artist, like Daniel, but the similarity ended there. Her conversations with him became more intimate and revealing each time. She thoroughly enjoyed their talks with him.

But having him there, in Daniel's loft, in her home, felt awkward. He kept his distance physically, sometimes simply catching her eye in a brief acknowledgement he knew she was in the room. At times, Jenna caught herself wishing he would pull away from Aaron to visit with her. She also caught herself purposely avoiding him when he did start to approach.

He left with Joan to stay at Denise's. Jenna considered offering her couch so they would have a chance to talk, but she couldn't be quite that daring, especially since she didn't have a separate room, but just a space hidden behind a curtain. He and Joan were only staying in town until the day after Christmas. Not long enough.

After putting Aaron in bed and cleaning up, she wandered into the studio and picked up the little box Alan brought. She hesitated only a moment before tearing the paper off. A gold pin, shaped like an artist's palette, with different-colored gems sparkling here and there. It was beautiful, but she didn't wear pins. Shouldn't he know that? She was twenty-four. He had known her for thirteen years. He should have noticed she didn't bother much with jewelry. She generally left the same pair of stud earrings in day after day instead of taking the time to change them. Another way of pushing her to be more, she assumed.

~~~

Fighting against the heaviness of her eyelids, Jenna realized it was early. Her walls reflected a light cast of the sun's rays, painting them a beautiful translucent, deep navy. She lay still and allowed her mind to awaken as she wondered how hard it would be to imitate the effect. It was the perfect color for her loft, though maybe with a purple cast instead of navy, to go with her lavender. Her mind now fully active, Jenna rolled out from underneath her heavy blankets, pulled her robe over her shoulders to protect them from the loft's morning chill, and scuffed into the kitchen to make her tea. Warm cup in hand, she went to claim her rocker, eyes fixed on the awakening sky.

Aaron would rise soon to his first Christmas morning, not a thrilling one for him with only her as company, but there were a few
~~~

toys from Santa in front of the gift table. The year before had been both better and worse: the excitement of being pregnant, waiting for her son, tempered with knowing Daniel would only have a short time with him, if any. But at least Daniel had been there.

Denise's household would be roused already, her kids clamoring about wanting to open their packages. Jenna hoped they would like what she found for them.

Aaron stirred. She could barely see him from the oak rocking chair; his divider needed to be moved. Jenna already missed nursing him since he was fully on the bottle, and she wondered whether she should have stopped so soon. It did make it easier for her to leave him with a sitter when necessary. So far, she had only done that twice, but if she was going back to school... How would she now? She couldn't possibly leave him with Cheryl, not after what happened with Alan.

His stirring turned into a soft complaint and Jenna went to get his bottle. Well, she wasn't sure she wanted to go back to school. There had to be something she could do without it. As Aaron greeted her with a huge hug and sloppy kiss, Jenna decided it didn't matter. Her current plans were already set and the future she could deal with as it came. Taking care of her baby, rocking him and seeing his satisfaction was enough.

When his tummy was full, Aaron pushed the bottle away and lay still. A chubby hand pulled softly at her hair and grabbed her mouth. He loved to play with her teeth and get his palm tickled by her tongue, and his hearty laugh always made her smile.

He bolted to sitting when the doorbell rang.

"Are you expecting company?" She chuckled at the question in his gaze. "Okay, let's see who it is. But if it's Alan again, I'm not opening the door."

"Ah dah."

"Door? Yes, I heard the door. But thank you." She kissed his head and propped him against her left side.

Jenna checked the peep hole. Trevor? Why was he there so early? Had Joan sent him so she wouldn't have to spend the morning alone?

"Ah dah." Aaron reached out and banged on the door.

There was an echoing bang in return.

The baby laughed and hit the door again, and again came the echo.

"Okay, you two will wake the neighbors." She stopped another bang and opened the door, barely.

"Good morning and Merry Christmas. Hey, buddy."

Aaron smiled and reached for him.

"Can I come in?" Trevor took Aaron's hand.

"I'm not dressed yet. Is Joan here?"

"Nah, it's amazing. There are actually cabs in this little city. I brought food if that'll work again. And I can wait here if you want."

"Um, come on in. Just don't look at me. I'm horrendous in the morning." She moved back.

Completely ignoring her request, Trevor allowed his eyes to roam her frame. He grinned.

"I told you not to look at me."

"I know, but you're wrong. You're ravishing."

She chuckled. "Okay, I already let you in. You don't have to lie."

"I don't, ever."

Jenna finally looked into his eyes. She believed him completely. "Thank you, really. But I need to change."

"No thanks needed, really." Switching a bag from one hand to the other, he slipped out of his coat and dropped it onto the rack, in the same manner as Joan. "Come here, buddy, let's warm up these rolls while your mom..." He approached to take her son, then studied her face. "You don't have to change on my account, you know."

He was closer than he needed to be. And her uncombed hair, no makeup, and old robe didn't bother him in the slightest. Daniel would have teased about how she looked like an old housewife. Or maybe he hadn't been teasing.

Jenna pushed hair away from her face. "I'm glad I'm not bothering you, but I'll be more comfortable dressed." She hoped her breath was okay.

His grin changed, holding something in.

"I'll be back in a minute." She edged away and knew darn well he was watching her cross the room.

Jenna stared out the van window at the darkness. Touches of gray snow lingered on the grass alongside the road from the light showers they'd had two days earlier. Denise's children had spent much of the day checking for new snowfall and singing "Let it Snow" in hopes of encouraging it to come. It hadn't. But Jenna accepted Trevor's offer to drive her and Aaron home.

She also spent more time with him at Denise's than she had the night before. He didn't push it; she did. He was a great antidote to her fear of spending Christmas without Daniel. Jenna constantly found herself drawn to him. And now, in the silence of the van, even that was comforting.

She felt a kind of déjà vu when Trevor parked her van in front of the apartment building and walked in with her. Except he insisted on carrying the baby. And Jenna felt no hesitation inviting him out of the biting cold and into her home.

While she busied herself pulling Aaron from his coat and changing him into pajamas, Jenna half-watched Trevor walk around the studio, studying Daniel's sketches. He had looked at them briefly the night before but hadn't remarked on them. In fact, he only mentioned art when Joan or Denise pushed the issue. He'd seemed more interested in his bartending job than in his painting. Jenna found that curious.

"So, I expected to see some of your work displayed."

She set Aaron down to find his toys and wandered closer to her guest. "Why?"

"Why are you not proud of your art?" His eyes penetrated hers.

"It isn't anything. It's just a hobby."

"I don't believe that's true. I saw the drawings you left at Joan's."

She averted her face. If he saw them...

"I was tempted to take the one of old George in to the gallery. I know he'd get a real kick out of you thinking he was worth drawing."

Her cheeks grew warm.

"Joan showed me. After that phone call when you were so upset, I went over to talk to her. Maybe I shouldn't have, but it worried me and I thought maybe she could have Denise..."

Jenna looked up at him. She knew he talked to Joan or he wouldn't be there now, but she had never expected him to admit it. "How much did you say?"

"I told her I enjoyed your company. She figured out we'd been seeing each other, casually. It doesn't seem to bother her."

"She wants me to move to Chicago. Did she ask you to convince me I should?"

"Yes."

Jenna turned. So that's why he was there: one more person trying to tell her what she should do with her life.

"But I told her I couldn't do that. I wouldn't be much of a friend if I tried to talk you into something you weren't sure you wanted. And since you've spent so much time redecorating, it must not be what you want."

"I don't want to leave him."

"Leave who? The friend you were yelling at?"

"No. Daniel. If I leave his home, it would be like leaving him. And I can't do that."

"No? Then why did you redo the loft into something you don't think he'd like?"

She whirled back to argue ... and stopped. She couldn't argue. She had almost completely changed Daniel's studio until it wasn't his anymore, painting him further out of her life.

Trevor moved in and caressed her cheek with his thumb. "You know, it doesn't matter what Joan wants, or what the friend you were yelling at wants. And it sure as hell doesn't matter what I want. As you told me about my art, do what's best for you. Stay here, move to Chicago, run back and forth. Hell, move to Alaska if it strikes you. Don't let them push you. Mourn your husband as long as you need. But you have my number if you want to talk, and I'm always willing."

She stared. He could act very mature when he decided.

"I should go. It's been a long day and I know you have to be tired. You did great trying to act like you were in the Christmas spirit." He grinned and moved away.

She called a taxi while he picked Aaron up to say goodbye, hung back while he talked to her son, then walked him to the door and took the baby.

Trevor slipped into his coat and pulled a round tube from the bag he'd set on the floor. "I brought something for you."

Jenna hesitated. She felt funny accepting a gift when she didn't have one to return.

"It's not wrapped. I never seem to get that done. But I want you to have this." He pulled the cap off one end and shook the tube to dump out the contents. Propping the empty container under his arm, he carefully unrolled the yellowed paper.

Her heart nearly stopped. It was Daniel's. A drawing of her he did before their marriage, again with the suggestion she was unclothed, which she might have been.

Finally, she collected her thoughts enough to speak. "Where did you get that?"

"At an estate sale, several months ago. Apparently they had no idea what its real value was because I picked it up for next to nothing. A shame for them, but nice for me since I couldn't afford its real value." He paused. "I was surprised he would sell something that looks so personal."

She shook her head. "He didn't. A folder of his work was stolen, just after he started to become a name. He was devastated because there were several ... well, personal, more than that. Not meant for the public. I keep hoping they won't surface, although he made them ... um, kind of disguised. Still... I've regretted letting him do it ever since." Jenna set Aaron down to take the drawing.

Trevor nearly whispered. "I hope they won't. But I'll admit this one caught my eye and I couldn't walk away. This is what made me start studying his work. Of course I'd heard the name, but... Jenna, I have wanted to meet you ever since I found this."

She raised her eyes to his. "Me? Or Daniel?"

"You. I became interested in his work because of you, because I expected the only way I'd ever get to know you would be by studying the man you married. I never expected to get closer than that."

"So you recognized me the first time at Joan's. That was an act."

"No. I didn't, at first. And when I heard your name, I was trying very hard to act normal so I wouldn't scare you off."

She returned her gaze to the sketch. "You're giving this back?"

"Yes, but I debated it for quite a while. It's not easy to give up."

"You didn't have to. I never would have known you had it."

"Knowing you means more than having some sketch, even if it is by the great Daniel Rhodes. I thought it might mean more to you."

Jenna allowed the paper to roll itself up again. Holding it carefully in one hand, she gave him a half hug. "Thank you. It does."

His head pressed closer and both arms surrounded her. It wasn't uncomfortable. She didn't pull back. He wasn't as scrawny as she had originally thought, but sturdy, muscular. She felt protected.

Minutes passed, and still, he held her. He wore different cologne. It was fresh and spicy. A young scent. Vivid. But soft. She felt Aaron grab onto her leg and pull to his feet. He wasn't used to sharing her so much.

A loud horn in front of the building pulled them apart. The taxi. Jenna picked up her baby and asked Trevor to call when he got into Chicago. More snow was expected during the night.

"I will. Merry Christmas, Jenna. Take care, buddy." He shook Aaron's hand and stepped into the hallway.

"Trevor?" She gathered her nerve while he turned toward her again. Stepping closer, Jenna slid her free arm around his back, inside his coat, and leaned in to kiss him.

Twenty-one

Trevor was abrupt, slightly distant, when he called to let her know he and Joan arrived safely in Chicago. Nothing was said after the kiss. He simply searched her eyes then fled to the taxi's impatient horn.

The phone conversation left Jenna with mixed feelings. Maybe she assumed too much. He didn't necessarily want to be kissed just because he wanted to be her friend. Was she doing to Trevor what Alan was doing to her? Jenna cringed. She wouldn't make that mistake again. And she wouldn't call and bother him. He had her number.

Wandering around her home, Jenna gave up and sat in her rocker. The loft was clean enough. Aaron was napping. She supposed they could go out for paint when he woke, but she hadn't decided what color to use on her walls. Besides, Jenna had lost interest in decorating.

After staring out at the melting ice dripping from her trees, she stood again, wandered over to check on Aaron, walked along Daniel's mural of drawings and into the supply closet. She picked up the gallery. It had to be finished, one way or another, no matter how it turned out. In a half-trance, Jenna pulled out her supplies: easel, paints, brushes, turpentine. Returning to the back corner of the bar in her mind, she tried to recall Trevor's paintings. The small versions wouldn't have to be detailed. She only had to remember well enough to get the main idea, and the right colors.

Aaron woke before she finished and Jenna grudgingly set the brush aside. She took care of his needs and was thankful he settled down with his Christmas toys and plastic books so she could return to her work. Glancing over what she had done so far, Jenna noticed it was distorted. Trevor's paintings hadn't stood out so much in reality. It was appropriate, though, that they took over as the main theme of her painting. The musician, sitting at the table, letting his cigar burn away, hadn't been their reason for being at the gallery. He only added to the atmosphere.

By evening it was done. This one felt like much more than a hobby.

Over the next three days, she finished another and started a third. The therapeutic effect of the Chicago paintings calmed her enough to pick up the phone when she heard Alan's voice. She agreed to have lunch with him two days before the New Year.

<center>~~~</center>

Alan stood to pull out the high chair and waited until the baby was strapped in, then held Jenna's chair.

She insisted they meet at Northwoods Mall, in the little food court, so if they were recognized it wouldn't look like they were trying to hide anything. The middle of the weekday wasn't a busy time and the tables beside them were empty. Still, Jenna glanced around as she got settled. "Have you been here long?" She pulled a snack from the diaper bag to keep her son occupied.

"Only a few minutes. What do you want? I'll get it."

She tried to hand him money for her order but he refused, as she expected. Aaron talked to passers-by while they waited, with more friendliness than could have rubbed off from either of his parents. Alan finally spoke to the baby when he returned. Aaron didn't hold grudges. He offered part of his soggy teething biscuit.

"So, what inspired you to decorate?"

Jenna pushed the plastic fork through the wrapper and picked at her rice. The mall's stir-fry wasn't as good as Trevor's Chinese take-out, or maybe it was only his company she missed. "Boredom, I guess. Didn't have anything better to do."

"Not painting again yet?"

She looked up. "Why does it matter so much to you?"

"Because it matters to you." He set his fork down. "I know I've been overbearing, but I hate that you've been so stifled. I miss the fire I used to see. Believe it or not, I do have your interests in mind."

"I know you used to."

His chest rose and fell. "I've been ... going through some things recently. Cheryl and I..." He stopped to let people pass. "I don't know, Jen. She wants to move back home, and I think she should feel like she is home, with me. Not to mention my business is here. She complains that I'm always gone and I know I work a lot, but that is how we can afford what we have. It's not like I spend it gambling or whatever. I want to make sure my family is comfortable. I don't understand how she expects to have it both ways."

"Alan, don't you see what you're doing?"

He raised his eyebrows and waited.

"The same reason you criticized Daniel. For putting his work ahead of me. You don't have to work so many hours. Your guys are very capable. I know. I've watched them. But you're so obsessed with it that you won't let go, even a little. That's what bothers her, like it bothered me. And that's why I don't paint. Not much, anyway. I won't do that to my son. And you shouldn't do it to your wife."

He stared at her, silent. Nothing more needed to be said. In lecturing her friend, Jenna realized Alan had been right. Daniel's obsession had stifled her. She couldn't allow herself the freedom of giving in to her own interests because she was too occupied with trying to compensate for his. She'd always had to be available for those few moments he was willing and able to give her his attention. She had geared herself to be the constant full-time parent because he wouldn't have been. She'd pushed herself aside to make up for his overpowering presence, and then, for his overpowering absence.

Aaron banged a tiny fist against the table and Jenna looked over at him. She would have to give him space as he grew. She would have to have something of her own so he could do the same. So he wouldn't be completely wrapped up in, and stifled by, her need of his attention.

"The artist, Trevor, he does mean something to you."

Jenna turned back to Alan. She nodded.

"He seems awfully close to Aaron."

"He likes kids."

"He's young."

"So am I. I just haven't felt like it recently."

Alan picked up his fork, held it, set it back down. "You're going back to Chicago, aren't you?"

Jenna held his gaze, wondering if her friend's marriage would be easier if she wasn't so available, how much better it would be for her and Aaron if they weren't so isolated. How much more palatable Trevor's take-out had been. How much easier it was to be in Trevor's company.

She allowed herself a slow, cleansing breath, holding back tears, feeling a door begin to close. Back to Chicago. "Most likely."

~~~

Pulling out her suitcase, Jenna packed it with her warmest clothes and threw in most of what Aaron had. She didn't buy him much at a time since he grew out of it so quickly. It didn't take long to pack. The two canvases she wanted to take were already beside the door.

Finally, she called Denise to tell her she wouldn't make her New Year's party. The idea of driving to Chicago alone made her nervous,
~~~

but it was late morning, there was plenty of daylight left, and the warmth of the sun had dried the roads.

Trevor hadn't called and she didn't blame him. Maybe he wouldn't welcome her visit. If not, she would stay with Joan for a few days and come back home. Her mother-in-law gladly accepted her self-invitation and agreed to watch Aaron for the evening. Joan was having a few people over, as usual, but she never went out on New Year's Eve.

As she settled into the van, Jenna took a deep breath. Aaron was happily babbling, always ready to go anywhere. She was terrified. But she wouldn't back out, not this time.

Her stomach settled as she drove down the interstate singing along with her music. She loved the cassette player Daniel put in the van for her. Approaching Chicago, however, the energetic strains of Sawyer Brown had to soften. She needed more concentration to get through city traffic. With her nerves flared again by the time she reached Joan's apartment, Jenna was extremely relieved she didn't have to parallel park. She could have managed it in the Mustang, but with the van it would have been impossible.

Joan met her with a hug. "Jenna, honey, I was surprised by your call." She took Aaron. "I wasn't sure whether to actually expect you."

"I hope it's okay. I know it's last minute."

"You know you're always welcome, whether or not you call first. Use your key."

Mrs. Covington rushed up to welcome her the minute she stepped inside. Jenna resisted the woman's attempt to pull her in farther. She wanted to take a few things out of the van before slipping out of her coat and shoes, a much easier task than loading it had been, since she didn't have to cart Aaron along with her on each trip. Dropping onto the couch, she felt fatigue settle in with the warmth.

"Joan says you have plans. I didn't realize you had friends here."

"Aaron, no." She got up again to take him away from the lamp table before he grabbed the crystal dish on top. "Oh, just one."

Joan rescued her from an explanation as she moved the dish to a safer spot. "What time is he picking you up?"

"I'm taking a cab. I'm not sure enough of the directions to drive."

"Alone? Wouldn't it be better to have him come get you?"

She understood Joan's concern and appreciated it, but it had to be done that way. "He doesn't know I'm coming and I may not stay long. But he told me which taxi to call if I ever needed to. It'll be fine."

"He? It's a male friend?"

Jenna looked over at the nosy lady. Jenna kicked herself mentally; it would spread quickly that she was dating again, whether or not it was an actual date.

"Oh, Edna, how you pry. She has an artist friend who happens to be male. Don't make so much of it."

"An artist? Do I know him?"

"Possibly. Jenna, why don't you lie down a while before dinner so you're refreshed for this evening. You are going to eat first?"

She was more grateful to her mother-in-law than she could show. "I won't leave until around eight, but Aaron's getting hungry."

"Give me what he needs and go rest. I'll take care of my grandson and call you when dinner is ready."

She nodded and went to get Aaron's bag. A nap sounded good, and maybe a shower. Traveling always made her feel not-quite-clean.

Jenna spritzed her favorite perfume and checked the mirror, judging her outfit and her figure. Still following the plain and dark rule, she'd chosen black khakis with a black stretch-knit mock turtleneck covered by a glittery black and gold lace hip-length vest. Appropriate for New Year's Eve, but not too dressy. Her black walking shoes would have to do. Pumps made her feet sore too quickly and she wasn't sure how long she would be standing. And maybe it wouldn't matter. Trevor wouldn't necessarily want her to stay. She knew he was working. He mentioned it on Christmas, giving her the impression there was nothing he would rather do to celebrate the end of the year.

The nerves returned when she kissed Aaron and headed out to the taxi. Jenna was out of place in bars, since she rarely went to them. And she worried about Trevor's reaction. Would he be embarrassed to have some girl check up on him? Though that wasn't her intention. She only wanted to try to keep him as a friend, if he was still willing. Maybe he had a girlfriend. That would explain why he sounded so strange during their conversations. She would be with him tonight, his girlfriend, if he had one. If so, she would act like he was just an artist friend.

The buildings and street lights moved past, taking her courage away with them. She sensed the driver watching her but didn't dare look at him. He would have told her. Trevor would have mentioned a girlfriend if he had one.

Unless she was new. Or a New Year's Eve date. Jenna couldn't see a guy like Trevor without a date for the New Year. A pressure in the back of her neck moved into her skull. A bad idea, going to Trevor's bar unannounced. What was she thinking?

The taxi rolled to a stop in front of the Rocky Oyster. It seemed different at night as light streamed from the small windows and couples stood around the entrance. Jenna looked out into the darkness and debated. She could go back. He would never know.

"This the right address?"

She glanced at the driver. "Yes. I'm just..."

"Sure you wanna go in there alone? It's not the Ritz, ya know."

The Ritz? The black suede trench coat Joan insisted she borrow must have given the driver the impression Jenna was more important than she actually was. Her mother-in-law was right; it was warmer than her short denim coat, and it did match her outfit better. But it was far too elegant for her, and for the bar.

She realized she was stalling and pulled a few bills from her bag to hand up to the front. "I have a friend here, thank you."

"Want me to wait and make sure?"

Jenna considered his offer. What if Trevor had cancelled for some reason? Or if he asked her to leave? She took a deep breath and pulled her chin up. "No, thank you. Happy New Year." Jenna pulled her coat tighter, not sure whether the shiver was more from the biting cold or her fraying nerves. The couples by the door stared. Doing her best to ignore them, she pushed the metal handle, careful not to brush her skin across the old, splintered wood.

Music and laughter drummed into her ears and smoke burned her nose. Her heart hammered. She didn't belong here. Maybe the taxi had waited. Starting to turn, her path was blocked by a group coming in. There was nowhere to go but in farther. Stares caught her eye. What was wrong with her that made her stand out? Many of the women were dressed as well as she was. But they didn't look nervous. Possibly, her fear showed too much.

"Looking for someone?"

She started at the voice. It was slightly familiar. He was terribly tall and broad-shouldered. She didn't recognize him.

"In the wrong place, maybe? Someone give you bad directions?"

"Is this a private bar? Should I not be here?"

His explosive laugh made her step back. "Nah, it ain't private. I'm Nate, the owner. Haven't seen you around before, that's all. You're very welcome. Come on in, and if any of these malcontents give you any hassle, just yell for me. I don't put up with harassment in my bar."

Jenna relaxed. His eyes were friendly and his voice ... the guy who answered the phone when she called. She wondered if he recognized hers.

"Find a seat and I'll send someone over. What's your name?"

She tried to find the right face through the swarm. He wasn't behind the bar.

"You have one, don't ya?"

"Sorry." Did she want to tell him? How could she refuse? "I'm Jenna." She had to yell over the music and surrounding voices. "I was actually looking for someone who works here..."

"Jenna?" His eyebrows furled.

She waited, wondering if he did remember.

"Come." He took her arm without asking and half-pushed people out of his way, leading her ... somewhere.

The twinge returned to her stomach. He was taking her to the gallery, in the back corner of the bar. Thoughts of escape began to surface, but how would she get through the crowd, away from this huge man who had a firm, though gentle, hold on her arm? She should have called Trevor, at least let him know to watch for her.

He stopped. She began to panic.

"Hey D-day, ya have company."

She looked up and saw Trevor turn. The man had recognized her name, not her voice. But she hadn't given her name over the phone.

Trevor's grin changed to surprise. Not sure whether his reaction was good or bad, she tried to figure out what to say as he set the tray of empty glasses on the nearest table and moved in close to her, very close. Stares surrounded them. She didn't care. His thoughts were all that mattered.

"What are you doing here?"

Jenna could easily have touched him if she reached out. If her arms weren't frozen at her sides. Just friends? Maybe that wasn't what she wanted.

She had to say something. "It's New Year's Eve. I... I know you're working, but..." Gasping for a breath, she stepped back. She sounded like an idiot. "I shouldn't have come. I'm sorry." Trying to turn in to the crowd, her arm was again bound by a firm hand.

"Jen, wait."

Her eyes on the floor, she avoided the stares but allowed him to turn her back to him. His hands on both of her arms, he left barely enough space between them for air to move through. "Why are you here?"

Hell. This was it. She had already stepped across the line and it was too late to back out. Yanking courage from somewhere in her past, Jenna met his eyes. "I wanted to spend the New Year with you. If you want me to leave, just say so and I'll go back home. But I drove all the way up here ... because I had to... I'm painting again. I've actually finished a few, which is unusual. I seldom finish anything. But it didn't feel like a hobby. I brought one for you, the sketch you saw at Joan's ... I painted it. It was the first real thing I've done." She froze. His stare didn't waver. "Trevor? Do you want me to leave?"

He slid his hands up her arms and pressed closer. "No. I want you to come home with me tonight."

Jenna's heart pounded against her chest. She could barely breath as he lowered his mouth to hers. Finding his shoulders, she held tight ... for support. The space between dissipated and a strong hand cradled the back of her head. The other held her body against his. Her tension drained down through her toes and into the floor.

Twenty-two

She awoke in his bed. Alone.

Taking in her surroundings, Jenna remembered being embarrassed the night before when his aunt heard the door and came out from her room to wish Trevor a happy New Year. She seemed surprised he wasn't alone, which surprised Jenna. Trevor introduced her to Aunt Nina casually, as though he hadn't taken her home for a particular reason, Telling her goodnight, he led Jenna down to his "space," as he called it, in the house he shared only with his aunt.

He had the basement to himself, a very large space considering it was an actual house and not a townhouse like Joan's. Their home wasn't quite as particularly decorated as her mother-in-law's, but it was nice and gave the appearance of comfort. The basement was a separate world, rather messy and dark. She couldn't imagine how he painted with such little light, and looking around, Jenna had to wonder if he had a hamper. Clothes were dumped in small piles here and there, with a couple of shirts hung over worn chairs. The furniture looked as if it had been salvaged from street curbs or thrift shops. But his artwork was everywhere. It fit in well with the mess.

Even the headboard was a Trevor Dade original: a simple hand-made wooden frame painted with a mural. Mostly, the subject matter was undecipherable, but other parts made her cheeks flush when she studied it long enough. She chuckled as she thought about how her parents would react to Trevor and his work, and she almost wished he hadn't been such a gentleman the night before.

"Good morning."

She jumped at his voice and pulled the blanket higher around her. Silly, since she was still mostly dressed.

"Cold? It does get chilly down here."

"Oh, no, I'm fine."

"Aunt Nina said I should see if you're ready to eat."

"What time is it?"

He pulled his wrist up to check the too-large black watch. "Nearly eight-thirty."

"Eight-thirty?" She threw the blankets back and jumped up, but faltered. She was still tired. "Joan must be worried to death. I shouldn't have stayed."

"I called her." He waited to make sure he had her attention. "I told her we talked art too long and you fell asleep. Aaron's fine. She said not to wake you and you don't need to rush back."

Jenna sat again and wrapped into the blanket as the coolness of the basement caused a shiver. Would Joan believe all they had done was talk about art? Most likely not, though it was true. Well, nearly. They talked about a lot of other things, as well, including Daniel and Alan, and a bit about her parents, and his. Trevor being an orphan and living with his aunt since just after his fifteenth birthday explained the black he always wore. He had been very close to his parents.

His kisses enveloped her even now, along with the memory of her head cradled against his shoulder, her hand on his chest. His muscles flexing with his movement...

He offered a large sweatshirt and helped pull it over her head and arms. "I'm glad you came back."

Jenna loved the way his eyes constantly reflected a spark of mischief but were always true to their target. And she enjoyed being their target. With a light kiss, she traced a finger from his chest to his stomach. "You know, when you brought me here last night, I really expected..."

"Yeah, so did I." He gripped her fingers and shrugged. "But I was digging just getting you to talk so much. And it got late."

She noticed how his hair was tousled, apparently uncombed. It was charming. "I would have."

He grinned and brushed a strand of hair from her face. "You know where to find me."

Joan greeted her like it was an everyday occurrence for Jenna to have spent the night with a man. She debated telling her mother-in-law nothing happened, though Joan didn't ask and didn't seem bothered. And would she believe her anyway, considering Jenna agreed to meet Trevor at the bar again that night? Actually, he insisted on coming to pick them up early enough to have dinner with him and his aunt, both her and Aaron, and Aunt Nina offered to babysit afterward.

Jenna liked Trevor's aunt. Down-to-earth and friendly, Nina shared her home with Trevor as an equal. They kept track of each other, but not too close. They ate and slept and had company on their own schedules. She went away with friends now and then, and he did the same. Nina had no children of her own and doted on her nephew, who was perfect as far as she could see. He was the exact image of his father, her favorite brother. Jenna hadn't found out whether or not Aunt Nina had ever been married. It wasn't mentioned and Jenna wasn't sure she should ask. But she expected Aaron would get along with her fine. If not, she would have to cancel plans to go to the bar with Trevor and either return to Joan's or stay and visit with his aunt until he got home.

Sitting with Aaron on the floor, pretending to be interested in the toys he handed her then took away again, Jenna hoped her son would cooperate. She very much wanted to go to the bar with Trevor, not only to chat with him during his breaks and whenever possible while he worked, but also to watch him work. He even made serving drinks an art form, over-emphasizing his movements with varying distances between the bottles and glasses while he poured. And he was an exceptional conversationalist.

He introduced her to most of the regular patrons. A few recognized her name. All obviously enjoyed talking with him and did their best to talk with her. Jenna hoped her lack of socializing skills hadn't been misunderstood. She'd had trouble trying to fit in and add to the conversation since her early marriage and pregnancy prevented the normal single social life. It made her an outcast in the noisy bar.

Whenever Trevor heard a song he especially liked, he'd given himself a break and escorted her to the dance floor. He was a good dancer, relaxed and smooth. Jenna felt like a crutch next to him: wanted, but a bit damaging to his image. She wasn't used to dancing as a couple, either. Daniel would never dance in public and he had been too busy at home.

A sudden slap at her face made her jump and she caught Aaron's arm when he lost balance. He'd pulled himself up to standing and she felt the little hands pinch into her skin, but she apparently didn't show the proper respect for his accomplishment.

Jenna took his hand when he raised it again. "Don't hit. I see you."

He smiled and planted a sloppy kiss on her cheek.

"Time for your nap." Wrapping an arm under his legs, she felt his instinctive grasp of her neck. He would be walking before she knew it, before she was ready.

Aaron's comfort with Aunt Nina was nearly as spontaneous as it had been with Trevor. His unwillingness to complain even slightly about Jenna leaving him was both reassuring and disconcerting. He wasn't old enough to not need her yet.

Trevor closed the door and waited for Jenna to continue down the stairs, away from the house. "He'll be fine. We'll call now and then."

Jenna perused his face as she pulled her coat tighter against the sudden chill. He wasn't pushing and likely wouldn't have complained if she suddenly changed her mind, but she still heard no noise on the other side of the door. Aaron was fine the previous night with Joan. And she wanted to go with Trevor.

She grasped his arm.

A taxi took him to Joan's, and would take him back from Joan's after he dropped Jenna and Aaron off there. But she saw no reason to spend the money on taxis all night when her van was available. She let him drive. Actually, she was glad he agreed to drive.

The wind yanked at the door of the old vehicle, gusting frigid air from Lake Michigan. She shivered inside the van, smoothed her hair back down, and watched Trevor walk around and claim the driver's seat. He quickly revved the engine and switched on the heater. "Nasty tonight, isn't it?" He rubbed his bare hands together.

They'd kept their distance through dinner and while visiting with Aunt Nina. Now, alone in the cold darkness and relative privacy, Jenna wanted more. She scooted to her left until their thighs met, completely ignoring her common sense telling her not to get attached, to not start anything.

She didn't have to.

Trevor pressed his mouth against hers, grasping her head to pull her closer. His heat was more intense than the air blowing from the raucous fan. Jenna let her free hand slip under his coat, rest against his side ... move farther around his warm body. Cold fingers caressed her lower back, groping until they found bare skin underneath her shirt.

She broke the kiss and struggled to find her voice. "Do you have to work?" It came out as a whisper.

His mouth brushed against her neck. "Yes."

"Can you get off early?"

Trevor met her eyes, his fingers still exploring the naked curves of her back. "Are you always so pushy?"

"Not always. Sometimes. Should I stop?"

"Only if don't want to encourage me." With a slight grin, Trevor pressed back into her lips.

She fully wanted to encourage him. So she did. Almost too much. But his touches felt incredible. He half-groaned as he said again he had to get to work.

Making herself moving away enough to let him drive, Jenna shivered. She knew it wasn't from the toe-numbing cold that seeped through the floorboard. Or from the van's heater blowing loudly to try to overrule the outside air. She wasn't in love with this man. She barely knew him. But she was glad she had returned to Chicago.

~~~

After eight days of vacillating between Joan's and Trevor's and the bar and a couple of art museums Trevor had talked her into, Jenna appreciated the snowfall and light howl of the wind giving her cause to simply sit still. Aaron fell asleep in the middle of playing in Joan's living room and Jenna only moved him enough to be on top of his blanket, covering him with another. She called to let Trevor know they were staying in with Joan. She didn't admit she also needed time away from whatever was evolving in their relationship.

They had kept things friendly, so far not much more than heavy flirting. Twice, Jenna expected it to transform ... merge, but she hadn't pushed it and neither had he. She was thinking she should go back to Peoria and hadn't admitted that, either. There was no real reason to go back other than the opaque fact that it was home. But it called to her.

One night of hibernation became three. Trevor phoned, once on the second morning, twice on the third day. Something inside wouldn't let her go see him. He didn't call the next day. Jenna decided to leave in the morning.

Before she could go, she had to drop off the painting.

After dinner and clean up, she stole to her room to change out of her house clothes. Winding her hair into a neat bun, Jenna stood back and checked the mirror. She hadn't worn it that way for a long time. Again, it made her look older. It suited her mood.

She grabbed her old coat and pulled it on while stepping into the living room to find Joan. "I need to go out for a little while. Would you mind keeping Aaron for me?"

Her mother-in-law glanced up from the newspaper. "Is he picking you up?"

"No. I'm taking the van. I've been watching. I can get there fine." And the canvases were still inside.

Joan nodded. "You will be careful. And call me when you're on the way back so I'll know to watch for you."

"Oh, I won't be long. I just..."
~~~

"You're going to tell him goodbye?"

Her stomach fluttered. Goodbye sounded so final. "Well, I have to tell him I'm going back." She picked up her son to give him a kiss. He whined when she tried to set him down.

Joan rattled the paper, set it neatly on the side table, then stood to take Aaron. "You get to stay with me, sweetie. And Jenna, don't be too abrupt. He does care about you."

Joan thought it was a break-up. It wasn't. At least Jenna didn't think it was.

The drive made her nervous, though traffic was fairly slow on week nights after rush hour and the snow had melted off the roads. She planned to arrive a half an hour before he had to leave for work, plenty of time to say she was going home and to give him the painting.

Sawyer Brown soothed her once more, until she pulled into his driveway. After a deep breath, she got out, retrieved the canvas from the back, and made her way to the door. It was strange to knock and wait for a reply after all the times she had walked right in with him.

Expecting Nina to answer, Jenna was taken aback by Trevor's sudden presence. He wore jeans and a T-shirt like ordinary guys. No loose, hanging shirts. No black covering his real personality. "Come on in." Not even a trace of annoyance in his voice.

"I can't stay." She avoided his eyes and checked for his aunt while brushing past him into the foyer.

"She's not home. She'll be away a couple more days visiting a friend." He closed the door and stayed beside it.

Jenna turned back. "Oh. I'm sorry I missed her. Will you tell her I said thank you?"

"For what?"

"The hospitality. I should have brought her something, but this is last-minute."

"You're leaving?"

A deep breath helped her continue. "Yes, I need to get back."

"Why?" He waited for an answer that didn't come. "Something I did? I'm not pushing, ya know. I know you've been pushed enough."

"No." She stepped toward him, gripping the canvas so tight it made her fingers throb. "It's not... I'm just going home for a while. I'll be back."

"Back to Chicago? Or back to me?" He leaned against the door, not advancing or retreating. Waiting, for something she couldn't give him.

"I brought this for you and kept forgetting it. The sketch I painted. I told you..."

"The first real thing you've done. I wondered when you would show me." He came to her, close enough to pull at the brown paper covering the canvas.

"No. Wait until after work or something. It's not very good and I don't want you to have to try to act like it is in front of me. Don't keep it if you don't want it." She moved away to prop it against the wall, and bumped against him when she straightened.

"You belong here, Jenna." A hand slid behind her neck. His kiss took her in.

She pulled away. "I'll call you ... when I get back ... if you want."

Trevor dropped his arm in retreat.

Rushing to open the door, she glanced back, started to speak, and changed her mind. Jenna fled half way down the sidewalk then slowed almost to a stop. Then she did stop.

What was she doing? She didn't want to leave.

Motionless and surrounded by the icy black of an empty winter night, Jenna allowed the biting wind to whip her unbuttoned coat around her thighs. She couldn't stop the moisture in her eyes. She didn't love him. She didn't want this. It was too soon to be involved again, too soon for the longing involved with a relationship.

It had to stop now, before it was more than she could handle.

Forcing her feet to continue, she wiped at her face. The cold made her eyes sting. She would have to stop the tears immediately in order to drive through the city at night.

Her fingers shook as she fumbled with the keys.

"Stay with me tonight."

She jolted at his voice, turned, then shielded her face. The tears hadn't stopped. She couldn't let him see...

He pulled her chin higher. He hadn't bothered to find a coat. "Stay with me, Jen. Only for tonight. No promises. No pressure. Just come back inside."

She shook her head. "I can't."

"Why not?" He shivered.

"You need to go in. You'll freeze. You don't even have shoes..."

"Why not?"

Jenna stood staring at him. She had no idea how to answer.

"I opened the painting. You have no reason to play second string to someone else all your life. You can stand on your own just fine. And

I'm not looking for obligations. Hell, I'm twenty-two and I like being a part-time bartender right now. I don't want obligations, but I don't want you to walk out like this."

"Twenty-two?" Jenna studied his face. He couldn't be two years younger than she was.

He shivered again. "I thought you didn't realize. Does it bother you? Or does it convince you that I'm not..."

"I'm not getting married again. I'm not in love with you. I don't want to do that whole thing again."

He shrugged. "So just sleep with me. I can deal with that."

She pivoted toward the van. If she went that far...

"I'm kidding, Jen." He caught her from behind; his face nuzzled against her hair. "You're not ready for that so let's not even bring it up again. We're friends, right? Come to work with me and hang out, relax. I'm not gonna add to your stress."

Reluctantly, she allowed him to take over, to guide her actions. They returned to the house and he left her to calm down and check her face while he changed into work clothes. She called Joan before they left, trying to keep her voice steady.

The bar was too noisy. No more than usual but it irritated her in her present state of mind. There was no room to hide in, to get away and pretend she was elsewhere. Instead, she stayed inside herself and avoided conversation as much as possible.

They began to leave her alone. Trevor tried to ger her to talk to him as well as he could, but she didn't know what to say to him. She didn't want to talk. She wanted to go home. Which home she meant, Jenna wasn't quite sure.

Strains of a familiar song caught her attention and Trevor looked over from where he was mixing a drink. It was their song, their first slow dance.

He knew she recognized it. Handing a drink over the counter, he ignored other yelled orders and walked around the bar, focused on her. He took her hand. "One dance?"

She tuned into the singer's voice as she followed to the small space reserved for the few who used the bar as a club.

Jenna kept some distance. He didn't complain or try to move in. She felt, or thought she felt, people stare, wondering why there was so much space between them, why she hadn't been to the bar in nearly a week after being there every night. It made her tense and she scuffed his toes more than once.

"Relax, Jen. It doesn't matter what they think."

She met his eyes. How did he know? He was right, though. It didn't. "But what are you thinking now? About me? Us?"

He paused his movement and released her hand to brush fingers against her bare neck. "Me? I'm enjoying your company while I have it. Trying to frame every detail so I at least won't lose the memory."

Jenna stared. He didn't expect her to stay with him. Maybe he never had. He wasn't trying to run her life, or change it. He was simply there.

So don't hold back, it's not a game we're playing... Of yours, and mine, and nobody else's...

She kissed him. As timidly as their first kiss. And he pulled her in.

They blended into the song, heard the music change, become heavier, faster. Couples turned into groups, swarming around them. Still, they remained transfixed.

Trevor didn't bother to ask if he could leave early. He informed Nate and took her home. And though there was no music in his basement, Jenna heard it still: the heavy beat, pounding tempo, changing into a slower melody. She was peaceful, lying against his bare skin.

Twenty-three

Jenna set her hand against Aaron's forehead. It was no warmer than usual. Giving in to his insistent fuss, she pulled him from the playpen. The bags could stay packed for the time being. Her son rarely demanded so much attention, and even if he wasn't sick, he wasn't happy. Maybe it was two weeks away and the long drive home. She didn't remember him being as fussy after their last trip, though.

Settling in her rocker, Jenna cuddled him, soothing them both with the gentle swaying motion. He would be nine months old in a few days. Nine months. It didn't seem possible. How could she have dealt with so much in the span of less than a year? And her son couldn't be so close to his first birthday. He was still so small.

She'd spent too much time away from him while running around with Trevor.

Jenna focused her attention on the changes in the loft and nearly regretted inviting Carrie to stay with her. She didn't mind the evidence of her friend's presence. It wasn't that she was particular about her decorating. And sleeping on the couch wouldn't bother her. She did that fairly often, anyway. But she'd lived alone for nearly eight months and would have to adapt, again.

Through the window, beyond her trees, a translucent red-orange glazed the darkening sky. Despite the bitter wind chill, it had been a good day to travel, with no snow and only a few clouds sifting the bright rays. The old "red sky at night" proverb told her the following day would also be sunny and calm. Her heart wasn't easily convinced. She left Trevor, without further warning. He must have thought she would change her mind after their night together. And she nearly had.

While in his arms, his bare skin warming hers, Jenna couldn't even consider leaving. His light touch was a balm; his gentleness nurtured her soul. To leave him the next morning had been callous.

Jenna pushed the memory from her consciousness and took Aaron to his crib since he fell asleep. He barely stirred as she covered him. With a shiver, she went to turn the heat up.

Shuffling into the kitchen, she filled a cup with water and set it in the microwave, mesmerized by the slow circular motion until the beeping roused her enough to pull it out again. The mint tea was gone.

She'd forgotten to get more. Finding several herb blends, apparently Carrie's addition to the pantry, Jenna pulled out the first one she found and dropped it into the warm water.

She wandered back to the couch and pulled the afghan over her legs, let her eyes drift toward Daniel's studio ... and his sketches along the wall. Guilt crept into her thoughts. First, the guilt of walking out on Trevor, slowly replaced by how she had broken her promise to Daniel. She promised to stay true to him.

Sipping the spicy liquid, Jenna's hand shook. Only eight months. It had only been eight months and she had already turned to another. A queasiness overcame her insides and she set the cup on the side table, scrunched her body lower on the couch, and pulled the afghan to her chin. The weight of horrendous guilt mixed with confusion and lonliness suddenly overwhelmed her brain. Dusk turned into dark. Her eyes clenched against it, all of it.

Darkness didn't block it out. The fuzziness of mental and physical fatigue didn't block it out. A throbbing of her temples didn't block it out. It became stronger the more she tried to run from it. Giving in, Jenna focused on it, on her husband. Her promise...

She stroked his hair, trying not to let him see her pain. He had enough of his own.

Daniel's face was drawn, pale, much too thin. It killed her soul to think of how the cancer was devouring the once young and healthy body. It wasn't fair. He had so much left to give. So much...

"Jen." His voice, with only half the strength it used to have, stirred her insides. "It's okay. You're strong. You'll be fine."

Fine? No, not ever again. She attempted a smile. "Don't worry about me. Is there anything you need?"

"Just listen. I'm tired, but I have to tell you..."

"Rest then. Tell me tomorrow. I'll be here." She leaned in to touch his lips. They were cold; it scared her. "Daniel?"

"Jen, I am so sorry ... for everything I didn't do ... for you ... that I should have. For not..."

"No. Don't."

"I have to..." His eyes clenched.

"Is the pain bad again? Do you need more..?"

"Just listen. I wasn't fair to you, by not telling you..."

"It wouldn't have mattered." She fought tears back as she caressed his hair. "It wouldn't have mattered if I had known. I would still be here."

"My angel. You have always been ... my angel, my true inspiration."

Her head dropped. He was trying to say goodbye and she wasn't going to have it. It was too soon.

Daniel's hand raised to her face. Jenna noticed the effort it took and grasped his fingers, let him borrow her strength.

He gasped for air. "Promise me something."

"Don't do this, Daniel. Don't say goodbye."

"Jenna, I'm tired of fighting. You have to let go now."

"No. Daniel, no." Her tears fell onto his hand.

"I will be here with you, in our son. Tell him ... how much I wanted him, that I'll be watching ... over him."

She caught her breath. "I don't want you to leave me."

"Promise me, that ... you will let yourself ... be who you are. More than anything, I want you to promise me that."

Jenna stared. He was worried about her. Through all of his pain, and fear, he was worried about her. She rubbed a hand across her eyes, forcing a calm she didn't feel. He didn't need to worry about her now.

"Promise."

He was getting weaker as she watched. She nodded. For his sake, she would promise him anything. "Okay."

A slight curvature of his lips told her Daniel had accepted her agreement. She laid his arm back down on the bed, keeping hold of his fragile hand. "Rest now. You're too tired."

"So are you. Lie down with me."

She hesitated. It was late, nearly midnight, and she was more than tired. How would she keep herself from falling asleep?

"Jenna."

She nodded and reclined carefully, aware of how movement caused him pain.

"Stop worrying, honey. It's beyond that now." His words were softer, barely audible. His face began to relax.

She moved in closer. "Daniel, you will always be my only true love. I will love you forever. And your son will know you."

His head turned, barely. "Raise him ... to be like you. I love you, Jenna. I love who you are."

She met his lips, then cuddled her head on the pillow against his, a hand atop his chest, barely feeling the heartbeat. It used to be so strong. She had loved to lay her head against his chest, listening to the strong melody. She imagined she could hear it now, pounding ... pounding...

Jenna awoke suddenly. She hadn't moved. She still cradled Daniel's head. Her arm was numb and tingled when she rose enough to see the neon light of the now-unused alarm clock. Just after two a.m. and only the slightest moon glow from the windows. She looked at her husband. His face was purely relaxed, with no trace of pain. She was glad he was getting some sleep... Her hand didn't detect the heartbeat. But she could vaguely see his chest rise and fall, barely. Then it stopped.

"Daniel?" She pushed herself up onto the still-tingling arm and brushed her fingers across his face. "Daniel?" No reply. No movement. She felt for breath she couldn't find. "No."

As she realized he was no longer with her, Jenna surrendered into the mattress and let her tears flow. What difference did it make? He was gone. She was alone again.

She had to call Joan at Denise's. They would want to know. Not yet. She couldn't pull away from him yet.

"Jenna?"

A voice nagged at her head. Joan? No, not Joan.

"Jenna? Wake up. What's wrong?"

She opened her eyes, aware of moisture on the pillow under her face. Carrie. Why was she... With consciousness alighting, Jenna bolted up. He wasn't there. A dream. No, a memory. She hadn't just lost him. It had been months...

She rubbed a hand across her wet eyes and saw another figure.

Alan. He sat beside her. "What is it, Jen? Did something happen in Chicago? Why didn't you tell me you were coming home?"

"No. A dream. Daniel..." It was still too vivid. She couldn't relive it enough to tell him.

He became her best friend again as she sank against him and let it out. Blindly accepting tissue from Carrie, her breathing finally calmed, the tears dried. She still held him.

"What happened in Chicago, Jen? And I want the truth this time."

She blew her nose, still sniffling. "I... I spent every day of the week with him ... then ... I stopped. I was going to leave and I ... went back ... to say..."

"To say goodbye, to the painter." Alan's voice wasn't accusatory, only questioning, but he wasn't asking. He knew. "And you couldn't."

Jenna shook her head, wiping again at her nose.

"So don't, Jen. If you want to be there, maybe you should be."

"But Daniel ... I promised..."

Alan forced her release of him. "Promised what? You fulfilled your promise. You were devoted, and faithful." He was careful with his word choice in front of his sister. "He didn't ask you to be alone forever, did he? I can't imagine he would have wanted that."

"No, he..." She stopped and held her breath a moment. He hadn't asked her... Thinking back through the dream, the true memory, Jenna shook her head. She'd had it all mixed up. Her emotions had turned things around. She hadn't promised to never date again, only that he would be her only true love. He hadn't asked her ... anything except ... to be who she was. He had to know she would need companionship. Daniel would know that. He would never have wanted her to be alone.

She went to check on her son and turned back to her friends. She couldn't speak. She just stood there, looking at them, seeing a distance she'd never seen before. They belonged there, in Peoria. Jenna didn't. And she no longer had a reason to stay.

Alan came to her and set a hand aside her face. "Call Joan. I'll help you move. And I imagine the Art Institute has a teaching program."

~~~

Jenna pulled the van in front of Alan's, turned off the engine, and checked inside the large box from where constant yips seeped through air holes. The puppy tried to jump out to her. She petted him until he calmed, grabbed him around the stomach, and cuddled him in close.

"Okay, you're fine. And you're going to like it here." She stroked the golden hair. He was a beautiful little thing. It would be hard to give him away, but Aaron needed to be older before she took on care of an animal. Fortunately, Denise offered to keep her son while Jenna was running this last errand. She wasn't sure how she would have managed the baby and the puppy both.

Bright sunshine took the bite out of the January cold enough she didn't mind holding the puppy while waiting for someone to answer. She was glad it was Alan and smiled at him.

He raised his eyebrows. "Wouldn't it have been easier to get a dog after you moved instead of just before?"

"It's not mine. It's for Justin."

"It's what?"

"I told you he needed one and you haven't bothered yet, so..."

"Jen."

"Alan, this will be good for him, and since I'm taking his playmate away, I couldn't resist bringing him another." She could see him start to give in. "Go ask Cheryl." She waited as he obeyed. The puppy was an active little mutt. They would have their hands full with him.

Cheryl gave her a smile. "Oh, he's beautiful, Jenna. What a sweet little thing!"

Her friend's eyebrows were still raised. "Dogs are a lot of work."
~~~

"Oh, so are kids, but we have three of those. Justin will love it. The twins always leave him out. It'll be good for him, and the yard is plenty big. You can build him a house when it gets warmer and he's older so he isn't always under your feet."

Jenna smiled at him. With Cheryl on her side, she knew she won.

He sighed. "Come in. I'll get Justin."

The boy was thrilled. Jenna watched him play with his new best buddy while the twins kept their distance. They weren't sure about the wiggling puppy. But Justin gave Jenna a big hug. "J.R., that's his name. Doesn't he look like a J.R.?"

Jenna smiled. "Yes, I would say he does. Is that a friend of yours?"

"It's you. I can't name him Jenna, since he's a boy."

"My initials?" Justin nodded and she kissed his head. "I want you to teach him to like little kids so when Aaron comes to visit, you can all play together."

His whole face lit up while hugging his new pal.

She stood and faced Alan. "I have to go, but I have something for you, too. Will you walk out with me?" Giving her farewells to Cheryl and the kids, Jenna led her friend to the van. She pulled the side door open and carefully grabbed the canvas. "I want you to have it."

Alan's eyes widened. "You're giving me the zoo painting?"

"You said you've always loved it. It's my way of thanking you for always believing in me. For pulling me through and helping me move on. This is what I want you to remember. This is who I am."

"I know. And this is how I have always thought of you, Jen. In a T-shirt and shorts, your hair down and your feet bare. Down-to-earth and content to be there. He captured you at your best. Thank you for this, and don't throw anything away. Save it for me."

She chuckled. "Okay." Pulling the sliding door until it latched, she opened the front door.

"You know, I'm sure Carrie will have the loft filled in no time, but we do have a guest room. And Trevor is welcome, too."

She nodded. He was letting her go. She loved him for that.

He held the painting with one hand and touched her arm with the other, planting a kiss on her cheek.

On his driveway amid the bustling neighborhood and windows Cheryl could have been looking out of, Jenna leaned in to touch his lips. Briefly, but warmly. And she released him. "Bring Cheryl and the kids up to see the art museums and galleries. I'll be your tour guide."

Twenty-four

Jenna knew in which neighborhood she wanted to search for an apartment, on the outskirts of the area college students had invaded and made their home during their years at the Institute. It was also not far from Aunt Nina's suburb, an easy drive or nice walk, if Trevor still had any interest. She wouldn't blame him if he didn't, but it would have no factor on whether or not she stayed. Chicago fit her well. She could blend in with other artist-types and non-traditional families. Being a young single mom wouldn't stand out as much in the city as it would in her hometown. And Peoria was too close to her hometown, providing less cover from the image people expected her to have because of her parents' careers.

A career: something she would have to work on. While looking through the classifieds for apartments, at Joan's kitchen table, Jenna scanned the employment ads. She wasn't real sure what to look for or exactly how she would deal with working, going to school, and taking care of her baby, but she would have to have something. Figuring her current availability of funds along with rent paid for the loft would cover rent in a decent neighborhood for somewhere between two and three years, it didn't give her much time to get a degree and start making a real income. Of course, they had put money aside, in a long-term fund Daniel insisted on having for their retirement, or for an emergency. She hadn't realized why it was so important to him until he became sick.

He had known, somehow. Jenna finally admitted to the pain she felt about not being told he'd had cancer as a child. Until it came back. Daniel felt lucky to have the years he did after being told he wouldn't reach puberty. He insisted he hadn't told Jenna because there was no need for her to worry about it. She truly believed he meant he could beat it again since he had once. She couldn't be angry, though. At this point, she wasn't sure she wouldn't have done the same.

She flipped the page. Nothing pulled her interest other than a few that required experience she didn't have. Skimming though the art section for her own amusement, she caught glimpse of a small ad. A part-time gallery assistant, no experience needed, some art knowledge required. She recognized the street name and tried to place where it was. Fairly close to Joan's gallery, if she remembered. She wondered whether she would dare use her mother-in-law as a reference. Joan offered to get her a job at the gallery she supported, but Jenna refused. That was Daniel's territory; she wanted to leave it that way.

With a deep breath, she dialed the number in the ad. The line was busy. She tore the piece from the paper and set it aside to try later.

By the time Aaron woke up, Jenna had a list of apartments. Only three were in the neighborhood she wanted, but several others were noted as back-ups. She didn't have time to be too particular. Most of her furniture had been left for Carrie, but the books and art supplies and her personal belongings and baby things were either packed into the van or stuffed into the guest room at Joan's. So far, Daniel's sketches still hung in the loft. She planned to take them down to relocate to her new apartment when she went back to trade the van for the Mustang. She saw no reason to keep both vehicles in the city and the van would not be practical in downtown Chicago.

She would need to learn to use public transportation. Trevor generally took the metro. She could do that if he would show her how to keep from getting lost, though she would prefer the El whenever possible. Daniel had taken her on it a couple of times, when she'd asked, but he preferred the more private taxis. She chuckled. They really did have different ideas about a lot of things.

Handing Aaron his bottle, she glanced at the clock. Trevor would be painting now, she assumed. Late afternoon was his chosen studio time when he was in the mood. Otherwise, he would be out. Doing what, exactly, was hard to guess. Playing basketball down the street or just hanging out with friends. Maybe wandering, looking for someone to chat with. Jenna couldn't imagine Daniel playing basketball or just "hanging." At twenty-two, Daniel found her and was rushed into marriage. But maybe that was exactly what he wanted. She hadn't pushed him. She offered to free him. It was his choice.

The phone pulled her from her thoughts and she set her baby in his walker before answering. Aaron liked to talk to people, in person, on the phone, however.

"Jenna, honey, I'm going to be rather late tonight. Can you find something there or should I stop? I'll have a sandwich while I work, but I do want you to eat."

"I'll find something, Joan. It's fine."

"Are you sure? It's no trouble."

"No, really. I'm fine." After convincing her mother-in-law she was well able to spend the evening alone, she replaced the receiver and looked over at Aaron. "Well, what should we do tonight?" He smiled and banged his free hand on the small tray, bottle still stuck between his teeth. Lurching for the phone cord, he ran the walker into her legs. "Sorry, Charlie." Jenna pulled it up and draped it over the top of the phone. "And just who do you think you're going to call, anyway?"

"Ah dah dah dah."

"I know you want to talk, but I have no idea where you got that from." She rubbed his head and returned to the table. He scooted over next to her and set a hand on her leg while he sucked on the bottle.

She sat watching him and let her mind wander. Joan asked the night before whether she intended to let Trevor know she was in town again. Jenna had been in Chicago four days already and had thought about it nearly every minute but still couldn't answer. How? After walking out the morning after they slept together, how did she just go back? Call? Show up at his door? They'd had no contact for over two weeks. She missed him and thought about him constantly, but would that matter to him?

With a glance at her list of apartments, her eye caught the job advertisement. First things first. She had to get settled. Returning to the phone, she tried the number again.

"Elucidations. Can I help you?"

~~~

It was a new, small gallery, but very friendly. As proof she knew something about art, Jenna had taken the sketchbook she worked in before leaving Chicago. She'd added three new sketches in the past couple of days: one of Justin and the puppy, one of Alan's home that emphasized the landscape, the other – her goodbye to Daniel – their loft, as she had first seen it, with him standing at an easel. It didn't resemble him, or anyone. Again, fairly surreal. And she nearly removed it from the sketchbook. After a long debate in her mind, she decided to leave it since no one at the gallery would understand the sketch.

The manager in charge of hiring loved it, all of her work, and apparently had been impressed with Jenna herself. Not only did she hire Jenna immediately, even knowing she was a single mom, but she pulled Jenna through the gallery to a secluded office to introduce her to the owner. He was young, surprisingly young for an owner, and Jenna wasn't at all sure he wasn't flirting. They even agreed to hold the job for the two weeks she needed before she could start.
~~~

She flagged a taxi and headed back to Joan's office to pick up her son. Her mother-in-law, of course, was delighted although she would have preferred for Jenna to work in "her" gallery.

"Did they recognize your name?"

Jenna hesitated. "Well, I didn't exactly tell them. I used my maiden name for the interview. I wanted to get this job on my own."

"You plan to use Givens instead of Rhodes, to stay in hiding?"

In hiding? No, not any longer. "That was only to get the job. I'll tell them when I go back to return the paperwork." Her mother-in-law seemed only partially relieved. "I'm not giving up my name, Joan. That is who I am now, and I'm very proud of that. I am Jenna Rhodes, for better or for worse."

~~~

The sun sifted down from the sky taking its time. The more the day progressed, the more Jenna wanted to share her news with Trevor. If he knew she had a job, that she was getting an apartment, maybe... Suddenly unable to control the restlessness, she used Aaron's nap to change clothes and fix her hair. Dinner was ready for Joan when she got home from work, but Jenna couldn't eat. Instead, she thanked her mother-in-law for keeping her son and left to find the catalyst who prompted her return to the city.

It was early. There likely wouldn't be much of a crowd at the bar yet. He would be getting things in order and chatting with the guys.

The confinement of the taxi did little to warm her, with bitter Lake Michigan wind seeping through the windows. The driver was sullen and uncommunicative, which was fine. Jenna hugged her arms around herself for warmth and tried to figure out what she would say to Trevor, and what she would do when he told her to leave. Give up, or try to change his mind? Maybe he would have a girlfriend there with him this time.

The ride ended almost too soon and she forced her half-frozen fingers to open the door. She supposed she would have to invest in a pair of gloves, although she didn't like them. In Peoria, she hadn't been outside for long enough or often enough in the last few years to worry about it. On the city streets, though...

She stopped outside the old wooden door and turned. Through frozen breath, Jenna surveyed the area. Chicago. Her new home. For a moment, she was slightly intimidated by the crowded, narrow buildings reaching into the sky and the bustling locals paying no attention to her
~~~

as they hurried home to dinner or out for their evening entertainment. Then she smiled, at no one. She had done it. She had broken away from her parents, her past, her insecurities. Traces of fear still dwelled within, but they no longer ruled her. This was her home, her space.

With a deep cleansing breath, she turned back again and opened the door, unconcerned about the splintered wood. The familiar smell of alcohol, nicotine, and mustiness surrounded her, lured her in. The clinking of glasses and voices welcomed her. Trevor was behind the bar chatting with one of the regular patrons. Several tables held faces new and recognizable. Nate looked up. She grinned and motioned for him not to give her away.

Jenna was nearly to the bar when Trevor turned, ready to greet whoever approached. She stopped.

He didn't look as surprised as she expected. "Welcome back."

The casualness of his greeting caught her off-guard. But what did she expect in front of his friends? She supposed it wasn't fair not to do this privately so he could say what he thought. "Hi. It's freezing out there tonight." She rubbed her hands together, berating herself for sounding so stupid.

He grinned. "Yeah, you know it's January, right? Pretty typical for the Windy City. Have a seat and warm up."

Jenna slipped out of her coat, hung it over the back of the barstool closest to where he stood, and hoped something intelligent would come to mind soon. Propped on the worn, leather-clad seat, she tried her best to look relaxed. She felt stiff, again out of place in his world.

Trevor maintained his professional stance. "What would you like to drink? It's on the house."

"Oh, you don't have to do that."

"I know I don't. And you didn't have to come back."

Her stomach tightened. He had lowered his voice. His eyes were friendly, but wary. The guilt she felt this time was for him. She had hurt him by walking away so quietly, so viciously. "Yes, I really did. Have to come back." Jenna suddenly had so much she needed to say. She caught her breath as a tingling sensation rose from somewhere inside, somewhere she couldn't quite place. "Trevor, you were right, you know. This is where I belong."

He leaned in against the bar, arms crossed atop, his face inches away, eyes drilling into hers. Jenna could feel the stares surrounding them. "Do you trust me?"

The tingle moved through her arms down into her fingertips. The conversation was getting too intense for public view.

"To choose your drink. I know something that'll warm you right up."

She controlled the urge to lean forward and kiss him. "Of course."

"Right back, don't go anywhere." He strolled to the other end of the bar, hiding from her view the concoction he was mixing. He also spoke quietly to Nate, too obviously about her. She began to wonder if she should accept any drink from him. Just as quickly, she scorned herself. Too many movies.

Her heart rate had nearly dropped to normal by the time Trevor returned with a steaming mug, crowned with whipped topping. "Careful, it may be too hot yet."

"Thank you." She cupped her hands around the mug. The heat stung her fingers.

Nate sent Trevor around to sit with her. The silence was awkward until he asked about Aaron and she asked about Aunt Nina and his painting. The few patrons there so early left them alone and kept their distance while they talked about nothing. That was awkward, too. He didn't ask why she left, or why she returned. Jenna could tell he wanted to say more, but he kept it in.

She wanted to touch him.

"I better get back to work. Can you stick around?"

She pulled her eyes away. "Actually, I shouldn't stay long."

"You're not going back again right away?"

"No. I..." He had stood to walk away from her, but waited. Jenna studied him. No black tonight, simply jeans and a T-shirt. He looked incredible. "I was wondering... I got a job today and I really need to go apartment-hunting tomorrow since I only have two weeks to get a place and move in and..."

"A job? Here?" He sat again.

She longed to move closer. "A gallery assistant, part-time, nothing big. But it'll work for now."

"You're staying?"

"Maybe I shouldn't ask, since ... it wasn't right of me to leave that way, but ... I was confused ... about a lot of things." Jenna took a breath. He was watching her, waiting. "Yes, I'm staying. And I really hoped ... that we could at least..."

"Did you find what you kept going back to Peoria for?"

Her heart pounded. He had leaned closer again so he wouldn't be overheard and his scent was stronger than the cigarettes and alcohol, his original scent, the one she couldn't place. "Yes. And it had to stay there, where it belonged."

He smiled.

"Anyway, I have a van full of stuff and Joan's guest room is packed and she's being nice about it so far, but..."

"You can stay with me."

The tingling returned. Her breathing was forced. Jenna opened her mouth, tried to speak, and looked away. Move in with him? Briefly, she saw herself in his basement, her clothes hanging over a chair alongside his, their easels adjoined. But Aaron...

"Think about it. I have to get back to work. We can talk when I take you home." He stood, then leaned in to kiss the side of her head.

Jenna raised her face to see his eyes. Trevor didn't care who was watching or what they thought. When he leaned toward her, asking for more, she wrapped a hand behind his head and pulled him in.

~~~

She wandered around the spacious three-bedroom apartment. Still mostly empty, except for her art room, it gave out a light echo in reply to sounds. With aching feet, at the end of three days of apartment hunting and three nights of accompanying Trevor to the bar, Jenna knew it was exactly what she needed a moment after she stepped inside. Under process of remodeling, only the apartment's kitchen and two of the bedrooms had refinished floors, but work had stalled. Jenna was able to get a good discount for taking it as it was. And it worked well for her plans. The unfinished bedroom turned into her art room. The tiles had been scratched up and stained, so she wouldn't have to worry about spilling paint. Meant to be the master bedroom, it had two wonderfully large windows on adjoining walls. Jenna didn't need that much space to sleep. The smallest room was large enough for her bed and dresser and would serve as a guest room if needed. A daybed could turn the studio into a sleeping area. The mid-sized room would work well for Aaron's crib and changing table and a play space when he got older.

The tiny kitchen was no problem since she didn't like to cook, and the living room was open and airy, also with large windows. They were the selling point. Her paint-splattered rug added life to the apartment. Jenna's first thought had been to put it in her studio, but she changed her mind. She liked the casualness it provided by being the first sight from the front door. So far.
~~~

Trevor did all of the searching with her. They were both tired, but they put in the fourth day moving her things out of Joan's guest room and the van and into her own place. Aaron stayed with Aunt Nina in the evenings and during the move and was perfectly content there. Joan stopped by the apartment briefly. She didn't quite approve but was sure Jenna would turn it into a nice home. She'd been friendly to Trevor and invited them both to dinner on his next night off.

Brushing a hand across the sculpture Joan allowed her to take from Daniel's bedroom to relocate in a corner of her new living room, Jenna sighed and drifted into the studio. She propped herself in front of a window and looked down at the rooftops of neighboring houses, thinking about the extreme difference in the view. She would miss her trees and the river, but the activity below was energizing. She could let herself daydream about where her "neighbors" were going and what they were thinking...

Strong hands brushed around her waist. She covered his arms with her own.

"Tired?" Trevor's voice was soft against her ear.

"Exhausted. And you should rest before work tonight."

"I'm not going to work tonight."

She turned in his arms, welcoming his kiss. Then she pulled back. She hadn't allowed him to get very close. Although she and Aaron were essentially living with him and his aunt until the apartment was ready, they weren't actually living together. Jenna insisted on staying upstairs in the guest room with her son. It was just easier to go to his place after being at the bar so late than to pick Aaron up and go back to Joan's. Convenience only, or so she told herself. But she refused his offer to move in with him. She wanted to stay more in control than she had the last time.

"I should get Aaron. I imagine your aunt is tired of babysitting."

He backed off. "I'm sure she's not, but okay."

She handed him the keys to the van automatically.

He was quiet, though, too quiet. Even at his aunt's house, while they talked about the apartment and how Nina loved to take care of Aaron, Trevor barely joined the discussion. He did watch Jenna. She caught him staring several times until she became uncomfortable.

Her son yawned and rubbed a fist over his eyes.

She kissed his head. "You're ready to get settled in. Want to go see your new home?" The baby raised a hand to her face then let his head drop against her shoulder.

"Can I take you home? I'll take the metro back."

Jenna touched Trevor's eyes. "I hoped you would. I'll even offer Chinese take-out if you can find the restaurant for me."

He stayed late, talking with her and playing with her son. Jenna wandered a bit in between and pulled a few more things from boxes. After Aaron was asleep for the night, she moved into her art room. Part of her was anxious to initiate the space, the rest of her opposed the thought. What made her think she needed a studio? She could easily turn it into a guest room instead and use it as a den in between guests. If she was going back to school, she could use the desk for homework. Daniel's desk, the only piece of his furniture, other than easels, that she relocated to Chicago. Her bed was new, a simple frame purchased quickly the day before, just after she signed the apartment lease. Trevor did that with her, too. It felt strange, with the salesperson assuming they lived together and Trevor making jokes about trying the bed out in the store. She chuckled.

"What's so funny?"

Jenna turned at his voice. "Oh, I was thinking about how the woman looked at you yesterday."

"Yesterday?" Trevor handed her a cup of steaming brown liquid. "About trying out the bed?"

"Thank you." She could smell the mint. "Yeah."

"I'm used to those looks." He grinned.

With a sip of her tea, Jenna went back to digging through the open box with her free hand. She was tired of unpacking but it was a useful distraction. As she pulled a few miscellaneous objects out to place on the desk, she found her memory albums. Maybe it was a good time to stop. She had never shared them with anyone.

Trevor came over and reached in to grab the book. "Artwork?"

"No. It's just ... well, there is some of that, but mostly..." She set her cup on the desk and took the album. "It's a journal, except with more pictures than writing. Some scribbles here and there, but..."

"Can I see it? Or is it personal?"

Jenna held on to the album, keeping her eyes averted. It was the first of five she had done that held childhood mementos and photos and drawings, a few chorus awards and art show ribbons. It was very personal, even Alan hadn't seen it. Neither had her husband.

She looked up at her ... boyfriend? Friend? She wasn't sure what to call him. "Only if you won't laugh. There are some old pictures of me and I was an awkward child, not nearly as graceful as Mom wanted me to be."

"You would laugh harder at mine. My parents were horribly permissive. I had green hair for several months."

"Green?" She chuckled. "Well, I guess you can see mine if I can see yours."

He raised his eyebrows. "I think we've already done that."

As his meaning sank in and made her cheeks warm, he kissed her. Quickly, without asking and without expecting anything in return.

They sat on the floor, against a wall, and she shared not only the first book, but all five.

She felt movement and opened her eyes. He was still there. Somehow, she hadn't expected him to be. It was dark; the glow of the moon through her bedroom window provided the only light. He was completely dressed, other than his shoes, and she had changed to sweats and a clean T-shirt before dropping onto the bed at one o'clock in the morning. The books took forever to go through, only because he wanted the stories behind the pictures and drawings. He loved her surrealist touch.

His aunt would expect more had happened between them since he stayed the night. Or maybe she thought he was at work.

Jenna sat up, turned to look at him when he moved, then left the room. Just after five, if she could see the clock well enough. Not sure what to do with herself so early in the morning, she went to check on Aaron. He was sound asleep and didn't even flinch when she stroked his head. She should be asleep, too. She was exhausted.

Wandering into the living room, Jenna peered through the bare windows. Street lamps reflected a light snow and highlighted the cold metal of passing cars. Apparently, she wasn't the only crazy person up too early.

With a yawn, she moved into her studio. The easels were still propped against the wall. Several paints and a few canvases sat on the desk. Switching on the light, Jenna squinted until she adjusted to the sudden brightness. She crossed to the desk and sifted through partial paintings. Trevor had praised her on all of them. He said he would love to see them finished.

She ran her fingers over her favorite painting: Trevor's bar. It was dark, the age of the building emphasized. And a single bartender taking care of a full counter. With a deep breath, she pulled an easel away from the wall and kicked it to standing with one foot. She placed the painting on it and stood back to get an objective view. It needed ... light. There was no light source.

Amid the rubble on the desk, she found a brush, a palette, and a few paints. The work felt smooth and quick as though something guided her hand. She stood back again. It was done. Satisfaction swelled inside. Yes, she was home.

"It's wonderful, Jen."

She jumped, nearly dropping the brush.

"Sorry. I didn't mean to scare you. Do you always paint so early in the morning?" His voice was rough, sleepy. His hair was mussed.

Jenna studied him, standing in the doorway, his clothes wrinkled from lying in her bed. "No. I couldn't sleep."

"I moved around too much."

"No." She went to find turpentine to clean her brush. Where was it? While she searched, she watched him approach the easel to study the painting and began to get irritated that everything was in boxes.

He came to her, took the brush from her hand, and set it on an unopened box.

"It'll dry out." Her irritation faded with the touch of his fingers sifting through her hair.

"I'll find it. You need to sleep. You're too tired."

Jenna watched his hand move to her shoulder and slide down her arm. His touch overwhelmed her. She did her best to stay in control. "I ... guess I felt it calling to me. It had to be done."

"So, now that it is?" He moved closer.

Her body tensed. A palette would have trouble fitting in the space between them. And it was too much space. Jenna stared into the eyes of the man in her painting, the man who cheerfully waited on others, putting their needs first. Putting her needs first. She raised a hand to his face, touching him to ensure he was real. He grasped it and kissed her palm. Cold shivers consumed her, heightening every sense.

Jenna kissed him, slowly, deeply, allowing him inside her world. Letting him fill a void she had never noticed. "Trevor." Her fingers slid onto the warmth of his back. "Move in with me."

Epilogue

Jenna flexed her calf muscles in a slow rhythm, causing the old oak rocker to sway back and forth. Trevor moved it from the loft to their apartment as soon as she realized she would have need for it again.

"Aaron, honey, sit down."

The eighteen-month-old stared a moment before he obeyed. Jenna was glad he was still an easy child, especially since the one in her arms likely wouldn't be. She was fidgety and constantly insisted on being held. Jenna didn't mind sitting and holding her, although sometimes Aaron showed his irritation at the attention his sister received. He only climbed up to stand on the couch while Jenna rocked Anna.

Mid-October. A year ago, four and a half months after losing her husband, Aaron had been in her arms as she stared out the window wondering how she would be able to live alone. Now she had two babies and a live-in boyfriend. It hadn't taken her long to get pregnant again. Trevor often joked about having a house-full within five years. He didn't seem to mind the thought. He also didn't care that she still had no interest in being married. They were doing fine as they were.

She finished one semester of school and Trevor became so interested in her career while helping her study that he decided to follow her lead. He would be a good teacher. Already, he volunteered at the nearest school and immensely enjoyed teaching art to grade school kids. The bar still beckoned to him and he put in a night or two a week there. He was selling quite a few paintings but had taken the more commercial road. His work hung in office buildings around Chicago and other cities in Illinois, Indiana, and Michigan. Joan had connections in those states, as well. She didn't quite believe in the commercialization of artistic talent, but Trevor was pulling in enough money to support Jenna and the kids until she was ready to get back to work. And he painted for himself as he felt the need.

Jenna worked at Elucidations until she went into labor, assured she would have a place whenever she was ready to return. She enjoyed the gallery so much she had second thoughts about returning to school. Either way, at the moment, she was content to stay home and take care of her babies.

A rattle at the door caught her attention and sent Aaron running.

Trevor watched for the boy as he opened the door and swept him into his arms. "Hey, buddy. How was your day?" As Aaron babbled his toddler talk, Trevor came over and leaned down to give Jenna a kiss. "How are my girls?"

"Girl? I'm older than you are."

"And you're never going to let me forget that, are you?" He grinned and planted another kiss on her head.

"Sure. When we're old enough I'll want to start hiding my age."

"You plan to stay with me that long?"

"Well, the kids are kind of used to you, you know."

"A two-week-old can't be too used to anything. Isn't that right, my little Anna?" He stroked his daughter's silky hair. "And I guess we better space them farther apart, so by the time the youngest is over being used to me, you'll be too old to want to run off with some younger guy."

She laughed. "I don't think I could handle anyone even younger."

Trevor took her hand and kissed her palm. "I've missed you today. Come sit with me."

Jenna rose, letting him help her weakened stomach muscles by pulling her arm gently. Anna fussed about being disturbed.

"Okay, bud, let me take your sister for a few minutes." He set Aaron on his feet and claimed the baby. She continued the soft cry until he sat on the couch and laid her against his chest. Jenna sat next to them, turned enough to hold his free arm. She was tired and glad he was home to take over. Her son grabbed a book and claimed his other side. Listening to Trevor read a story he had to know by heart, Jenna leaned against his arm and let her eyes close, surrendering to the peace.

Final Strokes

"Art washes away from the soul
the dust of everyday life."
Pablo Picasso

One

A whiff of condescension mixed with arrogance swirled through Jenna's senses in the guise of strong cologne, alcohol, and a ton of sparkle and cleavage. Grasping Trevor's arm over his silky shirt sleeve, she fought the urge to bolt.

The parties were the only side of Trevor's life Jenna didn't like. They were necessary, she knew, since networking was maybe even a larger part of an artist's world than was putting paint on canvas. She hated to feel that way, but truth couldn't escape when it slapped into her face. It was part of her life now, also, since she had unwittingly chosen an artist as a mate, again. Though she regretted the lifestyle at times, she never regretted her choice.

She adored him. She loved him. What could she do?

He set his hand over hers and caught her eyes. "Relax, Jen. Enjoy yourself. We have the whole night alone..."

"This isn't exactly alone." She glanced around the crowded room.

Trevor moved in front of her and touched her chin. "Not yet. But no kids tonight. We'll show our faces for a while, have a drink, and hit the buffet." He stepped closer and slid a hand around to the small of her back. "Then I'll take you home, where we will be alone, and I'll make this up to you." He met her lips and gave her that look, the one she always found irresistible. "I can't tell you how much I look forward to making this up to you." He played with the hair alongside her face. "So you keep telling me just how much you hate these things and I'll have that much more to have to make up."

Jenna stroked a finger from his shoulder down his arm. "I hate these things." She brushed his lips. "The noise. The arrogance." She moved her mouth beside his ear. "The fakes who think they can paint and talk so loud about how little they really know." She kissed under his ear. "The false flattery when they don't understand anything you do but won't admit it." She returned to his mouth, nearly kissing him, but holding back, teasing. "And I am really ... really, very annoyed that I have to be here only because..."

"Because why?" He skiffed fingers down her hip.

"Because I adore you so and I don't want you here without me."

"You adore me?" He grinned as his fingers moved farther back, nearly enough to be indecent.

"I adore you." She gave in to a real kiss, light and quick. "And you are so horribly, horribly handsome tonight that's it's almost worth all of this just to be able to look at you, to be on your arm, and to see the girls who are showing most of what they have wish they could take you away from me."

He looked around. "Where?"

Jenna pulled his face back to hers. "Never mind. You're mine. And if you forget, I'm sure the kids will remind you."

Trevor grinned, his eyes sparkling. "Not something I'll forget, Jen. I love you. And I've been thinking, maybe it's time to add another little soul who would happily remind me how much I'm yours."

She pulled back, stared.

"Anna will be two in another month. Sales are going well. We can afford another."

"Yes. Maybe it's time."

"Yes?" He smiled and pulled her closer again. "So how about we start working on that tonight?"

"*Trevor.* Where in the hell have you *been?*"

Jenna turned to the loud interruption and sighed. Now it started.

Another baby. They'd barely talked about the possibility of a third child, sometime in the future, but this was the first she knew he was seriously considering it. She only hoped it wouldn't bring back that other conversation she didn't want to have.

"Hey Luke, it's been a while. What's up?" Trevor kept his arm around Jenna's back as he accepted an outstretched hand from a tall willowy man with too much facial hair.

"Yeah it's been longer than forever. Damn, it's good to see you again." The guy glanced at Jenna and shifted to pull a skinny brunette to his side. "Mandy, you gotta meet this guy. He does those incredible abstracts I've told you about. Still gotta take you to see them." Without letting her respond, he turned back to Trevor. "This is Mandy, my fiancée. She's a legal secretary. Can you believe it? I guess one of us has to have a real job."

"That's great, man. Congratulations." Trevor's voice changed but he took their hands and smiled.

"And this must be the wife?" Willowy guy studied her.

Trevor rubbed her back. "This is Jenna, my girlfriend."

She gritted her teeth through the fake smiles from the couple.

The artist of some kind leaned in, lowering his voice. "So, I heard you were hitched. Sure hope you know what you're doing bringing a girlfriend to this thing. Or doesn't the wife care? Do you have one of those open marriages?"

Jenna wanted to punch him in the jaw. If she was a girlfriend with Trevor's wife at home, she'd be humiliated, not that she wouldn't deserve to be. But did he think she couldn't hear him?

"I'm not married. Jenna's the only woman in my life." Trevor's voice was still tense; his arm around her stiffened.

"No? Is the rumor you have kids false, too?"

"We have a couple of kids. A little girl who's nearly two already, and Jenna's little boy who's three and a half. They're with my aunt tonight so Jenna could be here. She loves these events."

The guy believed Trevor's pithy joke, his way of letting her know this wasn't someone who mattered to him. The fiancée either didn't approve of Jenna's rather plain navy skirt and blouse or of her having two children with different fathers. She couldn't fathom caring any less about the girl's opinion no matter how hard she tried to care, if she'd wanted to bother.

"Hey man, you oughtta just make an honest woman out of her, you know. If I can take the plunge into unholy matrimony for the sake of my girl, you can manage it." He winked at Jenna. "Let's meet up for dinner this week and I'll help you work on him."

"Thank you." Jenna answered before Trevor could. She was not having dinner with this man. "But I don't want him worked on, and if I'm anything, it's honest. Maybe too much so..."

"That she is. And you'll have to excuse us." Trevor shifted to take her hand. "We were about to go find out what's on the buffet."

Jenna allowed him to cut her off although she wanted to tell them they had no right to judge her or their relationship. *Fiancée.* That was nothing but a divorce waiting to happen. She could see it.

"Should have had a hamburger before we came." Trevor perused the buffet. Elegant, yes. But as usual, only tiny bits of taste testers, nothing like Joan's spreads when she hosted an art opening.

"I told you to."

"And you were right, as always." He gave her a grin as he handed her a thin plate.

"I don't want anything." She set it back on the stack, regardless of how rude it was.

"Come on, Jen. I know you don't want to be here, but give it a try. It looks edible."

"Why did you cut me off?" She accepted the plate as he gave it back to her. She could at least grab a few shrimp.

"I didn't cut you off. What do you think this is?" He held up something greenish topped with brown specks.

"You did. And I wouldn't know." She shook her head when he offered the thing she couldn't fathom putting in her mouth.

Trevor leaned close to her ear. "He's a talker, and he pulls a lot of strings in certain places. I haven't seen him in forever by choice. I try hard not to see him." With the heart of a true adventure hero, he took a bite of the thing. His face was priceless as he swallowed it quick and then tried to kiss her.

"Huh uh. Wash it down first." She grabbed a glass of Champagne and handed it to him.

He swallowed half the glass and tried to share that, too. "Aw, come on, Jen. I know you love Champagne as much as you love these events." His eyes sparkled with his mischievous grin.

"My next boyfriend will not be an artist." She walked around him to get to the shrimp.

He laughed and gripped her tight around the waist. "Then I guess I shouldn't introduce you to the tall, sexy, stud of a realist I know who asked for an introduction."

"Oh? He's sexier than you are?"

"Easily." Trevor kissed above her ear.

"Hm. I might change my mind, then. Wouldn't be the first time."

"And I keep hoping it won't be the last." He met her lips. The man knew no shame. There at the buffet table with people everywhere, he lowered his hand to her rear as he kissed her.

"Trevor." She pulled his hand up farther.

"No one cares, baby. This isn't Joan's gallery. It's far lower class than that. Why else would my work be here?"

"That may be, but you'll blow your chances with that far-sexier-than-me blonde over there staring at you. Go ahead and look. She might as well know I know she's staring."

With a grin, he took Jenna's plate and handed them both to some guy next to them. "I have a better idea." Showing every bit of his strength, agility, and grace, even if he wasn't all that strong-looking, Trevor leaned her back in a low dip and kissed her deeply. A smatter of applause and some cat-calling surrounded them as he lifted her. And he looked around the crowd. "If anyone wants to talk about my work tonight, they better make it quick, 'cause soon, I'm taking my gorgeous girlfriend home to work on baby number three."

Jenna felt her face get warm and he pulled her in close, his arm around her head. He was awful. Why did she put up with him? When she pulled back to see his face, she knew why she put up with him. He made her happy. And loved. And secure.

Plodding her way through the chit-chat, Jenna tried to keep Trevor pulled in as she forced herself to be content that she was there with him and without the kids. She almost never left them other than for work, only part time. Elucidations wanted her to increase her hours and part of her wanted to agree, but Anna was still a baby and Aaron... Jenna sighed. Aaron, her easy and quiet child, had become quite a handful. Aunt Nina, Trevor's Aunt Nina, had trouble keeping up with him. If she moved to full time, Jenna would have to find a sitter who could handle the three-year-old better. But she was fairly sure part of Aaron's problem was that Jenna was already away from him more than he wanted her to be. He was wonderful on weekends. The other five days were something else. And Trevor wanted another.

Part of her did, too. On days Aaron and Anna snuggled up close while she read to them or watched television side-by-side or laughed together, Jenna wanted another. But then there were those days she could hardly take time to breathe and went to bed exhausted after work, and after their bickering and getting into things drove her crazy. Those days, she couldn't possibly imagine wanting one more.

Of course Trevor did. He was great with them, and he only had one. As much as he claimed Aaron, her son wasn't his. He was Daniel's child. It was horribly obvious at times, especially since his previous friendly-to-everyone mode had switched to shy mode, just how much he was Daniel's child. Jenna worried about him so much more than she could ever admit out loud. If he had a few days he barely ate, her own stomach hurt. When he caught a virus, she hovered too much. Her mother-in-law, Daniel's mother, had warned Jenna that making herself sick would help no one, even if her fear came to pass. She couldn't answer Joan. She'd lost her husband to cancer. She would not lose her son. So what if she made herself sick or ran herself too ragged if it meant she would notice it early? It was worth the risk.

And that was the other thing. Did she want the worry for another one? How much did she have in her before it went too far? Eventually she wanted to do something of her own, even if she wasn't quite sure what that would be. How could she if she kept adding complications?

Trevor touched her face. "Are you ignoring me?"

"Oh. No, I'm sorry."

"What's wrong, Jen? Do you need to leave already?"

"No, I'm fine. I just got lost in my thoughts for a moment."

He eyed her before giving in and returning to the conversation with a couple who admired his art.

She should have stayed in her own thoughts. The couple had been married for twenty-five years, as their graying hair proved, the woman said. Their kids were on the verge of leaving home for school and they looked forward to their time alone, but regretted that it came so soon.

Trevor got quiet as they talked about the challenges of marriage and child-rearing. Jenna slid an arm around his back and felt his surprise. She didn't often show him affection in public; it was no one's business. But she was enjoying the rare night out alone, even if it was an art party, and she wanted him to know. It didn't matter if they were married. Jenna couldn't even imagine being without him anymore. He was comfortable, secure. But he was more. It wasn't anything like her marriage to Daniel. Trevor wasn't an escape. He was her destination. She truly believed he was the one she was meant to find, and part of her wished she'd found him first.

She cringed at the thought. She'd loved Daniel. She had. It was the pain she could have missed. Losing him so fast, so soon, and watching it happen for so long, feeling so helpless as he slipped away, she could have missed. She could have happily lived without knowing how that felt. It scared her more than she had ever told anyone, even Trevor. Although she guessed he knew it did. She guessed it was why he was so patient with her. He knew the pain of losing his parents. Suddenly. Too early in life. An accident. He knew the pain of loss.

Still, she figured it was different. He hadn't had to watch it happen.

Two

Jenna pushed the cake pan into the oven and set the timer. She could wait until it was baked and cooled before she mixed the frosting. Her limited cake decorating skills wouldn't allow anything spectacular, but it would be decent enough for a two-year-old's party. Washing the remaining batter from her fingers, she decided to relax in her rocking chair for a few minutes before she finished preparations. Her baby was about to turn two. It didn't seem real. Trevor hadn't mentioned more children since the party. She wondered whether he changed his mind. Maybe she hadn't sounded interested enough, and she wasn't sure she was. Maybe. But she wanted time to recuperate from her first two first. The more she thought about it, the less she could imagine being pregnant while taking care of a 2 year old, a 3 and a half year old, a part-time job, and an energetic boyfriend.

She grinned thinking of Trevor's boyishness. It still attracted her. It also exhausted her. She was glad he decided to take the kids out, to wear them out so they would sleep better. In the meantime, Jenna would enjoy the quiet of the apartment. It was sparse still, since she hadn't taken time to do much with it, so she turned her eyes to the window. Wanting to feel the fresh fall air, Jenna rose again to pry it open. Trevor had said it was perfect run-around weather. The chill that swept in told Jenna she was right to insist her kids wear their jackets. He could always take them off if they got too hot. She expected Anna to come in without hers since she generally stayed warm, as Trevor did. Aaron would insist on keeping his firmly zipped and likely with the hood tied around his chin. Jenna wasn't sure if he was actually that cold or if he just liked the security of being wrapped up, as she did. Cuddling under a thick comforter or wrapping in a few layers without overheating was one of the best things about fall, as far as she was concerned.

Her other favorite fall activity was watching the leaves turn to reds and yellows and oranges and shades of brown, then tumble lightly to the ground. She especially liked to be out in the wind as leaves tossed around her feet, singing their own melody. She didn't get much of that in Chicago, though. The wind was plentiful, but there were few leaves. And the air didn't smell like it had from outside her loft in Peoria, with the scent of the river mixed in. Lake Michigan smelled like a lake. It wasn't the same. Or maybe the city odors changed it before it reached her senses. Thinking back to the architecture tour she had taken with Trevor on what was technically their first date, Jenna sighed. No, even out on Lake Michigan in the boat, it was different. The lake smell had been obvious, of course, but not the same. It smelled of fish. The Illinois River just smelled like ... the river.

With a shiver, she closed the window and stood beside it to watch the activity below. She needed to finish cleaning since everyone would be there the following day, but it was too quiet. She scolded herself as she remembered the constant lack of quiet and the constant longing for it, and returned to work.

Then she stopped. She didn't want to prepare for their daughter's party alone. She wanted Trevor there to help, or just to be there.

Distracting herself, she went to the little stereo she'd had since high school and pushed in one of the cassettes always sitting on top. The Oak Ridge Boys would keep her company without the mindless chit chat or relentless advertisements on the radio. Maybe instead of cleaning, she'd go through unopened mail.

It didn't take long. Most of it was junk. Filing the rest, she looked around. The floor needed to be mopped, but there wasn't much point in that until morning. The kids were sure to spill or drop something when they got home. Deciding to straighten the bedrooms, Jenna went first to Aaron and Anna's. So far, they still shared. She supposed she and Trevor would have to give up their work space, or combine it with their bedroom. Where did he think they would put a third child in the small apartment? Anything bigger would cost far too much.

With another sigh, Jenna changed her mind yet again and went to the art room to check her current work in progress. It had been in progress for quite some time. She was always too tired to work on it after she got home, fixed dinner or cleaned – depending on which was her turn, spent time with the kids, and got them in bed. Saturdays were errand days. Sunday family time.

With a scan of the scene's half-formed background, she spotted a part that had to be reworked. A few minutes with it wouldn't put her too far behind.

The contentedness she too rarely felt with her work settled in and refused to let her stop. She was in her *art zone*, as Trevor called it. She couldn't remember the last time she had been there. Her hand took over and added bits she hadn't considered before, changed colors, defined deep, drastic highlights. When her feet began to ache, Jenna checked the time. Too long. She had spent too long... The cake. She forgot the cake.

Dropping her brush onto the palette, she scurried into the kitchen. The scent of chocolate mixed with a tinge of overdone. Shoving the oven mitts over her hands, she pulled it out and grimaced. It looked more like scorched charcoal she could draw with than like something anyone should put in their mouths. She coughed at the smoky air.

Now what? Not only had she lingered in the work room too long, neglecting what she should have done, but the cake was a disaster and the apartment smelled awful.

Jenna went to open the window again and noticed it was nearly dark. Where was Trevor? The kids would get cold, even with jackets, when the sun went down. And she had to go get another cake mix, which irritated her nearly to breaking point. It took forever to go do anything in the city by the time she got through traffic. So much for a nice, easy birthday party. Maybe she should try to relocate it, have it at a pizza place as others did, but there was no time to make reservations now. Everything would have been booked long ago. Why had she wanted to move up to Chicago?

Without much choice, Jenna gritted her teeth and shuffled through a drawer to find paper to leave Trevor a note in case he got home first. Part of her hoped he would. They were out late. The other part hoped she could get back and fix things up before he got home so he wouldn't walk in on the mess.

Shifting the grocery bag to her other arm, she tried to block out the too-loud conversation in the elevator. While at the store, she remembered she didn't have snacks of any kind and frantically tried to come up with something palatable for all ages. Her niece and nephew were picky eaters. So was Joan, although her mother-in-law wouldn't complain. And Alan and his family were staying for dinner after the party. Jenna apologized to her friend for having it on a Sunday since he would have to either drive back to Peoria late at night or miss half a day's work on Monday, but she couldn't imagine preparing during the work week. He assured her it was fine and they looked forward to it.

Jenna looked forward to seeing him, all of them. It had been a few months, nearly a year. Far too long.

One of the women brushed up against her as they got off on their floor and Jenna sighed relief at their departure. She couldn't imagine why it was so necessary to talk so loud in such a confined space. Did they really think their conversation was interesting enough everyone needed to be subjected? She cursed when it stopped again at the next floor and clenched her teeth when her stalker stepped in. Not an actual stalker, but close enough. She dreaded getting caught anywhere with the woman who grabbed her to talk, for far too long, about nothing interesting, every time they ran into each other.

Forcing politeness, Jenna answered questions about where she had gone and discussed how things were with their separate families. She hated that the most. The stalker-woman always changed her voice when referring to her and Trevor and the kids as a family. They *were* a family, regardless of their technical legal status. They spent more time together and enjoyed each other more than most families Jenna had seen, and she emphasized this to the woman just to see the jealousy at how well Trevor treated her.

Of course, he might not be so tolerant tonight, since she had the whole day at home and he'd arranged for her to have much of it to herself and there was nothing but mess and burned cake to show for it. Lurching away from the stalker-woman at the next open door, Jenna made her way to her apartment and adjusted the grocery bag again to find her keys. She took a deep breath, ready for questions and kids climbing all over her and the aroma of scorched sugar.

As she turned the key and stepped inside, she frowned. There was no noise. And no scorch. She was sure she closed the window before she left. Even on the fifth floor, she refused to have it open while they were away. But it smelled fresh, and clean.

Trevor looked over from the kitchen. "Hey, I was getting worried. It's dark."

Jenna glanced around the apartment. No toys were scattered around the floor or on the coffee table. The pieces of torn paper and dust had disappeared from under the dining table where Aaron had been doing his own art the night before. Pillows were settled on the couch in an orderly fashion and the blanket she kept there for cool evenings was neatly hung over its back instead of bunched up and half on the throw rug that needed to be cleaned.

"I felt guilty that I left you to do everything while we were out playing."

She nearly blushed as he came to her. "I didn't do anything..."

"You toasted a cake." He grinned and took the bag.

Jenna followed him to the kitchen. "You didn't have to do this. I got distracted and lost track of time. I didn't mean to leave it for you."

"You were painting." He pulled the bags of chips and vegetables from the bag, stowed them away, and set the cake mix on the counter.

"Yeah. And I only meant to fix the area I wasn't happy with, only for a few minutes, but…"

He set both hands on her waist. "I'm glad you were painting. It's been too long. And it's coming along well. Very nice, Jen."

She kissed him and gave him a strong hug. Her hero. It sounded corny, even in her mind, but she couldn't help thinking of him that way since he made everything okay, always. "It's quiet. What are the kids doing?"

"Can't tell you. You'll have to call Aunt Nina and ask if you need to know. I left them with her and she'll bring them in the morning. I wanted us to celebrate our daughter's birth alone tonight, holding you quietly the way I did the night before she was born, this time without contractions interfering, of course."

Overnight? She hadn't been away from them overnight in … well, never from Anna and only a couple of times from Aaron.

"I brought dinner." He pulled away and opened the oven door to pull out a grease-speckled brown bag. "The oven was still warm when I got home, but I think this is cold by now. Let me heat it while you get cleaned up."

While he spooned Chinese take-out into oven dishes, Jenna moved closer. The kids would be fine. She would call and tell them good night, reassure herself at the sound of their voices. She wrapped her arms around her boyfriend from behind, let her head rest against his back, and reveled in the way he paused what he was doing to wrap his arms over hers and hold her in. He never shrugged her off as Daniel often had because he was busy and didn't want to be interrupted. Trevor never shrugged her off. Ever.

He turned to give her a light kiss. "Go shower and warm up. It'll be ready when you are."

Jenna lingered in the shower longer than she should have. The hot pulsing water did wonders for her spirit. She always stressed too much about having company, but she wouldn't let it bother her tonight. She would put the new cake mix in the oven after they ate and everything else could wait until morning. With Trevor's help, it would work out.

Slipping into a baggy sweatshirt and sweat pants that came close to matching, she went back out to find him. The room was dark, except for the glow of candles. Tons of candles. She couldn't even count them. She felt under-dressed in her own apartment. "Should I change into something more..." Her words fell back when he turned from lighting the final candles. He'd pulled off the loose outer shirt, leaving only the fitted navy tee that highlighted his frame.

"You know you don't have to change for me, Jen." Trevor set the lighter down and moved toward her.

She should have dressed nicer, or less. But then he had no reason not to wear something form-fitting and sexy. He was sexy. He was in incredible shape, more sturdy than when they'd first gotten together, as he'd finished growing up. At twenty-two, he'd been mostly finished but not quite there. Three years had allowed him the time to become truly a man, fully formed, not large, he was still a small medium, but ... but fully formed. And he no longer wore his clothes hanging off him as he had when they met.

Jenna, on the other hand, was already too flabby when they'd met and had gone the wrong direction. Not that she was obese or anything, but she had baby flab and baby fatigue and ... and not the will to do much about it.

He didn't appear to mind any more than he ever had. His hands found her waist, her too-round waist, and slid down her hips over the bulky sweats.

"I can... I didn't know you were..."

He kissed her, not a light kiss as earlier, but deep and lingering. She couldn't do more than catch her breath afterward, with her head against his shoulder. It had been some time since he'd kissed her that way. "Let's eat while it's warm again."

She gave in to his soft voice and his hand pulling at hers.

Through dinner, she was reminded of their first meal together, at Joan's, when he'd come to see her bearing a greasy bag of Chinese takeout. She'd tried to keep distance, but he'd pushed in, brushing against her skin and peering into her eyes. She wasn't always sure if the connection was truly there from the beginning or if he'd simply worn her down with asking.

It didn't matter. The connection was deeply there now.

He cleared the table, rinsed the dishes, and refused to let her wash them. Instead he took her to the couch where she gazed at the candles and snuggled close. "Jen?"

She turned to his voice.

"Are we still considering another child? You haven't said anything. And you're still protecting yourself. Don't you need to be off it a while before we..?"

"Oh." Jenna felt her lungs expand and made them release the deep breath. "I don't know. Are we?"

"You're not ready? Why did you say yes at that party?"

"I don't know. I mean I don't know if I am."

He nodded and gripped her hand. His eyes moved away from hers.

"Trevor, I ... I'm still always tired, and Margaret is pushing me for more hours. I barely give Aaron and Anna the attention I should. It's good that you do, but I'm not sure it would be fair to them..."

He raised a hand to her face and forced her full attention. "Never mind what Margaret wants. Never mind what the kids want for the moment. What do you want?"

She couldn't. Maybe Margaret's wants could be overlooked, but not her children's. "I want what's best for my babies. You know that. I always have. I can't imagine..."

"I know, Jen, and you're a wonderful mom. Truly. Even if your time is limited, when you're with them, you are *with* them. They feel it. You're doing fine."

"Maybe. But I'm tired. And I don't know how I'd..."

"Cut down on your hours."

Jenna shook her head. She needed her part-time at the gallery.

"I can pick up more hours at the bar to make up for it."

"What good would that do? Then I'd see you less."

"You'd have more time with the kids, and to rest. Being out around people wears you out too fast. If you limit that..."

"Trevor." She brushed against his lips. "I need time with you, too. What's the point otherwise? You keep me sane."

He grinned and leaned in, pressing her back against the couch. She should have dressed less.

"Jen." He whispered beside her ear. "Marry me."

Her stomach cringed.

He pulled back. "At the end of the month, it'll be three years from the day we met. Marry me that day. September 27th."

"You remember the day."

"Of course. It's the day my world changed."

Jenna felt her eyes water.

He brushed fingers against her cheek and then her eyes, spreading the moisture along her skin. "I love you, Jen. I want to be more than your boyfriend. I want to be your husband."

She nearly gave in. But she couldn't. She'd done that before, gave in, to Daniel's bed, than to his proposal, to his lifestyle and what he wanted. "I can't." Her voice was nearly a whisper. "I don't want to be married. I want ... what we have."

"It won't change just because we get married."

"Yes it will. It always does. It did. I can't."

"Jenna..."

"No. Trevor, don't. I love you. You know I love you. You know I want you here, and I want us together. I don't want that to change."

"It won't, Jen. I won't." He kissed her nose and wiped more tears.

"You don't know that."

"You don't know I won't if we don't get married, either. It doesn't matter, if we are or if we aren't. If I change, I do, no matter..."

"Then there's no need. If it doesn't matter, let it go. Please. Just let me have this." She slid her hand under his shirt and caressed his back.

He sighed and snuggled his face against her neck. "I won't give up." Before she could think of how to answer, he kissed her, deeply. And he didn't bother to move them back to the bedroom.

Three

Jenna handed the steaming cup of rich coffee, black, to her friend, glad he and his family were the only ones still in the apartment. Party was over. Dinner was over. She was tired but gratified it all went well.

"Thank you. I would have helped myself." Alan gave her a grin.

"You came all the way up here for my daughter's party and you're giving up a half day's work. The least I can do is bring you a cup of coffee." Jenna glanced over at Anna's squeal and found Justin tickling her. Cheryl told her son to stop.

"Actually, I'm giving up two days of work. And so are you."

"Why am I giving up two days of work?"

"We're sight-seeing." Trevor slid a hand along her back. "Tour guiding, so to speak. But we need to keep it at least part educational so Justin's teacher won't throw a fit."

"He brought his camera along and wants to fill it with Chicago, all in two days." Alan sipped his coffee. "Well, a day and a half. We have to head back mid-afternoon Tuesday. Trevor has everything planned, so don't make yourself crazy wondering where to go or how to get there, as I know you would."

Jenna threw her friend a half-amused scowl. "Maybe I don't do that anymore."

Trevor chuckled. "Yeah, she does." He squeezed her shoulder. "Not this time. We're pushing everything else aside for a couple of days. Only fun. No obligations, except for poor Justin who has to prove he learned something."

Alan scuffed his son's head. "That's fun to him. He'll be fine."

Lowering to the couch, Jenna listened to talk of the Children's Museum and the Art Institute and Navy Pier and the Sears Tower in between Justin talking to her about his dog and that J.R. was sad when they left him with Alan's parents for the weekend, since his dad wouldn't let him bring him along. Jenna assured him J.R. would be happy for a few days with his grandparents, more than he would be in a crowded car and in the hotel. He said the car wasn't crowded and Alan said it sure would be with a 60 pound hairy dog jumping around. The puppy Jenna gave Justin when she left Peoria, a mixed breed, grew bigger than she expected, but Justin didn't mind at all.

Aaron came over and cuddled into her side as she talked with Alan's oldest. He was tired. His sister was still running full steam, still entertaining the twins, Alex and Rae, but Aaron breathed a deep sigh and played with Jenna's fingers.

"Feel okay?" Jenna raised her other hand to his head in the guise of stroking his hair. He felt fine. Normal.

He nodded.

"Just tired? It's been a long day, hasn't it?"

He nodded again. Not much of a talker, her Aaron. Like his father. She kissed his head and cuddled him in, then focused on the two men standing and talking together as Cheryl supervised the kids and talked in between. Trevor was like their Anna, still going full steam and with plenty to say. As funny as it sounded, Jenna found it more relaxing than Daniel's silence had been. It meant she didn't need to try to start conversation or fill silence. He did that. And when there was silence, she never minded. Not that there was much.

She also found it relaxing that Trevor got along with Alan so well. Her husband never liked Alan, or maybe he didn't trust him. Actually, Jenna knew he hadn't trusted him. There was reason, to a point, but she could never get it through to Daniel that he didn't need to trust Alan, or any other man. He only needed to trust her, and he could.

She grabbed a deep breath and turned her attention to her son. Trevor knew. Jenna had told him everything: how Alan had hoped to marry her, how he tried to get her to leave her husband for him when she and Daniel were having so much trouble, how she nearly let him get to her. Only because she was so lost, so lonely. Still, Trevor didn't hold it against her friend. He said he understood why Alan would want her and he was glad she didn't want the same. And he let it go. Not once since had it ever come up.

"We should go. Tomorrow will be a long day." Cheryl told her not to get up and gave her a half hug from the side. "I remember the days of my kids being so little. It's exhausting. Don't worry. It gets better."

Alan raised his eyebrows. "Or you get so used to being exhausted you don't notice."

Jenna chuckled. "Is that it?"

He took a last swallow and eyed her. "Is eight too early for you? We can start on our own and meet somewhere if it is."

"No, not at all. If not for you, I'd be at work by then."

"That early? Thought you worked at ten."

"I changed it. I get home sooner that way." She knew he wanted to argue, but he moved conversation along to verify plans with Trevor and went to grab Rae when she complained about leaving.

Jenna got up to see them out and brushed fingers through Aaron's dark straight fine hair. "Bath time, and bed. You'll have fun with Justin tomorrow, you think?" Her son had always looked up to Alan's oldest who was seven already. He paid less attention to the six-year-old twins but Anna adored them. They were more active and that pleased her to no end. Aaron only nodded and Jenna felt his head again.

"He's fine, Jen. Stop worrying." Trevor swept him up, turned him upside down to make him laugh, and carried him to the bathroom.

~~~

It was unusual for Trevor to come on to her two nights in a row, and she was tired from so much walking around the city in between jumping on the metro which Justin hated and the twins loved. He did like the El, though, and Jenna had to agree, with both. She didn't much like the metro that went underground, but she liked the El that stayed above. Her feet ached. Her body was exhausted. But Trevor had been so wonderful all day, Jenna didn't have the heart to turn him down.

Luckily, he didn't draw it out too long and she was glad to cuddle against his side and set a kiss on his chest. "Thank you."

He chuckled. "Was I better than usual tonight?"

"No, I mean..." She propped herself up to see his smiling eyes. "I never have a complaint. You know that. I mean about today. Taking off work and going out of your way to be sure they saw what they wanted and... It was very sweet. Thank you."

"You don't have to thank me, Jen. They're my friends too by now, right? I kind of thought they were."

"Yes, but..." She stopped. She supposed it was true. At least with Cheryl and the kids, but Alan... No buts. Not between them. "Of course they are. It was still sweet."

He rolled her onto her back, brushed a hand over her forehead and into her hair, and kissed her. "You need to stop thinking that way. I know with you and Daniel, you had your friends and he had his, but I'm not him and I don't work like that."

The use of Daniel's name startled her. He hadn't for months, maybe two years or so.

"What's mine is yours, Jen. Anything and everything. And I think you would feel more the same if we were married and..."

"No. It wouldn't matter. I didn't with... I didn't. But I don't think
~~~

he even had friends or wanted them so it's not even close to the same. Yes, I want that with you. I have that with you. I do. Already. Alan and his family are yours as much as mine and Nate and Keisha are my friends, too. I agree. So just take the compliment I gave you and don't make so much of it."

"It's hard not to when you do."

"I don't..."

"You do. In little things you say. You did all day long. Hell, we've been together for three years. Can you maybe let the past go by now?"

She squirmed out from under him.

"Now you're mad."

"No. I'm tired."

"Whatever you say. Night, Jenna." He kissed her shoulder and rolled away.

She sighed. Let the past go. She had. Maybe she hadn't, but how? How did you just tell yourself none of it mattered anymore when it did? Weren't you supposed to learn from your mistakes, from the past? How could it be both ways?

~~~

Trevor bowed out of sight-seeing the next day. The school needed him, he said. His sub had called in sick. Jenna found it hard to believe he coincidentally couldn't go after he got mad at her the night before, but she also didn't want to believe he wouldn't just tell her the truth as he always had. At least as far as she knew, he always did. She hoped she wasn't only being naive again.

Jenna found Alan easily in the semi-crowded restaurant where they'd decided to meet. He was alone, looking as though he didn't fit in with the big-city-dwellers. And he didn't. Honestly, neither did she. She just kept trying to tell herself she did, or could. At times, she believed it. At other times, she thought of packing up and moving. But Trevor was a city boy. He didn't want to be anything else.

Making her way to the table, Jenna smiled when he looked over. He was alone, which was nice since they hadn't talked alone in forever. She thanked him when he pulled her chair out. "So where are Cheryl and the kids?"

"Tired from yesterday. We'll stop by and get them later. And your family?"

"Trever got called in to work. He took the kids to Nina's although they both threw a fit. He asked me to apologize to you for him."
~~~

"Not needed." He signaled a waiter. "Hope you don't mind having breakfast with only me. If you do, we can leave, if you think it would bother Trevor..."

"Of course not. It's fine." Jenna ordered a cup of hot tea. Bother Trevor? She wondered what would actually bother Trevor other than the marriage issue which was mostly a non-issue by now. "Did the kids have fun yesterday? Mine went straight to sleep. A miracle."

"They had too much fun, I think. We had a hard time getting them settled enough to sleep." Alan sipped his coffee. "I hope Trevor didn't get too bored playing tour guide, and that they didn't drive him crazy with questions."

"No, he enjoyed it. He's great with kids. And he's a teacher, Alan; he's used to questions."

He looked down at his coffee for a moment, then met her eyes. "So how are things, Jen? You seem to be doing okay, except..."

"Except what?"

"I don't know. But there's something. Are you happy?"

"Yes." There was no hesitation in her answer. No doubt. "The kids try my patience at times, but you know, I expected that."

"But?"

Jenna waited for an explanation. Nothing happened for Alan to ask about. The day had gone well. Alan and Trevor got along and they all helped with all of the kids and...

"Has he proposed again?"

She sucked air into her lungs. Had Trevor mentioned it? Did he think Alan would help push her to accept? She bit her tongue long enough to order a cinnamon roll and scrambled eggs and waited until they were alone again. "Why do you ask?"

"Because I know how much he wants it."

"And he knows I don't."

"Yes, but will it be worth it to hold your ground if everything on top of that ground slips away?"

"What makes you think it will?"

"I know how you tend to look past things you don't want to see. I just hope you're not this time."

"I thought you liked him."

"I do. I can't say I was sure at first, but he's good to you and good with the kids and I think you're happy overall, so that's good enough for me."

"Then what are you doing? Why are you questioning this?"

"I'm not questioning your relationship, not at all. I'm questioning your lack of…"

"Commitment?" She waited while he didn't reply. "Alan, you don't have to be married to be committed to someone. I'm faithful. He knows that. And I'm always there. I'm home with him at night and I go with him to his art parties. What I feel and how I act mean more than that piece of paper. I'm more devoted to him than a lot of wives are to their husbands, you know, and vice versa. He knows that, too. It's more than a lot of spouses have." Jenna knew it was at least a little nasty to say as much, to be so pointed, but she had to wonder if Cheryl would still be with Alan if his wife knew he'd come on to her. Before Trevor. During Daniel. And after Daniel. While Alan was married, he'd come on to her.

Alan's expression said he full well understood her comment, but he let it go. "It bothers him to introduce you as his girlfriend and Aaron as your son he claims, like he did yesterday when we ran into those art people. It bothered him."

"He says it's okay." She sipped her tea. It was still too warm.

"He's Aaron's father, Jen. By all rights, he is. He's the one who's been there for him since he was a baby. And he acts far more like your husband than Daniel ever did. Let him be that. Make it all legal. I think you'll be far happier…"

"Don't tell me what'll make me happy. I think I know that better than you do."

Alan nodded, that patronizing nod that always put Jenna on edge.

It did again. "We're fine. Don't look for trouble where there isn't any. And you can stop slamming Daniel now. He's been gone nearly four years. You can stop."

"Fine, I'll drop it. I was just concerned."

They paused the conversation when the waiter returned with their food, and they forced safer conversation. She listened to the updates on his business that he avoided mentioning the day before when Cheryl was around. He'd promised his wife long ago not to talk about work during dinner, holidays, or family vacations. She supposed Cheryl had mostly decided to let them alone this morning so Alan could talk about his landscaping business with her. Jenna loved to hear about what he was doing and had thoroughly enjoyed going out to his sites while he and his crew were planning and planting and constructing. If she let herself think of it too much, she missed it. Mostly she didn't let herself think about it. Or how she missed her trees in general. Trevor was a Chicago boy. She wanted him enough to stay.

Maybe once Alan left, Jenna would pick up the kids and go to Humboldt park gardens since she had the day off. She didn't like to go without Trevor, though. Women did it all the time. She knew they did. But her small town upbringing still made her skittish of the idea. When the kids were older, she'd be more comfortable.

Her time alone with Alan was too short, even if she was annoyed with him, and Cheryl decided they should take the kids, all of them, to the harbor. Jenna didn't want to go to the harbor, and she didn't want to take her kids there, not without Trevor who kept up with them better. She gave in, of course. At the harbor, Alan put Justin in charge of keeping hold of Aaron while he took main charge of Anna himself. He enjoyed the girl, he said, since she was so like her mom. Jenna thought she was far more like Trevor, but if he wanted to wrestle her, she wouldn't argue.

Cheryl took the chance to amble along Jenna's side and ask how her job was going. Surprised to be asked, Jenna filled her in on the small promotion, on how she shared an office now with another girl, a younger girl who'd taken to Jenna's side to learn the business. She told her Margaret, the gallery's general manager, wanted her to add hours but she hesitated because the kids were so young.

"They're doing great. Not that I think you should add hours, but it's not hurting them for you to work." Cheryl pushed a clump of blonde hair out of her face. "I've been thinking of looking for a job."

Jenna was surprised enough she stopped walking. "Really? Alan's business is doing well, it sounds like. He's not holding something back from me?"

"Oh, no, it is. It's not because I need to, just because I want to. Or I think I want to. The kids are in school all day and I get terribly bored. Alan says I should take up a hobby or find other women to go out and lunch with or so on. But I want more than that, only part time, during the day when they aren't home. It wouldn't hurt anything."

"So do that. What are you looking for?"

"Office work. It's what I studied. But I don't know if it'll be worth the fight. Alan wants me to be home."

"So what?" Jenna wasn't sure if she was more annoyed at Alan for being such a dictator with his wife or at Cheryl for letting him do it. "Who cares if he wants you home? He doesn't get to make all of the decisions because he's the man. Don't let him."

Cheryl stared as though Jenna slapped her. "It would be a fight..."

"So? Tell him when the kids aren't around so they don't hear it, and stand your ground. It's your choice, not his."

"It should be our decision together. That's what marriage is."

"Is it? Then how come he gets a say and you don't? How is that *together*? And don't look at me like that. I know what I'm saying. I was married. It was all about him and his wants and..." She stopped. She'd never admitted she felt that way. She wouldn't hardly admit it to herself. "Just tell him you're getting a job. It's your choice. And if he complains to me about it, I'll straighten him out. You know I'm not afraid to do it."

"You didn't in your own marriage." It was snippy. And pointed.

"No. But I should have. I was too young. Too needy. I'm not anymore. I wouldn't do that to myself again. And I won't. Trevor is pushing for another kid, too, but that doesn't mean I have to. It's my choice. I'm the one who has to..." Jenna shrugged. "I don't have to. And if I want to add hours at work, I will."

"I didn't realize..." Cheryl relaxed again. "I thought things were good between you. It looked like it."

"They are. And I plan to keep it that way."

She picked Trevor up for lunch before Alan and his family had to leave. The atmosphere was tense between the adults and siblings squabbled with each other and Cheryl joked about everyone being too tired. It was nearly a relief when it was over.

While his family got situated in their car, Alan came to hers as she strapped Aaron and Anna into their seats.

"So what do you think of the old Mustang now?" Trevor ran a hand over the edge of its roof.

"Jenna said you had it painted for her. Looks good. Nearly new."

"Yeah, they did a good job, but she still bitches at me about it."

"Why? Looks like the right color."

Jenna stood between the car and the door and rolled her eyes. "It was too expensive. I told him it was."

Trevor shrugged. "It was that or a stock color and amateur work. The car deserves better. She's holding up as well as my old lady."

"Better than me." Jenna slid an arm around his waist.

"She's younger than you." His eyes teased.

"Thanks. You could have argued."

"Doesn't do me any good to argue with you." He wrapped her in a hug and kissed her head. "But you are wrong. And even as beautiful as she is now with her new coat, you're far more beautiful."

"Uh huh." She pushed away. "I better get you back to work."

He grinned and took Alan's hand as he told him to have a safe trip back to the *little imitation city*. Alan invited them to come visit whenever they wanted to get out of the oversized, overpriced wind trap. Their usual sparring.

Jenna handed Trevor the keys and gave Alan a long hug. He wanted her to move back to Peoria. He worried about her in Chicago. He wanted them to get together for backyard cookouts and other occasions, as best friends did. She couldn't argue. Since her friend finally liked her choice of partner, it would be nice. She wanted it, also. But Trevor was entrenched in the city. She couldn't see him leaving it. And maybe Daniel wasn't still there, but his mother was. Joan was a real mother to Jenna, unlike her own.

Daniel had hated Chicago. He was so opposite Trevor in so many ways. Except for the artist boy thing. He'd been older than Jenna instead of younger. Not that Trevor being two years younger was a big deal. Her four year difference with Daniel had been a bigger deal. It struck her that both Daniel and Trevor had been twenty-two when she met them, but Jenna was seventeen when she first slept with Daniel and twenty-four with Trevor. That had made the biggest difference.

She met Daniel because he wanted her to model for him and he often sketched her. She met Trevor because of Daniel's art. Trevor never asked to paint her. He never sketched her. He had no interest in either. She hadn't bothered to ask why. Jenna figured she might not want to hear the answer.

With a "take care of yourself" and quick goodbye, Alan agreed to let her know when they got home.

She slid into the Mustang's passenger seat. Her '66, a gift from Daniel that Alan had called a bribe when he bought it for her. The paint job was Trevor's gift for her twenty-seventh birthday. It did need it. Rust was setting in. He knew it worried her and said it would be worth the price in the long run to stop the rust and help preserve it. Before winter, he wanted to find a place to garage it, to keep it out of the heavy winter salt. She could have the van, he said. He'd use public transportation. Actually, both vehicles were hers – she had them when they met, but she hated driving the van and it worked well for Trevor to haul his canvases, as well as his sports stuff he toted around in case of a last minute call from a friend to play basketball or tennis. The Mustang was horrible to drive on snow, but during the winter she hadn't gone in until ten and the roads were pretty clear by then. It worked. Of course he was right about the salt.

"Did you have a good visit?"

She looked over at Trevor as he waited to let Alan pull out first. "Yes, it was nice enough. I don't suppose you can ditch the second half of the day so we can take the kids to the park."

Anna nearly bounced out of her seat at the suggestion and Trevor looked apologetic. "Can't. I shouldn't have taken so long for lunch. We're fighting for class time as it is. I have to meet with the board at four, so I'll be late."

"I don't know why you bother. They'll cut it at the first sign of needing to save money, anyway. You know they will, never mind it does a lot of those kids a lot more good than science ever will. How many of them will ever need to know the table of elements or even remember any of it?"

"I know. Not that learning anything is ever a bad thing, whether or not you use it later, but I know, and I keep telling them how good art is for kids' brains. They just don't get it." He swerved around a car that slowed to double park long enough to let someone out. "Actually, I'm thinking I might start working toward my master's and focus on that especially, on the research behind it."

Work on his master's? That would mean less time for the kids, less play time on weekends. Not to mention the expense.

"What are you thinking, Jen?"

"I think you should if you want. It'll make it harder for them to let you go, too."

"Or if they do, I could move to college level, although I'd rather not. But it would be an option."

"You're worried about your job."

He shrugged. "Not now. Just trying to help protect the future. But don't worry. Nate always wants me at the bar. I can pick up whatever hours I need."

"Or I can accept the hours Margaret wants to give me."

He didn't respond until several minutes later when he pulled in front of the school and put the car in park. "Does that mean you've..." He glanced at the kids. "You've decided to stick with two? Long term or temporarily?"

"It doesn't mean anything of the sort and I don't know. If we do that, it would still give me a year or there-about to work full time."

"Nina can't handle them full time, Jen."

"I know. I'd have to find someone."

"And then it takes anything extra you'd make."

"We need to do that, anyway, as you've said."

"Okay, we'll talk when I get home. I have to run." He leaned into the back to give the kids a kiss, and met her outside the car. "Jen, you know once you start full time, you'll have a hard time escaping that again. She'll promote you and you'll get too indispensable."

"Maybe I want to be."

He sighed with a light nod. "Are you going to the park?"

"Not without you."

"Jen..."

"It's fine. I appreciate the time you already took off." She kissed the side of his face. There were too many people around to do more than that. "Good luck with your meeting."

Alan called as she was getting dinner. She assured him he wasn't interrupting anything and Trevor wasn't home yet.

"Good."

She felt her eyebrows raise as she told Anna to sit her butt on the couch and quit standing on it. "Good?"

"That sounded worse than I meant."

"You're annoyed. What's wrong?" She shaped hamburger into patties one-handed as she held the phone in the other.

"You told Cheryl she should get a job?"

"What? No, she said she wanted to get one. It wasn't my idea."

"But you said she should, despite what I think. Was that payback for my comment about Daniel?"

Jenna wasn't sure what comment he meant since Alan did it so often she ignored it by now. "Alan, really, if she wants to get a job, why shouldn't she? Your kids are half grown."

"You have actually *met* my twins, right? They're far from half grown and Alex is far too dependent on her still..."

"Maybe he shouldn't be. It might be good for him."

"It's not that easy. And you do understand she's only talking about it because she's bored, not because she wants to work."

"So? Why shouldn't she?"

"Because I have a name in this town and anything she does other than the kids and the house, she does half-assed. I have to do the bills because she rounds everything and guesses at the balance. If we have business calls of any kind, I have to do it because she'll let them walk all over her. She won't stand up for herself, not even to me, and I can just see... Hold on." He said something away from the phone. Then came back. "I wanted to let you know we got in." Covering. Cheryl must have entered the room.

"Well maybe it's time she learned to be less dependent, too."

He cleared his throat. "Hold on a second."

Jenna knew he was mad at her, but he'd get over it. Letting Cheryl be so dependent wasn't any better for her than it was for himself. And she was smart enough to figure out how not to be. She only acted like she couldn't because she didn't want to. Jenna didn't dare say that.

"Look." Alan's got quieter. "There are things you don't know, so how about you talk to me first? And by the way, why didn't you tell me that you were thinking about having another baby?"

"What? Did Trevor tell you that?"

"No. Jen, he has never said anything about your personal life. He respects you too much."

"Then how did you..?" Cheryl told him. "Doesn't matter. I didn't say anything because I don't know if I want to do that so we aren't trying yet. And we may not."

"But Trevor wants it."

"Yes. But as I told Cheryl, he doesn't automatically get his way just because he's the man of the house."

"Oh for hell's sake, Jen. Get off that, would you? You're going to lose him with that attitude. He's not trying to force you to do anything. He's not Daniel and he's not your father. Get over it. Move on. See Trevor for what he is because he's good for you, and you're going to lose him if you don't get over yourself."

Seething, she nearly slammed the phone down. "I have to finish supper. Take care of your own issues, Alan. We're fine."

"Okay. But don't tell me I didn't warn you."

"Knock it off. You're only mad I wouldn't accept you and you're taking it out on him, or on me through him."

"You're kidding me, right? Jenna, I don't want that anymore. I have no interest in that anymore, so you can get over that, too. Don't bother to take it as an insult but I can see clearly by now it wouldn't work. We'd just argue more. So as I said, get over yourself. Trevor's a good guy. I like him. I enjoy seeing you together. He's exactly what you need. Marry the guy already before he changes his mind. And right now, I'm not sure I'd blame him."

Change his mind? Jenna felt something deep inside her sink. She knew what it was. It was that constant nagging thought that Alan was right, that Trevor would change his mind. "If he's going to change his mind, it'll be easier if we aren't married now, won't it? It won't stop it. It'll only make it harder..."

"Jen, I didn't mean he would. I only mean..."

"No, you're right. There are things he wants that I don't, and things I want that he doesn't, and we can't even work those out very well. So yes, he might. As long as I still think he might, I can't marry him, can I? I've already lost a husband through death. I don't want to lose one through divorce."

"And you think it'll be easier if he leaves if you're not married than it will be if you are?"

"Yes. Maybe." Maybe she was wrong. "I don't know. But I know how hard it was when it nearly happened with Daniel. It nearly killed me, Alan. I know how hard that was. And we never really got back to where we had been. You can't go back once it's gone that far."

"You barely knew Daniel when you married him. It's different."

"Is it? Is it time that makes a difference, or the contract that says you're legally bound whether you like it or not, that makes you take each other for granted so much you lose each other? I think people stop trying hard enough when they're married, not like when they're still dating and trying to make a good impression. I think it's ... a disaster waiting to happen, and I can't stand the thought of ending up that way with Trevor. I love him too much, Alan. I don't ever want to feel that way with him."

Silence came across the line. "We need to talk more." Alan's voice was gentle, apologetic. "I have to go right now, but let me call you... When would be a good time to talk?"

He meant alone, when his family wasn't around and when Trevor wasn't home. That rarely worked well. "I don't know. But it's fine, okay? We're fine." She heard him tell Cheryl he was coming.

"I'm glad. But call me if you need to talk. I'll make the time, Jen. I'm happy you have him and I don't want that to change. Honestly. Despite what you may think."

"Thanks. I have to go, too. He'll be home any minute." Anyway, she hoped he would be since he was already an hour late. With a quick goodbye, she gritted her teeth and finished pounding the beef into hamburgers.

Four

She should have accepted Joan's offer to babysit so Jenna could be at The gallery while Trevor worked behind the bar. At her suggestion, Nate had renamed The Rocky Oyster and gave it the nickname for the back corner room. Trevor now bartended at *The gallery*, with only the *The* capitalized to show it was supposed to be pronounced with a long E which sounded more distinctive, so Nate said, a couple of nights a week. She knew it was more because he enjoyed it than because they needed the money. They weren't all that tight. She still had the money from her husband's royalties put away, and with Joan's help, it was growing. If Jenna did decide to go back to school, it would cover her costs. Alan kept telling her it was fair to use it that way since Daniel's work and needs had kept her out of school.

It wasn't true, though. She kept herself out of school. She didn't see much point when she was still unsure what she wanted to do. She couldn't even decide whether or not she wanted more hours at her own gallery, an *actual* art gallery where, whether Trevor liked it or not, she was already becoming more indispensible. Or whether or not she wanted another child.

As she fought with Anna to get her in the bath and in bed, Jenna couldn't imagine why she would want to start this all over again. It was easier for Trevor. He went on about his business, his job, the bar, his painting, and she dropped them off before work and picked them up, got dinner, cleaned up their messes, read to them, bathed them, and stayed home with them while he went to play with his friends. Why wouldn't he want more? He did play with them when he was home. He often took them out on the weekends to give her a break, but why was that for her? Why wasn't that just because they were his, too?

Well, Anna was his. And she was the harder one. Aaron was never any trouble for him. He was getting to be some trouble for Jenna, however. He hit his terrible twos a year late and just loved to tell her *No* at any opportunity. Anna was already doing it. She hit it just before she turned two. Why would she want to start all of this all over again?

And yet, once they were tucked in and their beautiful little arms had given her big tight loving hugs and their beautiful little faces were peaceful against their pillows, she changed her mind. She did love to sit and hold her babies. Many of the best times of her life was when she'd simply sat in her rocking chair and enjoyed her tiny child created from love who so willingly returned her love.

Those times, and the times Trevor was fully in tune with her, were her favorite times. It would be hard to choose one over the other. She couldn't keep having babies just to be able to sit and hold them, but those times with Trevor... Jenna hoped like hell to have many, many more of those over many years.

With a sigh, she wandered into the art room. He had several canvases stretched and prepared, ready to use, in different sizes. When he got in the mood to paint, he wanted to be able to just pick up the size he wanted and go with it. If he had to do prep work first, he often wouldn't make himself. Jenna also hated the prep work. If she had to do it, she'd just go buy the premade canvases. Trevor wouldn't do it. Neither had Daniel.

But then they were real artists. She only played at it.

She spent several moments looking again at Trevor's work, some done, some in progress, some abandoned waiting for new gesso and a new start, then grabbed a canvas he'd already given up on and covered. It only had one light coat of gesso over his swirled bright paint. Maybe she would use his work as a starting point. Would he mind?

Of course he wouldn't. He preferred to start again on new canvas. Rarely would he use the reconditioned canvases, since they apparently already held emotions he drained into paint that didn't mean enough to keep. He had a lot of them piled up.

Changing her mind, Jenna grabbed a new one. He would fuss at her, teasing that he'd have to make another that size, but since he prepared them and didn't use them, she had to wonder if he'd rather they not be used. Maybe he had plans for them.

With no idea what she meant to paint, Jenna fell back to her old standard. She brushed some light denim blue across the canvas and deepened it toward the bottom, leaving a strip big enough for forest green and gray. Then she changed her mind and took the blue all the way to the bottom, and lightened it again so it resembled a wave of color that came at her and receded.

Wiping her brush on a paper towel, she picked up brown and gray and a touch of black and shaped trees over the blue. No leaves. Winter trees with plenty of reaching branches.

Her feet were tired by the time she got in as many as she wanted along with lots of little tiny shoots poking off the main branches that always reminded her of fingers just waiting to grasp anything within their reach. Stepping back to get a wider perspective, Jenna considered adding some green on the bottom as a sort of anchor. It looked too ... floating. Ungrounded. As usual, reality mixed with the surreal. She never did anything anymore that didn't have her surrealist touch, even when she aimed at reality.

She jumped at a hand on her back.

"Sorry." Trevor moved beside her, his chest against her left arm. "I tried to wait till I wouldn't interrupt. Am I? You can say so and I'll leave you alone." He skiffed her spine from top to bottom.

"No. Just surveying it. How long have you been home?"

"A while. You were absorbed in your work. It was nice to see."

"I'm sorry. I didn't hear you come in." She turned enough to drop the brush in the cleaner, then set her arms over his shoulders, careful not to touch his shirt with her painted fingers. "You can interrupt any time. You know that. You're far more important than any canvas. This is just ... a hobby. Nothing. You know that."

"It's more than a hobby, Jen. You can admit it to me. And to yourself. Honestly, you can." He moved in closer. "Besides, I like to watch you paint. It turns me on, and you know that." He kissed her neck just below her ear, the spot she found irresistible, which he darn well knew.

"Everything turns you on. I can be covered in flour with my hair a holy mess and you say it turns you on."

He chuckled. "Can I help it if I find you so sexy?"

"Hm. Or at least available." She gave him a light quick kiss. "And usually willing. But I have paint all over my hands."

"As you always do when you paint. That turns me on, too." He lowered his hands to her hips, pulled her in against his.

"Trevor." Her body tried to give in to him. She rarely had any control of it when he decided to press the issue. "I'll get it on your shirt. You're wearing a good one."

He released her, gave her a glinting smile, and pulled it off to toss onto the stool he bought to keep her feet from getting sore, never mind she said she didn't want it and never used it. "You can get the paint on me instead. I wash."

"What time is it?"

He kissed her neck again. "Just after midnight. I didn't mean to be so late."

"You'll have trouble getting up in the morning."

"Maybe, but I won't tonight. Come to bed with me, Jen."

"You must have had a good night."

"It was good enough. Want to make it better?" He ran his fingers along her hips.

Jenna nuzzled her face in against his flowing locks. "You smell like smoke."

"Mm, sorry. I'll shower." He met her lips and pulled her in tight. She gave in to his bare skin against her arms, to his mouth teasing, his fingers sliding up under her shirt. "Looks really good, by the way."

She glanced down at herself as he pulled her shirt up. "No I don't. I've gained weight. You don't have to act like you don't notice."

He caught her eyes and smiled. "Jen, I meant the painting."

"Oh. I'm not sure about that, either."

"Stop being so hard on yourself. You are wonderfully talented." He pulled her shirt over her head and slid his fingers over her breasts. She'd taken the bra off long ago. He loved that she hardly ever wore it in the house. "And classically beautiful. I like real-looking women. You know that. I don't want you to be a stick."

"But I'll be bigger than you are if I'm not careful."

He stepped back, the glint still in his eyes. "Was that a slam? I know I'm a scrawny little artist boy, but really Jen..."

"You are a scrawny little artist boy." She smeared her fingers down his chest. "And you're too young for me." Wiping the back side of her hands on his stomach to rid them of any still-wet paint, she gripped the top of his jeans and undid the snap. "But I might be able to make a man of you yet."

"Good luck, old lady. But you're welcome to try." He yanked her in against him and kissed her, then nibbled her ear. "Come help me wash this paint off."

~~~

"I told Nate I could work tonight."

Jenna heard the slight annoyance in his voice over the phone. She hated to hear him annoyed. It bothered her more than she should let it, but she'd already told Margaret she would work late. "What time does he expect you?"

"Seven."

"Why so early? The bar isn't busy then."

"We have a big shipment coming in. It needs to be checked before the driver can leave, and then stocked. You know the drill, Jen."
~~~

"Okay, and we have a big show tomorrow. Margaret needs me."

"Until when?"

"Until it's ready."

"You're supposed to be part time. She should have others doing that."

"She does, but the girl called in sick. Probably partying since it's Friday night, but either way, we're short staffed." Jenna listened to his silence and sighed. "Fine. Bring the kids here on your way in. I'll figure out how to handle them."

"Won't Margaret throw a shit fit about having kids in her gallery?"

"What do you want me to do? It's either that or nothing, from the way it sounds. They're not going to the bar." Jenna grabbed painting tags she still had to put up and glanced through her list. She needed a couple of hours at least.

"I'll take them back to Nina's and you can pick them up there. Guess I'll see you when I get home. Make sure you eat something."

Jenna agreed, although she probably wouldn't bother. He was too annoyed about taking them to Nina's, and she understood. They were already there so often. Unable to put her head into work without finding a better option, she picked up the phone again. Joan readily agreed to keep them so Jenna wouldn't have to leave before her job was done. Anything to keep her working in art, she supposed. And Joan would call Trevor herself to tell him to bring the kids to her. It would be more out of his way, but he could deal with it. It was more out of her way to pick them up, too.

By the time she got off, her whole body was tired and it was snowing. With a grimace at the thought of driving to Joan's, corralling the kids into the car, and driving home again, by herself, after dark, Jenna determined to find a sitter, preferably one who would go to their apartment. Maybe only two or three days a week. Nina could do the other days and Aaron and Anna wouldn't always be stuck in the house.

But how would she find someone she could trust that much? There were too many horror stories about nannies and sitters ignoring the kids or worse. She wasn't worried about the apartment. They had nothing anyone would want. The only thing of real value were Trevor's paintings and she couldn't imagine anyone being that bold, especially since he didn't demand a high price for his work yet. But she did have several of Daniel's paintings hanging in the open. That could be a risk.

Maybe a day care center would be better. Did they accept two day a week care? Jenna sighed as she got out at Joan's. She didn't want that, either. They would constantly pick up colds and everything else and give them to Jenna and she didn't relish the idea of them being just two of a big crowd of kids. They would get enough of that once they started school. Anna would probably love it. Her Aaron, though... Maybe he would. He was friendly. Not overtly friendly, but sociable. He might be okay with it. She needed to get him around other kids more before he started school. Two days a week might be good for him, as she'd told Alan about Alex.

But he got sick so easily and it worried her to death. She never slept when he was sick.

Joan greeted her with a hug, said she looked tired and that the kids were settled in with colors and newsprint pads. Joan would not let her grandchildren use coloring books. She wanted them to use their own imagination to draw what they wanted. Jenna understood her point, but she didn't see that there was any harm in learning to stay in the lines, at least sometimes. She had coloring books at home. She also had plain paper. They chose which they wanted.

She believed in choice.

Her babies ran to her and she crouched to give them hugs and then looked at what they were doing, listened to whatever they wanted to ramble about, and in between, answered Joan that she hadn't eaten and yes she would love whatever leftovers there were from dinner.

She could stay that long. She was starving. And she wouldn't want to bother when she got home.

By the time she ate, she was too relaxed to want to go out again, and the snow hadn't let up. Joan asked her to stay. Jenna couldn't argue. She called the bar. Trevor was busy so she asked Nate to let him know she wouldn't be home.

Five

Pulling her skirt over the black slip, Jenna grimaced. It was tighter than it should be, but the sweater draped over top would hide that, she supposed. To tame her nerves as she got ready for the school's Christmas party, a family party for Trevor's job, she focused on the television playing in the other room. *Star Search* was her guilty pleasure. She'd found Sawyer Brown that way and this season she was rooting for Phil Vassar. Trevor teased her about it. He didn't listen to country. He liked heavy metal. How he could listen to bands with names like Napalm Death, Savatage, and Anthrax she just didn't understand, especially since he was one of the sweetest and most upbeat people she'd ever known. He said he didn't pay attention to the words. He liked the heavy demanding beat. They'd made a pact: he didn't play that around her or the kids and she didn't play her country around him, other than the few more pop sounding bands he could stand. She gave in to him about Celtic Frost, on some of their softer songs.

At least he enjoyed her all-time favorite band. Of course it wasn't country. She still often pulled out her Raucous albums while she was cleaning or cooking because the upbeat rock made it far less boring. He never minded, and now and then, he'd pull her away from her chores to dance with him to one of their songs. Usually a slow one. Often, whatever chore she'd started didn't get done.

And he allowed for the exception of *Star Search*, even if he did tease her heinously about it. There wasn't much country on the show. It had a variety of acts, so a song or two here or there didn't get to him. The spokesmodels drew his attention enough to make up for it.

Jenna sighed as she clasped her necklace and stood back to peruse the mirror. She was far from spokesmodel material, even from model material, especially with the extra weight. She'd have to do something about it when she could find the energy.

And she didn't want to go to the party. Trevor knew she didn't. He knew as well as she did that they would raise their noses at her for the way she was living. Jenna couldn't care an iota less what they thought, except for the way it could affect him. She'd been sick the year before and couldn't go. Maybe she could fake being sick again.

"Hey. Ready?" Trevor stepped into their room and Jenna knew

she couldn't back out. He was excited to finally show off the kids. He was excited she would be there with him. And he looked amazing in his black pants and dark green shirt with thin black stripes. His long blond locks stood out against the dark clothes and highlighted his green-hazel eyes. The hell with what anyone thought. "Yeah, I'm ready enough. And I'll do my best not to embarrass you."

With a grin, he came to her and slid his hands down her waist to her thighs. "*The* Jenna Rhodes will try not to embarrass *me*? You're hilarious. One of the things I love about you. You do know I always get lots of points just for having Jenna Rhodes on my arm."

"I can't imagine why. I've done nothing worth anyone caring about."

"Other than inspiring the great Daniel Rhodes to greatness."

"It had nothing to do with me."

"Oh Jen, tell yourself that all you want, but no one will believe you. He said too often that it did."

"He was being nice."

"Either way." He raised a hand to her face. "It's easy to see how you would. And you know that's the only reason I'm with you, right? I figure it should work for me, too." The grin returned, along with a sparkle in his eyes.

"Is that so?"

"Mm." He nuzzled his face beside hers. "That's so. Well. That, and that everything you do turns me on."

"You're easy to turn on."

He chuckled. "Funny. I didn't used to be. Come on, we'll be late."

It wasn't quite the torture Jenna expected. They were all polite to her, even if it was often rehearsed politeness. A couple of people did mention Daniel's work but Trevor veered them in another direction fast enough it didn't get uncomfortable. And they made a nice fuss over Aaron and Anna, both of whom actually behaved fairly well, at least as well as any of the others and better than many.

She was glad to get home, and she was glad the kids were worn out so they went to bed without a fuss. Stripping out of her too tight dressy clothes, she slipped into a long nightgown, the floor-length black one with a lacy trim accenting her cleavage that he liked, and went to look for him.

He was in the studio, kicked back in a chair with one foot hiked onto the desk, a drawing pad resting on that leg, a charcoal pencil in hand. Sketching. He rarely ever sketched. Generally, he took the image in his head and just laid it onto canvas. The picture of him, the abstract artist all dressed up, relaxed onto an old chair with charcoal in hand made her want to catch him on paper. She'd never done it, although she thought about it often.

Jenna stood and watched until he looked up and she went to join him. "Am I interrupting?"

"Never. What do you think?"

She tilted her head to see the sketch. Part of a building, a falling down building. Perfectly rendered. When he tried, he could draw more realistically than even *the great Daniel Rhodes.* He only tended to prefer not to focus much on realism. "It's beautiful. I love the detail. What is it? Is it a real place?"

"My old school. I was thinking of it tonight. Things were much simpler back then, weren't they? Back when we were in grade school?"

Simpler? "No. Not for me."

He raised his eyes. "No? Honestly?"

"Honestly." She ran fingers through his hair. "They're simpler now, here with you. I'm happier now. I'm where I want to be."

"Are you?" He set the pencil and tablet aside and coaxed her to sit on his leg. "I've wondered recently if you are."

"What? Why?"

He slid his arms around her waist. "When Alan was here and they were talking about the zoo and his house and yard, I had the feeling you miss that. Having a yard. Less traffic. Less congestion. Do you?"

She allowed a deep breath before she answered. "Sometimes. But if I was in Peoria, there would be things about Chicago I would miss, too. I'm happy here. With you. At work. I am. So you don't have to wonder." It was true enough. Trevor made her happy. Her work at the gallery ... well, sometimes it made her happy or at least productive and it was hers. She knew he wanted more of an answer, but there was no point. They were where they were. She'd made her choice.

Jenna kissed him and released the top button of his shirt. "You've been turning me on all night looking so hot and having those women flirt like they wished they could come home with you."

"You're imagining things."

She wasn't, but she didn't want to argue. Not tonight. "Okay." She released another button. "Should I leave you alone to finish what you were doing?"

"Absolutely not." He reclaimed her mouth and helped her up.

~~~

Jenna hung up with Karla and half considered taking her cousin up on her offer. She hated to Christmas shop alone. It was better with the kids, better and worse both, but it would be worlds more fun with Karla. In Boston. Not that Jenna could just pick up and go. Trevor wasn't off until a couple of days before Christmas to a couple of days after New Year's. Jenna didn't want to travel then. Seeing Boston in December would be nice and she'd love to do it, but she wanted to do it with her boyfriend, not without him.

With the kids fed and in bed, Jenna kicked her feet up on the couch. She'd expected him home by now. It was Sunday. How busy could it be at the bar? She picked up the novel she'd barely started the other day, read a couple of lines that didn't get through to her brain, and set it down to go find a cup of mint tea.

As she waited for the water to heat, she wandered into the art room. Her latest tree painting was still on her easel. She'd thought it was done but it wasn't right. It was just trees. There was no heart to it. Returning to the kitchen to drop a tea bag into the cup, Jenna went with it to her front window. Snow fell through the night and blurred the buildings across from hers. She missed the trees outside her own window. The loft's windows. Daniel's. Not hers. Technically it was still hers. Carrie was renting it. Alan's sister loved the place and so did her new husband, so they stayed. This was her window. Her apartment. She chose it, with Trevor's help. She signed the lease. She paid the rent. He paid everything else. And he put money back in savings, to travel on, he said, although they hadn't been anywhere. Jenna put nothing in savings from her own income. There was little left after rent and the few groceries she bought and she spent that on the kids or on art supplies.

Not that it mattered. She had Daniel's savings.

With a sigh, she went back to her painting. The last time she'd looked out the loft's window, it was foggy, as though the trees were already receding from her life.

Fog. Maybe that's what it needed. But did she know how to paint fog? If not, she could gesso over the whole thing and try again. Except some of the trees were among her best. The shading and highlights were perfect. Real. Only a couple of them. The rest were lifeless.

She set the cup down and picked up her palette to add white, a touch of black, and a bit of cadmium blue. She mixed different shades
~~~

of blue-gray white and thinned it with a bit of mineral spirits. Maybe a mistake. Alkyd might be the better choice. But she wanted to try. If it ruined the perfect trees, so be it. What did it matter? It was only paint.

When her feet throbbed too much to stand, she went to check the time. Nearly one. He wasn't home. And he had work in the morning. So did she.

Jenna cleaned her brush, glanced at the canvas, and decided to think about it more another night.

She was asleep when she felt him lay beside her, cuddle in to tell her good night, and apologize for how late it was. He smelled like smoke. And perfume. With a cringe, she rolled over and ignored it. A lot of women at the bar wore too much perfume. It was hardly the first time he smelled of it.

Six

"Oh Anna, stop already."

"I want Daddyyyyy…"

"Then get your coat on and let's go find him."

"*No*. Daddy come *here*. I not go home with you. *No*."

Jenna sighed as Nina took over with the girl, told her not to talk to her mom that way, and forced her coat on. Anna was mad at her for working late again, but Trevor was supposed to pick them up. He'd called and said he had errands and asked her to get them.

It was past dinner time. They were also cranky from being hungry. At least Aaron didn't yell at her. He was quiet. Withdrawn.

But she had to work more hours. Having nothing left over after rent and a few tidbits wasn't good enough. She'd given up working for long enough after Anna was born. It depleted her own funds. She had a right to build them again, to be able to take care of herself. And if he would pick them up at four-thirty when he was off, they would be home plenty early to relax before dinner. It was only fair. She got them out of bed, dressed, fed, and dropped off every morning. He could at least pick them up.

She tried hard not to let her frustration at him reflect on her babies as she thanked Nina and hustled them into the car.

By the time they got home, after Anna finally hushed and Aaron found his voice to complain the whole way about one thing after another, Jenna was annoyed that he wasn't even home yet. She pulled out a box of Goldfish and poured some on the table to hold them. Taking two minutes for herself, she changed out of her work clothes, washed her face, and pulled her hair into a ponytail. The kids were fighting by then. With another sigh, she forced herself out to break it up and gave in to let the girl have a cookie that she yelled for.

"Fine. Here. Now quiet down and find something to do until I have supper ready." Macaroni and cheese with hot dogs and green beans would have to do. She couldn't deal with more than that. Have another one? Was Trevor crazy? Jenna was giving her already neglected babies hot dogs and macaroni for supper instead of a real supper. Why should she inflict herself on another innocent victim?

By the time it was done, Jenna realized it was far too quiet and went to find them, hoping like hell they'd fallen asleep. They weren't in their room, or in Jenna's room on her bed where Aaron liked to sit and read. With a cringe that ran all the way through her body, she checked the art room and stopped at the door. "*What* are you *doing?*"

They were covered in oil paint. And so were two canvases. Two in-progress canvases. One of Jenna's, her trees in fog painting that was coming along well enough she almost felt like a real artist, and one of Trevor's, his newest, just finished.

She was almost ashamed of the way they jumped when she yelled, since she never yelled at them, but she couldn't quite be ashamed. "I *told* you *not* to come in here. You *know* better. *Only* with me or your daddy. *Look* what you *did.*"

Their little eyes were wide and their bodies were frozen in stop-motion. Her painting had big red finger streaks across it. Trevor's had red and yellow messy brush strokes. The colors on the ruined canvases matched the colors on the transgressors' clothing and hands. "*Get* to the bathroom. *Now*. And *don't* touch anything."

By the time they were cleaned up and in their room, with their clothes in the trash, Jenna had yellow and red paint on her own clothes and she was exhausted and frustrated.

"Hey, why's the food sitting on the stove cold? And hot dogs? For dinner?" Trevor, at the bathroom door, scanned her. "You've been painting."

"No. Your kids have been painting. I've been trying not to scream more than I already did. Cold hot dogs will just have to work. Could you at least feed them? I can't even eat now." She brushed past him to her own room and slammed the door.

Jenna was almost ashamed of being so nasty to him, too, but she couldn't bother. She pulled off her favorite house shirt, turned it inside out so the paint wouldn't spread farther, and dropped it on the floor alongside Trevor's sweats that he usually kept on the floor instead of on the hooks she put over the closet door to keep his clothes *off* the floor. She rifled through her drawer to find another warm house shirt, pulled one out, and sat on the bed, holding it on her lap.

She'd yelled at them. She never yelled. But they destroyed her painting. Her trees.

Her door opened. "Kids are eating... Jen?" He closed it again and came up in front of her. "Hey, it's just paint. Come on, come eat with us." He ran fingers along her bare shoulder.

"Don't." She jerked away and pulled her shirt on. "Did you see what they did?"

"Haven't been in there yet. They didn't get anything of Daniel's, did they?"

"What? No... Hell, I didn't check. I don't think so." She swerved around him and to the art room to check her husband's paintings that were still low enough to reach. They were fine. With a deep breath, she figured she shouldn't be so bothered, but now she was bothered that she hadn't even thought of it. Daniel's art. There wouldn't be any more of it. She needed to get them put up higher.

At Trevor's chuckle, she turned to see him holding his ruined canvas. "It's not funny."

He shrugged. "It's just paint on canvas. Maybe we have a couple of budding artists on our hands."

"I hope not." She muttered it before she could stop herself. At his raised eyebrows, she changed direction. "How doesn't that bother you? You put a lot of time into it and..."

"And I enjoyed doing it. That's what it's about, right? Enjoying it? If others enjoy my work, that's great, but that's not what it's about. Not to me." He set it back on the easel.

"But it's also about what you put into it. It's not just paint. It's..."

"Emotion. Passion. Yes. But it served that purpose. And I kind of like it this way, maybe better than I did before." He glanced back at the canvas. "Definitely better than before." He turned back to her. "They only got mine, right?"

She felt her head shake and gritted her teeth.

"Not your trees..." He went to her easel, which sat angled away from his but adjacent, so they both caught the light from the windows and where she could see out into the apartment, and shoved a hand through his hair. His short hair. He'd cut it. "Oh Jen. No wonder you're so upset. I'm so sorry. This was just gorgeous."

"What did you do to your hair?"

He looked over as though he didn't know what she meant. "Oh, cut it today. We might be able to get most of this off since it's wet."

She wandered over to him but she couldn't look at the painting. "Why?"

"It's nice, Jen. I've enjoyed watching your progress." He grabbed a cloth and started toward the canvas.

"Leave it." She took his hand to make him turn to her. "Why did you cut it?" She slid a hand around his head. The beautiful silky hair she was jealous of was trimmed back to his nape, his forehead nearly bare. "Trevor?"

"It'll make things easier. And it's just hair. Let me clean this for you. Go eat, Jen. You look wiped out..."

"No, it doesn't matter anymore. Leave it be. Why are you more bothered by that than your own?"

"Didn't like mine much, anyway. What did you plan to do with this one?" He looked at her canvas again, as though it had a magnet drawing his eyes and hand. "Sell it? I hoped you wouldn't although you could have. Maybe you still can if I can clean it up and you can touch it up..."

"No. I can't." She walked away from him, out to check the kids. They were actually eating, thankfully. Aaron peered up at her, his head ducked. "Finish eating." Jenna went to her rocking chair beside the little apartment window and looked out, but there was nothing worth looking at, so she got up again and turned on the television. The rule was always no television during dinner, but this wasn't dinner. It was no more than keeping them from being hungry so they could go to bed soon. If they quit eating to watch, she figured they weren't hungry enough still to worry about it. Jenna would make up for it with a good breakfast instead of the usual cereal and fruit.

She heard Trevor talk to the kids and he came to sit beside her. "Talk to me, Jen. What's going on in your head recently?"

"Nothing. I'm just annoyed. They know they aren't supposed to be in there."

"They're babies nearly. I'll put a lock on the door, a hook high enough they can't reach. Okay?"

"I don't like locks. You know that."

"But Jen, you should be able to cook without worrying about..."

"I'll put the paint up higher. It was my fault. I shouldn't have left them down."

"You didn't. You never do. I did, and I'm so sorry. I was working on that thing late last night and... I'm sorry. Let me try to fix it." He caressed her face and pulled her eyes to his. "Okay?"

"No."

"Jen..."

"Some things can't be fixed."

"It's paint and canvas. It can be fixed."

"That's *not* all it..." She got up and told Anna to use her spoon instead of her fingers. How did she explain? How did she tell him they were her trees? *Her* trees. On the last day she lived in the loft. How could he possibly understand? He couldn't. She didn't have the words to make him understand. She'd had no intention of selling it. It was … for her apartment, to bring her trees back to her home. There was no view in her apartment now and she wanted her trees. Now, she would never be able to look at it without seeing those red streaks, no matter how well Trevor cleaned it up, no matter how well she could fix it, if she could. They would still be there along with the way she'd screamed at her babies. She wouldn't forget that, either. It was useless to her now.

Just like songs she used to love until her mom heard them and bitched about how stupid the words were and she couldn't ever hear them again without hearing that, too.

It was the same.

Some things couldn't be fixed.

He tried again to get her to eat. She ignored him and went to the studio, moved the painting from the easel, and faced it against a wall on the floor. She didn't care if she got paint on the wall. Red paint. It didn't matter. The stupid walls were faded white, anyway, from before they moved in. She hated white walls. They had far more nail holes in them than their lease allowed and they'd have to give up their security deposit because of it already. Why did it matter if there were paint splotches on walls that looked like hell when they moved in? Maybe she'd paint them. Regardless of the lease. If they tried to do more than keep the deposit, she would argue that the room was unfinished when they moved in and they couldn't be charged for painting an unpainted room badly in need of it. Depending on her mood, maybe she would argue about the holes, too.

Jenna grabbed a new canvas and added reds and oranges to her palette. And dark green. A touch of yellow. No neutrals for shade and highlight. This one would only be colors.

She barely heard him say the kids were in bed and he didn't come in to see what she was doing. Rarely did she not want him to come in to look but he always knew when she didn't. She barely heard the television turn off and the radio turn on. With a half a thought as to what he might be doing in the living room with only the radio, Jenna dismissed it and continued.

I'll put a lock on the door.

She cringed. No. No locks. She'd even changed out the bathroom door knob so it wouldn't lock. If one of the kids walked in on one of them, so be it. They were still nearly babies.

And she'd screamed at them.

By the time they were old enough it would matter if they walked in, they'd know better. They didn't need locks, except for the front door which she always double-checked at night, both the deadbolt and the chain.

She'd never told him why. Trevor didn't argue about the bathroom door lock. He did argue about the bedroom door, for privacy reasons, but he let it go. He asked why. She wouldn't say. It didn't matter. She didn't like inside locks. He didn't have to know she'd been locked in her room when grounded once because she wouldn't stay there and was then forgotten because they often forgot she wasn't around. Some things were private.

She would not get accidentally locked in any room of her own apartment, and neither would her children. She'd throw every canvas and all of the paint out the window first.

~~~

"Morning."

Jenna opened her eyes to Trevor's fingers running over her forehead. He sat on the bed, dressed and ready for work.

"Sorry to wake you, but you didn't wake me when you came to bed last night and I wanted to be sure you're okay before I go."

"I'm fine. What time is it?"

"Nearly six. Feel better by now?"

"Why are you up so early?"

"Stopping by the bar for a delivery."

"Why?"

"Nate needs help with it."

"But he has help for that."

"The guy's sick, as I said. Bad bronchitis. Can't lift anything. Jen..." He slid a hand along her shoulder. "You've been doing a lot of hours. Call in. Take a break. Come meet me for lunch instead and..."

"I can't."

"Jenna..."

"You take off today and come lunch with me."

"I can't just take off..."

"But I can?"

"Okay." He leaned down for a light kiss. "I'll see you tonight. Love you. Have a good day."

She couldn't even answer him. She turned over and tried to go
~~~

back to sleep but her alarm buzzed as she was close.

"I have to go." Jenna shook her head at Margaret's third attempt to get her to stay and went to get her purse. It was nearly seven. She was tired. And she hadn't even said anything to him the night before, or that morning when he was trying to be nice, helpful. She should have left at four as she was supposed to so dinner would be ready. Maybe he'd give them hot dogs, although she'd never known him to do so, no matter what time he picked them up or how tired he was. He always fed them well, maybe because he wanted to eat well.

So did she. She'd barely touched the lunch she brought.

The drive home felt much farther and she heaved a breath of relief as she walked in.

"Jen?" Trevor had the phone in his hand and spoke into it. "She's home... Yeah, I think we got our wires crossed. I'll come get them." He hung up and shrugged his hands. "You forgot the kids?"

"No, you were... Are you kidding me? You didn't get them?"

He came to her and tried to help her out of her coat. "I'll go. Dinner's ready. Eat if you want."

"You were supposed to get them."

"I left a message. Are you going to let me take your coat?"

"I didn't get it, and I'll go. I'm still..."

"Tell you what." He ran a finger along her face. "Stay bundled. I'll call Nina and ask her to feed them and we'll go out first. Just the two of us. It's been a while since..."

"You said supper was ready."

"It'll wait till tomorrow. Let's make a date of this mistake and pretend it wasn't a mistake." He kissed the side of her face.

"They've been there long enough."

"It'll be fine."

"No. I'll go get them. I'm sorry, I'll ask tomorrow why I didn't get the message." She tried to slip back out the door. He stopped her, tried again to turn it into a date. She was tired, too tired. And irritable and...

He threw his coat on, grabbed his keys, and walked out.

Jenna sank onto the couch, still in her coat. Why was this getting so hard?

She insisted on cleaning up after he complained that she shouldn't have waited and asked if there was something wrong with it since she barely ate. The second time he asked, she said it wouldn't hurt her to lose a few pounds, which she needed to do, anyway.

As he put the kids in bed, she turned on the radio low and picked up their things and swept the floor and wiped oily handprints off her stereo which they also weren't supposed to touch.

"Want to dance?" He set his hands on her waist from behind.

"Too tired."

"Then why are you still cleaning? Let it go for tonight. It'll still be there this weekend and then I'll help you."

"They've been running around with food or unwashed hands. Look at this."

"So what, Jen? Stop obsessing with their messes and just enjoy them."

"Easy for you to say." She turned. "You're as messy as they are."

He grinned. "And you love me anyway. How about you enjoy my good side tonight and be irritated with me some other time?"

"I'm not irritated with you."

"Of course you are, and I'm sure you have a right to be. But I've been missing you lately and..."

Jenna pulled away to take the rag to the sink. Did he not hear her say she was too tired? He didn't listen.

Trevor grabbed her arms and turned her to face him. "Stop doing that."

"Doing what? Let go of me."

"Walking away. Keeping so much distance. Holding everything in. I'm trying to be patient. I know you have stuff going on in your head you won't tell me, although I don't know why you won't, and I guess that's your business, but stop pulling away from me." When she pushed his hands off her arms, he moved them to her head, on each side, forcing her attention. "Look at me, Jen. Tell me what's going on. Since Alan was here, you're completely someone else. You hardly talk to me. You're so far back inside yourself it's like you were when we met, when you didn't know me. But you do now..."

"Do I? I'm not the only one different and it has nothing to do with Alan."

"I'll take your word for that. About Alan. If you insist. But how am I different?"

"Why did you cut your hair?"

"I told you, to make things easier. Why does it matter?"

"The school told you to, didn't they?"

"They suggested it would be a good idea."

"And you gave in. You're not the same. You gave in. You've been giving in to them. I've seen it."

"I give in to you, too. I've always been that way, the peacemaker. You knew that when you fell for me. Why is it wrong now?"

"You don't give in to me. We talk. We compromise…"

He backed away and shook his head. "Funny that what you call compromise, I see as me giving in. You don't want to be married, so we're not. You don't want another child, so we're not. You want to work full time, so you are, never mind how grouchy the kids have become. You don't want to go out, so we don't. How exactly are we compromising, Jen?"

She was so frustrated, she couldn't even say it. She was working full time? Only for the past couple of weeks. Temporarily. So what? He was working full time plus another job, and he wouldn't need the other job if she stayed full time and they could be together every night and all weekend. She gave in to it because he wanted it. She was still in Chicago instead of just outside Peoria where she could have a small house and a yard and a garden and trees because he wanted to stay. How wasn't she compromising?

She had to get back to the original subject. "You have changed. You used to live as you pleased, do your art as you pleased, and just bartending in between painting was enough."

"I used to be single. And I mean really single, on my own, with only myself to take care of, not a family. That changes a person, Jen. You know that. Or it should."

"Why? I didn't ask you to change, to give up anything. I told you I could take care of myself, of the kids. I didn't ask you to move in with me to chain you down, only because I wanted to be with you. And now, you just let them *tell* you how to dress and how to wear your hair? You're a good teacher and they know it. The kids love you. They learn so much…"

"They won't if I get fired."

"They can't…"

"Yes, they can. They've been lenient, but after the party when … our *living status* became so public, things have changed. I won't push you to marry me to appease them, so I figured the hair cut was the better option."

"It's not their business."

"I'm in charge of their kids, so they say it is. I don't want to lose my job, Jen. I like my job. So I'm still doing what I love. How I look while I'm doing it is besides the point. It's just a thing."

"It's not just a thing. If you give in once, they'll push for more. I know how it works. The more power you give someone, the more they take until they think they can run everyone's life and tell them what they can and can't do..."

"Don't go there again. Not everything is about that."

"Yes, it is. *Everything* is. You know it is. Even relationships are about power and who's in charge and who makes the rules. Everything is, and you're giving in to it. There was nothing wrong with the way you dressed, or with your hair. You were clean and neat and..."

"And unless you want to marry me, I have to do what I have to do to appease them. It's that simple, Jen. That's the way it works. They hold my job in their hands and it is their right to say so. It *is*."

"So quit. Or threaten to quit. They won't let you leave. You're..."

"I *like* my job. There are plenty of better trained artists ready and willing to step in. I was lucky to get it in the first place. All those hours of volunteering got me in but it won't keep me in." His voice lowered, his shoulders slumped. "And ... I need to get my master's. For that, I need their cooperation. I can't get good recommendations by being rebellious. What I want long-term matters enough to give up small fights. It's for the greater good..."

"Your master's?" Jenna slumped onto a dining chair. "I thought you decided to wait."

"Do you object?" He sounded wary, daring.

She met his eyes. "I want you to have whatever it is you want. You know that. You've always known that."

"Except for the one thing I want most." Another dare.

"You know, maybe you're willing to give in that far, but I'm not. I won't be forced to get a legalized piece of paper just because it's *the thing to do*. I did it once. I won't again."

His chest rose and fell. "Okay, Jen. I get it. I do. But don't yell at me for doing what I have to do to keep what I want. I'm doing my best for us."

"And I'm not?"

"I didn't say that."

"You said the kids were grouchy because I'm working full time. Never mind how many hours you're doing."

"They are. And I haven't changed anything. It's you they miss."

"That's not fair."

"Jenna, you don't *have* to work so many hours. I'm taking care of it, as I said I would when you told me you were expecting Anna. I am. You don't *have* to."

"Neither do you. If I stay full time, you can quit the bar."

He opened his mouth to talk, then grabbed a deep breath and checked his watch. "I have to go."

She stood. "Go where?"

"To work. Nate's expecting me."

"This late?"

"Jen..."

"Fine. Go." She pulled away when he tried to move in for a quick kiss, as he always did before he left. To work. At nine o'clock. On a weekday. When he opened the door, she couldn't help but ask. "Is there someone else?"

Trevor turned to stare. "What?"

"Are you working or ... is it another woman? Tell me if there is."

The stricken look on his face nearly made her regret asking, but she had a right to ask. With all the hours he worked at the bar, she didn't see the extra income. Not that she had to see it. They still had separate accounts, but they still lived fairly tight and they usually talked about their checks, their income, their expenditures. She had the right to ask.

His head shook. "I can't believe you asked me that." His voice was low, hurt. "Jenna, I love you. I adore you. I would never in the world hurt you that way. Why in the hell would I badger you to marry me if I wanted that? Hell, I'm free enough still that if I wanted to take up with or off with another woman, I could easily enough. I don't want..." He lowered his head. His shoulders rose and fell. "I can't believe you asked me that. And I should probably stay right now, but I can't. I have to go."

As the door banged, Jenna slumped back onto the chair. Why was it so wrong to want him home at night? Why was it wrong to guess why he might not want to be? And why should he get so hurt by her question when he kept hinting about Alan? He *knew* she didn't want Alan, and she could have easily had him if she'd wanted him, too. He *knew* that.

Seven

She hated it. The trees were flat. The blue gray atmosphere was flat and the wrong color. There was no life in it.

Jenna set her palette down and paced the art room. She paused at Trevor's most recent. A still life. Realism. Beautiful. Full of life and energy. Like he was. Suddenly, she was so jealous of him she couldn't stand herself. Everything just seemed so easy for him. He wanted to teach, he jumped in and was hired. He wanted to paint, he jumped in and it came out perfect. He wanted her, he got her. He wanted Anna and she was fully his daughter. Recently, even Aaron was getting closer to Trevor. He charmed everyone. He talked easily to anyone. He trusted. Carefully, but he did. He still could.

He had wonderful parents. He lost them too early, but he'd had them and they were good to him and they were lenient about what he wanted to do, interested in and helpful with anything he decided to try. They'd spent plenty of time with him. And his aunt was the same.

Jenna didn't remember when she last spoke to her parents, or wanted to. Sometime before Anna was born. They approved even less of Trevor than they had of Daniel, which was so crazy Jenna couldn't figure it since she was twenty-four when she hooked up with Trevor and seventeen with Daniel and... They'd never even seen his daughter. Her daughter. They hadn't seen Aaron since he was a baby. Three hours away, or less in good traffic, and they hadn't bothered. She'd been to Alan's, across the street from their house and they would had to have seen her Mustang, but they hadn't bothered. Neither had she.

And she spent so much time working at Elucidations because it was what she had, other than the kids. Other than Joan, Daniel's mother, and Nina, Trevor's aunt, Margaret and her co-workers were the only people she talked to. And Nate and Keisha. Trevor's friends. And Alan, her only friend who was actually *her* friend.

Trevor wanted them to go out as a couple, to meet more people their age and hang out, but it wasn't easy for her. She wasn't charming. She wasn't good at conversation. None of the couples they'd tried so far had half enough in common with her to be close to understanding who she was or her outlook. They were all Trevor's crowd. And they were nice people. Charming. Good conversationalists. It only made her feel more awkward than she always had.

Returning to her canvas, she spurted yellow and red paint on her palette, dipped her fingers in it, and scribbled over top of her trees. Like Anna had over the one Jenna actually liked, but more, with more aggression, with more red. Then she felt childish and wiped it with a dry cloth. The browns and greens that hadn't dried yet smeared in with it and she traced the tree outlines with a clean corner of the cloth.

But then it needed more color again, so she dipped her fingers in the brown and white and ran them along the partly dried tree trunks. Over the red and yellow transparent smears. More blue. She dabbed her thumb in the blue and patted it along the background, behind the smeared-fixed trees, sometimes overlapping them. It was an odd effect, not close to realistic, but maybe she'd had enough of realism. If Trevor was headed that direction, she'd swerve and go a different direction. She couldn't compete with his realism. His realism was beautiful, lively, perfect. Hers was messy, surreal. In everything else, her house, her kids, herself, she wanted neat and tidy. Not on her canvas.

"Surprised you're still up."

She jumped at his voice. He was propped against the door frame, watching her. "What time is it?"

"Guess we should put a clock in here. You're not tired? It's after two."

"I don't want a clock in here. It's distracting."

"Doubt it would be the way you've been so absorbed recently while you paint. I've been home for at least fifteen minutes. I watched a while, went to shower, and..."

"What?" She was stunned at herself that someone was walking through her apartment, around her children, and she hadn't noticed.

"Mind if I look?" He ambled closer, but waited for permission.

"It's... I don't care, but it's just ... nothing. I'll gesso over it so I don't waste the canvas."

He took her side. At least he didn't smell like smoke and perfume. He smelled of soap, of clean male. And he hadn't put a shirt on, only his old sweat pants. "That's ... interesting. New technique?"

"No, just... I didn't like it, so I..."

Suddenly, he pulled her face to his and kissed her. She only fought it for a few seconds. He didn't give in. He held her, made it deeper, explored her mouth with his tongue, her body with his hands.

"Trevor." She whispered in his ear when he moved his lips to her neck. "My hands are full of paint."

"Hm, I saw that. I have nothing on I'm worried about." He caught her eyes. "Jen. My sweet Jenna, there is no one else." He kissed her nose. "I'm sorry if I've done something to make you wonder, but..."

"Perfume."

"What?"

"I keep smelling perfume on you. Strong. When you come home late. And you've ... been more distant, working more hours. I can't... I just can't be naive, you know, not anymore. No matter how much I don't want to think..."

"Keisha." He stroked a thumb down her face. "The bar's in trouble, Jen. We're revamping it, making it more elegant, trying to attract people ... like you, more upscale. I wasn't supposed to tell you. It's supposed to be a surprise. Nate wanted me to finagle some of your canvases from you, your pretty scenery paintings, as he called them, for the main room. He even has me painting things that look like real things. He wants to make it artsy, but classy. Wasn't sure how I would get your work there without you knowing. But Keisha's there every night, in charge of redecorating. She always wears too much perfume and she always hugs me in thanks as I'm leaving. Jen, I would never cheat on you."

She threw her arms around him. "I'm sorry. I am. I..."

"Stop doubting yourself, Jenna. It's your biggest fault, and you have no reason."

"I do. You know I do. I'm ... I'm not charming. I'm not friendly enough. I don't fit in with your friends. I'm overweight and I'm tired and I usually have smeared food on me somewhere from one of the kids although I try hard not to, and I... No matter how hard I try or how much I work at it, I can't make my art into anything worthwhile that anyone would want. Not like you do. Not like... My job is what I'm good at..."

"It's beneath you, beneath your talent and ability. You should be farther up the rung by now and you know it."

"I can't be, not without staying full time."

He sighed. "Okay, I give. Stay full time. I'll go to school later when the kids are older. When the redecorating is done, I'll have more time with them and things will settle down." He kissed her neck. "I'll pick them up. I'll have dinner ready. Go ahead, Jenna. Just give me about three weeks first, okay?" He ran fingers under the back of her shirt. "And you're wrong. About your art. The only thing it's missing is your belief that you can. Nate wants them. He's willing to pay for them, although you might have to take installments with fingers crossed that business picks up. If he has to close, he'll give them back."

"It's always crowded. How can he be having trouble?"

"It's almost all a beer crowd, a cheap beer crowd. He doesn't make much from that. That's why he's redecorating. It's a big risk, but given the location, it might work." Trevor closed in more. "Enough of that for tonight. It's late. We have to work in the morning. And I really want to..."

"He can have whichever of my paintings he wants. It'll clear them off the floor."

Trevor caught her eyes again. "No. You take payment. You earned it. They're worth it. So are you."

"He's your friend. Think he'd appreciate you not letting him have them free when he's struggling?"

"Yes he's my friend, but you ... you're my heart, Jen. My love. I'll put no one before you."

"Trevor Dade, if you're trying to butter me up, it's unnecessary. Help me get this paint off my hands and then take me to bed before I'm too tired."

With a grin, he laced his fingers with hers, held them up to their sides, and kissed her, pressing his body in close. She felt the paint squoosh between their hands, like a lubricant, while he moved his fingers as though he was mixing it on a palette. Breaking the kiss, she pulled her hands from his and drew on his chest with the orangish-brownish streaked oily colors. A large heart, with the tail of the heart sliding down the concave middle of his hairless chest and stomach. Jenna added more red to her fingers from the palette to give it more life, more vigor. He stood still, his lips hitched lightly with amusement, until she stopped.

"Not fair, when I can't do the same with you." He dipped his face in for a quick kiss.

"Hm. Don't move." She went to their makeshift clean up sink and rinsed her hands with mineral spirits, then dipped them in the soapy water bucket she always refilled before she started. He disobeyed and turned to watch her go over to close the door. As she returned to him, she pulled off her shirt, slipped out of her sweats, and pressed her naked body up to his half naked body, to imprint the heart in reverse onto herself. "You are my heart, too, Trevor Dade. Don't ever forget that."

His strong arms wrapped her close, painting traces of the meshed colors onto her back. They didn't bother to move to the bedroom. They couldn't, not without taking time to clean off the paint first and neither was willing to take the time.

"Trevor." Jenna caught her breath as she lay against him on the cool wood floor. "We have to go to bed before I fall asleep right here." She kissed a spot on his shoulder where there wasn't paint.

"I love you, my sweet Jenna." He returned the kiss, to her head. "Okay." He rolled away and stood, then offered a hand.

They wiped what they could off their skin with a fairly clean rag and went to shower. She figured it was better to leave paint remnants on her body than to bathe in mineral spirits. They used old towels to dry and didn't bother to get dressed before snuggling in bed.

He stroked her hair. "There's something else you're wrong about."

Now? He was finding something to criticize now?

"You are definitely charming. At least you are when you want to be. I think mostly you don't want to be, or won't let yourself, but you are when you allow it. How can someone who'll paint her boyfriend's body and rub herself against it not be charming?"

"That's different." She closed her eyes and took a deep breath. She never could have been so playful with Daniel. He didn't want paint on his skin. On his clothes, yes, but not his skin. And he was too likely to roll his eyes if she suggested anything silly. "I'm not. You are. It's part of why I fell for you, a big part of why I fell for you. I love your charming playful side, which is most of you. And it's why it bothers me so much to think you'll let them change that."

He squeezed her with a kiss to her head. "You worry too much."

"I have reason."

His chest rose and fell strong and soft and he caressed her bare shoulder. "I know. But you don't really think I'll lose my playful side, do you? The one that is so in lust with the way you tease me it's like a little boy with a dangling popsicle always within reach? As long as you stay that quiet hidden little tease no one else can see, I'll be that playful little boy tagging your heels like a puppy begging for attention." He grinned and rolled half on top of her. "Don't worry, my sweet Jenna. Doesn't matter what I have to do for work. I'm still here with you."

She wrapped her arms around his shoulders as he kissed her. It still felt like it had at first – sweet, wanting, wondrously passionate. She felt it deep within her soul, down to her toes, the wanting of him, the need to be closer, to let him farther in, to possess him fully.

Too soon, he moved back beside her. "Jen?" He sounded nearly asleep as he entwined her fingers in his own and rested them against his chest. "Was Daniel charming?"

She wasn't sure she heard him right, and hesitated.

"Should I not ask?"

"I don't think you ever have. Asked anything personal about him, I mean. Ever."

"Ah well, jealousy can be a real bitch. What can I say?"

"Jealousy? You're not jealous of Daniel."

"Like hell, I'm not." It was almost a whisper.

"Why would you be?"

He let out a quick snicker. "Other than how much you still miss him and that I know I can't hold a candle to him or to the hold he has on you, but hell, you look up to the man like crazy, and ... I guess I haven't asked because I didn't really want to know why you do. Yeah, he was good at art. I get that. I agree. But there's more. So was he charming? Debonair? I also get that he was handsome and girls kinda fell all over him. Still, you're deeper than that, so what is it?"

"He was debonair. Yes. Joan raised him to look and act elegant to fit what she wanted for him. But charming? No. He had trouble with critics because of it, because he hated shows and he hated mingling, so once his name was out there well, he pretty much refused to talk to them. Honestly, I'm not sure he liked people much in general. No, he wasn't charming. He was ... really nothing like you, other than being an artist."

Trevor frowned, silent.

"Why? What are thinking?"

"I don't think you want to know."

Jenna adjusted closer, leaned in against his body, her hand along his face. "I want to know. We tell each other everything, right? I tell you everything. Be honest with me. What do you want to know?"

"Then what was it about him that hooked you so hard? Was he good at conversation? Was he ... that good in bed? Maybe I shouldn't ask that. But what was it that made you so willing to marry him when you won't marry me? What is it?"

Her heart nearly stopped. She felt her breath pause. She couldn't imagine he didn't know. "Trevor." It came out as an expelled whisper. "How can you not know?"

"You won't talk about it. I've hinted. You change the subject. And I know, it's after three a.m. and we have to work tomorrow, but ...

damn, tonight turned me on, not just physically but mentally, more mentally than anything, and it reminded me full force why I love you so much and I want this to keep going. I have to know."

She gave him a soft kiss and stroked his face. "I could never be this way with him. Never. If you think I don't love you as much, you're wrong. No, he wasn't good at conversation other than art and no, not ... not so much in bed either. He was always ... so in control. So in charge and sure of himself and ... and I wasn't. Trevor, I was seventeen and feeling rebellious and largely unwanted and uninteresting and he made me feel like I was worthy of his attention, like I was interesting, and he wanted me. Yes, I looked up to him. To his inner strength. His calm. The way he never got ruffled. At the time, I needed that because I was so ruffled myself, always. So unsure. He was ... so far above me, you know? It was like ... being Degas' model. It elevated me to what I wasn't..."

"Oh Jen..."

"No, I have to keep going now or I won't. I don't talk about it because I don't like to admit it. I loved him because he wanted me so much. I'm ... not sure it was ever much more than that. I never felt with him what I do with you. He was in charge. I didn't work because he didn't want me to. He wanted me home with him and available. I was... Alan was right. As much as I fought him, he was right. Daniel was an escape. And yes, I loved him. I still do, but it's ... kind of like..."

"Falling for your rescuer?"

She pressed her lips together to stop the emotions threatening to overwhelm her body.

"All this time." He stroked fingers through her hair. "I was sure I couldn't live up to him. And Jen, he didn't deserve you. You can think all you want that he was above you, but it's not true. Not close."

She felt her head shake. "You ... let me be me. It's not because you can't live up to him. You are so much more. I have so much more with you. You don't make me feel stupid. You don't laugh at me for my odd ways and odd ideas. And I can tell you anything. I love you, Trevor. Truly. Inside out love you. I didn't need rescued when you came along. I just ... enjoyed your company, maybe more than anyone else in the world, ever."

"Enjoyed? Past tense?" His grin said he was trying to lighten the mood.

"Past." She brushed his lips. "And present. You're the only person on earth I'm this comfortable with. You're the only one I'm ever around who doesn't make me want to stay guarded to some extent."

"Do you expect that to change in the future?"

"No." She kissed his neck and cuddled down into him.

He wrapped his arms tight around her. "Then marry me, Jen. It won't change me, since I already feel married to you."

"Then leave it at that. It's working, right?"

"Jenna..."

She pulled back to see his face. "What I did to myself made me never want to get so stuck again. I can't stand the thought of it. Not because I couldn't have left. I could have, but I wouldn't, because I let myself think..." She grabbed a deep breath and held it. "That I had to stay because I said I would. I took the vow to stay. And I would have. I can't... I just can't do that again. I want this to be because I want it and for no other reason."

Jenna wasn't sure if he gave up because he understood or if he just fell asleep because he needed to sleep. Jealous. She felt horrible that he'd been jealous for so long, and she didn't know. He hadn't said. Maybe they weren't quite as open with each other as she'd thought.

Of course she'd exaggerated slightly. She'd loved Daniel more than she admitted, but she didn't know how to explain why without giving too many personal details. And some things belonged only to her.

Eight

Jenna could feel spring in the air. It was still cold but less frigid. She took it as a good sign since it was her first day as regular full time after the three weeks Trevor had asked her to wait, and she couldn't wait to tell him about her promotion. Margaret said they had only been waiting for Jenna to be ready; the position was waiting for her. Her manager also complimented her on the lost weight. It did matter, professionally ... just like Trevor's hair. She shouldn't have jumped him about it. Things were as they were. You could only fight so much.

She felt better anyway, was less tired at the end of every day, felt less irritable. Her mom had always told her she'd feel better if she lost weight. Of course at the time, she was only ten pounds above what the experts suggested for her 5'5" average frame, not enough to be badgered constantly by her perfect mother who only looked gaunt to Jenna.

Shoving the thought away so it wouldn't ruin her mood, she took the stairs up to her apartment instead of the elevator. She couldn't make herself do it when the kids were with her, but alone it was easy enough. At least it was getting easier. And she didn't have to run into her neighbors since none of them bothered with the stairs.

Jenna turned her key in the lock and stepped in to a luscious smell. Something Italian, she guessed. Maybe with lots of cheese. She would let herself splurge tonight, in celebration.

Trevor met her to help her out of her jacket and gave her a warm hug. "How was your day?"

"It was good, and it's better now." She grinned and set a light kiss on his lips as Anna came running up to grab her legs. Jenna rubbed the girl's head but kept her attention on her boyfriend. "Something smells wonderful."

"Hope so. Want to change while I get it on the table?"

"I can do that. You already..."

"I got it, but don't take your time. I'm starving." He patted her on the rear as she headed to her room. Usually she didn't appreciate it, but his wicked grin when she turned to scold him changed her mind.

She gave her babies big hugs, changed quickly, and gave Trevor a soft hug from behind when she returned. "I have news."

He set the pan down and turned to her. "Do you? Good news?"

"Hm. Yes. I got promoted. I'm now officially an assistant manager instead of officially just an assistant."

"Yeah? Nice, Jen. Ready to eat?"

Nice? "You know it'll pay twice as much."

"Yeah. That's good, Jen. I'm glad you're happy." He planted a kiss on her cheek as he passed by to the table and called the kids over.

"You're not."

"Can we talk after dinner? Like I said, I'm starving and this won't stay warm much longer. Made one of your favorites."

She breathed in the cheese and tomato sauce smell of his version of lasagna. He made it with linguini instead because he didn't like how the top layer of lasagna noodles slid off the beef and cheese mixture when he tried to cut it. Jenna always teased that his Italian ancestors would roll in their graves, but he figured they'd get over it.

It was as luscious as always, but she had trouble enjoying it after the way he shrugged off her promotion. It was a big deal. She was making something of herself, not only working for a paycheck. It was her first job she could actually brag about when they went out with his friends and he talked about his job and all the other women bragged about theirs. Now she could, too. She'd earned it, the hard way. It was a big deal.

He asked if she wasn't hungry. She truthfully said she was full already. Her sparse meals over the past few weeks made it impossible to eat much at a time without feeling nearly sick. As good as it was, it wasn't worth that.

Jenna insisted on cleaning up and listened as he tumbled around with the kids and complained about his too-full stomach as they kept pushing on him and laughing.

"There's mail for you. Anna, okay, hold on just a minute." Trevor pulled away from the girl and picked up a letter from the stack on the little desk Jenna ignored until she couldn't.

"Can it wait?" She dried her hands and rubbed lotion on to prevent the dry skin tug she hated. She was well ready for spring.

"I'm not sure. It's from someone named Givens. Not your mom. A *Delores* Givens? Recognize it?"

"My aunt. Are you kidding? Why?"

"I didn't open it."

Jenna fingered the envelope that looked like a card of some kind.

"Did I miss your birthday?" He was teasing.

"Right, because I wouldn't say something if you had. I doubt she even remembers when it is."

"So open it and find out."

She wasn't sure she wanted to open it. "No."

"Jen…"

She gave it back to him. "You can if you want. I'm not interested."

"Do you want me to?"

"I don't care. I haven't heard from them in nearly four years. Why should I care now?"

"Maybe someone died?"

She shrugged. "They have my phone number or they can let Alan know and he'll let me know if I need to." Jenna went to plop on the couch and smiled at her babies as they swarmed her with little arms and legs. "Were you two good for Aunt Nina today?"

Aaron nodded. Anna scrunched her mouth and looked away.

"Miss Anna? Were you not good today?"

"She got in trouble." Aaron whispered loud.

"Uh oh. For what?"

"She run fast in the house and breakded a plant."

"Broke, honey, not breakded. Oh Anna, not Aunt Nina's favorite plant? The big Jade?"

"No." Trevor came over with the opened card in his hand. "The small ivy thing on the corner. Not a big deal. She scolded Anna, who of course cried, and then she felt bad about scolding her."

"Anna Elaine, you know better. You made your aunt sad, didn't you?" At the girl's pout, Jenna gave in. "Okay, just don't do it again, right? Tell her you're sorry tomorrow."

"Yeah, not tomorrow. She has plans. We'll talk later." He held up the card. "An invitation to your parents' thirtieth anniversary party."

"Throw it out."

"It asks for an RSVP."

"Does it? Maybe I should have tried that for my events that never mattered to them. I'm not going, and I'm not answering."

"You don't at least want to show off our babies? Maybe they'll change their minds once they see how beautiful they're turning out, that they're well cared for…"

"It won't matter. No."

Trevor sighed and tossed the card back on the table. Why didn't he throw it out as she asked? Go to their anniversary party? Just so she could hear, again, about how she hadn't bothered to get married or to see her children get snubbed by their own grandparents? Not likely. What made her aunt think she would?

She got up and grabbed the card to drop in the trash.

He followed with a shake of the head. "I'm going in to the bar a while. I won't be late. And I have a sitter coming in the morning to keep the kids for the day. If all goes well, she may agree to three days a week to give Nina a break."

A sitter? In her house? With her babies? "Who is she?"

"She's a part time student. Keisha's sister recommended her, said she's great with her kids."

"Have you met her?"

"Me? No, but..."

"Are you kidding me? We're not leaving them with some student we don't even know."

"Keisha knows her well. She said..."

"I don't."

"She'll come an hour before you go to work so you can get to know her. Okay? And Jen, we need to talk when I get home. I know you're in a tizzy about the invitation right now, but we need to talk."

"I'm not in a tizzy. I just said no. So talk. But don't yell at me for being protective of my children..."

"*Our* children, and so am I, but something has to give."

"*Not* our children's safety."

"Fuck Jen, you think I'd risk that more than you would? She's safe and she's good with kids and unless you have a better option, we're kind of stuck tomorrow otherwise."

"Don't use that language with me. Save it for the bar. And I'll call in tomorrow..."

"You're going to call in three days a week?"

"No, but..."

"Then we need a sitter."

"I'll find one."

Trevor shoved a hand through what little hair he had left. "Right. Up to you, I guess. I'm heading out."

"Fine, but I'm not waiting up. I'm tired."

"Fine." He hugged the kids, told them to be good, and half slammed the door behind him.

Once they were in bed, Jenna plopped down onto her rocker, got up again to make a cup of tea, and paced until the microwave beeped. Had to talk. They *had to talk*? She dropped the peppermint tea bag in her cup and returned to the rocker, but there was no view worth looking at so she went to the couch and turned the television on low. Soon bored with it, she turned it off again and went to the art room, but she didn't want to paint, either. She stared down at the street, the wet gray street with neutral-colored cars drifting or speeding along – why did so many people buy boring neutral cars instead of something with color, with life? – and hardy Chicagoans in winter coats and hats or umbrellas, mostly neutral-colored umbrellas, mostly just black, and felt a huge scream well up inside. She wouldn't release it. Her babies were asleep and the apartment walls were thin and she'd been well-trained not to release it, to keep it in.

Except with her art.

Jenna set her cup down, scraped her palette of any color still there, and squirted on white and black and a touch of brown. Nothing else. She traced in outlines of buildings with a mixed light gray and a thin brush, then switched to a thicker brush and dabbed in darker gray, swirled white highlights at edges, added black for shadow directly on the canvas. Usually, she mixed the colors she wanted on her palette and then transferred them. Tonight she mixed them on the canvas as she painted. Grays. Neutrals. With brown here and there for accent. Buildings, short and tall. Streets. Cars. Umbrellas.

It was a fast painting, just an impression of her window scene mixed with her stirring thoughts. As she stepped back to look from a distance, Jenna decided it was fine as it was. She liked the sometimes sharp and sometimes blurred building edges. She liked the messiness of the sidewalk that made it look rainy. She especially liked the brown sky echoed by touches of brown on the windows and the sidewalks.

Grabbing the small brush again, she touched it to the brown left on her palette and signed her name as she always did if she bothered to sign them: *Jenna*. No last name. No last initial. Only Jenna. Appropriate for her artwork.

Thirtieth anniversary. Why had her aunt sent an invitation? Did Alan get one? Of course he would. Her mom absolutely adored Alan.

Dropping her brushes in the cleaner, she checked her hands, amazed there was no paint on them, collected her now-cold tea, and went to call Alan. It was late, nearly ten, but he would be up.

Jenna started when the lock turned in the door and looked at the clock. She hadn't realized it was so late.

Trevor gave her a curious look.

"Hey, I have to go. Sorry I kept you up so late."

As Alan said not to worry about it, Trevor told her she didn't have to get off the phone just because he was there.

Alan's voice interrupted. "Jen, you should think about it."

She nodded over the phone line. A bad habit. "Maybe. We'll see. Are you going?"

"Only if you do, for your support. There's no point otherwise."

"Thanks. I'll think about it." She caught Trevor's second curious gaze and said good night to her friend.

"Thought you weren't waiting up."

"I didn't. I mean I didn't realize it was so late. I'm going to bed."

"Jen." Trevor grabbed her arm. "I'm sorry I've been touchy. I have a big opportunity but I know what you'll say since it means you'd have to give up your job and..."

"No." Jenna pulled back. "I'm not giving up my job."

"You don't want to hear why?"

"Why does it matter? You already have your opportunity. You've had it the past three years. I gave mine up to stay home with Anna. Teaching was my idea, you know, and I gave that up since she came along so fast and you jumped on it and that's great. I'm glad. But Trevor, it's my turn."

"I'm not trying to take anything from you..."

"Yes you are. You just said..."

"Listen to me a minute."

"No." She set her cup in the sink and went to her room. Why should she? She'd done it before. She'd done it all her life, played second string, worked around everyone else. Why should she give up her job, her promotion?

"This could be good for both of us." Trevor came in and sat on the bed as she changed into her nightshirt.

"Right. Me giving up what I just earned and deserve would be good for me? How do you figure? Because you figure if you get more of what you want, it'll ... rub off? Support me better? I don't want you to support me. If I wanted that, I'd marry you and then it would be your place to do that, right? I can support myself, and my kids..."

"*Our* kids, Jen, and if you'd listen..."

"Ours. Right. But I'm the one who has to work everything around them while you go off and do anything you want to do, until all hours of the night so they barely see you and I barely see you. No. I'm not giving up my job. And I'll meet the sitter in the morning to see if she's okay since I had no notice...”

“I've been telling you Nina needs a break. I've told you.”

“You've also said it was fine.”

“It was, while you were part time, but Jen, she's nearly sixty years old and she has friends and her own interests and things she wants to do while she feels good enough...”

“Fine. Okay. I agreed. You fought it...”

“Because I thought you were...” He took a deep breath and stood. “I'm not sure this is an opportunity I can miss.”

“Fine. Then do it. But I'm not quitting. And I might go to the anniversary party if you want to come. It's up to you. I haven't decided yet but...”

“You changed your mind? That fast?”

“Alan thinks I should. He said it might be a good idea. At least for the kids, because they should have a chance to at least meet them.”

Trevor paced to the other side of the room. “Yeah, so did I. I've said that often. It didn't seem to matter.”

“Don't be like that. He knows more. He knows my parents...”

With a nod, he grabbed underwear from his drawer. “I'm going to shower. I have to sleep.”

When he crawled into bed beside her, he kept distance and just closed his eyes. Jenna held still, silent for some time, then rolled over to snuggle against him. “You know I love you, right?”

He grasped the hand she set on his chest. “Love you too, Jen. Night.”

She should have asked him, she supposed, about the opportunity. Maybe Nate wanted to make him a partner in the bar. Maybe the redecorating worked and it was picking up and ... and she hadn't asked. “Trevor?” She waited for the *hm* that said he was still awake enough to hear. “How's the bar doing? Going okay? You haven't said.”

“You haven't asked.”

“I don't usually have to.”

He was silent a while, then his chest rose hard and fell again. “It's doing well. Your uppity crowd is helping things along, so I guess I shouldn't bitch about it anymore.”

She pulled away and turned to her side. Her uppity crowd? There was nothing uppity about her. It was her parents' crowd, and maybe Alan's crowd, not hers.

Trevor rolled over and hugged her from behind. “It was supposed to be a joke.”

"I'm not uppity just because there are things I want and things I won't do because they don't work for me."

"I know, Jen. It was a joke. I'm sorry. Yes, Nate's doing well and it should be fine."

"Good. I'm glad."

"Are you? I was getting the idea you'd be happier if it went under."

She turned to face him. "I would never wish that. Why would you think so? Just because I get sick of never having you home? I won't apologize for that. I like your company. But I would never wish Nate and Keisha harm. You know I wouldn't."

"I know, I'm just... I enjoy it there, Jen. There's such a mix of personalities, of stories, of warm and open people who like to just sit and relax and talk about nothing. I enjoy that. I'd like it better if you were there but I understand it's overwhelming for you. I'll cut back now. I'll go less. And maybe you can go with me, just now and then..."

"Okay. You were right about the sitter. Thank you for finding one. I trust Keisha; it just makes me nervous. But I'll feel better about going with you if we don't overwhelm anyone with our kids."

He kissed her. A light kiss, grateful maybe. But it turned into more than that. And she was happy to let it. She'd sleep ... sometime. Over the weekend.

Nine

The drive to Peoria had her nerves on fire by the time they arrived. The late March overnight snow dump had been packed along the edges of the roads when they started out. Then the flurries began again and turned into huge flakes that made vision nearly impossible. Trevor didn't seem bothered. He slowed to the speed of the rest of traffic and just coasted along the interstate. It took nearly twice the time it should have. The kids started fussing after the first two hours. She kept them as calm as possible, trying not to let them add to Trevor's aggravation, even if he didn't seem aggravated. Anna finally fell asleep, and a handful of fruit snacks distracted Aaron. He settled for looking at books afterward, without his little sister annoying him.

Jenna calmed as they drove into the heart of Peoria and she looked out over familiar buildings. Her eyes caught the Civic Center and as always, she studied the modern building. She couldn't say she much liked the style, but Trevor did, and she had nice memories of it. Back in Eighty-two it opened with a Kenny Rogers concert, a big deal for her small city, or at least she thought it was. She was still married to Daniel then and she'd begged him to go with her. He had no interest, but Alan gave in. He also took Cheryl and Carrie so it wouldn't only be the two of them. Three years later Kenny returned, accompanied by Don Williams and Sawyer Brown. Jenna was in Chicago by then, living with Trevor, barely. Trevor agreed to go although she knew he didn't enjoy it a lot, but he didn't laugh at how excited she'd been not only to see her *Star Search* band live, but to see them in her hometown. He reminded her Peoria wasn't her hometown. She grew up fifteen miles away in a little no-stoplight town, but she claimed the city since that had been her home with Daniel, her choice to live with him there.

Jenna wasn't sure why the town your parents put you in should be more your hometown than the one you first chose on your own. To her, it wasn't. Well, she supposed it was. After all, it was where she'd met Alan, where she grew up with him, where she'd spent so much time walking around town, getting an ice cream cone, ambling around the park, or playing bad tennis games with friends who were equally as bad, usually her cousin Karla. And they didn't care how bad they were. It was for fun.

She guided Trevor to Alan's house since he only part remembered. It had been far too long. As they pulled into the drive, Jenna let out a huge sigh of relief and Trevor took her hand. "I got us here fine."

"I wasn't worried about you. It's everyone else who won't be more careful."

"You'll be happier if you stop worrying so much about everyone else."

"What they do affects me. If they drive like a maniac because they choose to do so and..."

He raised a warm hand to her face. "Worrying won't make it not happen. Take things as they come. Because I know, as strong as you are, whatever comes, you can handle. Stop worrying about it."

She figured he'd moved the conversation from other drivers to her family. Maybe he was right. She could make herself sick worrying about it and it would change nothing.

Alan came out the door in greeting and Trevor told her to go on in while he got sleeping Anna and the bags. She wouldn't, though. She wasn't about to just go in and leave everything to him. She didn't work that way.

Aaron was nearly asleep, also, and Jenna picked him up but he was too heavy when he was tired. She felt a pain through her stomach. An odd pain. Trevor was right; she had to stop worrying about everything. She was probably giving herself an ulcer.

"Let me take him." Alan didn't give her a choice and Aaron didn't complain. She went around to claim Anna from Trevor instead and Cheryl called her inside from the door as Justin ran out in his snow boots and coat to help carry bags. Such a precious child. She absolutely adored the boy.

"We were getting worried." Cheryl tried to take Anna but her daughter refused, which didn't at all bother her friend's wife. Nothing much seemed to bother her.

Alan set Aaron on his feet beside her since he was awake from the movement, told Trevor to set the bags just inside the door, and yelled for the twins to come move them to the guest room. Always in charge. It was comforting. He let Justin get the rest from the car alongside Trevor – it struck her that Alan's son had leeched onto her boyfriend in the way Aaron had leeched onto Justin – and took Anna, who didn't fuss at him, to let Jenna get out of her coat and shoes.

Anna knew Alan better. At times, her friend had come up to Chicago to visit alone, or only with Justin. Cheryl didn't like the drive.

The twins were too much hassle too often.

"You look like you could use a glass of wine." Alan finagled Anna from her coat, with Cheryl's help.

"At least one. I'm still not sure I should have come."

"I'm surprised you did."

She shrugged. "Trevor thought I should. I think he hopes Anna will be able to know her grandparents on one side since she doesn't have his parents. I keep warning him it won't be that way but he's such an optimist and he can't imagine… I'm really more concerned for his sake because I know they'll insult him."

"I would guess you're right, but maybe it'll be good for him to understand."

"Maybe." She looked over at Trevor as he came in and hoped it wouldn't hurt him too much. She was too used to it. It didn't matter for herself.

"You okay?" He shrugged out of his coat and let Cheryl take it.

Jenna hugged him. "Just tell me you won't let them bother you."

He pulled back. "Stop worrying."

Cheryl grabbed her and half pulled her to the couch, commenting on how much weight she'd lost, and asked if she was eating at all.

"Not enough. I keep telling her it isn't." Trevor took Anna when she reached for him but the girl woke fast with the other kids running around and ran off to join them.

"Are you feeling all right, sweetie?"

Cheryl was such a mother hen and she wasn't enough older than Jenna to talk to her as a mother, but she played nice. "I've just been busy." She put her attention on Alan. "On top of going full time, I've been staying up far too late painting."

"Oh? What are you working on?"

"This and that. Nothing exciting, just getting the feel again."

"I'm glad, but not at the expense of taking care of yourself."

"Maybe you can convince her of that while we're here." Trevor ran a hand down her back. "I can't seem to do it."

Alan gave him a sympathetic grin. "I've never had much luck convincing her of anything."

Jenna pulled herself from the conversation and watched the kids instead. J.R. flitted between them with his tail wagging hard enough it shook his whole back end. Anna was afraid of him and jumped away when he came near. Jenna could hardly blame her since the golden-haired stocky mutt was bigger than the two year old, but under Justin's care, he was also sweet and mild-natured. Jenna went over to sit on the floor and called the dog. He came and sat beside her and rested his head on her leg as she stroked his head. "Come here, Anna."

The girl frowned.

"It's okay. He's a nice puppy."

"Puppy?" Alan stood watching. "He's three years old. He's a dog. And if he's bothering her, I'll put him outside."

"He acts like a puppy." Jenna smiled at her friend's rolled eyes. "He's fine. She needs to get used to him. Anna, look, scratch behind his ears like this and he'll love you forever." With more encouragement and Justin at her side, the girl came over, slowly, and stepped back when J.R. raised his head to see her. "It's fine. Come here." Jenna reached for her hand and brushed the dog's head with it.

Anna smiled wide and plopped down beside them.

"You'll have to watch her around dogs now that she thinks they're safe." Alan crouched beside her.

"Thank you, I know. Not that she has much chance to be around them. This is good for her. Maybe I'll want one some day."

"In your apartment?"

"Well, no. But someday." Jenna couldn't count the times she'd pleaded with her mom to let her have a puppy since she didn't have a sibling and could rarely leave her yard until she was fourteen. She still wanted one, and it shocked her to realize how much she did. And a yard. A fence. Trees.

<div align="center">~~~</div>

Jenna woke to a pounding headache. She heard Trevor stirring in the room and called his name. "Ask Alan if he has something majorly strong for pain. I don't care what it is." She tried to look up at him but the light hurt her eyes. She heard him leave the room and heard him come back.

"Here sweetie." Cheryl put something in her hand. "Alan takes these for his work headaches. He said you should try it, but you should eat. Can I bring you something?"

"Can't." She swallowed the things with water and Trevor's help to sit up just enough, and set a hand on her stomach. He told her to just lie still and rest until it eased, he would take care of the kids.

Maybe it would be a good excuse not to go. She hadn't felt this bad since just after Daniel's funeral. Why should a family party bother her that much? She didn't care what they thought. Trevor said it was fine. But she was nauseated. And her head thumped. No matter what she told herself, she smelled disaster in the air.

Jenna at least looked decent in her black skirt and pale blue blouse, tucked in at the waist to emphasize her new figure. She still felt out of it from the pain medication and the pain still nudged at her, but she'd managed to eat some toast and a poached egg and she was on her feet.

She made herself walk to the car, and she made herself look calm and okay as Trevor followed Alan to their old neighborhood. But then she saw her parents' house and all of the cars lined up in front of it down the small street and she wasn't sure she wouldn't be sick.

Trevor parked at Alan's parents' house as directed, beside Alan, turned the engine off and asked if she was okay. She gave him a nod and he got the kids out. Jenna stayed put. No, she wasn't okay.

He opened her door. "Getting out?"

"No, let's go home. I can't do this."

"Jen, it's just your parents."

"You don't understand." She was going to be sick.

Alan's family came out to greet them and they were all bubbly and talkative and so okay with the whole thing. And she couldn't get out of the car. Trevor tried again. She didn't budge. Carrie tried to call her out for a hug. She couldn't. If he wanted to go, he could. She would wait right there.

"Jenna." Alan crouched beside her open door. "Come on."

"No. I can't do this. I ... I don't feel good enough..."

"It's nerves. An excuse. Come get it over with and then you'll feel better. If you leave this way, you'll feel worse."

"No I won't."

"You're the bigger person, Jen. You always have been. Show them you are. Walk in there with Trevor and with your gorgeous children and hold your head up as you should." He touched her face. "Because you have no reason not to, and you know you don't. So do I." He took her hand and stood. "Come on."

Alan at least knew part of what she felt. His own father abandoned him when he was young. Jenna knew he still saw the man at times and he was okay with it by now. But he was stronger than she was. And she wasn't sure being so insulted so often wasn't worse than if they'd left her for someone else who did want her. Alan's step father was wonderful to him. She could at least have had that.

He urged her again. She gripped his fingers tighter. "Don't go far."

"You know I won't."

Aaron clung to her as they got to the door. Jenna had to wonder if he remembered being there, but it wasn't likely since he'd been a baby. Her babies didn't understand the word *grandparents*. Joan was Grandma Joan, and as far as they knew, that was just her name.

Her heart raced when the door opened. The aunt who sent the invitation stared before recovering enough to speak. "Well Jenna. I didn't expect you. Since you didn't respond."

Jenna figured she meant she never expected her to accept. "We weren't sure if we could. You remember Alan and Cheryl and their children." She waited through polite agreement. "This is Trevor Dade, and Aaron you know, I think. This is our daughter, Anna."

"The boy has grown since I last saw him. It *has* been a long time. I'm sure your parents will be glad to see you."

Jenna bristled at the way her aunt ignored both Trevor and Anna but her boyfriend rubbed her back and gave her a wink, and half pushed her to follow.

As they were noticed, Alan and his family got nice greetings and Jenna got mostly stares. She set a hand on her chest when her racing heart got to her. Nerves. She had to stop. It didn't matter what they thought; Trevor wouldn't leave her because of her parents. It didn't matter.

"Are you okay?" Trevor, with their daughter in one arm, pulled her close with the other.

"I don't feel good. Let's just go."

"Jen..."

"I'm serious, Trevor. I'm..."

"Okay." He turned to start to tell Alan but a voice interrupted.

Karla. She gave Jenna a big hug. "Oh, I was *so* hoping you would *be here*. Don't tell me these are your *babies*. They're so *big*. Aaron was just *tiny* when I saw him last."

Jenna stroked her son's head when he ducked farther into her and introduced her daughter to her favorite cousin.

"They are just *beautiful*, Jenna. I can't *believe* I haven't come to see them. I kept thinking I would, but work keeps interfering and things just keep stacking up, you know, right? Mister Aaron, you are going to break hearts in a few years." She smiled when he pulled back and turned her attention to Anna. "She looks like you. She's so beautiful, Jenna. And this *has* to be the young stud I've heard so much about." Karla gave him a hug around the baby. "It's about time we met. I really have heard *so* much about you. I think everything Jenna ever says revolves around you. And the kids, of course. I'm Karla, the one who runs up your phone bill by talking her ear off. Jenna, wow, you weren't exaggerating. He *is* a doll."

Trevor chuckled. "I've heard plenty about you, as well. You're the one I'm supposed to keep the kids away from, right?"

Karla laughed. "Jenna, you've been talking too much. What have you told this innocent boy about me?"

"He's not all that innocent. He's with me, after all."

"Oh, I've *missed* you." Karla hugged her again, around Aaron. "And Alan, you haven't changed a bit. You still look forty."

"And it's still as much of a compliment as it was ten years ago."

"You know I'm kidding. You're still on my doable list, you know, right?" She winked and said hello to Cheryl and the kids, assuring Alan's wife it was just an old joke. "Come on, my sexier half is here somewhere. I want you to meet him."

"I have met him. I was in your wedding."

"I was talking to your young stud, silly. You and I can catch up later. I'm getting to know Trevor now that I can." Karla slipped her hand around his arm and nearly dragged him through the crowd, but she stopped at Louise Givens's voice.

Jenna turned to her mother. The racing heart that had started to calm picked up speed and her head began to thump again. She greeted her as politely as she could while people around watched.

"I didn't expect you would come." Louise Givens barely glanced at her then looked past her. "Alan, I suppose I have you to thank for making her attend."

"Mrs. Givens, I have never had any luck trying to force Jenna to do anything. I think you give me too much credit."

Her mother pulled her chin higher. "Yes, I suppose that would be asking too much of anyone."

"Actually, Trevor talked me into coming. I wasn't going to."

Her mother only glanced at her boyfriend. "Isn't that the name of that boy with hair in his face you were *with* at some point?"

Jenna's face heated.

Trevor chuckled. "That was me. I cut it for work."

"Oh?" Her mother was apparently on good behavior. She spoke directly to him. "And what is it that you do?"

"I'm an art teacher slash bartender. The teaching job brought the cut. Bar patrons don't care how I look as long as the drinks come out right."

Her mother stiffened. "I would imagine that's true, although I haven't personally had the experience to know. Do you teach college level? You look young for that."

"Grade school."

"Ah." There it was. *That* look. "Well, you are still ... together, I suppose, since you're here with..." She glanced at the kids.

"With our children." The heat spread throughout her body. "Yes, we're still together. You don't have to look surprised."

"*Our* children? I don't recall receiving a wedding invitation that would make him able to claim both."

Jenna clenched her fist behind Trevor's back. "There hasn't *been* a wedding, not since the one you chose not to attend. This is your granddaughter, by the way. Her name is Anna in case you wondered." She caught sight of her father approaching as Trevor answered about calling them both *their* children. Jenna soothed herself by rubbing Aaron's head. He reached for her to pick him up. Even as bad as she felt, she gave in and Aaron hugged her neck.

Karla jumped in and talked about how beautiful the kids were, claimed Anna who seemed fine with it, and pulled her husband up to introduce. Alan and Cheryl joined the conversation and Jenna backed away as far as she could. She pressed at the spot on her head thumping the hardest.

"Is it coming back?" Trevor spoke quietly in her ear.

"As soon as we walked in the door."

He took Aaron and brushed fingers against her temple and into her hair. "Don't let her get to you, Jen. It's nice that your cousin's here. Just enjoy spending time with her, and ask them over whenever they can. It would be nice for you. I'll agree so they know I'm happy to have them."

She nodded and leaned against him when he offered his free arm. Jenna heard Karla tease about being "lovebirds" and moved even closer to her boyfriend in response.

"Is that *necessary* to do here, in front of everyone?"

Jenna turned her head at her mother's voice. "Do what?"

"This is still our house, I want you to understand. Our rules still apply and we will have none of that here as long as I am still alive to enforce it."

She felt Alan's guarding stare but he stayed silent. Trevor began to move away. She held him tighter. "None of what, Mother? Affection?

Heaven forbid there be any affection shown in this house, right?"

"Jenna, lower your voice."

Something inside Jenna's head exploded, other than her throbbing skull. "Lower my *voice*? Say what you mean. You want me to leave."

"I did not say that. I'm *not* the one who wanted you out of this house. I simply expect my rules to be followed."

"No, you want me to be you. And that can't happen. I believe in showing affection, to my children, and to the man I love. I understand I didn't learn that here, but I do believe in it."

"It is bad enough that you embarrass me by bringing this man into my home, but you could act respectably as long as you are here."

"Embarrass you? I'm *embarrassing* you?"

"Did you think it wouldn't? The unmarried daughter with a *live-in* and two children from two inappropriate relationships? That was not how we raised you and I don't see why you have to throw it in my face, at our anniversary party, no less."

Jenna stood silently, feeling the stares, the tension surrounding her. *Embarrassing her*. How dare she? Who was embarrassing whom?

Alan moved up to her side. "Let's go, Jen."

She looked up at him, grateful for the assistance.

"You see, you're embarrassing your friend, as well. The only man in your life who would have been suitable for you, if you had been intelligent enough to listen to us."

Jenna glared back at her mother, but Alan stepped in. "No, she isn't. I have never been embarrassed by her. I think she has put up with enough of this and we don't need to stay any longer."

"Alan..."

"Mrs. Givens, Trevor is a good man, and he's good to your daughter. There is no need to insult him."

"Then why hasn't he bothered to marry her? Before they had a child preferably?"

Jenna cut him off. "I don't *want* to be married. He *has* asked, more than once. I like the way things are. I like living together just because we *want* to be together and not because some piece of paper says we're *supposed* to. I don't know why you think the way you did things were so right when you're so ashamed of the way I turned out. Maybe I didn't want things to turn out that way. I don't *want* my kids to resent me. I love Trevor, and I adore him, and I don't care who knows that, or who sees it, and I don't even care *what* you say about me anymore, but *don't* be rude to him. *That's* why I didn't want to come. I *knew* you would..."

"Jenna."

She started at her father's voice.

"Do not speak to your mother that way again."

Jenna's confidence bashed against the wall of her father. It always had. She'd never been able to stand up to him as she occasionally had with her mother. She'd rarely ever spoken to him.

"Maybe it's time for you to leave, as you did before."

Her insides tightened, fighting tears that tried to come. She was being kicked out of her parents' house, by her father, in front of everyone. And she couldn't argue.

"You don't deserve this, Jen." Trevor stepped in front of her, in between her and her parents, and touched her face. "Let's go. I'm sorry I pushed you to come. I didn't realize."

Mrs. Taylor put her arm around Jenna and told Louise Givens that if she had any sense, she would not only cherish her daughter as she should, she would be mortified at her own behavior. Her husband invited them next door to visit, agreeing with his wife and telling Jenna and Trevor to pay no attention.

Alan invited Karla and her husband. Jenna was glad they accepted. She refused more wine, a little nervous about her palpitations that by now were calmer but still there. She also refused the pie Mrs. Taylor offered, which got raised eyebrows from Alan since Jenna never refused her pies, but her stomach was too full of nerves. She leaned against her boyfriend and told herself she could at least be glad Trevor would never ask her to go back again. He understood now. Maybe it had been worth that.

Back at Alan's, she slipped into her sweats and sat with her kids and the puppy. It calmed her more to have the dog lay its head on her leg while she stroked its long soft fur. Maybe she did want one. They'd have to move; their apartment complex didn't allow pets. Maybe they could move close to a park in a place that would allow a big dog so when she took the kids out, she would feel safer. And when Trevor worked late and the kids were in bed, she would still have company.

Maybe getting away from her parents wasn't the biggest reason she'd accepted Daniel. Maybe it wasn't even because he needed her so much. Maybe it was mostly because he was always there; even when they didn't talk, he was there, every night, always. Until he left her.

Ten

Alan walked her out to the car as Cheryl waited on the front step to wave goodbye. "Are you okay?"

Watching Trevor buckle Anna into her car seat, Jenna sighed. "I said too much. I think I embarrassed him."

"Don't let your parents' issues be yours, Jen. You're different people. Remember that."

"They *are* my issues. We're supposed to learn from the past, aren't we?"

"Learn, yes. But, Jen..."

"Don't. Okay, just don't. I can't deal with more lectures right now. I'm tired and I just want to go home." She pulled away and went to her car door, started to get in, then looked back at her friend. He hadn't moved. He just stood there, waiting. She sighed and went back to give him a hug and an apology.

"Call any time you want to talk." He moved away and called across to Trevor. "Don't wait for a special occasion next time. We're always here if you want to get out of that horrendous city."

"And when you want to remember what a *real* city is like..."

Alan chuckled. "Have a good trip home. Let us know when you get in." He walked up to the car with Jenna, held the door, gave the kids another farewell, and told her to get more sleep.

She watched him as they pulled away. Part of her wanted to stay there, with Alan, where nothing was expected from her, where she didn't have to get up and go to work the next morning, where she felt more settled than she had at home recently.

Staring out at the houses along the hillside, on the little road that wound through Peoria's suburbs, she thought more about having her own house with a yard. No stairs or elevators to get to her door. Room for guests. Walls she could paint freely.

When they crossed McCluggage Bridge, she saw the Illinois River again as if she was standing in the window of the loft, watching for the Julia Belle that could no longer come. Her trees were all bare, stripped by winter's frosty fingers. They were still beautiful, gracefully powerful. If she ever had a house, the yard would be bordered by maples, and maybe a few apple trees. Apricot trees were possible, too, only because of her memories of the one hanging over the Taylor's driveway that made everyone dodge splattered apricots every summer. She supposed she wouldn't put it beside the driveway.

"Do you miss him more when you're here?"

She looked over at the jarring of her thoughts. "What?"

"When you're in his city. Does it bother you more?"

"Alan?"

Trevor's raised eyebrows told her she answered wrong. "Daniel, Jenna. I just wondered if being in his city made it harder."

"Oh. I wasn't..."

"What were you thinking about?"

She looked back out the window. They were off the bridge but she still caught glimpses of the river through the trees, whenever buildings didn't block the view.

"Alan?"

Jenna returned her gaze, silently. His tone sounded accusatory.

"He's who you miss?"

"Trees. I was thinking about the trees, and the river. I miss my trees, Trevor, the way I used to sit at the window and see hundreds of them and watch them change during the seasons. I miss that."

"You're not still happy in Chicago? You said you were."

She paused. Yes, she supposed she was. More so before he started holding the marriage thing over her head. Before she realized it was starting to come between them. But that had nothing to do with where they lived. "Yes, I'm happy in Chicago. I just miss my trees. It's not a big deal."

~~~

Jenna was glad she'd gone to the bar with Trevor the night before, but it upset her stomach again. The antacids controlled her symptoms well enough that she was eating better but she should have stayed with iced tea instead of the sweet cocktail Trevor mixed for her.

It was fun, though. They'd acted like a new couple. He hung on her, danced with her, teased mercilessly, and requested their song. Yes, she knew for certain her parents were wrong. Affection was absolutely okay to show. The way he'd gazed at her through the night said he was very thankful she believed it was.

She looked at the clock and knew she should get up. It was Sunday morning, though, and she allowed herself more leeway on Sundays. She'd stirred earlier when Trevor got up. He kissed her and told her to
~~~

go back to sleep and she moved over into his spot where the warmth left from his body penetrated hers and she was out again before he even closed the door behind him. He always kept the kids quiet while she slept in. And it was quiet, enough she nearly jumped when the door opened.

He sat next to her, pressing his cold cheeks against hers.

"You're freezing."

"It's nippy today."

"You were out?"

He grinned. "Ready to get up? I'm making brunch."

She slid her arms around his neck. "I love you, you know."

"Maybe I should make brunch more often." His eyes sparkled.

"Not because of that."

"I'm glad." He brushed her lips, softly, slowly, then pulled back. "Make sure you're covered. We have company."

Before she could ask, he slipped back out of the room.

With a yawn, she covered herself in decent sweats. Company likely only meant Joan or Nina, but she brushed her hair quick and her teeth, and went to find him.

She stopped just inside the main room. Trees. She had trees in her living room. Not real trees, but...

"What do you think?" Trevor took her side. "They were as close as I could get to your trees that would survive in an apartment, and they're supposed to be easy to maintain; just give them a drink now and then and feed them twice a year. If you want, I can paint their leaves in the fall, pull them off in the winter, and hope to hell they grow back again in the spring."

"Why...?"

"You said you missed your trees, on our way home from Peoria. You know what today is, right?"

Jenna struggled to remember the date so she could hopefully remember the significance of the date.

"Three years exactly from the day you asked me to move in with you. I'm using that as anniversary, so you can call it an anniversary gift, if you wish."

Her stomach cringed at the word, at the thought of the anniversary party. At his mixed in hint. But she had trees in her living room. "How did you do all this so fast?"

"With some help." He nodded across the room at Nate and a couple of guys she recognized from the bar who were entertaining the kids. "And I promised food in return, so I better get back to that."

"Trevor." She hugged him close. "You're too much."

"Do you like them?"

"Yes, it's wonderful, but the kids..." She could see them knocking them over and pulling off leaves to chew on.

"All non-toxic, and they've been told to leave mommy's trees alone." He went back into the kitchen, talking so she could still hear him. "I asked Alan about which to get and he gave me instructions to keep them alive."

She stood staring while he ran the kitchen and the guys across the room teased him about wearing the apron in the family. Trevor raised the egg whisk and suggested they shouldn't irritate someone about to serve them food. Then he looked over at Jenna and asked if she was just going to stand there or go in and sit down.

She caught his eyes. "I love you, you know."

"I know." He winked, and grinned, then returned to beating eggs.

Eleven

Jenna hung up with the second artist to cancel for her first show, the first she was fully in charge of, grabbed a deep breath, and went to tell Margaret. Her boss beckoned her in as she talked into the phone stuck between her head and shoulder, and made notes. She grimaced as she ended the call. "Please tell me you have good news."

"Should I come back later?"

"If you don't have good news."

Jenna threw her hands up and backed away but Margaret called to her. "I'm kidding. Mostly. What's up?"

"Neil just cancelled on us, on me. It leaves me with only four artists. Any ideas who else I can try to pull in last minute?"

"Part of your job to find them, Jenna."

"I know. Short of calling my mother-in-law, though..."

"So call her. Joan always knows the hottest new artists. I can't imagine she wouldn't help you."

"Except that I chose not to work for her gallery so I feel funny..."

"Jenna, this is business. Stop being so nice. You have it in you to do this. I know you do. That's why I kept pushing. Let yourself loose and do this. Find me an artist or two who will make us some money."

Let herself loose. As Trevor kept saying. It wasn't that easy.

"Of course..." Margaret stopped her. "You could always get that sexy boyfriend of yours to join the show. Isn't he a modernist? Buzz is really good about him, Jenna. Wouldn't hurt either of you to pull him in. I know Joan's studio is trying hard to get him."

"What?"

"You didn't know?"

Jenna felt her face warm. "No, I didn't know. But I can't use him to advance myself. It's not fair to ask."

"He's an artist. It's what he does..."

"Not so much anymore."

Margaret came around her desk, pulled Jenna back inside, and closed the door. "What's going on? I'm asking as your friend now, not your boss. You've been quiet lately. Are things between you..?"

"No, we're fine. He's just been more interested in teaching than painting lately. He has plenty for a show but I haven't heard him talk of doing one in months. He's talking about grad school, for teaching."

"Yeah? That's great. He's moving himself up." Margaret tilted her head with a curious gaze. "Why don't you look happy about it?"

"He's an artist. That's what he should do. The teaching is just to support us, although I keep telling him I can support myself and the kids with just a bit of help. He doesn't have to do this. And I wouldn't care, but he hasn't painted in weeks."

"All artists go through dry spells. Maybe this show will help pull him back, fuel him up. You should ask. Run it by him and see what he thinks. Don't push it, though. I would never risk your relationship for a show. If we have only four, we'll go with that and keep it low key. It'll be fine."

Fine? Nothing with the show was fine. She had glitches at every turn. Margaret constantly assured her it was only first show initiation; it happened. But it made Jenna wonder if she was in the wrong business.

Returning to her office, she hesitated, then obeyed her boss and called Joan to ask for a couple of names. She could ask Trevor if he was interested, for himself, not for her, but she wanted a couple more in line so it didn't look like she was desperate, like she *needed* him to do it for her.

Her mother-in-law chuckled through the line. "Well, yes, I can tell you the hottest name in modern art in the city right now, the one everyone is looking to grab."

"If you're not comfortable with that, I understand, Joan. Really, I don't want to swoop in on your territory..."

"He's not my territory. I would say you have first pickings."

"Me? I'm no one yet. Everyone I call tries to shrug me off."

Silence came from the other end. "What name are you using?"

"My name."

"Jenna Rhodes? They're shrugging off *Jenna Rhodes*?"

She paused. "Well. No. They're shrugging off Jenna Givens."

More silence.

"Joan, I know, I said I was only using it long enough not to get the job with Daniel's name, but then it seemed like I would be using his name to get ahead and I just don't feel right..."

"But it's who you are. It's your name."

"Technically."

"Technically? It is your name, Jenna. There's nothing wrong with using it. I used it to advance our gallery, as you know, along with his work. He understood it was business. Use your name. Get things rolling. They'll see you know what you're doing and you have every right to call yourself who and what you are."

Maybe Joan was right. But Trevor agreed with Jenna. Of course, maybe that was only because ... because he was jealous of Daniel. Or because he didn't want her to advance so far in her job.

Would he?

"Jenna, think about it, anyway. You *are* Jenna Rhodes. There's nothing disingenuine about using your name."

"Even if I feel more like Jenna Dade by now?" At the silence, she wasn't sure she should have said it. But she did, married or not. She felt more like Jenna Dade than she had ever felt like Jenna Rhodes, or even Jenna Givens, her maiden name. She was Jenna Dade. Even if not technically.

"Well, if you feel that way, maybe you should be. And before you argue or decide further, the hottest name I can give you is that one. Trevor Dade. I can sell anything he wants to send along to me, but then, so can Elucidations, if he's willing to do a show. We've been trying to get him. He keeps turning us down, as I'm sure you know."

She couldn't admit she hadn't known. But if he turned them down, Jenna sure couldn't ask him to do hers. Joan's gallery was the better bet, longer established, attractive to big spenders. Elucidations was coming along, but it wasn't there yet.

Joan did give her a couple of other names she thought had promise but her gallery didn't want them yet. It was a bit of a slam, but at least it was honest. She liked that about Joan; the woman was always straight-forward, although she did it politely.

Jenna called them both and asked if they would bring samples to her. They both jumped on the offer. She sure hoped at least one of them was good enough.

With the kids in bed, Trevor captured her against a wall, kissed her, and made her tell him about her day and her conversations with Margaret and Joan since she'd shrugged it off earlier when he asked. She told him everything except for the last name. She didn't mention that part of it. She did ask why he kept turning Joan down for a show.

He ran his hands along her sides and kissed her neck. "I have other interests right now." He peppered her face with soft kisses and paused longer at her mouth.

Other interests? Jenna stroked a hand over his head, pushing him away just enough to find his eyes. "Why? Tell me. A few years ago, you would have jumped at it. Tell me why you didn't. I want the full truth."

"Okay." He grasped her hands, pulled them up to her sides, and pressed them against the wall, then kissed her again. "Because you hate that world. You hate the parties, the attention. If I go that way, you would be drawn right back into it and I figure it's hard enough trying to get you to marry me, I don't need to make it harder."

"Trev..."

He stopped her with a deep kiss. As he released her, he spoke into her ear. "Jen, I'll do your show if you want it. It's up to you. Or I'll stay away from the whole thing as long as I can. But I want something, too. I want you to go away with me. I have an opportunity I can't pass up. I've wanted it too long, and I want you to go. For a year. All of us..."

She pulled back. "A year? I'd have to quit."

"Yes, you'd have to quit, but I'm sure they'll take you back."

"No, Trevor, I'm just... I can't pick up and leave for a year."

"You don't want to know where? You might change your mind."

"I finally have something of my own. I can't just..."

He released her and walked away.

"It's not fair to ask." She hardly heard her own voice, but she had to stand her ground. She'd worked too hard, given up too much. "If you have to do it, then do it. I don't want to hold you back. But I'm not moving. I'm not quitting. You'll have to go by yourself."

He turned and stared.

She almost backed down. A whole year away from him? She would hate it, but she could do it. She'd been through worse. He would be back. His daughter was there. Aaron, who he claimed as his son.

"Right. I guess I'm not *stuck*, am I? Okay, Jen. You've made it clear enough. I'll stop asking. Don't wait up." He grabbed his keys and coat and walked out.

~~~

Jenna knew the quality of the two artists Joan sent her wasn't as up to par as the rest of the show, but she agreed to them both. They had potential. Their color use was good. There was enough apparent symbolism that she could see something in it. Thank goodness Trevor had helped her understand modern art. It was her weak point. She had to wonder if it was a test that Margaret chose that for her first show. Knowing Margaret, Jenna wouldn't be at all surprised.

She would not suggest again that her boyfriend join her show. She wasn't even sure he would attend. He didn't wake her when he got
~~~

home the night before or when he left in the morning. Jenna felt him there but she made no move toward him. It wasn't fair to ask. She had no reason to give in. If he went, he would come back to see them, at least the kids. Or they could drive out to wherever he was for a vacation. She didn't like to fly, but she could if it was too many states away. Jenna supposed she should have at least asked.

Throwing her head back into work, her show, she looked over the arrangements so far. She had seven artists since Neil changed his mind suddenly and agreed to be there. A decent number, five canvases each. A small show but good enough for her first one. Margaret said she could keep it casual, low key, and Jenna was glad to do so. But she wanted every detail perfect. The theme was Local Inspirations and she contracted with three restaurants within a couple of blocks to provide a variety of finger sandwiches and other easy to eat foods for the buffet. Since she had space, she invited local high schools to choose two of their artists to display separately, not for sale, only for show. Jenna figured it would pull in the students' family and friends and they'd feel obligated to look at the work for sale, as well. There was a good chance no sales would come of that, but it would be a crowd and a good experience for her artists.

"Jenna, it's after six. You might want to go home."

She looked up at Margaret in the doorway, in her jacket, with her handbag tucked under her arm. "I didn't realize it was so late."

"The show will be fine. You're doing a great job. Go home to your sexy artist and your beautiful kids and come in late tomorrow to make up for the hours you've been working."

"Oh but I still have to..."

"There's time. I insist. Go. Get out of here so I can."

Trevor had the kids fed by the time she got home but he waited and ate with her, quietly, across from each other at the table while Aaron and Anna watched the Ninja Turtles, a video Trevor bought for them Jenna didn't like. Anna just loved it. Trevor's kid.

She asked about his day and he said only that it was fine. The quiet bothered her so she talked about the show, about her new artists, how it was fun to work with high school kids who were excited about being shown in a real gallery.

"I guess you decided not to have my work?"

She looked at him in surprise. "You didn't seem interested."

"I said it was up to you."

"Well." She sipped her lukewarm tea. "This is a little casual show. Obviously, since I had to add two amateur artists. You deserve more than that. Take Joan up on it if you want. Don't let me stop you."

He tossed his fork on his plate and pushed up from the table.

"Why are you upset?"

He shook his head and started to clear the kitchen.

"I'll do that. You cooked."

"I got it."

She stopped him and slid her hands up his stomach to his chest. "Why are you upset?"

"Hell, Jen, there are too many things..." He shook his head again and dropped his gaze, turned it toward the kids.

Too many things? "What have I done? I'm not trying to hold you down. If you want to hit big in the art world, do that. It's your choice. I can deal with it. It won't change how I feel. But don't do it because I asked. It has to be your choice. I won't push you into anything. You know I don't think anyone has a right to push someone to do anything they don't want to do."

"Shit, Jenna, does *everything* have to be about that?" He shrugged her off. "Does it *always* have to be about politics, about rebellion?"

"It's not about rebellion."

"The hell it isn't. Everything you do is always a fight against your parents. Shit, let it go already."

"What are you talking about? It has nothing to do with..."

"Jen, let it go. You proved your point. You went against what they wanted for you, but you're still allowing them to control you, and it's hurting you." He touched her hair. "Let it go."

"That's not true. How can you say that when I'm doing what I want to do?"

"Are you? Then why haven't you gone back to school? I know you want a degree, to teach or ... something else maybe, but I know you do and you won't because it's what *they* want."

"That's not true. We're tight enough as it is. I'd have to give up my job, or at least drop some hours and I like my job..."

"We're not that tight, Jen."

"We would be if I spent money on school instead of working."

"Use the money Daniel left you. What else is it doing?"

"No."

"Why not?"

She shook her head. She couldn't use that. It was her safety net.

"Because you don't trust me to be able to take care of our future? At least until you're done with school?"

"I won't do that to you. I didn't ask you to move in to take care of me. I can take care of myself."

Trevor's chest rose hard and fell slowly. "And see, I want us to depend on each other, to take care of each other. Why does that scare you so much?"

"Because I know it doesn't always work that way and I won't be in that position again."

"So you'd rather keep counting on Daniel's support than mine."

"No..."

"Or on Alan's."

"What?"

He walked away a few steps and kept his back turned. "Why did you let Alan talk you into going to that party when I couldn't?"

"That's not true. *You* got me to go."

"You said no to me and yes after you talked to him. And then you wouldn't get out of the car until Alan talked to you. Why?"

"Trevor ... why are you bringing him into this? He has nothing to do with anything."

"I thought that for a long time, Jen, but I'm not sure anymore."

Not sure? What was he not sure about? She went over to stand in front of him. "What is this really about?"

"Do you actually not have feelings for him? Or do you just tell yourself you don't because your parents want it? If they'd obected to him, would you be with him instead?"

Jenna felt her jaw drop, but she couldn't even start to put her confusion into words. Feelings for Alan? No. Never. Nothing other than friendship. If there had been, she would have given in to him before, after losing Daniel and before Trevor, when he'd tried. Her parents sure would have objected to that, too, since Alan was married. It had nothing to do with them.

"See, at this point..." He ran a hand through her hair. "I'm not sure much of the reason you're with me is because they don't approve. I hate to think so, but I can't figure why else you would..." He sighed and dropped his hand. "I'm not a political tool, Jen. I'm just a man. A man who adores you completely and loves you passionately, and I need to be more than that. I can't be your political tool anymore, your way of getting even with your parents."

"You're not... No, Trevor." Her stomach hurt. "I love you. You know I love you."

"Enough you're willing to let me go away for a year by myself. Jen, I... I don't know if I can keep doing this. I think you're not sure what you want and until you do..." He backed away. "I'm going to stay at Nina's a while. I think we both need time to think about this. We jumped into it too fast and..."

"No." She heard her kids laughing at the television and did her best not to cry. She let it hit her stomach instead.

He gave her a hug, a friendly hug. "I'll bring the kids home on the days they stay with Nina and come pick them up on Sundays and take them out so you'll still get part of your day off."

She pulled back. He had it planned out already. He'd been thinking about leaving her and hadn't said so. She couldn't even answer. Her tongue wouldn't work. He was leaving her.

Jenna felt numb as she watched him pack his important things and go hug the kids, telling them he would see them in a few days. It was Wednesday. He'd picked them up from Nina's. The next two days their sitter would come. And Trevor wouldn't be home.

Twelve

Jenna poured water in the base of her trees. They were starting to look dry already, though it had only been a few days since she last watered them. She scrunched her forehead, pausing in her work. How much was too much? Maybe she should call Alan and ask. She couldn't kill the things after Trevor put so much effort into getting them.

Two weeks. He'd moved out two weeks ago. He and the kids were out running somewhere. It was a beautiful day, fully spring, and she had every window open to catch any fresh air that made it past the buildings and factories. It wasn't like Peoria air, like the air when she sat outside with Alan and watched him and his men work.

She sighed. She wouldn't even care where she was if Trevor would just come back home where he belonged.

Monday was her big show and she didn't care about the stupid thing anymore. He wouldn't come. Why would he? She wouldn't if she were him. She thought about going in to work to recheck and make sure everything was in place, but Margaret gave her express orders to stay home and rest since Jenna had nearly passed out Friday. She was too tired, too nervous, too upset about Trevor. He didn't know and she wouldn't tell him. If he was going to come home, it had to be of his own volition, not for any reason except he wanted to be there.

Setting the watering pail down, she went to the window. Beautiful. Sunny. Warm. She should be outside in it, and if she had somewhere to go alone, she would, but she didn't. Maybe she should have asked to go with them. He hadn't offered and she couldn't make herself ask.

Jenna nearly called Alan, but she hadn't told him Trevor moved out and she didn't know how to talk to him without telling him and she didn't want anyone to know. Joan didn't even know.

With nothing better to do, she grabbed a book and stretched out on the couch. Margaret told her to rest, so she would rest and pretend the breeze coming in was fresh and crisp.

The door startled her and she pushed herself up. It was nearly dark, and she was chilled.

"Were you asleep?" Trevor turned lights on and eyed her from a distance as the kids jabbered about their day. They fed the ducks and sailed popsicle stick boats they made with him last weekend. Anna said something about loud noises that made her jump. Firecrackers, Trevor said. When they calmed, he asked again if she was asleep.

"I guess so. I was reading. Resting."

"Jen..." He told the kids to go wash their hands. For the first time since he left, he sat close to her. "Are you feeling all right? Seems like every time I see you, you're ... thinner or paler. Something. Maybe you should get a check up?"

"I'm fine. I'm just not sleeping well. Once this show is over... You know it's a big deal to me, right, even if it isn't a big deal show. It's not like Joan's or anything, but to me..."

"Yeah. Obviously. Enough to use your married name."

"What? No, I'm not."

He pulled a sheet of bright green paper from his back pocket and unfolded it. A flyer about her show. Jenna knew Margaret had them scattered... Jenna Rhodes. It said Jenna *Rhodes*.

Trevor stood and stared at her. "So you've decided, I guess."

"Decided what?"

"That this is your path? The wife of the great Daniel Rhodes now making her own name as a gallery manager? Or are you trying to work up to curator?"

"I didn't do this."

"Doing it yourself or letting Margaret do it is all the same. I knew she would..." He was interrupted by Anna's play yell as she ran over in and jumped at him.

"They've missed you."

He threw her a look. "Yeah, I have to go. Nate's expecting me. Jenna, the hell with the show. Take care of yourself. The kids need you healthy. Put them first."

She couldn't find her tongue enough to either yell at him or ... or press him up against the wall as he'd often done to her and kiss him. Ask him to stay. Tell him she missed him, too. Only her babies kept her from breaking down as he left. Put them first. What in the hell did he *think* she was doing?

~~~

Jenna felt her heart race again. There was no reason for it. The show was going well. Better than well. She had four sales already for three different artists, including one of the new ones. Margaret had looked at her sideways when she saw their work but said she trusted Jenna's instincts, and it had paid off. Even one sale for one of them
~~~

was good for a first show.

She wondered if she'd bothered to eat at all during the day. Maybe she hadn't. Trying to clear away from the crowd without notice, she had almost escaped when Margaret called her name. Turning, she saw Trevor. He was there. And dressed nice. Charmingly nice. Her sexy artist, as her boss called him. He looked every bit of it.

Jenna had finally admitted to Margaret that they broke up since her boss kept talking about seeing him there and Jenna couldn't let her think she would. She never expected him to come. Surprisingly, Nate and Keisha were with him. Since Jenna hadn't been to the bar in ages, and since she wasn't with Trevor any longer, she truly wouldn't have expected them to come. She felt almost guilty that they had.

Forcing her way over to greet them, Jenna tried hard to keep distance, to act professional, but Keisha hugged her in congratulations for her big event, and Nate gave her a huge smile and loudly enough for others to hear, said he came looking for more art to add to his own gallery. Jenna wasn't sure if it was just for show or if he was doing well enough by now to afford original art. She hoped he was, not for her sake or her artists, but for his.

"This is nice, Jen." Trevor's look of admiration was mixed with reserve she hated to see. "Congratulations on your first show."

"Thank you." She hugged him. She hadn't meant to, but he'd come to it, for her, even if they'd broken up, even if he didn't want her to do this, if it meant she didn't support him enough. He'd still come.

And he was wearing that scent again, that one she recognized from the beginning that she loved and couldn't think why it was familiar. She held him too long, enjoying the scent and his warm not-really-so-scrawny body against hers. He sighed and pulled her in tighter. He missed her, too. She could feel it.

Jenna backed up just enough to see his face. "I can't tell you what it means to me that you're here."

"You thought I wouldn't?"

"I thought you wouldn't, and I wouldn't blame you, but I'm glad you are. I'm..." She was suddenly light-headed.

He ran a hand through her hair. "You're not well."

"I ... haven't eaten. I was about to do that..."

"All day?"

Her head shook and when Margaret joined them, Trevor said he was taking Jenna back to her office to eat and she'd have to cover. Jenna tried to argue. He didn't allow it.

It was just the two of them as they waited for the runner Margaret assigned to take food to her and Trevor took her face in his hands. "You can't do this every time you have a show. You look like hell."

"Thank you. Nice of you to say when I have to go back out there and face everyone." Her stomach hurt, was queasy...

"Not what I meant. You're beautiful, Jen, and from what I saw you're charming the heck out of everyone. But I know you, and..."

She pressed her lips against his. She hadn't meant to, any more than she'd meant to hug him, but damn she wanted to take him home.

He snuggled her body in his arms and lowered his lips to her neck, stroked her back. "I love you, Jenna. I don't want us apart. Can we talk after the show?"

As she nodded against his shoulder, the girl came in with food and apologized for the interruption. Jenna couldn't care less if anyone saw them. He'd come to her show. He wanted to come home. She'd do what she could to make that work.

Her tension eased with Trevor there at her side and she ate well, quickly, and asked him to stay beside her for a while until she calmed better, admitting she was so stirred up inside she felt in a haze. She half expected him to say this wasn't the right line of work for her if she felt that way, but to his credit, he didn't.

Margaret nearly jumped on her when they went back out. Nate was at her side. "Why didn't you say you had such a big art supporter as a friend?"

Jenna was at a loss until her boss explained that Nate had picked up three paintings for his business. She glanced at Trevor. His look and the squeeze of his hand said he knew Nate's intentions when they came and it was fine.

"Aren't you Trevor Dade?" A young woman with punky baggy pink and black clothing and feathers dangling from her triple-pierced ears grabbed Trevor's arm. "You *are*. I follow your work. I don't see it here. How did I miss it?"

He gave her a grin. "Thank you, no, I'm only here in support."

"Oh, that sucks. When is your next show? I have a bunch of friends who say they'll come. Most don't have much money to buy but they talk a lot and they'll spread the word. It's so cool to meet you."

Someone spoke in Jenna's other ear and she squeezed Trevor's hand and released it to get back to work. She didn't go more than a few steps away; Jenna wanted him in her presence. She should have asked him again to add pieces to her show. For him. Not for her.

"So this is *the* Jenna Rhodes." A tall sandy-haired man pushed up in front of her, beside Margaret, and took her hand before she could offer it. "I thought you'd left Chicago."

"I'm sorry, have we met?" He was familiar, but she'd pushed so much of her past life away that she couldn't place him.

"No. We haven't met. I've heard your name. Of course. Everyone in the local art arena knows your name. You're not easy to find."

Something about him gave her the jitters and she pulled her hand away. "And why would you want to find me?" She saw Trevor's head turn. Paying attention.

Margaret stepped in. "Jenna, I'd like to introduce Kent Graham. He's been looking around at what you've done here and he's interested in sponsoring a show. I've asked him to come in during the next week to talk. You can verify a day. I wasn't sure enough of your schedule."

Sponsor a show? Her jitters became full-out uneasiness. Before she could figure out an answer, she felt a hand on her back and the guy looked beside her with a surprised expression. "You're Trevor Dade, am I right?"

"Yes." He nudged closer to Jenna.

The guy noted their closeness and a disdainful look flitted across his face, but then he smiled and offered his hand. "I didn't realize you were ... supporting Jenna's work?"

"And I didn't realize you were on a first name basis with her. You know each other?" Trevor didn't accept his hand. Margaret repeated the sponsorship interest.

"I heard. I think she's doing well enough without sponsorship."

Jenna cringed at Margaret's look. "Mr. Graham, it was nice to meet you and if you'll talk to Debbie, over there in the green blouse, she'll make an appointment with me for the coming week."

"I'll do that. And please, call me Kent. I prefer first names. It feels more friendly."

She felt Trevor tense and gave the Mr. Graham a polite smile, then excused herself and pulled her boyfriend away. "What are you doing?"

"You know him?"

"No. But he's a work contact and I'm at work."

"He's a sleazeball."

She was taken aback at his tone. She wasn't sure he'd ever spoken that way about anyone. "You know him?"

"Never met him, or heard of him. I can see it. You know he was eyeing you..."

"I noticed, but I can handle myself. It's hardly the first time I've been eyed, or hit on." Maybe she shouldn't have said it. "I can handle it. And I can't afford to lose what could be a good contact just because he was…"

"Okay, you're right. It was unprofessional. I'm sorry, but Jenna, I have a bad feeling about him."

She nudged closer, though not as close as she wanted since they were still in sight of art patrons. "Because he's part of that *uppity* class you always complain about." It was too obvious not to see it. His suit was expensive, perfectly cut and fitted, and his attitude matched.

"Maybe. But so were you and I didn't feel that way."

"No I wasn't. My parents were. I wasn't. You know that."

He held her eyes, silent a moment. "What time is this over?"

"Technically, ten. I can't say how long people will linger afterward and I have to stay until they leave. I can call when I'm done so you'll know. At Nina's?"

He stepped closer. "I'm staying."

Jenna wanted to think he meant staying with her, as in moving back home, but she couldn't assume. "Till the end of the show?"

"Yes. And don't worry, I'll keep my distance from that guy as long as he behaves well enough."

She smiled and backed away. She'd never seen this side of him. It was cute. Her sexy scrawny artist boy showing a jealous possessive side, ready to scrap with a guy in a suit just because he flirted a bit. It was really very adorable, too much to be annoyed at him.

Nate and Keisha couldn't stay long, but Trevor floated around talking with people, as charming as always, and always throwing the attention back at Jenna. She fielded a lot of questions about her husband in between, since Margaret had put his name on the flyer. Well, her name, but not her professional name.

By the time the last patron drifted out, it was close to eleven. A good sign, Margaret said, and sales were incredible. It would give Jenna a big bonus in her next check. Maybe she would use it to take time off and take her family on a short vacation somewhere, if Trevor could get the time off. They could wait until summer break. Maybe she would have another show before then and another bonus and make it an even better vacation.

As she organized her desk enough to be able to stand to look at it in the morning, she felt warm hands slide up her sides and turned to be enclosed in his arms and a nice long kiss.

"Ready to go?"

"Oh yes." She ran fingers through his hair. "Take me home, my scrawny little artist boy."

He raised his eyebrows and pulled her in tighter. "I think I'll have to remind you how *not* scrawny I am, or at least what I can do with what I have."

She grinned. "It hasn't been long enough I don't remember."

"Kids are staying at Nina's. I want to be alone with you."

As usual, she let him drive and they didn't talk on the way, or when they got home. He started to talk, but stopped, moved in, and kissed her hard, passionate, deep. They were mostly undressed before they ever got to the bedroom and for a second, she was reminded of the way Daniel made it up to her having to put up with his shows. She shoved the thought away as fast as it came and replaced it with the way she always felt far more fulfilled with Trevor. Always. In every way.

Breathing heavy, and lightheaded, she snuggled in against him and held tight, afraid to say anything to break the mood.

"Jen, come with me." He kissed her head. "I don't want to be away from you."

"Then stay." She returned the kiss to his chest, the soft skin that was already lightly tanned with spring's return. She had to wonder when he'd had his shirt off already. He tanned easily for a blond kid. His Italian roots, he said.

"I'm going to Italy."

She first thought her own thoughts interfered with what she heard and made it different than what he said. "What?"

"Italy, as I always wanted. I've been offered a teaching position there for a year. I'll see the work of the masters in person and part of my job will be comparing techniques and exchanging thoughts about similarities and differences of the classics and modern art. I'll do an article, peer reviewed, that'll be published. It's what I've always wanted to do and it's a huge honor. When I put in for it, I never expected to get it. I'll stay with a group of artists and ... I can't turn it down. Can you imagine what we can see in a year? Paid room and board. Four days of work, three of free time to see whatever we want to see. I leave in two weeks, during Easter break. Come with me."

Italy? For a year? "Two weeks?"

"I've been trying to tell you but you..."

"Trevor, I can't just take off for a year."

"Of course you can. Margaret will understand. You know she will. This is a once in a lifetime thing and it's only a year." He ran fingers through her hair. "This is my big dream, Jen. I never expected to be able to do it so soon. I've been saving all I can and we'll have plenty of run-around-Italy money. Let's do this, Jenna."

A year. Out of the country. "I ... I don't have a passport. The kids don't have passports. It takes more than two weeks..."

"Yes you do. I have them. The pictures I took of you... That paper I made you sign when you were too tired to ask what it was. We're all set. Just pack a few things you have to have and..."

"No." She sat up, pulling the blanket with. "Are you crazy? You got me a passport without my knowing? And the kids? How did you sign for Aaron? You're not his..."

"I'm legally his guardian. You signed that long ago, knowingly."

"For emergencies."

"For anything he needs." Trevor got up out of bed and stared at her. "Jen, I *am* his father. Just because it was Daniel's sperm, so what? I've been here for him since he was *six months* old. He calls *me* Daddy. You're making an issue of it now?"

"No, I just... I didn't know how you... It doesn't matter. Trevor, this is... I can't just pick up in two weeks and move overseas."

"Sure you can. I have someone who'll stay in the apartment and pay the rent to keep it for us. He's trustworthy, but if you'd rather, you can take Daniel's paintings to Joan to hold for you. I have everything set up." He sat next to her, fully nude and pleading. "Come with me. We'll soak up the culture, the artwork, the buildings you've studied and talked about. You can see them. I'll take you anywhere in the country you want to go." He slid a hand aside her head. "Come with me."

"They won't pay for me to go. And what would I do there when you're working?"

"Whatever you want. Paint. Learn Italian. Whatever. And ... they will, on condition."

"Condition?"

"If we're married, they will. And don't make a big thing of it. We can go to the courthouse, keep it simple. We don't have to announce it or tell anyone. It'll be nothing but a legality for the trip. You don't even have to change your name. In fact, with the passport in your current name, you probably shouldn't..."

"No." She heard it come out before she even thought. "Trevor, no, I..." Grabbing a deep breath, Jenna rolled out of bed and slipped her robe over her shoulders. And she went to him, stroked her fingers through his hair. "This is too much for me right now. I can't... I just can't. In a few years..."

"I may never get this opportunity again, Jen. Not a year, paid, with guarantee of a published article. You know how that will help my career? Now is when it's happening..."

"And you should go."

"Jenna..."

"You should. I want you to go."

He pulled her closer, between his legs. "Come with me."

"I can't. Go, Trevor. Go to Italy. I want you to write and tell me everything you're seeing, or at least the highlights. Call when you can, to talk to the kids..."

"And you think I want to leave them for a year?"

"I think ... you'll regret it if you don't. And they'll be fine. Call them when you can..."

He slid his hands under her robe to set on her waist and looked up into her eyes. "You'll move on. If I leave you for a year, we might as well call this off because you'll move on."

"Or you mean you will?"

He dropped his head against her stomach and she pulled back at the pain it caused. To cover, she lowered to her knees. "You know what? If that happens, then ... maybe it should."

"Jen..."

"We can't force it. It's why I wouldn't... I don't want you to feel..."

"Stuck?"

She nodded.

"Don't you get it, Jen? I *want* to be stuck to you. I *want* that. I don't want to lose you. I want you to come with me and..."

"If you're that sure I won't wait, why do you want me?"

He pulled her up closer, slid the robe off and let it fall to the floor. His fingers caressed her shoulder as his eyes wandered her body and returned to her eyes. "I want you ... because I love you. I've loved you since that night we met when I offered you a virgin drink and you blushed and then you kept watching me. I could tell you had no idea what to think but I could also see you were curious, interested, and I was so amused and flattered and ... and turned on. Damn Jen, I don't want this to end. I never expected as much as I got, as much I've had with you, but I still..."

"Things end, Trevor. Even good things end. You didn't want this.

As you told me, you weren't looking for anything steady or however you put it. You got more than you bargained for. And I'm glad you stayed this long. I've loved..." She swallowed hard to keep control. It was ending. She felt deeply that it was ending. She'd never expected him to stay as long as he did, and yet it wasn't long enough. But he had to go. And she couldn't.

"You're saying goodbye."

She felt her head nod and her eyes water.

He gasped a deep breath and rested his head on her shoulder. "How about we don't say goodbye? We'll see how it goes. Because I can't..." He raised his face to hers. "We stretch our wings for a year and ... see how it goes? Just ... a separation."

"A separation between non-married people is a breakup, Trevor. You know that."

"But if I feel married to you? Then what is it?"

"I think if you did, you wouldn't be leaving. You wouldn't have moved out." She touched his lips to stop whatever he was going to say. "It's okay. It's not like I'm going to run off and get married or anything, right? You know I won't. So it's really more up to you."

He stood and pulled her up with him. "Your mind is set."

"Yes."

"Then I guess I should go. I'll be back for a few things..."

"Stay tonight." She ran fingers along his bare hip.

His head shook. "I can't."

Jenna pulled her robe back on as he dressed and walked with him to the door.

"If you change your mind, Jen..."

"I won't."

With a light kiss, he walked out.

Thirteen

"I told you not to look at me."

"I know, but you're wrong. You're ravishing."

She chuckled. "Okay, I already let you in. You don't have to lie."

"I don't, ever."

Jenna finally looked into his eyes. She believed him completely. "Thank you, really. But I need to change."

"No thanks needed, really." Switching a bag from one hand to the other, he slipped out of his coat and dropped it onto the rack, in the same manner as Joan. "Come here, buddy, let's warm up these rolls while your mom..." He approached to take her son, then stopped and studied her face. "You don't have to change on my account, you know."

He was closer than he would have needed to be. And her uncombed hair, no makeup, and old robe didn't bother him in the slightest. Daniel would have teased about how she looked like an old housewife. Or maybe he hadn't been teasing.

Jenna pushed hair away from her face. "I'm glad I'm not bothering you, but I'll be more comfortable dressed." She hoped her breath was okay.

His grin changed, holding something in.

"I'll be right back." She edged away. She knew darn well he was watching her cross the room.

Jenna woke up, alone, and realized she'd been dreaming of him, of the first time he'd come to visit her in Peoria, for Christmas, of how he acted like Aaron's dad from the beginning.

She shouldn't have brought it up, said he wasn't. He was. As he said, he was Aaron's dad. Aaron called him Daddy just as Anna did.

If I feel like your husband..?

Trevor. No. This can't be done. She had half a mind to call him and tell him she'd go to Italy. And do what? Just be the painter's wife again? How could she go back to that? She'd been so numb the night before when he left that she fell back in to bed and right to sleep. A glance at the clock told her it was nearly six. She had to get up and ready for work soon. Her job. The one that meant so damned much to her she lost him over it, and she didn't want to go.

Tears started slowly and she told herself to stop. But it turned into sobs, hard deep driving sobs that wracked her body. As hard as after Daniel's funeral when everyone went back home and on with their lives and she was alone with Aaron. Her parents hadn't even gone to the funeral. Nothing. She heard no word from them. She'd been stupid to go to their stupid anniversary party. It just showed a lack of pride that she would go after they didn't even come to her husband's funeral after not being there through any of the time she was losing him.

Trevor had apologized several times afterward for pushing her to go. He just didn't understand. He said he couldn't possibly understand. Why did they have her if they were going to be that way?

She couldn't answer. Maybe they didn't mean to... Jenna gasped into her wet pillow. Did they not mean to? Was she a mistake? Did they feel burdened with her when she was only an accident? She found herself laughing at the thought. Was it all because they got *stuck* with her? Was that why she was so worried about anyone, about Trevor, feeling stuck?

He had to go.

It served them right. If they hadn't wanted her anyway, it served them right to be deprived of her children, her beautiful children.

She went from insane laughing back to crying. She was depriving her children of their daddy for a year because ... because she wanted her own life. But why shouldn't she?

A sharp pain hit her stomach. She had to eat more, better, sleep more. Except she knew it wasn't lack of food or sleep. She knew.

But he wouldn't. Not until after he left. She would not hold him back. She wouldn't force him into anything, or out of anything, just because she... Not again.

<div align="center">~~~</div>

The phone stirred her with its insistent ring and she forced her swollen eyes open to see the time. After ten. No. She rolled over to grab it and cringed at another pain and wearily said hello.

"Jenna? Are you all right?"

Margaret. She forced an answer. "Sorry. I was asleep. I'm late."

"Are you all right? Am I interrupting? Trevor's still there?"

"No. You're not..." She shoved a hand against her stomach. "He's not here. He left."

"Left? As in..?"

"As in he left. We broke up." Tears started again and she did her best to stop them. Margaret tried to talk to her more but she couldn't. She said she'd be there in about an hour...

"No. Take the day off. Rest. Leave the kids with their aunt and just rest, honey. You've earned it. We'll talk tomorrow. Call me if you need me. I'll be here all day."

At the end of the day, she dressed as though she'd been at work and went to pick up her babies. Trevor wasn't there. She figured it was a good thing he wasn't because she would probably break down. Aunt Nina watched her with concern, or consternation, Jenna wasn't sure, and she didn't stay. She got the kids in the car, drove through a fast food stop, and went home.

Alone. She figured she might as well pull herself together and get used to it. When her alarm clock went off, it would signal a new start.

~~~

Tomorrow. He was leaving in the morning and although Jenna agreed to dinner with him alone before she picked up the kids, they hardly talked. She figured there wasn't much to say. For old times sake, they went to the Chinese takeout where he'd picked up lunch the day he'd come to badger her about going with him on the architecture tour. On the boat. Which she'd loved. If he fell for her the night they met, she fell for him on that tour when she found it so easy to talk with him and when the wind kept blowing her hair in her face and he brushed it away. Yes, she'd fallen for him at that moment.

He'd been so young and raring to go then. Unencumbered. Light-hearted. Easy to be with. Only three years ago. It felt so much longer.

They were the only ones in the restaurant that she couldn't quite call a restaurant. Two small tables were pushed against the one wall of windows with two chairs each that people normally used only to wait for orders. The tables were sticky and she hoped it was from cleaner. The black and white matte vinyl floor showed gray shoe prints. The counter was cheap and small and she could see over it into the tiny cooking area where they spoke rapidly and loud and she had no idea what they said. When the door opened, the newcomers had to try not to hit their chairs and looked at them as though wondering why on earth they would actually eat in there. But the food was good.

He told her more about what his job entailed and as he talked, his excitement was tinged with something he wouldn't say. Doubt maybe, about leaving the kids. He'd already left her, so she couldn't imagine it was much of that. They'd hardly talked since he moved out.

She couldn't finish hers, as she never could, and she put the lid on to take home for lunch the next day. He held the door as they left and
~~~

opened the car door and they stayed silent on the way back to Nina's.

They also didn't get out of the van when he turned off the engine. Her van that he drove because she didn't want to, and she wouldn't sell it as he suggested, as Alan suggested. It was Daniel's van. It didn't bother Trevor in the least to drive it except that he had to put gas in it more often than he appreciated. She'd sold Daniel's car that he got as he started earning well to his sister for too low a price, but Jenna didn't want it and she didn't need three vehicles.

"Nina says you can leave the van parked here."

Jenna nodded.

"You're quiet tonight." He peered at her, his hands on the steering wheel.

"I don't know what to say."

"Say anything. Just talk to me. We used to talk over the phone all the time before you moved to Chicago. About anything. Just to talk."

"Before you left me. Before I knew you would."

He dropped his head and his hands with a sigh. "Okay. Guess we better go in. I want time with the kids tonight before you go."

She nodded again and got out. What was there to say? She walked with him to the door, let him open and hold it as always, and let the kids take over. She did her best not to think of how they would miss him, or how she would, and she pushed the time way too late before she made herself pull them away.

He walked them to her car and told them he loved them and to be good and to draw pictures for Mommy to send to him and he would draw pictures to send back to them. Always the artist. Jenna nearly laughed, and would have, if her heart hadn't sunk so low into her stomach she could hardly breathe.

He again opened her door. Jenna stood beside it trying to figure out what to say. It didn't matter. Whatever she said, he was leaving the country in the morning.

"Take care of yourself, Jen. Start eating better, okay? Nina's here for you if you need her. Nate said to call him, too, any time. He's good at fixing things so if something happens and you can't get the building maintenance there fast enough, call him. Okay? Tell me you will if you need."

"I'll be fine. I can..."

"You can take care of yourself. I know, Jen, but we all need a hand now and then. There's no shame in asking. So tell me you'll call Nate if you need help."

She doubted she would, but she supposed it was possible. "Okay."

"And watch out for that Graham guy. Something about him truly bothers me. It's not jealousy. I've seen guys hit on you and it didn't worry me at all, but he's..."

"I will. Just take care of yourself around all those pretty Italian girls. Make sure you leave time for your art, too." She tried to grin but it didn't come out well.

He set a hand on her face. "They won't hold a candle to you, and I don't care how mushy that sounds. I mean it. Tell me you'll talk to me when I call."

"Of course. But I need to go and get the kids in bed. It's late..."

He slid the hand down her arm to touch her fingers, and stepped back. "I love you, Jenna. You're the first person I want to see when I get back. Remember that. Because I won't change my mind, either."

She gritted her teeth with a light nod and got in the car. But she couldn't close the door. She sat a few seconds, put the key in the ignition, and got back out. Covering the few steps quickly, she threw her arms around him and kissed him hard, glad he returned it just as passionately. When she finally made herself release him, she stroked his face. "I love you, too, my scrawny little artist boy. I want you to have fun and learn a lot and teach a lot and ... and come home to us. And we'll see where things go from there. Yes?"

"Jen, if you're still free in a year when I come home, you damn well better hold onto your socks. You have a year to think about what you want and I'll want to know by then. One way or another." With a light kiss, he released her. "Call when you get home so I know you are. Or should I come with you and..."

"No. It's hard enough this way, and I have to get used to it."

<center>~~~</center>

Jenna congratulated herself on holding it together at Nina's the night before, and on letting him leave for Italy without a fuss. The one year deadline grated on her but it also comforted her. He didn't act like it was over, just on sabbatical. Maybe that was all they needed. A year would give her time with her job to see if it's what she wanted to stay with, as she thought she might, although she still didn't like the party-like shows. He didn't understand why she always complained about going to his and then signed up to organize them for strangers. It was different. At Trevor's shows, she was only his girlfriend and had to act right for his crowd. At work, she was in charge, or at least mostly in charge, and how she acted affected herself, not him. She could be who she was. As Daniel made her promise.

Aaron had cried when they left Trevor behind since he understood enough to know his daddy would be away a long time, and Anna cried because Aaron did. Jenna didn't. She was the mom and she'd prepared herself for it and everything was fine. It had to be fine. She was lucky to have had what she did with him.

She was late for work due to comforting the kids as she dropped them off and promised she'd get off early and take them for pizza and ice cream with lots of sprinkles. It worked, although the thought of pizza and ice cream made Jenna nearly sick. She knew she should make an appointment but she wasn't ready yet. Without confirmation, she didn't have to acknowledge it, other than to be careful what she ate.

A meeting with Kent Graham was not what she needed, but she was prepared for that, as well, and she'd put him off a week longer than he wanted already.

When Margaret knocked at her office door, Jenna stood to greet him and asked him to come in and have a seat. She still didn't like him, and Trevor's warning buzzed her head, but it was business. She could handle it.

He made himself quite comfortable, and again, Jenna felt like she should know him. As she pulled her thoughts and her papers together to set aside, he pulled his chair closer to her desk. "Have we met? Of course I mean other than at your show. I have a feeling we have."

"Do you? I wondered, also. It must have been at another art show or at an artist party."

"You must be right, but it would have been at a show. I can't say that I've ever been to an artist party."

"Lucky you."

He smiled. "If you don't like them, why do you go?"

"When you're with an artist, that happens."

"Ah. You mean your husband dragged you to them? Or your ... boyfriend? Should I not assume Mr. Dade was your date?"

"I think we should get to work. What kind of show do you have in mind? Do you have certain artists you want featured?"

"I like realism. And no, I'm not in touch with artists."

"Then why the interest in sponsoring a show?"

Mr. Graham leaned back with an annoying smirk. "I like art. I don't have to personally know artists to like art, isn't that true?"

He was a condescending ass, but she tried not to let that thought show on her face. "There's generally something in it for anyone willing to sponsor a show. I know how it works. I *am* in the business. So what's in it for you and what is it you want from me?"

He leaned forward again. "Loaded question."

She didn't like his expression. "No. A simple question."

"I suppose it might be, if you want to keep it all business. Before I put my foot too far in my mouth, is Mr. Dade your ... regular date?"

Not anymore. But she wasn't stupid enough to say so. "That's not pertinent to the show, and yes, this is and will be only business."

"Well then." He straightened and said he was fortunate enough for his own business to being doing very well and wanted to give back to those who afforded his relaxation when he was away from work. He'd been to galleries across the nation and overseas, listing museum names that made Jenna terribly jealous – the Louvre, the Prado, the Uffizi. Italy's Uffizi, which she could go see with Trevor if she'd been smart enough to do it. She brought herself back enough to hear him say art was a passion he had no talent for, although he tried, so he wanted to support those who did have it.

It seemed honest enough. Jenna figured she could work with that.

<div align="center">~~~</div>

She should have gone with him. Jenna's first waking thought after her now everyday thought of hating her alarm clock with a passion was that she should have gone with him.

She expected him to call in sometime during the day, although he would call Nina, not her, since she was at work and he wouldn't want to wait for a receptionist to patch him through, but Nina promised she would let Jenna know just as soon as she heard he was in safely.

Calling in to tell the kids to get up, she went to make a small pot of coffee and wondered if it was too late to go. Of course it was too late. They had to be married first and they couldn't do that with an ocean between them. And she didn't want to marry him; she only wanted to be with him. How many men would jump at that? Why couldn't he be happy enough with it?

"Ari not getting up." Anna's precious little sleepy voice preceded her into the kitchen.

"Oh I think he'll have to. Mommy has to work." She rubbed her daughter's head. "Come on, baby. Help me get him up." Jenna started to lecture Aaron since he was awake and stubbornly just lying there, but he didn't look right. "What's wrong, sweetie?" She set a hand on his forehead. It was warm. "You don't feel good?"

He shook his head and pointed at his neck.

"Oh baby. I'm sorry." She smoothed her hand over his dark hair. "I'll bring you some chicken broth and some medicine, okay? We'll get you all better. Come Anna. You can help me." Maybe she could keep the girl away enough she wouldn't get it, too, though that was unlikely as much as they climbed all over each other.

Shoving a cup of water in the microwave, she called in to work, added chicken bouillon crystals into it, and let Anna stir as she went to find the children's Tylenol. A bad day to miss work. Mr. Graham had an appointment with her and Jenna had a hundred things to do since she left early the night before.

As she started to take the cup in to *Ari*, the phone rang. She nearly ignored it but if Trevor was in, he would call there as this time of the morning. It wasn't Trevor. Margaret threw a fit about her calling in. Jenna asked what she was supposed to do. Take them to their aunt's as usual, her boss demanded.

"I can't take them there sick so she gets it, too. I already hope they didn't give it to her."

"Heavens, Jenna. Get yourself a real babysitter you can count on. Full time. I need you today. Call someone."

With a promise that she would try, she went in to her son and sat beside him. Leave him with a fever and sore throat? How could she? He shook his head when she tried to get him to take a swallow, so she offered the medicine with a promise it would make him feel better. He was so good about it, always, but he hesitated.

"Aaron, come on baby. I know it hurts but this will help." She stroked his hair above his warm forehead. "How about if I lie down with you?" He nodded and she made a deal. Medicine first. She nearly cried at the pain on his face as he swallowed. "That's a good boy. Let me get Anna settled with cartoons and I'll come right back."

She also had to call Nina to tell her they weren't coming. Margaret would have to deal with it. She had to take him in to the doctor. A babysitter couldn't do that.

Strep throat. Three hours at the emergency room with both kids by herself and two prescriptions since Anna was starting to show the symptoms, and Jenna was exhausted. She called Nina to let her know she should get checked, but the feisty woman said she never got that and Jenna should bring them to her and try not to get it herself. She wouldn't. Not until Aaron looked better.

Trevor often enough hassled her about worrying too much, but he could hassle her to the ends of the earth and she would still worry. He was too much like his dad, built like his dad, sick easily. How could she not worry?

And Trevor hadn't called in yet. He should have. Where was he?

~~~

She told Margaret with a hoarse burning throat that the kids were better but she had it and could hardly talk, and her boss said to take aspirin and get in there. She'd missed two days already. She could stay away from others as she worked, but she *had* to be there.

Her babysitter refused to come although it was her day because she was too susceptible to strep and wouldn't risk it. Jenna called Nina. The kids had been on antibiotics more than twenty-four hours so they were safe. Jenna would keep her distance.

Anna and Aaron were both bouncy like crazy since they finally felt good and Jenna had a heck of a time getting them ready since she didn't and she could hardly talk. She'd be late but Margaret would have to deal with it. By the time she got to Nina's she was so exhausted she could hardly move.

"Oh honey." Nina took her hand. "You look awful. Did you see the doctor yourself?"

She shook her head.

"Go do that."

"I have to work." She cringed at the pain.

"Like heck you do. The place won't fall down without you. Come here." Nina grasped her arm and pulled her to the couch. "Now just sit down and let me take care of things. I'll call your boss. She won't dare argue with me."

"Did Trevor call?"

Nina stopped, her energy suddenly faded. "Not yet. But I'm sure he's fine. You know how young men are. He's lost in where he is and what's he's seeing and just forgot. I know he's fine. Lie down, honey. I'm going to get you to the doctor's so you can get better."

She shook her head again. It did no good. Nina told Aaron to go find a blanket and forced Jenna to lie down on the deep couch.

"Jenna, honey."

She woke to Nina's voice and a soft shake. The light in the room
~~~

had dimmed. She must have slept a couple of hours or so after Nate brought her back from the hosital visit. It was Nina's idea for him to take her so the kids could stay in. The last thing she remembered was sipping at the homemade chicken soup.

"Sorry to wake you but Trevor's on the phone."

She shoved herself up. "Is he okay?"

"He's fine now. Seems he was down with the same thing and they had him locked in an infirmary. Aaron's talking to him now. He asked to talk to you. Are you up to it?"

She nodded. Her throat still burned but it didn't matter. At least they hadn't made her stay at the hospital more than a few hours while they gave her an IV and took tests, including a monitor for the baby that so far was surviving through Jenna's neglect. They lectured her about not eating, not sleeping, being sick for so long. And she was forbidden to work for the next week.

When Nina handed her the phone, she did her best not to let him hear it, but he'd been told. About the illness. No one knew about the baby. Not yet. She had to tell him first and she couldn't do that yet, either. He just got there. She wanted him to entrench himself in his work before she told him. If she told him. She was still undecided on that point.

"Hey, I hear you're down with this, too." His voice nearly made her cry, and she nearly changed her mind. She wanted him home. "So I don't want you to talk much. I just wanted to say I'm sorry for not calling in. I tried. The school was supposed to get you a message. Aunt Nina said they didn't. I'm so sorry."

"It's okay. I'm glad you're well."

"You sound awful."

"Thank you."

He chuckled. "I gave Aunt Nina orders to take care of you, so don't fight her. This thing is bad. I'm rarely knocked out like I was. It's good to hear your voice, Jen. I'll call back when you can talk without pain. Just wanted to say I love you and I miss you already."

She fought back tears. "Me too."

"Okay, I have to go. Give me to Nina and go back to sleep." He paused. "I do love you like crazy, my sweet Jenna. Remember that."

She pinched her lips together to prevent tears and gave the phone back. She wanted him home. Maybe she'd tell him she'd marry him if he just came home.

Fourteen

Nina fought her about it, but Jenna had to get back to work. She wasn't contagious anymore. She could talk. And she was tired but not so exhausted she could hardly make it to the bathroom and back.

Margaret asked how she was, with a touch of snippiness, and filled her in with a constant stream of business all the way to Jenna's office where she sat down to regroup. She was tired just getting from the car to her chair. She shouldn't have gone in.

"Mr. Graham will be here in about twenty minutes."

Jenna grimaced. "I'm not up to that today."

"His show is already behind schedule. You are a professional. A little illness can't hold you back forever." Margaret pulled a chair close. "I'm sorry. I should be more sympathetic, but Elucidations has a huge chance to grow with the Graham account and he refuses to work with anyone but you. I need you, Jenna. The gallery needs you."

Deciding to be flattered instead of angry, since she had no energy to be angry, Jenna sifted through her paperwork to try to figure out where they left off and where they needed to go next and felt a pain in her abdomen. She closed her eyes and breathed deep and slow until it subsided. She shouldn't have gone in.

"Let me take you to lunch." Kent Graham leaned over her desk. "We've made great progress. I'd love to thank you for it since I can see you don't want to be here yet. Are you feeling all right, Jenna?"

"Thank you, I'm fine, but I need to work through lunch. I'm way behind on everything."

"You can't get over that bug if you don't eat."

Something about him reminded her of her father, if her father had bothered to talk to her. She'd seen him be friendly with enough people in town to know he could be.

"Is your silence a yes?" He smirked.

"No. But thank you. I brought lunch with me."

"Ah, but I'm offering a nice quiet stress-free lunch at Petterino's. I can convince Margaret we need an hour for a working lunch. We don't have to actually work." He winked. "It looks like you could use good food, relaxation ... good company?"

Petterino's. Trevor took her there for their anniversary the year before, the anniversary of their first kiss. The man found anniversaries for everything under the sun. An Italian place. She loved it. But it was expensive, beautiful, more elegant than she was dressed for, and she would not go out with this guy. He would be too easy to encourage. "Thank you, Mr. Graham, but no. Like I said, I have a lot of work..."

"Kent. Jenna, please call me by my first name."

"It's unprofessional."

He sat back in his chair. "All right. We'll play it your way. How about I go pick up food and bring it back and we can keep working?"

"No. Thank you, but really..."

"I insist." He stood and told her not to bother with her sandwich from home because he was bringing lunch.

"Not Italian. Please." Jenna sighed when he smiled at the way she gave in. She didn't, really. She just didn't have the energy to fight it.

Tapping her pencil on her desk, she stared at the wall. Mr. Kent Graham. The name still wasn't familiar, only the face. It bothered her that she should know him. Maybe they had only run into each other at a show somewhere, but when? And why was he being so aggressive? There were far prettier girls working in the gallery, and everywhere else. Unattached girls. Energetic. Not exhausted mothers who ... who were adding to their brood unintentionally.

Jenna shoved a hand through her hair and wished her office had an outside window. It was barely big enough for a desk and the door was glass so she wasn't cut off from the rest of the building, but it was too closed in, especially now when she already felt too closed in. She wanted to be outside. Watching Alan and his men work on a new landscape.

She supposed she should call him. He'd left a couple of messages but Jenna hadn't made herself even tell him Trevor was leaving, had moved out, was in Italy. She supposed she should. Talking about it would make it feel more real, though, just like ... the baby. Trevor's. That he didn't know about. She supposed someone should know.

For now, she had to throw herself into work. At least Graham's art interest wasn't abstract or modern. He liked realism, as Daniel had. The artists she'd found for the show weren't Daniel's quality, or Trevor's quality, but at least... She frowned. What would make her think they weren't Trevor's quality when she didn't even understand abstract art? Because she'd been told it was quality work? Because she wanted to believe it was? With Daniel, there had been no question in anyone's mind. It was right there for anyone, even a non-artist, to see. But Trevor ... yes, she could see it had a quality to it, even though she didn't know why. Of course, she loved surrealism and easily picked out quality in that genre when others looked at is though it was just weird. It was weird; that's why she liked it. She could see what it was and what it meant but it was off the norm, different. Her mom hated it. She'd always nodded at Jenna's work when she was young just to say she saw it, but she always said if Jenna couldn't get it *right*, then she should do something else.

She never seemed to get anything else right, either. And she was getting tired of constantly starting over.

Grabbing a deep breath to calm the heart flutters as they started again, she focused on her other tasks of the day. She did it successfully enough that she was startled when he appeared in the door with a light knock and a plastic bag, stuffed full and wafting an incredible scent.

"Interrupting?"

"Yes, I... Um, no it's okay." Jenna set the photos and query letter from one of a stack of envelopes from artists looking to do shows aside and picked up Mr. Graham's folder.

He set the bag on the other side of the desk. "Oh please, put that away. Let's enjoy lunch leisurely and we'll get to that later."

"Mr. Graham, as I said, I'm behind, so this has to be a working lunch. I don't mean to be ungrateful, but..."

"Kent. And yes, I will correct you every time."

Which was bound to get annoying fast. She had to stop it now. She had no energy for that much annoyance. "Please don't. I'm still not sure why you insist on working with me, but as I've said, this is only business and I am a professional. I use first names for my friends and close coworkers. Not otherwise, and that includes clients."

His smirk annoyed her even more than usual as he handed her a disposable plastic container and hard plastic silverware with a napkin. "Well then, I was holding off with this, but I may have to fill you in better. Iced tea, no sugar, no ice." He set a Styrofoam glass with a lid beside the container. "Did I remember correctly?"

Jenna didn't bother to answer although she had no idea how he knew, much less remembered. "Fill me in? About what?"

"Eat, please." He opened his and waited for her to do the same. It was a sandwich with a roll for a bun and plenty of veggies.

"Ham, turkey, Swiss, and all the toppings that aren't spicy. Did I guess right?"

Guess? It was as accurate as the tea without ice or sugar. "It's fine. Fill me in about what?"

He grinned. "You're impatient, aren't you?"

"Sometimes."

"It's simple, actually. I'm a big fan of your husband's work. You are why I chose this gallery. I found you through a flyer for your show. The Jenna Rhodes, wife of Daniel Rhodes, now working in art circles yourself instead of circling them with your husband."

"Former husband. He died over three years ago."

"Yes. And I suppose I should have said former husband but these things are hard to know how to handle." He bit into his sandwich.

"Well, I guess I'm confused as to why you want me to run your show just because you like Daniel's work. One has nothing to do with the other."

"You don't remember me."

She hesitated. "You said we hadn't met."

"And you have a good memory." He swallowed and grinned. "We didn't officially meet. I was at Daniel's funeral. I'm an old friend of his, from high school."

Jenna's heart fluttered. This guy had known her husband, before all the publicity.

"I was into engineering and he was, of course, in the art crowd, but we crossed the borders occasionally. I tried to talk him into using his art skills as an architect since there was real money in it. His mother didn't appreciate it. She didn't like me much, said I was trying to hold him back in my 'humdrum' world, where he didn't belong." Kent grinned and sipped from his own drink. "I suppose she was right. He did well for himself with his art. I was glad to see it."

The stranger sitting in front of Jenna talking about Daniel smacked the reality of his existence back into her face. Most of the time since losing him, she had become fairly numb to the loss, locking it down into a place of its own that dulled her senses enough to prevent the sharp pangs of grief. Joan had become her own mother in effect well enough by now that she didn't cause the memories to stir. Neither did Denise. Jenna counted her just as her sister by now, a sister she only saw on holidays, but still...

"This is hard for you." His expression became more serious. "I am sorry. I expected since you have a boyfriend, you would have moved on enough it would be fine to talk to you about Daniel. Was I wrong?"

"No. I'm just surprised."

"I meant to break it to you more slowly, but considering your refusal to see more than a work relationship, I thought it might help to be more honest instead."

He should have been honest first. At this point, it was too late. Jenna didn't want to eat with him. She wanted to tell him to get out. But she was hungry and she'd neglected herself, her baby, too much already.

"I should have kept in contact with him. Things just have a way of slipping past." He turned a ring on his finger.

"You're married?"

His voice lowered. "Divorced. I should take this thing off, but it's not something I wanted. Just another thing I let slip past. Water under the bridge. So now that I'm not only a run-of-the-mill client, maybe you could use my name."

Something about it bothered her, but he knew Daniel back in high school. Her husband had never talked much about it. Neither did Joan. It could be a chance to learn more, get to know his past.

"I'd love to meet Daniel's son. Is he much like him?"

Jenna wavered. She wouldn't say much. "In some ways, yes. He has his hair color, his particular nature."

"That must be fun." Sarcasm sprinkled with humor.

"He's a great kid, easy to get along with."

"That's nice for you. Maybe I could come over some day? It would be nice to be in touch with Daniel's son."

"Oh. I don't..."

"Too fast? Your boyfriend could be there."

He couldn't, actually, but Kent Graham didn't need to know that. "We'll see." She opened his folder and pushed the conversation back where it belonged. She had to have time to think, without those brown eyes and the smile so close to her. Daniel's friend. Daniel had never mentioned having friends from high school. She always thought he must have had.

Fifteen

"It's about your class reunion." Jenna snuggled up against Daniel's back as he studied his current canvas.

"Throw it out."

"You don't want to go? We could..."

"No one there I want to see. Throw it out, Jenna. And I'm trying to work so could we do this later?" He pulled away from her.

With a sigh, she let him alone and dropped the invitation in the trash. Maybe he wasn't interested, but she was. She wanted to meet the people he used to hang out with and ... and maybe he didn't want them to meet her. Maybe he didn't want them to find out she'd gotten pregnant and pushed him into marriage, although she didn't. And she wasn't pregnant. She'd lost the baby, and... and maybe he didn't want anyone to know. He and Joan had hidden her pregnancy so well, to make it look like it happened after their marriage, that hardly anyone even knew she had been. She supposed it was for the best.

She sipped her lukewarm tea and settled onto the springy couch on the other side of the loft. He didn't like the television on when he worked, or the radio, so she picked up a book.

Why had she not met any of his friends? Only art people, as he called them, for business reasons. He had to have friends. Everyone had friends to some extent. She wasn't particularly sociable but she even had a couple of friends. He'd met them. She made every effort to share them with him because she was so proud of him...

She supposed he wasn't as proud of her.

Jenna woke with a start and reached for Trevor for comfort. He wasn't there. And he wouldn't be there.

She wondered if she could get out of working with Kent Graham. She didn't want to work with him. She didn't want to see him. But she was a professional, as Margaret said. Funny how she didn't feel like it.

The phone's ring made her wonder if that's what woke her. It was only five a.m. She grabbed it and answered with a question.

"Hey Jen. Sorry it's so early."

She sank back onto her pillow. "Hey, I was just thinking of you."

He paused. "Why weren't you asleep?"

"I was. I mean when I woke I... Doesn't matter. How are things?"

"Good. Busy. Wanted to catch you before everything interfered tonight. Feeling well by now?"

Except for her stomach which, she realized, felt worse than it had been. "I'm okay. The strep is gone."

"Good. You sound better. You're still staying home for a couple more days, right? So I can call later if I find time? I have to run..."

"I'll be at work. I went back yesterday, but you can call there..."

"You're supposed to rest. That thing is nasty. It took me forever to get over and I'm usually a quick mend. Stay home. Margaret can make do."

"I can't. Mr. Graham will only work with me and I'm behind already and I..."

"Graham? Jenna..."

"Don't start, Trevor. It's my job."

"Find a different sponsor. Just *tell* Margaret..."

"It's okay. Really. He's an old friend of Daniel's. That's why he was familiar. He was at the funeral, I guess, though I don't remember, but I ... was pretty out of it, so... Anyway, it's okay."

Silence came over the line except for voices and laughter in the background.

"It's not okay, Jen. I'm telling you it's not. The guy was ogling you like ... not like a friend of your late husband. I don't care who he is..."

Jenna sighed. "You know what? It's my business. I'm here taking care of things because you don't want to be, so..."

"You know that's not true. I couldn't pass this up..."

"You'd already moved out."

"Okay, let's not argue. I only have a minute. Please, just be careful. Don't meet him anywhere but at work when others are around and..."

"I can take care of myself, Daniel. I told you I could."

Silence filtered through again and his voice lowered. "Trevor."

"What?"

"I'm not Daniel, Jen."

Heat flamed through her face as she realized what she'd done. "I'm sorry, I... It's just... He always gave me a hard time about other men and ... I just... I'm sorry."

"Have *I*?" His voice held anger, controlled. "Have I *ever* given you a hard time about the men who flirt with you? I see it. Plenty often. Have I *ever* said anything?"

"Trevor, I'm sorry. It's early. I'm half asleep..."

"Not an excuse." He was silent as she pressed her lips together. "I have to go. I'll check in with Nina and talk with the kids. I'm sorry I couldn't be what you wanted, Jen, that I couldn't be Daniel for you.

Goodbye, Jenna."

"No." She spoke to a phone that didn't answer. He'd hung up. And she couldn't call him back. He used a community phone. He was in and out and ... and she was such an idiot.

Tears tried to take over but she pushed them back. She had to work today. Her eyes were an awful mess for hours when she cried. It was part of why she'd taught herself not to cry. She didn't.

Oh Trevor. Call me back when you calm down. I'm so sorry.

She couldn't possibly sleep and it was too soon to get ready for work, so she shuffled into the art room. She hadn't bothered since he left. It was too empty.

And too full.

There were new canvases stretched over frames, in all different shapes and sizes, all primed and ready to use. A ton of them. Trevor. He'd set them up for her to use because he knew she wouldn't.

With a pain in her stomach and her head, and a burning hole in her heart, she lowered to the floor in front of them and cried. She was such an idiot. She loved him so. She wanted him. And his baby.

For the first time, she realized she wanted this baby, the one she kept fighting him about, the one she didn't have time or energy for. "What have I done?" She spoke to the blank canvases. If only she could gesso over parts of her old life the way she could over paintings that didn't work out right, Jenna would change so many things.

She'd marry him. In a heartbeat. In his baby's heartbeat.

Wiping her eyes with her sleeve and sniffing, Jenna fought the pain and the longing and went in to shower. She had to work. She'd given Trevor up for the damned job, so she might as well do it.

"Anna, get out. Let's go."

"No, I go work with you."

Jenna sighed. "Baby, you can't. I'll try to be early, okay? Come on. You love it at Aunt Nina's."

Anna pouted hard enough it nearly made Jenna laugh, or cry again, and she couldn't do that since she'd had such a hard time trying to stop it earlier and her eyes were still red underneath the brown liner and she'd have to make up an excuse. Allergies, except she didn't have any. She could say she got mascara in her eye. She'd done that before. It did make her cry, but not hard enough for her eyes to be red and swollen.

"Anna, please honey, just get out of the car."

The girl wouldn't give in, so Jenna reached in to pick her up. A sharp pain hit her stomach and she put her down again. "Okay. You win." Jenna tried to sound normal. "Mommy will stay here with you. Okay? Come inside now."

Her babies jumped out and headed to the door. As soon as Nina opened it, Aaron told her Mommy was staying, too.

"What's wrong, Jenna?"

"I have to sit." She pressed her arm against her stomach and made her way to the couch. Nina fussed over her but she said it was fine and she just needed to lie down a while and call in to work and she'd take the kids back home.

Nina tried to talk her into staying, but it was Trevor's aunt's house and she just couldn't. Not today. After he said goodbye. After she'd messed up so badly. At least the kids behaved well enough she got home without trouble. Margaret was upset. Jenna couldn't explain over the phone. She'd have to tell her. When she was able to go back in.

Barely in the door, Anna said she was hungry. Jenna said she just had lunch. The girl insisted so Jenna went in to find an easy snack for her ... and nearly crumpled to the floor. She didn't let herself fall. She grabbed the counter and lowered, against the cabinet, with the knob poking her back on the way down. Aaron ran to her side. "Baby, get the phone for me. Okay? Climb up on your stool..." She could hardly breathe, the pain was so intense.

Aaron didn't have to be told twice. He pushed his stool over to the wall, climbed up, and carefully got down to stretch it over to Jenna. She thanked him and told him to take his sister to their room. He didn't want to go. She asked him please and waited until they left.

She called Joan. Told her ... she was trying to miscarry, to come get the kids...

She woke up in the hospital. At least the pain was over. Jenna wouldn't think about the rest.

Joan came to her and asked how she felt. It wasn't something she could possibly answer, so she didn't. She asked where Aaron and Anna were and nodded when she said they had a sitter Joan trusted, not to worry. And then she complained that Jenna hadn't told her, about the baby, or about Trevor leaving. She'd called the bar looking for Trevor and got Nate, who was there at the hospital worried about her since Joan wouldn't tell him why she was there and Jenna couldn't respond except to ask Joan not to tell anyone. Not *anyone*.

Joan stroked her head and left the room. Jenna considered calling Alan and asking him to come be with her, but she couldn't tell him, either. She had to think about it too much if she talked about it and she couldn't. The first time, when she lost Daniel's baby, she thought about it non-stop until it nearly destroyed their marriage. Not that she had a marriage to hurt this time, or even a relationship, but she had her children and that was more important and they needed her. She just wouldn't think about it. She would go home and heal and refuse to let it in her thoughts and go back to work and ... and limit her hours again so she could be with her babies more often. If Margaret fired her, she'd move to Peoria.

It was that simple. Mind over matter. She would make it that simple.

It was dark when she woke again. To a familiar voice. Her boss.

"Jenna?" Margaret came to the side of the bed. "What's happened? They won't tell me anything since I'm not family."

"I have to take a few days off..." She was groggy, drug induced groggy, and her abdomen was on fire.

"Of course, but what happened? I've told you you aren't eating enough. Did you pass out?"

"I..." She couldn't talk about it. "I have to cut my hours, Margaret. I'm sorry. I thought I could, but with Trevor not here, I just can't..."

"Sweetie, don't talk about work. It'll wait. I'll take care of things. I'm concerned about you."

She saw Joan come in and was surprised her mother-in-law was still there, or there again. Joan took over, told Margaret visiting hours were over and she'd have to leave, that Jenna wouldn't be at work for at least a week, and that she and the kids would be staying with her at least that long. She already had it set up, had someone to stay with her during the day while Joan worked, which she wouldn't do much for the next week, either, so she could watch over her personally.

Jenna didn't argue. She didn't say anything to her boss as she left. She agreed to try to eat something when Joan pushed and told her she hurt and ... let her take over. Joan had asked Jenna if she should call her mother. Jenna told her absolutely not to call her. Or Alan. No one.

Sixteen

Jenna lingered at Joan's long enough. Two weeks. She hadn't needed to stay that long but it was nice to have adult company and someone else to help take care of things. She hadn't gone back to work, either. Margaret came by. Jenna said she wasn't up to it and part of her hoped to be fired. She wasn't. Her boss said to take her time. Jenna managed to tell her why she was in the hospital and she did it without emotion, at least not much, and said it was fine, she was fine, she just wanted time with her kids after everything, since they were still upset about Trevor being away.

Nina came to visit and took the kids a couple of times because she missed them. They'd talked to Trevor over the phone both times. Nina told him only that Jenna had a sitter so she didn't have the kids much. As far as Nina knew, she'd only gotten too exhausted after her strep throat. Jenna couldn't tell her more.

The sitter Joan hired had school-aged kids and wanted only some daytime hours, which worked well. She was great with Aaron and Anna, and Jenna liked and trusted her, so it was arranged for her to continue to watch them once Jenna went home. Joan was paying her. Jenna fussed. Joan insisted, said she'd done far more for Denise and her family than she had ever done for Jenna so she was due and there would be no argument.

Mary Beth also loved to cook and she was good at it and Jenna felt better than she had in months. Her face was less gaunt, less the way her mother's always looked. Jenna complained that she would gain everything she lost and didn't want to and it reminded her of Trevor saying he didn't like sticks, he liked her to look like a girl, not that it mattered anymore. Through the grapevine, meaning some of Joan's art friends who often dropped by, she'd heard Trevor was staying with a woman in Italy instead of with the other artists. Maybe she would marry him and give him kids as he wanted. Jenna heard the nasty tone in her thoughts as she thought it, but she hadn't talked to him at all since that morning. He knew she was at Joan's. Nina told him, and he hadn't called. Not that he should.

Every day at Joan's, Jenna thought more about heading to Peoria, about finding a little house with a yard, and declaring herself off limits to men. She also considered moving to Boston with Karla to hang out with her cousin, but it was too big. She wanted small and quiet. She wanted ... what she'd run away from.

For now, it was nice to be back in her own apartment. Joan came with her to help her settle in and went to open windows. Someone had taken care of the place. Trevor's trees were alive and pert, as though mocking her. She'd half wanted the things to die.

Shoving away from that thought, she went to make tea.

"Your answering machine is blinking up a storm. Should I play it?"

"No." She'd do that later, alone. When she felt like it. "Anna, put your raincoat on the rack, please, not the floor.

"My coat wet."

"I know, baby, that's why there's a mat under the coat rack. Hang it up so it can dry."

The girl frowned and looked at the coat but didn't make a move to listen. Aaron did it for her and Anna threw a fit. Before Jenna could jump, Joan did, in a matter of about two seconds. Jenna had to be amused. No wonder Daniel was so ... controlled. Finicky. Controlling. Trevor was messy, which annoyed Jenna to no end, and his daughter was just like him, but at least he ... he wasn't controlling. He let her be messy, too, in other ways.

With a sigh, she grabbed her tea, plopped the tea bag in, and lowered onto the couch.

Joan sent the kids to their room to find something constructive to do and grasped Jenna's free hand. "Now that you're home, do you want to tell me what happened between you and Trevor?"

She shrugged. "He got a better offer."

"Oh Jenna, don't believe those rumors about the woman in Italy. You know how people love to talk and how they exaggerate. I don't believe it for a minute and you shouldn't, either. Now tell me, did he give you warning at all?"

"Yes." She barely heard herself say it.

"And? You decided to let him go?"

"No. I held my ground. As I should, right? As you always have. As you've told me I should — take care of myself first, right?" She saw her hand shake and raised the cup to her mouth to make it stop.

"Well, that depends. Are you holding it for something you truly want and need or are you holding it just for the sake of holding it? There is a difference, you know. I hope I made it clear that the ground I held was always necessary ground."

Necessary ground. In other words, was she only being stubborn? A couple of weeks ago, she would easily have said yes, it was ground she truly needed. Now she wasn't so sure.

To be honest with herself, which she knew she too often wasn't, Jenna wasn't at all sure. She cast her gaze out the window, at the top of the buildings she could see, at the sky, the rain and clouds.

"How much do you love him, Jenna?"

Joan's soft voice, softer than normal, and her question, brought the tears to her eyes she'd refused since that morning. When she called him Daniel. It bothered her more that she'd hurt him than it did that he hung up, that he hadn't called since.

"Answer me. I want you to say it." Joan took her tea, set it on the table, and shifted to face her more directly. "How much do you love him?"

"Far more than myself. I... I screwed up. Bad. I was arguing with him, over the phone, and ... I called him Daniel. It was only because he was complaining about a sponsor I'm working with who flirts and he doesn't ever do that, not like..."

"Like Daniel did. I know he did. I talked to him about it."

"It doesn't matter anymore, but I hurt him and I can't take it back and he shouldn't take me back. He keeps asking me to marry him and I'm so stupid I wouldn't do it and there's no reason. I should have. The first time. Even when he was leaving me, I wouldn't. I've been such an idiot. Why should he take me back? Why shouldn't he find a sweet, pretty, together Italian girl and have what he should have?"

"Because he's in love with you."

"Why?" Jenna shoved herself off the couch. "I guess I just... I don't know why Daniel was and I don't know why Trevor is and..." She grabbed a deep breath and spread her fingers across the window. It was cool. Hard. Ungiving. It let everything go through it, sun, dark, cool, warmth, without being affected by it. It reflected back anything in its vision that was at the wrong angle to pass through. Otherwise, it was invisible, as she often felt. Just a window, a pass through, or a reflection, with nothing noticeably substantive of its own. Functional. Otherwise uninteresting.

Joan wrapped arms around her shoulders from behind. Unusual. Joan wasn't a hugger. "Your parents really did a number on you. Oh honey, you have to learn to say the hell with them. Just because they were too stupid to see what a beautiful treasure you are, you can't feel like you aren't. Daniel tried to convince you. I know how hard Trevor has tried. In the end, you have to do it. There are so many reasons Daniel loved you. And why Trevor does." She turned Jenna to face her. "And why I do. It's not because you married my son. You were the first I didn't try to pull him away from him, even with your young age, because I couldn't. I've loved you from the beginning, and I knew it could mean trouble for him, but there was something in you I loved and I could see why he did, and I didn't help him be careful enough, I didn't help you be careful enough, because I wanted my son to have you. I could list reasons, but it would do no good." She brushed the side of Jenna's head and wandered away to pace the room.

She turned back. "You need to take more time off work. I insist. In the meantime, I have a project for you, a paid project. As I did for Daniel, I will give you a salary comparable to your job and for the next month, I want you to stay home and work on your art."

"Joan, I can't take a month off..."

"Of course you can. I'll speak with Margaret and make it work for her, as well. And Mary Beth will take care of the children during the day, sometimes here, sometimes at her house so you have quiet... Don't argue, it's perfectly safe and it'll be good for them to get out around other children more. She's doing a beautiful job with her own; they're good kids and Aaron and Anna will do fine with them."

Joan came back and took her hands. "You have been a wife or a mother since you were just barely eighteen with very little support from anyone. It's time for you to be Jenna for a while. I want you to paint yourself. By that, I mean whatever is in your head, put it on canvas. Whatever is in your heart, put it on canvas. Or on drawing paper. Whichever fits. In between, do whatever else you like. Shop. Read. Go out with a friend. Whatever you like. I'll stop by now and then and I want to see progress on your art when I do.

A whole month to do whatever she wanted? Did she have enough in her head or her heart to fill a month's work of canvas? She wasn't sure she did. But she gave in. What else did she ever do but give in? Or hold her ground that maybe wasn't necessary ground.

When the kids were in bed, Jenna wandered into the art room. A whole month mainly to herself? Paid? She shouldn't accept. Joan was only kind of still her mother-in-law. Jenna had moved on from there and Trevor was ... was...

Still, Joan often supported artists just because she wanted to get them on their feet. Why shouldn't Jenna allow it? She doubted there were many who more needed to find their feet than she did.

She traced fingers down one of Trevor's paintings, and went to play the messages. Maybe he'd left one.

A few were marketing calls she deleted as soon as they started. A couple from Karla just wanting to chat. A few were Alan, and his messages grew more insistent. She stopped it and picked up the phone.

Cheryl answered. "Oh Jenna, where have you been? I swear Alan would have left in the next couple of minutes to drive up there and find you if you hadn't called. Everything okay?"

"Sorry. Yeah, I... What's up?" She lowered onto the couch.

"Here, I'll get Alan. He'll want to tell you."

She sighed and wished she hadn't called. What now? Her mother was angry and telling everyone how ungrateful she was? Or had he found out she was in the hospital? What would she tell him? Maybe he found out Trevor left..."

"Jen? Where have you been?"

"What's wrong? I just got your messages. You sound upset."

"Just got them? Were you away?"

"Yes. We... for a couple of weeks. What's wrong?"

He paused. When he started again, his voice was lower. "Jenna, your dad had a heart attack. Three days ago."

"Heart attack? Mom's a hospital administrator. She didn't know better how to take care of him?" At her pettiness, she sighed and tried again. "Is he home? Mom's freaking out, right? What do you want me to do? Help her take care of him? I don't think so..."

"Jenna." His voice was a scold. "He didn't make it. The funeral's in the morning."

Funeral? She sat stunned. Funeral. He was too young. She knew he ate greasy fast food a lot but he wasn't overweight, not much, and he was always active, always busy, always ... so stressed over his job. He worried too much, about everything. Her mom often told her she was too much like her father and she argued but...

"Are you okay?" Alan asked as though it made much difference.

"Yeah. Surprised. I didn't even know..."

"You should come out. Stay with us overnight. You can both miss a day for this, I would guess..."

"No." She stood and paced to the window.

"Jenna, I know how you feel but I think you might..."

"After what happened at the party? No. I'll just cause problems. It'll be better if I don't. And I'm..."

"Talk to Trevor. See what he says. Regardless of what's happened in the past, I think it'll still matter to you in the long run if you don't."

Talk to Trevor. She nearly laughed. "I can't talk to Trevor about it. He's not here. He left me, and the kids, and I just can't deal with this, too. I can't do it. So no, we won't be there. It was bad enough when I had a live-in but now I have his kid and not him and ... I just can't face that. And when have they ever been there for me? When? Do you have any idea..?" She caught herself. "No. I'm not going."

Silence came through the line as Jenna waited for him to try harder to convince her. "He left you?" Alan sounded more shocked about that than Jenna was about her father. "He would never leave you."

"If you mean what did I do to push him away, you're right. But I can't talk about it and I can't handle the drive to Peoria on my own right now and I can't... I can't, Alan. It's just too much."

"Okay. Jen, okay, I get it. Are you all right? Stupid question; I know you're not. Do you need to talk?"

"I can't. I'm going to bed. I..." She swallowed hard and shoved a hand through her hair. "Call me tomorrow. After the... After. Tell them I'm not well. Whatever you want. I don't care. I really just can't give even an ounce of shit about it and I know I'm horrible and I may be sorry later but I don't right now and I can't."

"Jen, I understand. You know I understand. We'll talk tomorrow. If you need me to come up next weekend..."

"No, I ... I need time. Okay?"

"Of course, but don't be too alone. I mean other than the kids."

"Thanks for letting me know. Nice that someone bothered." Jenna sighed as she hung up. No one had even told her. She had to wonder if they were under orders from her mother and wouldn't be surprised. She supposed they wouldn't be surprised, then, that she wasn't there.

Sipping her now cold tea, she dumped it, set the cup in the sink, checked the door, turned out the lights, and snuggled into bed. She reached a hand to Trevor's pillow and imagined touching his face, cuddling into his not-really-so-scrawny body. She could almost smell his cologne, that one he had one when they met.

Her body was exhausted enough to override her stirring brain and got heavy, mellow, unconcerned about anything beyond her mattress, beyond her thoughts of Trevor, of scent, that luscious curious scent...

"Come on, Jenna. If you want to meet them, you better hurry."

"I can't breathe."

"You shouldn't have worn the tight jeans. I told you..."

"No, I ... I'm too nervous."

"Oh please, you're twenty-one and you've been married for three years. What's to be so nervous about? I finally got you away from home, away from the cranky artist. Enjoy yourself and relax. They're just people."

"Don't call my husband cranky. He's not cranky. He's..."

"Jealous. Overprotective. Finicky. Yeah he's cute and all, but really, Jenna, you know he's not perfect. It took forever to get you here away from him. Let's have some fun. Just a little fun."

"I'm sweating, Karla. What if I get to shake his hand and it's wet? That's gross. He'll think I'm gross."

"What are you, twelve?" Her cousin rolled her eyes. "Besides, they just got off stage. They'll be too sweaty to notice you are. They'll never smell your B.O. over theirs. Trust me." Karla clenched her hand and hustled her backstage through the arena. She showed her badge to some big guy in a security uniform and smiled back at Jenna. "Perks of working for the fan club. Nice, huh? Relax. They aren't animals. They don't bite. I told you they're great with fans. Well, your guy might just bite. I've heard stories of him. I think it's telling that you chose the biggest pervert of the group as your favorite when you're married to... Well, I think it's funny."

Jenna heard plenty about Raucous from her cousin who had met them all several times and had photos to prove it. Karla's favorite was Mike, the lead, and she said she left her fiancé home tonight because she wanted to steal a kiss from the lead singer, just once, just because, although she'd told Peter it was so they could have a girls' night out. Jenna couldn't imagine having the nerve to ask one of them for a kiss, much less actually do it. Karla said he would likely be willing to do a lot more than that if she was one of those girls, but she wasn't. A kiss, Peter would forgive. He wouldn't forgive more than that and she didn't want that anyway.

The guard in front of the dressing room said they'd have to wait a few minutes; a couple of them were changing. Karla chuckled. "The two neat freaks. Not yours." She winked.

Jenna blushed as the guard looked at her. "Not mine. Stop calling him that."

When allowed entrance, Karla had to nearly pull her in. The first one she saw was the lead guitarist and damn if he wasn't even hotter in person. She stared although his attention was elsewhere and he didn't notice. She heard her cousin greeted by name and suddenly she was face to face with him. Stu. Of Raucous. Karla introduced them. Jenna's face grew hot. Her heart raced. His grin was even more adorable in person, too, and he drew her in for a hot sweaty hug. But sweet. And he didn't smell of B.O., not much. He smelled of... the most incredible cologne she'd ever smelled on a man. It suited him perfectly...

Jenna sat up. She was in bed. In her room. Her apartment.

That cologne of Trevor's she could never place. The same as Stu's.

The pervert of the group, as Karla said. But he was sweet. He'd talked to her the longest time. The others were friendly enough, but he was super friendly, although he didn't try anything. He was a gentleman.

Like Trevor. A gentleman, sweet, but not nearly stuffy or uptight or finicky or ... or possessive.

Karla had tried to convince the singer to give Jenna a good night kiss as they left, but Jenna had told him she was married, so he grinned and kissed her face, not her lips, with another sweet hug.

Trevor reminded her of him. It had never occurred to her. She'd longed for him even before ... while she'd been married to Daniel, she'd longed for what Trevor gave her.

She was such an idiot.

Seventeen

One month. She'd lost her baby one month ago. She'd last talked to Trevor a month ago. And she had seven new paintings complete along with a few more started. As Joan requested, she painted anything that came to mind. Her first was of the backstage scene at the concert Karla took her to in Boston in Eighty-one. Six years before. It felt much, much longer ago. She felt so much older.

She'd painted the *Julia Belle* faded in the background of a river scene, foggy and distant, with the buildings along the riverfront taking precedence on the right hand side where it was less foggy. She had a scene from the architecture tour, paintings of her babies lying on the floor beside her with paint of their own and translucent rays of light, two of them, shining spotlights on the floor beside Aaron and Anna – the two unnamed, unheld. She had two cloud paintings, one bright and one stormy. And the heart. She used her fingers to paint a fleshy shape of an upper body and traced a messy red and yellow heart over it, over the chest, trailing onto the stomach. Trevor's heart. She named it. She never named her paintings, but that's what it was: the heart she painted on his chest with her fingers.

Jenna moved that one into her bedroom, still wet, and hung it on her wall where she could look at it as she was trying to sleep at night. Trevor's heart. Her heart.

Joan hadn't been by to look yet but they'd talked on the phone every day and Jenna took the kids over for dinner when invited and she said she was making progress. Joan told her she looked better, healthier. Jenna said it was Mary Beth's cooking. She hadn't told Joan about her father. Jenna hardly thought of it. By now it was a non-event; it hadn't happened in Jenna's world. She'd been creating her own world the past couple of weeks and she simply didn't allow anything in it she didn't want there. She talked to Alan most every night after the kids were in bed, to appease him since he was worried. She said she was fine, and she was. She was painting. She had help and occasional company. She had her babies. And she had everything Trevor had given her. Even if he wasn't there, she was more grateful every day for what he left in his wake, for his understanding, his comfort, his talks – she missed talking to him the most – for the way he made her feel she was okay as she was, for his love. For whatever reason, Jenna knew deep inside that he did truly love her and as she painted, as she felt herself come out into the open onto canvas, her thoughts, her dreams, her memories ... she didn't find anything that scared her, that was so monstrously bad someone shouldn't love her. She painted light, some dark but never total dark. She painted beauty. Inspiration. Love. Every canvas held things she loved for some reason, even the dark clouds she loved because of their color, their form, their promise that they'd release their tears and then be bright and pretty again. That they were temporary.

She realized what an optimist she was and it made her laugh.

When Margaret called in the middle of the next day as Jenna was standing back looking at a big pond with trees reflecting from it and trying to figure out how to make it more glassy and wet looking, Jenna agreed to go back to work. Two days a week. Joan said she could do what she wanted with the rest of her time and Jenna wanted to go back to work. Part time. When her kids weren't home anyway. She would bring home the envelopes with show requests to peruse as she could. Maybe she would do it with her kids, ask their thoughts, teach them about art at the same time.

Her boss sounded surprised it was so easy, but the painting was going well and Jenna was in a good mood and she was ready for more company again. And she had a show to finish.

For today, she would finish her pond painting. It needed clouds. Vivid clouds. Grabbing her palette, she squeezed out globs of different blues, a violet, and white. Then she added plenty of gel to each, separating the white to add more gel to part of it and less to the rest. She wanted the luminescence, as close as she could get to that.

In the middle of adding hints of clouds to her current painting, Jenna had a thought and went to find another canvas. Blank. She put it on Trevor's easel and turned the thing so it was side by side with the other one. She dipped a large brush into the different blues alternately and spread background color across the top, variegated it with more white in the middle and then violet toward the bottom for a touch of contrast and depth. Without wiping her brush, she scooped a glob of white onto it, the less gelled white, and dabbed and swirled the undersides of several clouds. The paint already on her brush mixed gently with the white and she used heavily gelled white for the upper two thirds of the clouds. She smoothed it here and there, added a touch more violet, created wisps along the edges, and built other parts thicker, with more texture and less color.

They weren't terribly realistic clouds, but then none of what she'd done was terribly realistic, as usual. She liked it, though. They were clouds that fit in her own world, the way she saw them. Happy enough with it, she went back to the pond painting and used some of the same technique, but smaller.

By the time Mary Beth brought the kids home, Jenna was happy enough with both paintings. She dropped her brushes in the cleaner and went to give her babies big hugs.

Eighteen

"I'm warming coffee. I guess it's from this morning?"

"Yeah, but I'll make more. You don't have to reheat that." Jenna set a hand on his chest.

"It's fine. You know as hot as I warm it, nothing unsafe is gonna live in there." He grinned with a kiss to her hand, and held it out farther to see it better. "You've been painting."

"I got bored when it got quiet. Crazy, huh?"

"Can I see what you're working on?"

"It's nothing, really. Not worth looking at. Aren't you tired? It's late. The bar must have been busy."

"It was. And I want to see it." He ignored the beeping of the microwave and kept her hand to walk with her to the den.

She reveled in the simple touch of holding hands. The friendliness of his eyes. The interest in her painting. He praised the emerging cloud scene, then noticed a messy canvas against the wall that she'd given up on. She told him it was nothing, just playing with colors, and she'd gesso over it when it was dry.

Trevor looked up at her from where he knelt in front of it. "No, you're not."

"It's garbage, Trevor. Just a mess."

He stood, close enough she could feel his breath against her face. "It's not garbage. It's abstract. It's you, from inside."

Her eyes drifted to the canvas. If that's what she looked like inside, it was no wonder she was always so disorganized and lost. Was that how he saw her? Was that really how she saw herself? She shook her head. "No, I wasn't trying... I just didn't know what I wanted to paint. It's nothing but keeping my hands busy."

Trevor caught her face between his palms. "You should keep your hands busy more often, with no plans. It is you, Jen. It's whatever you were feeling inside. And it doesn't have to look like anything to anyone else. I know you've never understood my art. But look." He motioned toward the canvas. "Stop to let yourself remember what you were feeling at the time and really look at it. Then you'll understand." His eyes shined, excited. "It's only abstract to everyone else. To you, it's reality. And some day, I want you to explain it to me, what you were feeling at the time. Just don't paint over it."

Explain it to him. Some day.

Jenna stood staring at the painting he'd hung on their bedroom wall and now and then asked if she was ready to explain it. She kept saying there was nothing to explain. It was only colors. A lot of orange. Red. Red-violet. Gray. A lot of gray. A big box with a lot of gray inside and a lot of bright colors outside with only hints of those colors deep in the middle of the box.

It was her. She felt gray when she painted it but she wanted to be vivid, to explode vivid loud heavy emotions all over. To let the gray out because gray wasn't her, or it wasn't supposed to be.

She had to get ready for work, but first, she sat at her little desk and wrote it out, to tell Trevor. She'd said she would. Since he never called the apartment, she couldn't tell him personally, but she could mail it. She had his address. She'd never used it, but she had it.

Maybe she would.

~~~

Overwhelmed by all of the welcome back flowers in her office and the sweet greetings from her coworkers and bosses, Jenna had to fight herself not to cry. She never considered that her presence mattered so much, but she also had notes stacked high in her inbox and Margaret said some were work related but many were from patrons and artists, not only from their gallery but from a couple of others, as well, who heard she was in the hospital. Jenna sat down and picked up the stack of them. Mixed together were messages taken by one of the assistants and cards that had been mailed. Jenna never gave out her home address. She always said she was easier to find at work. She even had her home phone unlisted so they couldn't find her in the phone book.

She supposed she'd done it because Daniel had. Trevor argued, said he wanted to be found by old friends and work acquaintances if they wanted to find him. She said he could list his own name but to absolutely not list hers.

Unable to make herself open the cards, she put them all into her art case, a pretty brown leather one Trevor bought her that had a sturdy pocket inside for her regular paperwork and plenty of space to carry artwork safely, up to 26 inches. He'd offered to get a bigger one but Jenna didn't work big. It felt overwhelming. She rarely went bigger than 16 x 20. Besides, she already felt conspicuous carrying it. The good thing was the extra side pocket that carried what other women carried in a purse. She hated to carry a purse so the little pocket with her necessary stuff took care of that. Her keys were on a hook around the handle. Often she just stuck them in her jacket pocket instead, or her jeans. She only had the apartment key, the car key, and the work
~~~

key, plus the artist palette pin Alan gave her a few years before that she used as a key fob. She never wore pins. When she fussed at Trevor about it, he fixed it to be usable for her keys. Alan shook his head with a chuckle when he saw it.

What would he think when he got her letter? She'd dropped it in the mail on her way out so she wouldn't change her mind and she nearly did anyway. Hopefully the pretty Italian woman wouldn't find it first and get rid of it. He wouldn't be with anyone like that, would he? Jenna couldn't imagine he would. She had to try hard not to let herself see the woman in his arms, or in his bed, which hurt her all the way to her core.

"Am I interrupting?"

She jerked her head up from where she was doodling a sketch of Italy during her mind meanders. Kent Graham. Already. He wasn't supposed to be there until later in the afternoon. Margaret said she would have the morning to settle back in.

"I'm early. I know." He ambled in and stood in front of her desk with a quick glance at her doodle. "Making travel plans?"

Jenna grabbed a deep breath and slid the sketch into her drawer. "I'm not prepared for our meeting yet. I barely got in and…"

"That's fine. I'll be back later. Thought I'd drop off some notes I've been working on to help you prepare for our meeting, and I'd like to offer lunch before we get started. Thought I'd give you a head's up. I'll be back at twelve. Look forward to it." With a grin, he started out, and paused beside a bouquet of red and yellow tulips and forsythia branches. He tugged on the card attached with a quick glance back at her and another grin, then left.

Lunch. If he meant lunch out somewhere, he was bound to be disappointed. Trevor asked her to see him only at work, and of course she didn't have to listen, but something said he was right and she should have just admitted he was right when they talked. Even if the guy was Daniel's old friend.

As she sorted through her work, Jenna found herself thinking of her paintings and had a thought for another one. A house structure. No walls, only the wooden support beams and the wiring, the cement base, maybe a piece of furniture … no, an easel. Blank. Waiting as the house was waiting. An empty scratched up wobbly stool beside it. Red and yellow paint tubes on the seat.

Why had Graham pointed out the card, with the red and yellow flowers? Like the heart on Trevor's chest she'd painted.

Jenna went to look at it. "Glad you feel better. T." She flipped it over. Nothing more. T? Trevor would put his name, and he didn't know she was in the hospital. Did he? *Glad you feel better?* He wouldn't be so impersonal, not over something like that. He would call her. Wouldn't he? Red and yellow tulips. He knew she loved them.

She paced the office and read the other cards. Coworkers. Patrons. A small bouquet of white roses tinged with each of the primary and secondary colors was her favorite. To my favorite artist with healing wishes, Kent Graham. She grimaced and went back to her desk.

If Trevor knew about the miscarriage and didn't even call her...

She shook her head. He didn't. It was a bad joke. Who would do that to her?

He brought lunch in. Chinese. From the same takeout Trevor always used. "Is this all right?" Mr. Graham watched her expression.

"Fine. But you don't need to keep bringing lunch."

"I'd rather take you out, so let me know when you're willing."

When? What made him think she would be? Jenna set her dish to the side and moved right into business. A business lunch was far less intimate than simply eating together, even at her desk, and she had reopened her door that he'd closed. *I'm listening to you, Trevor. I am.*

The meeting went well enough. They accomplished a great deal. And before she knew it, it was time to go home. She didn't want to tell him what time she left now so she pushed him out with the excuse of another meeting she had to get ready for. He asked her to dinner. She said no and left it at that.

Since she got caught up in missed work and didn't watch the time well enough, her babies were home before she was and they flew at her as she came in. "Hey, did you guys have a good day?"

Anna's little arms circled her neck. "Good day, Mommy. You have good day?"

"Better now." Jenna kissed her little cheek.

"We talk to Daddy today."

She looked at Aaron. "Yeah? That's good. How's Daddy doing?"

"Anna told him come home and she cry to him. I was a big boy. I told Daddy Anna is okay and I take care of her."

Jenna pulled him in. "Oh Aaron, I love you so much. You *are* a big boy. Did you make Daddy feel better?"

He nodded.

Mary Beth said they both talked to him a good long time and then they went to the park to meet up with their play dates, a group of several women who went all together after school to talk with other adults as their kids socialized. Most of the kids were too young for school and a few were barely in school, as hers were. She offered to take Jenna, also, on one of her days off.

She found herself agreeing. With a thank you to her new friend who said dinner was in the oven and had twenty minutes left, Jenna saw her to the door and looked forward to the play date.

They'd talked to him a good long time... It struck her that meant he called the apartment. Usually he talked to them at Nina's. Was he looking for her?

~~~

By the end of Thursday, her first day off of the week since she'd agreed to work from ten to four Monday through Wednesday, with an occasional Saturday just before shows, Jenna had her newest painting done. The house structure. The whole canvas was in browns, mainly shades of sienna, except for the tubes of red and yellow paint on top of the wobbly stool that echoed muted red and yellow tulips in the green-and-sienna mixed grass behind the house's cement pad.

Trevor had called the kids the past two days but he hadn't called all day while she was there. He knew her schedule. How? Nina, she supposed. Was he really mad enough to call only when he knew she wasn't home? How long would the letter take to get to him in Italy? Would he even read it? If he knew her schedule, did he also know about the miscarriage and when she had gone back to work? Of course Nina knew about the baby by now. Jenna couldn't keep hiding it from her, and she'd cried for the longest time. Jenna hadn't. She couldn't let herself think about it that much. She supposed Trevor's aunt thought she was too hard-hearted for him by now. It was entirely possible she was right. Maybe she'd told him so.

Jenna grabbed another canvas, although it was late and her feet hurt, and set it on the easel. She stared at it for some time. It was too small. But they were all 24 inches or smaller since that was all she used and all Trevor set up for her. Stepping back, she looked out the door to the living area. It was dark. She had only the art room light and the small bathroom light on. Walking backward, she leaned against the window sill but didn't bother to look out at the street, the dark street. She looked at the white wall. The paint splotched white wall from
~~~

where they leaned canvases up against it. She hated white walls.

With a frown, she returned to her canvas and her palette full of browns. She used few colors. She preferred to stay with her usuals that she knew how to mix efficiently to get what she wanted. Trevor, on the other hand, had nearly every color he could find. He was addicted to finding odd paint shades and there were some he'd never even used yet. Many were barely used.

Jenna grabbed his box and his bigger palette and went to the left corner of the white wall. She could do a small scene along the bottom. Something ... fun. Vivid. With a sigh, she scuffed backward again, eyed the wall's proportions, and went to grab a pencil.

"You keep all of your needs in a small box, Jenna, and it's such a shame."

Joan's voice from just after she'd lost Daniel floated in. Her needs were far too large for a small box. They wouldn't even fit on the long white wall. But it would be a start.

Nineteen

Jenna hugged her friend too hard, and for too long, but she was so glad to see him.

"Are you all right?" Alan spoke into her ear as he rubbed her back.

She nodded against his shoulder and kept hold of his arm when she released him from the hug. "Come, I want to show you something I've been working on." With a quick invitation for Cheryl to follow, Jenna dragged him to her art room.

He went to her canvas on the easel. Another house painting, but finished this time, a complete house. "Is this the back of it?"

"Front."

"Where's the door? You have a porch and steps but no door?"

Jenna shrugged. "No one gets in that way."

"How do they get in?"

"Maybe they don't."

He turned to eye her but caught the wall and wandered over to it.

"This is what I wanted you to see. I have a bunch of paintings done, too, but this... It still needs work. I have more to put in it." She stopped talking and let her friends study her wall painting. A house from inside, and the art room door was the door to go out. The walls held framed paintings and large windows revealed shrubs and flowers at the bottom and around the edges. The windows were curtained but they reflected images from Jenna's distant past. The old bridge she'd painted. Tennis courts. Her room with the door closed. A cemetery. The framed paintings held recent memories. Over the door a tree grew out onto the ceiling a short way, and just above the door was a tree carving with Trevor's heart and *T & J* finger painted inside.

"Jenna..." Alan's voice echoed amazement. "This ... is incredible. I can't wait to see it finished."

"I hoped to have it done by now so you would, but I ran out of time. You'll have to come back when it's done."

"Oh absolutely." He wandered along the wall. "The detail in this... I'm stunned, honestly. You don't like ladders. How did you do this?"

"Makeshift scaffolding, which I also don't like, but it was good enough for Michelangelo, I figured I could make myself do it small scale." She heard Cheryl add her praise, but it was obviously praise from someone who enjoyed it but didn't understand it the way Alan did. Her friend was still intent on looking at details.

Cheryl moved to Jenna's canvases lined up along the opposite wall. Seventeen of them now, some better than others and smaller than others. "Wow you've been busy. These are nice. I'd love to have that one over my fireplace instead of that old painting Alan picked up at a yard sale somewhere. You could sell these easily, Jenna. Do you plan to do that?"

"Oh I don't know. It was an assignment, actually, from Joan. Just ... painting whatever came to mind." Jenna had to force herself not to laugh that Cheryl's favorite was her least favorite, a cloud scene that didn't come out quite right. "You can have that one if you want it. It's dry, one of the earliest ones."

"Jenna I couldn't. I was only..."

"Really, it's fine. I wasn't happy with it and didn't actually finish it the way I planned. I probably won't. It's yours if you want it." She caught Alan's half grin. "Tell her I mean it. She doesn't believe me."

He came to join them. "I'll be glad to put it over the fireplace instead of the other one." He walked along the row of paintings and shook his head. "I have to tell you, Jen, and don't take this wrong..." Alan crouched in front of the foggy trees and pond canvas. "But the great Daniel Rhodes had nothing on your talent. This is absolutely spectacular. Is it dry?"

She nodded and he stood with it, turned it toward the light from the windows. Shook his head again. "If you're going to sell this, I want first dibs. And don't under-price it for me. It would be perfect for my office where my clients will see it first thing. Of course it deserves a better place of honor, but I'm willing to outbid your highest offer. I don't even care what that is." He set it down and stepped back, still studying it.

Jenna hugged him again. It was her favorite, too. It had taken the longest. It reminded her of the days she'd spent outside watching him and his men work. She almost said he could have it, but she couldn't. She loved it. She rarely loved her work so, but she loved that one.

Alan loved to watch fireworks over Lake Michigan, so they went early and had a picnic dinner complete with apple pie Cheryl brought with her. It made Jenna nervous to have the kids in the middle of such a huge crowd of people in the park overlooking the harbor. Aaron wasn't a problem. He stuck to her side. Alan took over with Anna who wanted to wander. At one point, all four kids walked around with him and Cheryl asked about Trevor, if she heard from him recently. Cheryl was shocked to know she hadn't talked to him since just after he left.

She was writing to him, though. Usually three letters a week were sent overseas, telling him all the things she couldn't in person and should have. He didn't write back so maybe he didn't get them, and maybe it was okay if he didn't. While watching the fireworks, Jenna thought of him. He'd painted them once, the first year they watched them together; as soon as they got home, he went in and did a quick painting of the dark sky and bright lights. She'd stood behind him, wanting his company, and slid her hands up under his shirt as he painted, around to his stomach. He paused now and then to give her a kiss on the head and then set the palette down, swept her around to hold her in his left arm, and finished the painting with his right hand, reaching over to the palette to grab paint.

It wasn't the only time she'd made him paint that way. He hadn't minded. He often spurred her on if she held too still and left him too alone. He always said later he could see her touching him whenever he looked at those paintings.

Jenna wiped a tear. She missed him. She missed just holding him.

Alan put an arm around her and Jenna cried softly on his shoulder. Her first tears since ... since she wouldn't let herself remember.

"He'll come back, Jen."

She shook her head. She couldn't let herself believe it. When she sniffed and wiped her face, Anna crawled onto her lap.

They got the kids settled into their room, the girls in the two single beds and the boys in sleeping bags on the floor which they were more than happy with, and Alan poured wine for the three of them. She assured him again she was just fine on the couch, that it would hardly be the first time she slept on the couch. She gave Alan and Cheryl her room for privacy. Cheryl liked privacy and cared far more than Jenna did. Besides, there were two of them. Two wouldn't fit on the couch.

Her exhaustion, largely from the tears she wished she hadn't allowed, combined fast with the wine. She realized she hadn't touched alcohol in the longest time. Not since her miscarriage. Jenna wasn't at all sure she hadn't helped bring it on with the wine, and the headache medicine of Alan's she'd taken, along with not eating or sleeping well. Not that it mattered now, but she hadn't done any of those things since. Cheryl told her she looked better. She definitely felt better.

When the phone rang, she jumped and stumbled over the end of the couch, ramming her toe into the corner. She cussed, apologized to Cheryl, and saw Alan grab it for her before it woke the kids. He told the caller who he was...

"Yes, she's right here. Nice to hear from you." He held it out to Jenna and told her they were going to get ready for bed.

She cringed at the throb in her foot and the buzz in her head as she said hello.

"Hey Jenna."

She nearly crumpled to the floor at Trevor's voice.

"Are you there?"

"Yes. Trevor ... hey. How are you?" She lowered onto the arm of the couch.

"I um... I got your letter."

"One?"

"What?"

"You only got one so far?"

"You sent more than one?"

She made herself keep her composure. "Yeah. A few."

"Haven't checked recently. Jen, thank you. For explaining. I knew, though. I only wanted you to explain for yourself."

"I know. I wanted you to know I... Trevor, I am so sorry. For so many things..."

"Jen, don't. Okay? It's fine. How's work going?"

"It's... It doesn't matter. It's going well but I don't care much, to be honest. I'm painting a lot."

"So I heard. I want to see them when I come home." His voice was so distant, physically and mentally.

He heard? Maybe he did know, then. About the baby. Maybe the flowers were from him. She couldn't quite make herself mention it.

"Well, it's late there so I should let you go. I just wanted to touch base, to say ... happy Fourth." A pause. "Actually there's a lot more I want to say but I can't over the phone. Any chance we can talk when I get back or..?"

"Of course. Trevor, I..."

"I know, Jen. And I'll go check my mail."

"Maybe ... maybe you shouldn't. Ignore them, okay? I was just missing you and it was the only way I could talk to you but you can ignore them..."

"I miss you, too. Sorry I haven't called."

"It's okay. I understand. But I'm here, you know. I haven't moved on. I have in some ways but..."

"No boyfriend yet?"

She bit her lip to keep from crying. "One. But he's in Italy." At his silence, she figured she shouldn't have said it. "Sorry, I..."

"I love you, Jenna. And I'm sorry, too, about a lot of things. We'll talk when I get home. I have to run. We have limited phone time and I've used it on the kids."

"I'm glad. They miss you, too."

"Tell Alan I'm sorry I was rude. I just wanted you tonight."

She wiped a tear. "It's fine. Happy Fourth."

"It is now. Night, Jen."

Jenna sank onto the couch. He loved her. He only wanted her tonight. Maybe she was making too much of it, but she wanted him so.

Alan came back out to check on her and she said everything was okay and maybe he would come back, not just back, but back to her. She fell asleep leaning against her friend's shoulder but thinking of her Trevor. *Her* Trevor. He was.

~ ~ ~

After so much time working with Kent Graham on his show she didn't even want to do anymore, Jenna was glad to have the next three days off. She'd been doing more hours since the show was coming up in a week, but she refused to make it full time.

Trevor hadn't called again and Jenna spent a lot of time thinking of what he'd said and how he said it. After getting her first letter, he hadn't bothered to check for more. And I love you didn't mean he wanted to stay together. He was distant. Wanted to "talk" when he got home. Still, something about the conversation gave her some hope he still wanted to be with her.

She should have accepted his proposal. Over the phone. Should have just told him yes if he was still interested. Or she should have proposed to him, asked him to come home and marry her or asked to go meet him in Italy. She could sell some of her paintings. If they'd do as well as Alan thought they would, she could afford tickets to Italy for her and the kids.

She wasn't ready to sell yet. Trevor said he wanted to see them.

And she had the stupid Graham show to get through.

Jenna shouldn't call it stupid. The artists in it were worth showing. Most were nice to work with. A few weren't, but she overlooked that and would put their work in less conspicuous places, even if some were among the best. They would have to learn it wasn't smart to give so much attitude to someone who could potentially help their careers, or hurt them. She wasn't vindictive enough to hurt their careers, but she was more willing to help those who were nice to her. If the rude artists said anything about placement, she would shrug and call it luck of the draw. Of course they would know better.

The jerk sponsoring the show wouldn't stop asking her out. He threw tidbits of information about Daniel to her from time to time, like bait, as though she was a fish willing to get hooked on his line just for his dangled worms. Not likely.

Truthfully, it just didn't matter that much. What she had with Daniel was between them and that was it. More background wouldn't change anything, wouldn't give her more time with him. It wouldn't change the fact that he hadn't given her what she needed from him well enough. What was done was done. She told Graham she didn't need any information he had but he didn't believe she didn't. So be it. She could say no as often as it took.

~~~

Jenna was glad to have the day off but she didn't want to stay home alone. Skimming the paper Mary Beth always left for her after she finished reading it, she paused at an ad for the architecture cruise. She didn't have to think about it. Jenna left the paper on the table and went to get dressed.

It was supposed to beautiful and above 80 and she decided to trust that enough to wear shorts and a sleeveless blouse that fit her well. She added sunscreen to the exposed skin since she burned easily enough on dry land. With only a little pocketbook on a long strap she slipped over her head and one shoulder, she grabbed her keys and headed to the pier.

She knew it was a little sad that it felt like such an adventure, but she never did anything on her own. She had the kids or she'd gone with Trevor or Joan or Alan and she rarely took the kids just out on her own. It was sad she'd waited so long to do it, but she was doing it.

Her heart felt light and bouncy and she knew it showed in her attitude by the way people reacted to her. A few men turned to watch her walk by and that did nothing but boost her spirits even higher. She still had most of the lost weight off and gone, but had enough now to look healthy along with better sleeping.
~~~

Jenna bought her ticket, said yes, just one, without hesitation or guilt or self-pity. She wanted to be on her own today, out on the water, with her memories of Trevor at her side for their first date. Not really a first date, but it felt like it had been.

A guy a few years older than she was, so she guessed, stood next to her at the railing as the boat pulled from the dock and introduced himself. She played nice and gave her name. It didn't register with him, so he obviously wasn't in the Chicago art circle. He said he was a tourist and knew nothing of architecture or art and just decided to hop on and use it as a guide to places he might want to see while he was there. Jenna fudged the truth and said she didn't know the city well enough to help him so he might try someone else. He knew it was a hint. She knew his tourist-in-need line was a line and so she mentioned that if her boyfriend was there, he could do a better job of helping. Then she did what she'd never even thought of doing before: she took the ring Trevor gave her when Anna was born that she wore on her right hand, and moved it to her left, to the wedding ring finger. She'd taken Daniel's ring off not long after the funeral because she couldn't stand to see it. She'd always taken it off to paint so she wouldn't get paint thinner on it when she cleaned herself up and after the first painting she did after the funeral, she didn't put it back on.

She studied Trevor's ring. A pearl for Anna's birth month changed colors as she moved her hand and the three tiny diamonds forming triangles on each side caught the sun. Three. A sacred number, he said, and artistic. Every artist knew the effect of the number three.

Jenna always took it off when she painted, but no matter how tired she was when she stopped, she never forgot to put it back on. She'd forgotten Daniel's often, but he never wore his. He said he painted so often, he'd spend more time putting it on and taking it off than it was worth, and he never went out without her, so it didn't matter much. Everyone knew he was married. He didn't have to prove it.

It struck Jenna that he never got paint on his hands so he wouldn't have had to take it off. Funny she'd never realized that before.

Trevor never took off the bracelet she gave him. Never. Not to paint. Not to shower, to swim ... never.

She focused on the tour guide's voice as he told them about the buildings, but she heard Trevor's voice in her ear adding to what the guide didn't say. Maybe it wasn't too late to go to Italy with him. She could sell her paintings and just go. As soon as the Graham show was over, she could.

The next guy who started to flirt caught a glimpse of her ring as she purposely let it reflect the sun and assumed she was married. Jenna didn't bother to correct him.

She nearly jumped on the phone. He'd called the kids earlier, Mary Beth said, and would call back later. For her. To talk alone. She smiled at his voice and asked how things were.

"I uh... read the rest of your letters this morning. Jenna, I'm so sorry I wasn't there when you lost your dad."

She remembered that letter, where she'd ranted about how it was a non-event to her and it only mattered because she lost what she'd never had and could never have and otherwise she was just angry and she felt guilty for being angry.

She didn't want to think about it anymore. She wrote it out. It was over. And she'd had such an incredible day. "Doesn't matter. Guess what I did today?"

"Jen, we need to talk."

The tone in his voice dropped her mood right to the cracks in the floor. "Okay. But I should tell you..."

"No. Please. Let me do this first. It's only fair to you. And I have to do it fast or I won't. There's a girl here... And I thought about not saying anything because it was nothing, only... The night we talked and you called me Daniel, I kind of lost it. It's not an excuse and I'm not trying to make it one."

A girl. The rumor was true. She'd told herself it wasn't. With a fast gasp of air, Jenna lowered to the floor and leaned back against the wall.

"Are you still there?"

"Yes." She congratulated herself for not sounding furious. She was furious. And yet she had no right to be. She told him goodbye. "So, you have a new girlfriend. It's okay. Really. Like I said when you left, if it works that way, it should, right?"

"No, Jen, she's not... I was only with her a short time, until I got your first letter and I felt like holy shit because that one letter meant more to me than..."

"You know I can't..." She bit her lip, gasped another breath, and just said it. "It's okay. We broke up, right? It was your call. I told you it was. And it's okay. I think I... I've been thinking about going back to Peoria. I was only here for you and there's just no point now and ... I don't want this anymore. I'll give Margaret a month or so and help her find someone else and finish my obligations. But I think..."

"Don't call this done."

She gritted her teeth against his voice, the voice she loved dearly, the one that pulled her through so much for so long. Now it had been given to someone else. "I think you already did that. But you know, I'm glad you told me, that you didn't hide it, because that would be worse. I love you, and I always will, and you'll have to come see the kids because they need you..."

"And you don't."

Need him? Did she need him? Yes. And no. She'd spent so much time without him, without even talking to him, without any support from him of any kind, and she got through it. By herself. No, she didn't particularly *need* him, she supposed.

"Jenna?"

"You know what I need most now? To be honest with myself. To be ... who I am, as Daniel asked. The only thing he asked of me as he was dying was to be who I am and not let anyone stop that, and that's what I have to do. So you know, if ... if this was meant to be long-term, it would have been, but I've been through too much. I've floated along with the currents too long. I won't be here when you get back. I'm going home."

During the silence, she studied her ring, the opal and diamonds. She would leave it on, for now. Until she didn't feel like his wife anymore. She knew it would pass, as it had with Daniel. Maybe she'd fought against getting married because she wasn't meant to be married. She could find a boyfriend now and then and let that be enough. It suited her constantly flitting wants and desires.

"They're badgering me to get off the phone." Trevor sounded defeated and it nearly made her give in. But he turned to someone else. She'd turned to herself. They were at different stages. She couldn't back down. "But Jen, I'm... Can I come see you when I'm home?"

"Of course. As I said, you better keep up with the kids. They do need you and I know how much they do."

"Nothing could keep me from that, but it's not what I meant. Can I see *you*?"

She made him wait through a calming deep breath. "Yes. But I won't guarantee anything. Things change. It happens. It's okay."

"I love you, Jenna. I love you deeply and I'm so sorry..."

"Don't be. Do what you need to do. I want that for you, as I always have. And I love you, too." She wiped her eyes. "Goodbye, Trevor. Take care of yourself, okay? Don't be stupid like I was. I'll be here a while longer so you can call ... the kids, and I'll give you a new number when I have it. I'll leave it with Nina."

"Stay till I get back. I'll help you move. Jenna, just..."

"Trevor..."

"Please."

She rolled her eyes toward the ceiling. A few more months. Maybe she could. "We'll see. I'll let you know." She heard someone yell at him to get off the phone.

"I have to go now. I'll call back as soon as I can. I love you." The phone clicked.

At least half numb, Jenna stood to hang it up then went in to work on her wall painting. She had to at least stay until it was done, even if they painted over it when she moved. Just as well, she figured.

~~~

She was starting to love Saturdays and Sundays when she didn't work and the kids were home all day. She wanted to paint and they were buzzing around the house getting into things, so Jenna put old clothes on them and set them on the floor with old canvases Trevor had gessoed over and left. She dabbed oil paints of lots of colors on an old palette to set between them, gave them some old brushes, and told them to have fun. They looked at her like she was nuts. She never let them play in the oils. She had watercolors for them and some acrylics that were easy to wash from their skin, but Jenna figured the oils would fade off them the way it faded off Trevor when she painted him, on him. She did tell them not to get it in their hair.

She worked while they did, on a cloud painting she'd barely started some time ago. It was dry by now but it didn't matter. Her palette now held bolder colors, non cloud colors. That could be interesting, she figured. It wasn't turning out the way she wanted, anyway, which was why she'd left it for so long. Touches of dark green, burnt umber, and vivid red made their way into the clouds. Not pronounced, but just here and there with some white and sky blue and gray mixed in. She liked the effect, the swirl of the lines, the uncommon colors where they shouldn't be. And she went back to cover the gray she'd used. She didn't want gray in it. At all.

Jenna stepped back to get more distant perspective. What was that? It wasn't her. This wasn't her type of art, not her style. It was Trevor's style. Abstract. What was wrong with her? Couldn't she get him out of her brain long enough to just do her own work?
~~~

On the other hand, she liked the look of it. The clouds didn't look much like clouds. They were only swirls of color. Of emotion. Of what she was thinking about: Trevor. And the Italian girl. Her blond-haired scrawny little artist boy with tanned skin who talked more of his Italian roots than the rest of his heritage. He'd always wanted to go see all of the colors and shades of the Italian landscape and its people, he said. Jenna figured he'd darn well done that.

Maybe she'd go back to Peoria and find a home-grown boy. Not an artist. She wouldn't do that again. What would she look for or be attracted to? As she watched the kids make a colorful mess, Jenna realized she couldn't think of any particular thing that would pull her attention enough to be worth it, or of anything she particularly wanted from a man. She'd often thought about it with Daniel. She always felt guilty when she did, but she did. She didn't anymore. Not since the first time she'd taken Trevor to her bed had she thought of anything else she might want in a man.

Maybe she just didn't. Alone had its benefits.

Dropping her brush in the cleaner, Jenna grabbed another gessoed canvas of Trevor's and sat on the floor with the kids. She used her fingers as Anna did, and sketched in the image of her babies playing in paint. They both gave her big smiles. Suddenly, she missed the one she'd lost with a gut-wrenching pain. Maybe she did need a man, just for a short time. She had two kids with two last names, why not three? It was a more artistic number. But then she supposed they had that. Three. Herself, Aaron, and Anna. She was happy with that. Happy enough.

Twenty

Kent leaned over her shoulder, one hand on the back of her chair so his arm touched her as he pointed at a menu. "The shrimp would be nice as an appetizer to reflect the boat theme in what's-his-name's work."

"Daria. And he's a she. It would, but..."

"Hard to tell at times with her hair shorter than most boys and the baggy clothes she wears."

Jenna let it go. She liked Daria. The girl was young, but spunky, and she knew exactly what she wanted. Her paintings of boats on Lake Michigan were Jenna's favorite pieces. "Enough large shrimp for an estimate of sixty to seventy people would be pricy. We could do mini shrimp..."

"I don't do *mini* on anything, Jenna. You realize that by now, and I'm not concerned about the expense so you don't need to be."

"Okay. It's your show." She made a note to add large shrimp to the menu that was already looking like one of Joan's buffets.

He moved the hand from her chair to her shoulder. "No, it's your show. I'm only the sponsor. And to let you know, I have reservations after the show at Shula's. It's my thank you for all the work you've put into this."

"I really can't..."

"Of course you can." He shifted even closer. "Word has it Dade is having a fine time with a gorgeous Italian girl. Things get around, Jenna. You may fool others with that ring, but I know you've broken up. There's no reason you can't have dinner with an old friend of your husband's."

She stood, on the other side of her chair. "This is only work. And it's about time for me to..." Jenna stopped.

"I know that, too. You're off in fifteen minutes. How about we go pick up your children and hit a pizza place? We'll get to know each other better. I've yet to meet my old friend's son. Or your daughter. Surely, pizza with the children wouldn't be too intimate?"

"Thank you, no. So are we set on the buffet menu, then? I'll get it ordered first thing tomorrow if we are."

He came close and looked down at her. Too tall. He was far too tall for her average height. "You should be pampered and spoiled, dear Jenna. I can do that…"

She backed away. "You should go."

He threw a sly grin. "I'll go, but I won't let you refuse my dinner offer after our show. I insist."

As he left, Jenna knew she should have said he didn't have the right to insist on anything. But she was at work. So far, she still had to work with him. After the show that promised to do wonderful things for Elucidations, all bets would be off and she'd tell him to leave her alone.

A fine time with an Italian girl. Trevor said he wasn't still with her. Maybe that wasn't quite true. Maybe, after she'd said she was leaving, he changed his mind.

Unable to go home so frustrated, Jenna found herself parking in front of his bar. She hadn't been there since Trevor left and for some time before. She had no idea why she was now, why she wanted to be, but she did. Maybe Nate would know more… No. Jenna did *not* want to spy on Trevor. She only wanted familiarity. Conversation with those who knew him best.

Nate glanced over as she came in, then looked back, smiled wide, and descended on her with a huge hug. Jenna always felt so tiny around Nate and his football build. He was taller than Kent Graham but somehow it didn't feel as threatening. Nate could be threatening. She knew that. She'd seen it when patrons got out of hand. But except for their first meeting when he'd pulled her to the back room of the bar to take her to Trevor, she'd never felt anything but secure around him.

"What honor do I have today that Jenna Rhodes saw fit to visit my little establishment?" The sparkle in his eye said he was teasing. As usual. Nate was a huge tease.

"Thought I'd say hello. It's been a while."

"Are you feeling well? You look as though you do."

She knew what he was hinting. Joan hadn't told him why she was in the hospital, but he'd heard while he hung around waiting to see that she was all right. "I am well, thank you."

"And he still does not know of it?"

She shook her head.

"He should know, little butterfly."

"There's no reason. Especially since he has a new girlfriend."

Nate rolled his eyes. "Ah, the boy told you."

"So you knew?"

"After he called you, he called me, as well. Come." Nate took her hand. "Sit and I will make you something to drink."

"I have to drive home and I can't stay long. The kids…"

"I will not have you run in here and right back out. They are with Nina, yes?"

Jenna explained about her sitter and she had to go get her kids so Mary Beth could go to her own.

"I will take care of it. Pete, make the lady whatever she wishes. I will be right back. And she is a special friend, so you treat her right. Jenna, this is the new boy, not much of a replacement for D-Day but he is doing all right."

She smiled at the boy who looked about the age Trevor was when she met him, early twenties. "Don't mind him. He's always that way with the new help. Have you been here long?"

"A few weeks. Long enough to know his bullshit when I hear it. Excuse the language. What'll you have?"

Jenna wasn't used to being asked. "Um, something light, not too sweet, and very easy on the alcohol. I have to drive, whatever Nate says. Can I leave it to you?"

"Yes, ma'am."

Ma'am? Jenna suddenly felt ancient. She was also flattered.

Nate swirled back in and sat next to her. "Nina will go and take the kids to her house instead. They will be just fine there. She's missed them recently, she sure has. Have you been avoiding her for a reason?"

"No, I'm…" Maybe she was.

He set a large arm softly around her shoulders. "I told the boy he was a right fool for moving out. An imbecile thing to do, I said."

"He's not the only fool. I shouldn't have let him. I gave in too easily. It was my fault."

"You wish you had not let him go?"

Jenna nodded. She fully wished she hadn't let him go.

"My little butterfly, I have known that boy for a right long time by now. I have seen him do many foolish things. But I have also always seen him make them right again. He is only a fool on occasion, then he gets his head working and makes things right. Don't you worry, little one. If you allow him back, he will be back. Not that you should allow him back after this stunt, more imbecilic than any other I've seen. I reamed him good for it, you should know. He took it without stopping me, which means he agrees and he is sorry. Not that you should take the apology."

"No reason he should. We'd broken up. It was his choice."

"Broken up, had you? Not the way it sounded to me. That boy is full out in love with you and he feels lower than street tar under a horse's hoof by now, as he should."

"He hasn't called."

"Ah, because he is ashamed to talk to you." Nate withdrew his arm and touched her face. "Do you still want him?"

She nodded without thinking. Her eyes watered.

"He is luckier than he deserves." Nate hugged her close. "Come now. Pete has your drink ready and I have your sweet babies lined up for the night so you and I are going to chat a while and catch up and we will deal with the trouble that is Trevor Dade later. Yes?"

"My car's here. I..."

"I will take care of that, as well. Take a sip of that concoction and tell me if little Pete, here, treated you well enough. If not, I'll have him out on the sidewalk in a Chicago minute."

It was mint. With chocolate. A touch of alcohol, just enough. "It's wonderful. Thank you. Maybe remember this next time I come in and make it just the same?"

Pete smiled with a nod and went to take care of other patrons.

Jenna enjoyed sitting among Trevor's friends and acquaintances as it got later and the bar filled with the crowd that had pulled her in and was so welcoming when she started dating him and came to work with him so often. When they found she was carrying his child, Anna, they were even more supportive, and he'd glowed far more than he said she did when he told his friends, or when they talked to him about it, or when he talked of Aaron and every little new thing the boy was doing.

"What is wrong, little butterfly? Are we overwhelming you?"

She looked up at Nate's voice, unable to answer. She'd had too many grasshoppers. She was too tired. She missed him too much. Nate's comfort just upset her more. Somehow, she ended up in the passenger seat of her car with Nate behind the wheel. He took her to Nina's. He talked to her, but she didn't answer. His voice was concerned. Still, she kept quiet. It was too much. She would explode if she opened her mouth now.

Pulling into the drive and turning off the car, Nate got out and walked around to open her door. He accompanied her to the house. Someone had followed them, waiting to take Nate back to the bar. The headlights brightened the sidewalk.

Nina took over and thanked him, with an arm around Jenna.

Nate touched her face, his big dark brown eyes tilted down to hers. "Sleep and dream good things, little butterfly. All will be well."

Jenna had no choice but to stay over at Nina's. She couldn't drive, and the kids were asleep. She gave them soft kisses on their little cheeks and whispered good night in their ears and grinned as they stirred, their angelic little faces peaceful as they settled back in. Nina understood that she couldn't talk, she only needed to sleep. She chose to go down to Trevor's room.

In the dim light, Jenna opened a drawer where he used to keep his clothes and found a few old T-shirts still there. They were musty from disuse but it would work. She stripped out of her work clothes, into his T-shirt, and under his blankets. Fingering the headboard, the simple planks of wood Trevor had built and then carved roughly and painted, Jenna collapsed onto his pillow, wrapped her arms around it, clinging to it, smelling him within the fabric. He'd stayed there recently enough it smelled of him again.

As she calmed, she turned to her other side and spotted the photo of Trevor with his parents. He was so young. It had been years since she had seen the photo. Why hadn't he taken it to the apartment with him? He looked so much like his mom, it was eerie. She looked into the happy, smiling twelve-year-old boy's eyes, the boy who became her lover, her Anna's father. The photo was taken a year before he lost them. Such different eyes than she saw when she met him, when he was wearing only black baggy clothes.

Turning back again, unwilling to be haunted by those eyes, Jenna switched off the lamp. The blackness of the basement engulfed her. So did the quiet. She'd gotten used to the noise of the streets below her apartment, and the occasional slam of a door or moving furniture or arguing voices of the apartments flanking hers. Here, the only sound was the furnace kicking on and off and now and then a creak of the old house settling. She liked Nina's house, nearly as much as the Taylor's old Victorian. She hadn't been there in a long while.

Thoughts of the Taylors and evenings spent sitting with them around their fireplace or on their front porch, chatting and laughing with Alan's family calmed her nerves and she felt herself drift away into the peaceful dark nothing.

~~~

Jenna was exhausted by nine p.m. and Elucidations was still
~~~

packed full of people. Her artists, or Kent's artists, were doing well, both with sales and with socializing. Trevor had called only for a few minutes earlier to tell her good luck with the show and Alan called to apologize for not being able to get there as he'd planned, but he was swamped with work and the twins had school open house the next day. He hated going to the things but Cheryl always insisted he did, even though he knew most of the teachers already. She was to call him the next day to let him know how it went. She thought she might have to call tonight instead since it was going so well and she would need to tell someone about it before she could sleep.

"Looking good so far, aren't we?" Kent slid his hand down her back, too far down.

She shifted away only enough to give him a hint, wary of people watching. "It is going well. I'm glad. They deserve it."

"As do you." He stepped in again. "Jenna, I see a wonderful career for you ahead and I'd like to keep assisting that."

"Why?"

He raised his eyebrows. "Because you deserve it."

"Thank you, but I can manage without special assistance."

He smiled, an annoying smile. "You have to love an independent girl. All right, we'll keep playing it your way a while. Don't forget about our reservations tonight."

"I asked you to cancel them."

"I didn't. And we're expected. Several big names you know will be there. I'd hate to make an awkward excuse." He leaned in. "Even if you won't accept my further assistance, Jenna, you don't want to unmake a bed that's already made."

Maybe she did. She was leaving Chicago anyway. Wasn't she? The success of the party had started to change her mind and she'd yet to tell Margaret she planned to leave. Still, she resented the insinuation and his choice of words.

As he moved away into the crowd, Jenna sighed and put a smile on her face to greet new visitors. Her smile turned genuine when she saw Joan, even if Mrs. Covington was with her. She accepted a light hug from both and readily agreed to show them around.

"Jenna dear, you've done such a lovely job. Your artists must be terribly grateful." Edna Covington squeezed her fingers too hard.

"Thank you. I'm grateful they were willing to come. They're a nice group to work with." She wouldn't mention the few still giving her attitude about less spotlight.

Joan spent plenty of time studying their works and privately she asked why some of the better pieces were so out of the way, so Jenna told her why. Her mother-in-law laughed. "My love, you are fitting in terribly well, even more so than I thought you might. Good for you. I'm very proud of you. I hope you know I am."

She'd only said it once before and Jenna chose not to let her mind go back there. She was in a celebratory mood and wanted to stay that way. As the night wore on, Joan's comment started to bother her. She fit in well? With the crowd she'd always tried not to fit in with, to keep distance from so she wouldn't...

But she had. No wonder Trevor got so upset, had been so moody before he left. She'd turned into Daniel, not with painting, but with her job. She'd too often been too tired for her boyfriend. She'd talked to people all day and just wanted silence when she got home. She was grouchy with the kids and ... and it was no wonder he left. Through all of her badgering him not to give in to what *they* wanted, she was the one who did.

By the time the gallery had cleared out and they locked up, Jenna wanted to go home and just crash in bed and do nothing but be with her children all the next day. Actually, she wanted to go outside in the sun, to plant something, or take her easel and paints out in the fresh air and paint whatever took her interest.

She wanted to be away from this.

And there was still dinner at Shura's Steakhouse to get through, with *names she knew*. When Kent touched a hand to her elbow, all Jenna could do was sigh and go get it over with.

"Can I walk you up since it's so late?"

Jenna refused and backed up.

"Now you don't expect me to let a beautiful young woman go in and up that elevator by herself at one a.m., do you? I'm afraid I'm far too much a gentleman."

"I'm quite capable. Thank you, anyway." She held the building key in her hand but would wait until he left to open the door.

Except he took it with a grin and opened it for her.

"Mr. Graham..."

"Kent. Please. And I do have a reason. There's something you must know about Daniel. I waited until after the show so it wouldn't be distracting, but I think with the show over and therefore our work commitment over, you may not agree to see me again and I'll leave that to you if it's what you prefer. I do, however, want you to better understand why it is I chose to work with you."

"You told me, and there's really nothing I need to know that I don't already."

"Isn't there? So you know of his other family?"

"You mean his father he didn't know? His half siblings he never met? I know about them. I don't know them and I don't need to since they didn't decide to need to know him."

"Interesting. That's not the way I heard it. I know for a fact he'd met and knew his father and siblings very well."

No, he didn't. He said he didn't.

"Jenna, there's a good chance you'll be challenged for Aaron's inheritance. Please, let me come up for a few minutes. I'll make it brief but I don't think you want to talk out here."

"There can't be a challenge. Aaron is his only child."

"Is he?"

Her stomach lurched.

"Please. You may need my help more than you realize. Let me explain and if you prefer, I'll never contact you again."

She found herself accompanied up to her apartment and was glad the kids were at Nina's for the night. She offered coffee or tea as she slipped out of her jacket.

Kent grabbed her arms and held her close.

She tried to push away. "Let go of me."

"I wanted to do this differently but you keep rejecting all of my advances, so I'm afraid it'll have to be like this. Stop pushing at me, Jenna. It'll do nothing but hurt you more."

"You were *lying*. About Daniel. Just to get in my apartment? You're a *scumbag*. Let *go* of me."

"I wasn't lying. *He* was lying. He was good at that. You think you were the first little virgin girl he acquisitioned? You weren't close. He just screwed up and found one with parents in too high places to get out of it, or to let Joan get him out of it. He got *stuck* with you, *Mrs. Rhodes*. And you're too love-blind still to see it."

"That's not true." She tried to sound convincing.

He laughed, a sardonic laugh, and moved in to kiss her, but she yanked back and he grabbed her tighter. "I want to make you an offer. See, one of those little girls was my childhood sweetheart, the one I'd planned to be with forever, from the beginning, and have her only for myself. And your precious Daniel, the great Daniel Rhodes, ruined that. She wouldn't tell me who it was, not until after he was gone when she figured it was safe. But she never forgot him and she never failed to remind me that her son wasn't mine but she did fail to give me a son of my own, intentionally, by taking pains to be sure she couldn't, so I divorced her. And I've been biding my time." He backed her against the wall and pressed in.

"Don't." Jenna struggled to get away but he was tall and strong and her legs were pinned too much to knee him as she always figured she would if she had to...

"You haven't heard my offer yet, Jenna." He kissed her neck. "I figure if you're going to let yourself be taken advantage of, you could at least do it in style, with me. We'll sponsor each other, so to speak." He bit at the base of her shoulder.

"*Stop* it. You're *wrong*. He wouldn't... You're lying. It's all a lie."

"Is it? Ask Joan." He glared into her eyes for a second then shoved a hand under her blouse.

She pushed with everything she had and didn't even nudge him.

"I can be a father to your children. You're plenty young enough to have another, maybe even two or three more..."

"No." It was a desperate whisper.

"We could make a good team, Jenna." He slid his hand up farther and yanked her bra down. "I got your *boyfriend* that job, by the way, overseas, to get him out of my way. And I set that girl after him. She's a gorgeous, persuasive thing. It worked too easily."

She felt her head shake. All a set up. Because Daniel... But it wasn't her fault.

"So now I get what I've been working for. And *the great* Daniel Rhodes gets his payback. I just hope he knows..."

"*I* didn't do it. If it's true, you don't think I paid enough already? I've already paid for it. I *have*. She was *lucky* he didn't stay with her because he was never really *with* me. I was so damned *lonely* I could hardly stand it and I nearly..."

He stopped and met her eyes. "Nearly what?"

"Let *go* of me." His grip was painful. She'd have bruises.

"You nearly *what?*"

"I nearly slept with a friend because I was *lonely*. Is that what you want to know? You think he ruined *your* life because he was with *your* girl? What about *mine*? I've paid already, and *I* didn't do it." Jenna felt him release her just enough and she shoved him hard, got away, and ran to the kitchen to grab the biggest knife she had, one Trevor wanted she said they didn't need. Holding it out toward whoever the man in her apartment really was, she nearly laughed hysterically.

He took a step closer. "You won't use that."

"Like hell I won't. Get *out*."

"Fine. But I only wanted to know if those nude drawings of you are realistic. The ones in the folder he lost? Remember those? They weren't lost. He sold them. To me. To keep me quiet about his kid. So I've already seen everything you have, *Mrs. Rhodes*."

Her head spun. Her chest hurt, inside and out. "You're lying."

A sly grin slid across his face. "If you choose to believe that. But you might want to keep this little matter between us if you don't want them to go public, and I do mean very public. One quick phone call."

She took a step toward him with rage urging her on, and he backed up and out of her apartment. Jenna locked and dead-bolted the door and then slid down it, dropping the knife to the floor beside her.

He was lying. He was *scumbag* liar. Nothing more.

Ask Joan.

Fine. She would ask Joan. Trembling, she got up again and made her way to the phone. It didn't matter what time it was. She had to know. It rang four times and the machine picked up. She hung up and dialed again. On the third ring she got Joan's irritated voice.

"Does he have another child?"

"What? Who is this?"

"Does Daniel have another child?" She could hardly breathe and her legs shook and she slid back to the floor against the wall.

"Jenna? It's nearly three in... What did you just ask me?"

"Joan, I have to know."

Silence came across the line.

"*Tell* me."

"Jenna, who have you talked to? Who told you?"

Who *told* her? Jenna's hands shook and she clicked the phone off. Left it off the hook. He wasn't lying. Got stuck. Because her parents were too high up... No. Daniel, no. Maybe she didn't get everything she wanted from him, but she did love him and she truly thought he loved her.

She heard an electronic voice through the phone tell her that if she wanted to place a call... No. She wanted... Yes. She wanted to place a call. Trying to focus on the numbers, she dialed Alan. He didn't take long to answer. Caller ID. He knew who was calling and the first thing he said was "Jenna, what's wrong?"

"Come get me." She heard her voice shake as bad as her hands, or worse.

"Jen, what is it? Are you hurt? Do you need an ambulance?"

"Yes. No. No one... Just come get me. Please. Alan, please just come. Now. Please."

"Okay sweetie, I'm coming. First, tell me if you're hurt."

She pulled at her blouse, the pretty dark blue blouse chosen for the show, and pulled the bra back into place underneath with a quick check of herself. No broken skin. Just...

"*Jenna.* Talk to me."

"No, not ... I'm not..."

"The kids? Aaron and Anna are all right?"

"At Nina's. Yes. They're... He won't go there, right? Tell me..."

"He *who*? Jenna what happened?"

"I can't. Not over the phone. Just come. I... I have to go get my babies..."

"Are you at home?"

"Yes. The apartment."

"Alone?"

Tears rushed down her cheeks. Now she was. "Yes."

"The door's locked and you're not injured?"

"Yes. And no. Just come, Alan. *Please.* I need you."

"I'm on my way. Jenna, remember it'll take me two hours or so. I'll hurry. But you're all right until then?"

"I have to go get my babies."

"No, sweetie, you stay right where you are and keep the door locked until I come, okay?"

"My babies. If he goes there..."

"Cheryl's on the phone with Nina right now. They're fine. Asleep. She won't let anyone in and she's calling Nate to come over. Okay? They're fine. You stay put. I'll be there as soon as I can get there. Here. I'm putting you on the other phone with Cheryl and I want you to talk to her until I get there."

Cheryl? No. She wanted Alan. She wanted a shower, but she didn't dare. She had to watch the door.

"Jenna?"

At Cheryl's voice, she cried harder. She didn't want Cheryl. She wanted Alan. But his wife said to talk to her and he would be there. Stay on the phone and talk. Her kids were safe. Nate would be there with her babies. Strong secure Nate. They were fine. She had to stay put until Alan came.

She felt herself drifting away while Cheryl pushed her to talk, to tell her what happened. She was tired. Nearly three. A long day, week. A long few months since Trevor left.

Trevor. More than anything, she wanted him. Maybe not more than anything. She wanted to be home. Out of the city. Away from these people she didn't understand well enough and couldn't judge well enough. They were too different. She was face value. Alan was face value, even with his faults, he was what she saw. These people... No, she had to go home. Trevor was one of them. He wasn't what she thought, either. He'd left her. Then he cheated on her.

She just wanted to go home.

Cheryl kept pushing her to talk just enough she knew Jenna was still on the phone and still okay and a knock on the door made her jump. Her heart pounded so much she could hardly breathe. He'd come back. She told Cheryl someone was at the door. Cheryl told her to look through the peephole and tell her who it was.

Shaking, her legs barely willing to support her, Jenna crept quietly to the door and picked up the big knife she'd dropped there earlier. Joan. It was Joan at the door. She told Cheryl. Cheryl said to let her in. Jenna had to take a few deep breaths before she could make herself open the door.

"Jenna, I've been trying to call you..." Joan glanced at the knife in her hand and stopped. A man was with her. Jenna stared at him. Joan said it was a good friend of hers and she could relax.

"No. He can't come in. No."

"Jenna, honey, what happened? Put that down. He's a friend..."

"No." When the guy moved slightly, she raised the knife. "No."

Joan told him to wait in the hall and urged Jenna to let her in. Cheryl's voice called to her from the phone she'd set on the counter. She closed and dead-bolted the door against the man on the other side. Joan picked up the phone, talked to Cheryl, and hung up.

"*No.* Alan's coming. I have to..."

"I know, honey. Cheryl told me. What's happened, Jenna? Put that down and come talk to me."

"Daniel has another child."

Joan nodded. "Yes. But..."

She backed away, back against the island that separated her little kitchen area from the rest of the apartment.

"Honey, it hurt him too much to talk about it. So he didn't."

"I was his *wife*. Even if he got stuck with me, I was his *wife* and he didn't tell me and *you* didn't tell me."

"I couldn't go against his wishes. Jenna, put the knife down. There's no one here to bother you. But someone did. Who was here? Are you hurt? Can I help you?"

She jumped at the phone's ring and nearly hit herself with Trevor's knife. She wondered if she'd actually laugh if she had. Irony at its best. She wouldn't answer but Joan did. She didn't bother to listen. Her head was buzzing. Her heart was thumping. She felt close to passing out but she couldn't. She had to wait for Alan. She trusted Alan. She didn't want anyone else.

Alan. She should have just given in to him and married him to begin with. It would have been easier. So what if she didn't feel for him what she had for Daniel, for Trevor, not even close to what she'd felt for Trevor. He would still be there. He would be good to her, help her be whatever she wanted to be. She should have married him.

Joan hung up and told her again to put the knife down. She started to obey but her fingers wouldn't release it. Not until Alan came. And he would take her and her babies home.

She was too tired to stand so she slumped back against the wall onto the floor. Joan refused to come close until she put the knife down. Jenna didn't want her close. She'd lied to her. She let Daniel lie to her. Joan had thrown her knowingly to her son because she figured Jenna would be good for him. But what about her?

"Honey, I know you're too shaken right now to understand, but whoever talked to you must have made it sound horribly wrong. Tell me who it was. I might be able to fill in..."

"I don't want to know more. I don't. I don't care. I'm going home. Alan will take me home and it doesn't matter anymore."

"Jenna it does matter. We'll talk later, when you're calmed down. But you have to listen to me about one thing. Daniel loved you dearly. He did. He was far from perfect, I know, honey. But he did love you. You meant the world to him. I know you did."

But not enough to be honest with her. Jenna felt her eyes closing. She was exhausted. Three-something. A long day... Joan kept talking and then she stopped. When Jenna started to unclench her fingers, she heard Joan come closer and grabbed onto it again.

"Honey, let go of that thing before you hurt yourself."

She pulled it closer, against her legs.

"Jenna, please. Let me have it, honey. You're safe now. Whatever happened..."

A loud knock echoed through the apartment and she jumped.

"*Jenna*." Joan closed in. "*Give* me that thing. You've just cut yourself. It's bleeding. Let me..."

She saw the blood but she didn't feel it. Joan went to check the door. "*No*. Don't let him *in*." She struggled to her feet, and felt the cut.

"Honey, it's only Nate and Keisha. Put that thing *down*." Joan opened the door and Jenna held it up in defense...

Keisha started toward her but Nate held his wife back. Joan was talking to them. Jenna didn't hear what she said and didn't care. Nate stepped in front of them, his eyes on hers. "Come little butterfly. You are all right now. Let me have that. I will watch over you." He crept forward, reaching for the knife.

Jenna gave it to him. He set it on the counter behind her and she fell in against his strength, his protecting arms. She trusted Nate. Alan. And Nate. Even if Nate was Trevor's friend.

Joan said something about her leg and Nate carefully picked her up and took her to the couch. She clung to his large chest as Keisha checked her leg, said something about her hose, and Jenna didn't care.

"My babies." She looked up at Nate. "You're supposed to be with them."

"It is fine. We have just come from there. They are sleeping as little angels should be at this time of the morning. Whoever has scared you will not get near them. Two of my closest friends, my well-trained friends, are there at the house to watch whatever needs watching. They will stay until I come. No one will bother your sweet angels. No need to fear, little butterfly. Let me take care of everything now until your friend comes. Yes?"

She felt herself nod and felt a sting on her leg. Antiseptic, Keisha said. She lay back against Nate's shoulder. His big hand sheltered her face. She let herself give in.

"Jenna?"

She jumped at the touch to her face.

"Hey, it's me."

Alan. He was there. She bolted upright and threw her arms around his neck.

"Okay." He held her in close. "Okay, Jen. You're all right. Tell me what happened."

Not with Nate ... and Joan there. She shook her head. "I want to go get my babies.”

“They're still asleep. Joan just checked on them.” Alan stroked the side of her face. “Are you hurt? Other than your leg?”

Hurt? Her head was fuzzy. “I want to go home.”

“Yes, I'm taking you home to rest, to regroup...”

“No. I want to go home. To stay.”

He held her face in both hands. “Are you sure? Trevor will come back, Jen.”

“No, he ... has a girlfriend. Italian. He said he did. And Daniel... Daniel has another child. And I just want to go home.” She heard Joan ask Nate about the girlfriend. She heard Nate deny he was still with her. But it didn't matter.

“Okay, don't think about it now. You should sleep more and then we'll go get the kids and whatever you need right away and I'll come back for the rest in a few days. You can stay with us until you get on your feet...”

She held him again, and let him take her to her room to lie down, away from Joan, from Daniel's mother.

“Can you talk now?” Alan sat facing her. “Just enough to tell me what happened. Why did you have a knife?”

“He wouldn't leave. I didn't mean to let him in. He said... I shouldn't have let him in. I didn't hurt him. He left. But I would have. He...” She clenched her lips together and shook her head.

“He attacked you?”

She nodded.

“Jen...”

“No, he tried but I... I got away and grabbed Trevor's knife and he said I wouldn't but I would have if he'd...”

“I sure as hell hope you would have.” Alan stroked her face. “Who was it? Let me call the police...”

“No.”

“Jenna...”

“He has... I can't. Alan, I can't. I just want to go home.”

“Who was it?”

She shook her head. If he released those sketches... Daniel was a realist, an incredible realist. She couldn't bear to have those sketches public.

“Okay, baby, it's okay.” He rubbed a thumb over moisture on her face she hadn't realized was there. “Forget it for now. Rest.”

“I trusted him.”

"I know Jen. You wouldn't have let him in if you hadn't. It's not your fault."

"Trevor. No, I didn't ... not *him*. I trusted Trevor. I love him, Alan, I do, and I..."

"We'll talk about that later when you're not so shaken. You need to sleep, Jen. We'll talk tomorrow. I'll be on the couch..."

"No." She grasped his hand and moved over. "Stay with me."

"Joan's here."

"I don't care. Please. I can't..."

"Okay, sweetie. Just let me tell them they can go home and I'll come right back.

Jenna forced her eyes to stay open until he came back in and lay beside her, outside the blanket. He said Joan was staying and Nate and Keisha were headed to Nina's to stay with the kids. Nate would be with her babies and Alan at her side. She could sleep.

Twenty-one

Jenna accepted a hug from Cheryl and apologized for making Alan miss the kids' open house.

"Oh honey, don't worry about that. Are you okay?"

She couldn't answer so she rubbed Aaron's head as the boy again stuck to her, and Alan set Anna down to chase a cat out of the yard. "Anna, be nice to the kitty."

Cheryl waved like it didn't matter in the least. "That thing knows it's not supposed to be here. It digs in my flowers and drives J.R. crazy when he's outside. She's welcome to chase it away. Come on in." She called to Justin and he was instantly at the door. "Take the little ones to the backyard and let them run a bit. We'll leave the dog inside until Anna gets more used to him. Jenna, come in. Sit. I have coffee cake and tea. I even have mint tea for you."

Jenna gave Justin a big hug and told him thank you. Anna jumped on him and laughed, but Aaron took some convincing to release her. He had to be far too upset for him not to go tailing right after his buddy. Jenna rubbed his shoulder and Justin teased until he gave in.

She let Cheryl be in charge and let Alan get their bags to put in the guest room. J.R. sat on the floor next to her when she lowered to the couch. "Hey puppy. Are you being a good boy or are you driving Alan crazy yet?" He put his head on her knee when she scratched his ear.

"That dog is spoiled rotten." Cheryl rolled her eyes. "And my husband is one of the worst culprits. Don't let him fool you. He just loves that dog."

Jenna chuckled. "I know, and I figured he would."

At laughter from the back yard, J.R. trotted over to the window and whined to go out with the kids.

"I'll take you in a minute." Alan walked through and set the bags in the room then came back to sit by his wife. J.R. was right on top of him. "So, I have to run out a bit and check on the progress of one of our big jobs. You want to come or would you rather stay and rest?"

"Yes. I mean, I'd love to go see it but..."

"Go on. The kids are fine." Cheryl set a hand on Alan's leg. "Rae and I have supper started. It'll be ready in an hour. Enough time?"

"Closer to two would be better if it'll hold. If not, we'll make it a rush job, or try. Let me take him out for a few minutes so he doesn't whine for you the whole time."

"Oh you know he will. Don't worry about it."

"Can't we take him?" Jenna called the puppy back to her. "I'll hold onto him while you do what you need. Is it okay?"

With Alan's agreement, she went to tell her kids she would be out for a bit and to be good. Aaron ran over and hugged her waist.

"Baby, go on and play. I'll be back soon." He didn't let go.

Alan rubbed the boy's head. "Want to go with us?"

Aaron nodded with big eyes and Jenna crouched to his level. "It's okay, you know. Everything's okay."

"I want Daddy here."

Jenna choked back her emotions. "I know, baby. So do I." She said it before she thought. "A little while longer. It'll be fine." She held him tight and asked Anna if she was okay staying with the other kids. Her daughter smiled big and chased Alex the way she'd chased the cat, laughing the whole time. The girl would be just fine, Jenna assumed. Aaron would take more watching.

<center>~~~</center>

Jenna forced herself not to look at her mother's house as she followed Alan and Cheryl to the Taylors' driveway. They gave her a few days to settle in before asking if she would come out to visit and they were making a big Sunday family dinner of it. Carrie and Amber and their spouses would be there, also.

She'd spent the past three days at work with Alan and found ways to jump in to help. Cheryl said she didn't at all mind watching the kids but Jenna couldn't keep taking advantage, even if Cheryl said it was well worth having her there for Alan to talk to about his work so he wouldn't bother her with it.

Alan offered her a job, part time however often she wanted. Jenna didn't feel settled enough for that; she wasn't entirely sure yet if she would stay. The thought of going back to Chicago sent a hard shiver through her body and she wasn't sure she ever could.

Her dad would say to get right back up on that horse that threw you and show it who was boss.

Since when did she start hearing her father's advice from way back when he still gave it? She was too close to home. A glance over at her house, despite her promise to herself that she wouldn't, jerked on her last nerve so she turned away, toward the Taylor house she loved.

Except there was a For Sale sign out front.

Jenna could hardly make herself pull in beside Alan before she got out and stared at the sign. Her kids badgered her to unhook them and she pulled together enough to do so, to set them free out into the yard. And she looked again at the sign, and at the house, the one she loved, that had been home to her when hers wasn't.

"It's getting to be too much work for them." Alan took her side. "They wanted one of the girls to take it but they won't live out here. I'm too settled. It's hard to think about, though."

She felt herself nod and then was swallowed up by greetings from his family and Aaron still hung on her until Justin pulled him off away to the swing set in the back.

Jenna hugged and chatted and went inside with them but her mind was on that sign. How could they sell it? They could get help. But of course Mrs. Taylor wouldn't want a stranger in her house, taking care of her house. She was too independent. They were talking about a little one-story place close to Amber in Washington where Mrs. Taylor could still have a small garden for her tomatoes but no stairs to have to climb or the several flower beds she and Alan had set up through the years. With Jenna's help. Jenna had been given space for her own little flower bed one year where she planted gladiolus and hollyhocks. There were flower beds all along the front of the house, down the sidewalk, and scattered along edges and corners. It was a lot to care for, but they could just convert some of it back to yard. They wouldn't have to sell.

"You're awful quiet tonight." Carrie plopped down next to her.

"Alan's had her out doing landscaping the past three days." Cheryl teasingly scorned her husband. "She's probably exhausted."

"No, I'm fine. Three days of working outside is honestly so much nicer and less tiring than three days of work in the gallery."

"Are you going back there, dear?" Mrs. Taylor seemed not sure she should ask. "Alan didn't say."

"It would be hard for him to say since I'm not even sure. I don't... I don't think so. I think I might just stay here."

Carrie nearly jumped on top of her. "That would so *cool*. We could go shopping together and I can babysit. Jim doesn't want me to work while I'm carrying little one, here, and I don't either, really. I keep getting sick and it's not worth it..." She paused at Jenna's stare. "Did Alan tell you? I'm expecting. We just found out. I'm only six weeks and I'm so excited I'm about to burst. But I feel good and I can handle your babies if you want since they're always so good."

Jenna gave her a hug in congratulations and conversation moved to babies and illness ... and Jenna got up for more coffee.

Alan followed her to the kitchen. "Are you all right?"

She fell against him. Jenna didn't even know why she was crying. She was happy for Carrie and Jim and for their family who was all so excited for her and planning already and ... and she missed her baby, Trevor's baby he'd wanted so much. She also missed having a family who would have reacted that way for her. And she missed ... this house and the warmth and she didn't want it sold. And she missed Trevor.

"Let's step out back." He led her out the kitchen door to the dark yard that smelled of dusk and dew and grass and a touch of smoke from someone having a campfire, she supposed.

"You're upset about the house."

She nodded against him, again wrapped in his strong arms. She'd missed having strong arms around her, strong shoulders to lean on.

"That's not all. What is it, Jen?"

"I..." She pulled back and wiped her eyes and ambled out to sit on the bottom of the metal sliding board that had seemed so big to her when she was little.

Alan crouched in front of her. "Is it the thought of staying? Or only the readjustment?"

She shook her head.

"Trevor."

She sniffed hard to try to calm herself as her emotions threatened to break her down again.

"Tell me about the girl you mentioned."

"He said he was sorry, it was a mistake. But he was *with* her. A couple of weeks or so. It hurts... And I don't know if I even want him back and I don't know if I can deal with not having him back, if he's even willing and ... now that I ... I left the city... I don't want to go back. Even if I should go back just to convince myself I can, I don't want to go back."

"Why should you?" He wiped moisture from her face.

"Because it'll always scare me if I don't. If I let it win. I shouldn't let it win."

"Jenna, that's nonsense. If it's something you *want* to do and something happened to stall it, then yes, you should try again, but you never really wanted to be there so you won't win anything if you make yourself go back."

"It's Trevor's home."

"Well, you know, maybe he'll have to work around what you want for a while. He walked out. He saw another girl. If he wants you enough, and I think he does, then he can give in this far. Stand up for yourself, Jenna. That's the way you win. And I don't mean by being stubborn enough to let someone else's standards or obsessions affect your actions, but I mean for *yourself*, for what you truly want *inside*. What is it you truly *want*?"

"I want to feel safe. And I mean not only physically, but ... inside. I just want to feel safe. I know things happen. I understand that, but I mean..."

"You trusted him. Now you can't."

She felt her head shake. "I don't know. But I think... I think I need to stay. Here. Get myself set up and..."

"I agree." Alan squeezed her fingers. "Of course part of that's selfish because I love having you around, but I think the whole time you were in Chicago, you were just struggling with the daily things, with the fact that it scared you, and you couldn't get beyond that. Give yourself time here to find yourself, Jen. You know we'll let you stay as long as you want."

"I need my own place."

"Jenna..."

"I do. I have to..." She looked up at the house. "What if they rent it to me for a while?"

"Jen, this house is a lot of work. It's old, and maintenance..."

"I don't care. Alan, I need my own space. Cheryl needs her house to herself. You know she does. I can ask, right? I still have the money Daniel left. It'll help until..."

"You said you didn't want to use it."

"Well, you know, it's not doing me any good just sitting there." She swatted away a mosquito she could hardly see. The last bits of light were fading. "And I just can't deal with losing one more thing right now. I know, it's not mine. It's yours, your parents', but..."

"It's part yours, too." He skimmed the ridge of her face with the back of his fingers. "It was yours in a way before we even moved in. I still have those sketches. I know how you love the place, but are you up to that much work by yourself? Of course I'll help as I can..."

"I've done so much by myself by now I'll hardly think about it."

He slid the fingers up alongside her face. "It would be nice not to sell it to a stranger, but I have to say I was starting to think how nice it would be if you found a place just up the road from me, and if you'd accept my job offer. You wouldn't be so alone that way."

"This is just up the road."

"I meant a few blocks, not twenty miles."

Jenna felt herself try to move in closer. He was so sweet, steady. Safe. No, not safe. "I think twenty miles might be safer, actually."

He moved his hand to let it rest on her leg. "For me or for you?"

"Both. Alan, I... You know Trevor thinks the only reason I didn't accept you is because Mom pushed it so much. He thinks I would have if she hadn't pushed, or if she'd tried to pull us apart."

"I've had that same thought many times." He claimed her hand. "I think he could be right. It's a wonder he talks to me."

"Maybe I should have. Let myself. No one else has been there like you have and these past few days, I'm just..."

"You can't hide behind me, Jenna. I'm here to help, as your friend, and if I touch you too much, you'll have to say so. But I'm not leaving Cheryl. I won't do it to her or to the kids."

"I don't want you to leave them. I just want to feel this..."

"Comfortable."

"Yeah."

"You would get bored."

"Maybe."

He grinned. "I do love you. And yes, until you're settled, twenty miles might be safer. But I think Trevor will be back..."

"Not here, he won't. He won't stay here."

"And you want to stay. You're certain all of a sudden?"

"Yes. Except for two things."

"Trevor. And?"

"My mom's across the street. That, I'm not sure I can handle."

"Ah well, she never bothered to worry about what you were doing before. I can't imagine why she would now. There has to be an up side to that, right?"

Jenna slid her arms over his shoulders. "I love you, too. But yes, there is Trevor. Maybe. The thing is ... how do I take him back even if he wants to come back after he..?"

"You're still here with me."

"Different."

"Is it?" He pulled back. "I'm your friend. You trusted me when you were at your most vulnerable and I hit on you. Again. Like I am now to some extent, because I can't seem not to when you're this close and your guard is so far down. And still, you're here, still my friend.

You should give him the same leeway. After all, Jen, you really left him first, and I did warn you. Being in the same house isn't *being* there, and you know it."

Hitting on her. Was he? She supposed, and she supposed she should be annoyed with him, but he knew she wouldn't. He knew he was safe with her. She sighed. "I guess I wanted to be able to take him for granted the way I do with you, the way you do with me. I wanted that with him."

"But Jen, you have to do the same for him."

"I did. I..."

"No, you didn't. He was never quite sure enough you'd stay. That was driving him crazy, Jenna. It wasn't your job. It wasn't your refusal to have another child. It wasn't even your objection to marriage. He wasn't sure enough that you would stay. And apparently he was right, since you're here."

"No, that's not fair. I'm here because he left, because I don't like it there, because I ... I can't feel safe in that apartment anymore."

"Tell me what happened." He shifted to stretch out on the grass in front of her.

She told him the whole thing, their work relationship, the way he kept hitting on her, everything, including what he said about Daniel, and the sketches he had.

He was silent for a long while.

"Say something. Say I'm an idiot. I already know I am. You can say whatever you're thinking."

"I'd like to go up there and break every bone in his body. That's what I'm thinking. And, I wouldn't be too sure he wasn't lying about Daniel, maybe even about the sketches."

"How would he know about them?"

"It's no secret Daniel had sketches stolen, personal sketches, not meant to be shared. Easy enough to piece it together. And maybe he does have them, but as much as I didn't care for Daniel, I just don't think he ever would have sold them. I don't believe it. You should talk to Joan."

"I did. She asked who told me."

Alan shot his gaze up to hers. "About the child?"

"Yes. It's true. He does have."

"That doesn't mean it happened the way Graham said. He loved you, Jenna. He had a strange way of showing it, I know, but he did. You should never wonder about that. And why wouldn't he?"

"Why would he?" She heard herself say it before she could stop it.

Alan stood and pulled her to her feet. "Jenna, you listen to me. I have very nearly left my wife, who I do love, for you. I nearly left my kids who are the center of my world for you, at the risk they may never have forgiven me. Even now, I know I'm standing too close, touching you too much, when my family is just inside. How in the hell can you think you aren't worth loving when I..." He slid his hand along her face and leaned close. "When I love you enough to risk so damned much for you? Do you think so little of me that doesn't matter?"

"Of course not." Much of her wanted to grab him and take him away and make him stay with her. But it was only because of his words, because of the way he looked at her, touched her. It was *his* need pulling her in, not her own.

As she'd done with Daniel.

"I had a miscarriage."

He stepped back. "What? When?"

"About six weeks ago. I didn't even... I knew I was pregnant, but I hadn't really let myself accept it. I knew the day Trevor left, and I didn't tell him I was. He doesn't know, any of it. I didn't even let myself mourn the loss. I just couldn't. And then you called to tell me about my father, the day I got back home from Joan's, after she let me go home, and I just couldn't deal with that, either. I kept working and painting and..."

"How far were you?"

"Four months or nearly and it hardly showed at all. I felt too guilty to talk about it because I kept telling him I didn't want to do it again and when I realized I was it felt like karma slapping me in the face because he'd already moved out and I miss them both but I can't let myself deal with it."

Alan held her in a strong hug. "I think twenty miles might be too far. Someone needs to keep a closer eye on you."

She chuckled. "I don't know. I'm kind of used to just..."

"Keeping it all inside?" He released her enough she could barely see his face through the soft moon glow. "You need to tell him. Write to him, and tell him."

"I don't think I can."

"I won't let you fall apart. I'll be here."

"You two will get all eaten up by mosquitoes out there." His mom called from the porch.

Alan backed up more and took her hand instead. "In other words, we've been out here too long." With a light squeeze, he called over to say they were coming in. "Jen, I'm so sorry. For your loss. Even if you don't want to acknowledge it. I am sorry."

She felt tears push through and wiped them away as they ambled back to the house.

They got curious looks, especially from Cheryl. Jenna said they were talking about the house and asked if they'd be willing to rent it to her instead of selling. The Taylors were thrilled with the idea. Cheryl suggested she might go ahead and move in with them as they finalized things with their other place, so the kids could start adjusting.

A hint. She'd gotten far too close to Alan. Maybe she'd seen them out the window.

~~~

Jenna took Aaron's hand and led him into what used to be Alan's room. "So, what do you think? Do you want this room for your own?"

The boy looked up wide-eyed. "Myself. Not with Anna?"

"Not with Anna. She'll be next door. This will be yours and we can decorate it any way you want."

He nodded with a smile and walked over to the window. "Look. I see the swing set."

"You like it here, right?" She knelt beside him.

"Yes. I like the quiet and the grass and the flowers."

"Do you? You want to help me work in the flower gardens?" He nodded, but she could see something bothering him. "What is it, baby? What are you thinking about?"

"My daddy won't find us at home."

"He knows where we are. He can find us here."

"Daddy will come here?"

"He'll come see you. Of course he will. He loves you so much and he misses you. But Aaron, I don't know if he'll stay, if he'll be here all the time. If he's not, it's okay. We'll see him. He can come visit us and we can visit him." At his frown, she held him close. Soon, she would have to talk more about his real dad. He'd been told, vaguely, but she didn't want to make him think Trevor wasn't his daddy. He was. But Aaron would have to know more, after they were more settled.

"Anna can come sleep here too sometimes."

Jenna scuffed his hair. "If she wants. And if you get too lonely over here, I'll be right across the hall. You can come find me."

He nodded.
~~~

"And maybe Justin will come stay sometimes."

"Yes. And J.R."

"And J.R., too. In a couple of years, maybe we'll get you a puppy. Would you like that?"

"Yes. Not so big. Anna is scared of J.R."

"She won't be when she gets more used to him, but we can get a smaller puppy if you want." With her son content and settling in and thinking about how he wanted to decorate his new room, Jenna went down to where Anna was talking her head off to Mrs. Taylor.

"What does he think?"

Jenna lowered onto the couch. "He thinks he's going to be pretty happy here. And he's talking about a puppy. I hope that'll be okay."

The Taylors exchanged glances and Mr. Taylor answered. "We've been talking, Jenna. We want you to be comfortable enough to do as you please with the place when we move out, and if you'd like, we'll accept your rent payments as a rent to own arrangement. If you're not sure you want to stay, then we can leave it as rent, but if you decide to stay long term, we want to give you that option. We don't need an answer now, but please, think of it as your own. You don't need to ask us what you'd like to do."

Own it. She could just buy it. She supposed she could, once she got a job. They offered to hold the loan for her instead of going to a bank, no interest. They were well set. They didn't need the money, and they would be glad to come back and visit the place from time to time.

She told them she would definitely think about it. Something wouldn't let her make a final decision until she talked to Trevor. She had to talk to him. One way or another.

~~~

"Like this, Anna." Jenna helped her daughter hold the wooden mallet and hit the ball through the metal arch.

"*Yes. I did it.*" Anna jumped up and down.

Jenna rubbed her head and pointed out which arch to aim for next. Aaron was a near expert at Bocce Ball already.

As a woman about her age walked past with two kids on bicycles, one with training wheels, Jenna said hello. The woman returned the greeting. The kids stopped to see what Anna and Aaron were doing.

"You're a friend of the Taylors?"

"Yes. Long time." She introduced herself and her kids.

"It's nice to meet you. I'm Iris Wheeling and this is Kaedin and
~~~

Devin. They're six and four."

Mrs. Taylor came out on the porch and asked Iris to come on over and talk. The boys were still watching Aaron and Anna.

"Do you want to play?" Jenna grabbed two more mallets. With their mom's permission, Jenna took them over and left it to Aaron to explain the game.

"Anna won't feel overwhelmed with all of those boys, will she?"

Jenna laughed. "No, she's fine."

Iris accepted a glass of lemonade and stood on the driveway to help watch over the kids as they talked. She was new in town, also, from Wisconsin, but her husband was from the area and they moved back to help his aging parents. She did some bookkeeping work from her house in between helping her in-laws with errands, and her kids often stopped to talk to Mrs. Taylor.

"Maybe we can get them together for regular play dates?" Jenna felt horribly presumptuous for suggesting it so soon, but the kids were getting along, the boys were well-mannered and not upset by Anna's take-over nature, although Jenna kept telling her to behave, and she was enjoying the friendly chat.

"Oh absolutely. I'd love that. Most of the neighborhood is..."

"Old, like us." Mrs. Taylor laughed. "It's fine to say so. We know we are. And it's high time this quiet little street was filled with kids again. Almost makes me not want to leave."

"You know you're welcome any time." Jenna almost asked if they would just stay in the ground floor guest room they'd moved into. She'd gone so easily back to enjoying Janice Taylor's cooking, and Alan's mom insisted on cooking as long as she was there. The kids cuddled up next to Mr. Taylor at night as he told them stories, either one he remembered or one he made up. It was cozy and she wasn't alone and she didn't need all that space herself. But if Trevor came...

She shoved the thought from her head as Iris said she had to get back to make dinner, inviting Jenna to stop by any time. Anna fussed when her new friends left, so Jenna tackled the girl and rolled her on the bright green grass. Anna laughed and squeezed her neck and Aaron came to jump on top of them.

A car pulling in across the street caught her attention. Her mother. Jenna had yet to see her, and of course she would see her this way, with grass all over her clothes rolling around like monkeys.

Louise Givens got out of her silver Lincoln and stared across at them. Then she walked across the street and up the driveway to speak to Mrs. Taylor. "Your *For Sale* sign is down. Did you find a buyer?"

"Better. We had a little chickadee flit her way back home."

Jenna pulled away from her kids and asked them to pick up the game. She walked directly up to her mother. "I'm renting it."

"Oh? What happened to that long-haired boy?"

"Don't call him that. His name is Trevor, and he's working in Italy right now. He got a nice offer to teach and train there."

"So he just left you and his kid."

"No. I told him to go."

"You walked out on him? How do you plan to pay the rent?"

"I didn't walk out on him. And I'll manage just fine."

"Mommyyyy..." Anna ran up and thudded into her leg. "We cook out hot doggies tonight? I hungry."

"Miss Anna, we just had cooked out hot dogs yesterday. Go help your brother put the game away and we'll get ready for dinner."

To appease the girl, Mrs. Taylor said the casserole was nearly ready and they could eat outside if they wanted. She helped them finish picking up and left Jenna to deal with her mother.

"You didn't come home for the funeral." Her mother watched the kids as they left but didn't address them. "You don't think you owe us more respect than that?"

"Respect? You didn't come when my children were born. You weren't there for me when I lost my first baby and was devastated. You weren't there after I lost Daniel and was devastated. When have you ever been there? I didn't leave Trevor. I left Chicago. Because I was attacked and I don't feel safe there anymore. You didn't even know and I'm not sure you would have cared much if you did. You didn't know I just lost another child and you weren't there for me then, either. Joan was there. Every time. What do I owe you, exactly?"

"Attacked?" It at least sounded concerned. "Jenna..."

"Don't worry. I took care of that myself, too. I'm very good at that by now and I'll take care of my kids myself if I have to, also."

"And I suppose you're moving across the street to rub it in my face, so you can show just how much you don't need me at all."

Jenna was so shocked by the question, she could hardly make her brain work well enough to answer. "You know what? Not everything is about you. It just isn't." She walked away. It wasn't about her mother, or her father. It wasn't even about Daniel or Trevor. This was home. And she had plans.

Twenty-two

Breathing in the sweet smell of a new lavender plant, Jenna eyed Dave as he swept it away from her with a grin and took it to a new garden bed. She watched him arrange it with cypress shrubs around an established forsythia.

He looked back at her, his head cocked, and grinned again. "Want to come help dig?"

She ambled over. "I will, but that should go over to the side of the porch with the Russian sage."

"Hey, I'm following the boss's orders."

"I know, but I think he's wrong."

"You want to argue with him, go ahead. Otherwise, I'm sticking this thing exactly where he said to stick it."

At his teasing look, she couldn't help but play along. "You always take orders that well?"

"Depends. If I can find pleasure in it, I might." He winked.

She had to laugh. Of all of Alan's men, Dave was the most flirty of the group, and barely older than she was. He was built as well as Alan, muscular, tall, with gorgeous dark curly hair he kept short in the back and just long enough on top for it to curl. He was single, which Jenna found remarkable for as cute and funny and sexy as he was. The other guys said he was too jumpy, too unsettled, and his girlfriends tended to last about a week, two at the most. Jenna figured the right girl would change that.

"Dave, stop flirting with her before the boss fires your ass." One of the older guys shook his head.

"Hey, she doesn't seem to mind. Why should he?" He threw an amused look at Jenna. "So? Should I go ahead and stick this thing in?"

"No. You should move it over there."

With a glance at the other guy, he called over to Alan. "Hey boss man, your friend here says I'm doing it wrong."

Alan gave more instructions to one of the others and came over. "Doing what wrong?"

Jenna explained why she thought the lavender should go by the porch, at the end where it needed some kind of fence to conceal the blunt end and space underneath, and told him of her thought to use some of the cut logs from the tree they had to take down as steps off the porch to the yard in between the lavender and sage.

"They'll draw bees to the porch."

"Yes, but if we put a couple of big pretty pots on the edge of the porch and fill them with lemon balm, that should keep the bees on the outside, and keep mosquitoes away from the porch, too. Right?"

"It might. Hard to tell what bugs will do. But we've used the pots we had and I'm at the end of their budget. Big pots are expensive."

"Clay pots aren't."

"Too plain for this place."

"Not when I'm done with them, they won't be."

He grinned with a shake of the head. "Okay. Your call. Tell Dave what you want and he'll put them anywhere you ask. We're running low on time, though."

"I'll do them tonight and pot them tomorrow. Simple."

Alan rubbed a hand down her back and told Dave he belonged to her as long as she needed him, then turned back and told him if he wanted to keep his job, he would take that only the way it was meant.

Jenna laughed and moved into work mode. She had no problem with Dave or his flirting. To be honest, she was flattered. Grabbing two lavender plants and two Russian sage plants, she pointed out which logs she wanted and let Dave use his muscle to carry them to the side of the porch. They worked together to get the arrangement right and she used the small shovel Alan bought for her the other day to help dig holes. Pleased with the effort, she stepped back to study it and to plan how to paint the clay pots to best match and complement the new arrangement and the house.

Dave tilted his head. "You know you have dirt all over your face."

"Yeah? So do you. And?"

"And lavender in your hair." He reached over to pull it out.

"Hazard of the trade. Better than a bee in my hair."

"Now that, I'd almost like to see. Bet you'd squeal and run away from it, huh?"

"I don't squeal, and I'm not afraid of bees."

"No?" He stepped closer. "At the risk of my job, I have to tell you that I enjoy your company far more than any of those clean-faced girls who think they have to squeal to be a girl."

"Thank you. What if we add some of the extra river pebble around the base? It would help keep the weeds out."

"It would be a nice contrast with the logs, also. Good call."

"Complement."

"What? I guess it was..."

"No I mean it would be a nice *complement* with the log since the color is similar and they'll blend, not a contrast as in it stands out and emphasizes."

"Okay. I wouldn't dare argue with an artist." He grinned. "You ever teach art?"

"Only to my kids. What about a mix of larger river stone and small pebbles?"

"You should consider teaching. You have a natural way about you that makes people want to listen to what you say, without making them feel stupid as too many teachers do. You'd be good at it."

People wanted to listen to what she said? Jenna was stunned at the thought. "I don't have a degree. And I'm not big on school."

"So do it on your own. That might not work in your big city of Chicago, but around here, people would be happy enough to accept that you know what you're talking about. With your name and your big city art experience, what else would you need?"

"Chicago isn't my city. This is."

He smiled, a beautiful smile. "I have to agree with you there. But we better get back to work before we hear about it."

She moved over to the original bed he'd been working in where new plants had been set to replace the ones she'd taken and again helped dig holes. As she worked, she considered the thought. She could use the basement. The Taylor house had a big partly finished walk-out basement with glass doors and windows. She could turn it into a studio and start a new mural on the long plain wall opposite the windows. Her things were down there already, since Alan had gone back to Chicago to get them, including the canvases. He took his truck and one of his men to help and put her bigger things and brought what she asked for, to include her bed she'd picked out with Trevor and the kids' beds and dressers. Her miscellaneous furniture, she left for the friend Trevor lined up to take over the apartment until he got home. Nate knew him. He arranged it after Jenna left. Maybe Trevor would let the guy stay with him when he got home. Anyway, she needed new furniture. The Taylors were leaving part of theirs since it wouldn't fit in the smaller house. She'd fill in the rest as she could.

If she was going to make such big changes, though, she needed to just buy the house.

~~~

Jenna stood back to look at her work. The pots had turned out well. The lemon balm was still too small for them at the moment, but they would grow fast. She also put yellow and purple pansies around the edge to trail down over the sides to complement the purple of the lavender and sage and suggest the yellow of the lemon balm which wasn't actually yellow, but the yellow was inferred in the name.

The house owner wandered up next to her. "Very nice."

"You like the idea? The pots will fill out better as they grow and it's a perennial so if you cover it lightly over the winter, it should keep coming back without a problem. It's great for tea and cooking, too."

He smiled and set a hand on her shoulder. "Alan made a wise choice when he brought you on board, although I had my doubts."

"Thank you. I've watched him work often enough over the years, I figured I should be more constructive while I was out here."

He patted her shoulder with a smile and left to check on other progress around his yard. Jenna swiped her forehead with her sleeve.

"You sure impressed him." Dave nudged her arm.

"He's being nice because I'm a girl." She threw a wink, referring to his first comment when Alan brought her in to work with them, that he didn't expect to have to pull the weight of some girl along with his own job. She'd found it funny and by now had proved she knew how to pull her own weight.

"Okay, I deserved that. And you have dirt on your face again."

"Surprisingly, you don't. Guess you're not working hard enough."

He pulled a hand towel from his pocket and wiped the side of her face. "So, it's Friday. Feel like grabbing dinner tonight? What do you like to eat? I'm not picky."

"Oh. Thank you but..."

"I know. Alan said you're attached but in all the times we've talked I've only heard you mention your kids, not the guy you're supposedly attached to, so I thought you might not be too attached. Figured it wouldn't hurt to ask. You're not wearing a ring or anything."

She hadn't talked about him. Jenna knew she hadn't. Not because she wasn't attached enough, but because it hurt too much to think about him, to be so distant from him. She'd only taken the ring off so it wouldn't get scuffed or dirt packed. She still put it back on every night after her shower.

"So?" He picked something out of her hair, although she wasn't sure there was anything in it.
~~~

"Thank you, but no. I really can't."

"Can't? Or don't want to?"

She gave him a light grin and moved off to pull a few weeds out of an older bed. He bent to help but he didn't push. He asked about her kids, about her plans for the weekend, if she'd seen Arthur 2 yet. She had to admit she hadn't seen the first one and he said she should rent it because it was hysterical.

When Alan called her name, she answered without turning.

"You might want to take a break."

"I'm fine." She threw Dave a sideways glance when he chuckled and Alan tried again. She still refused.

"That's okay. It's a nice view from here. I can watch for a while."

Her stomach tightened. Trevor. She turned from where she'd been kneeling, reaching over... and he was smiling at her. Suddenly, she was furious. How dare he just show up while she was working and dirty and sweaty, without warning, and stand there looking so ... so sexy and calm and happy? "Why are you here?"

"I heard you moved."

"Yeah. And I'm not going back."

He nodded and the smile disappeared. "Can you take a break since your boss gave you permission?"

"I'll take a break when everyone else does. I don't need and won't accept special favors." She heard Dave chuckle again.

"Okay." Trevor looked at Alan. "All right if I lend a hand?"

"Fine with me. Dave, I need you to help George out back."

"Sure you do." He muttered only loud enough for Jenna to hear and flashed her a look as he got up. "On my way." He gave Trevor a light nod as he left.

"Did I interrupt?" Trevor looked far too amused as Alan walked away with Dave. Jenna could just imagine that conversation.

"I'm not going back." As he approached, she could see he'd let his hair grow out and the natural hightlights accented his nice tan. Such a beautiful mix.

"You said that."

"And I mean it." At least she thought she meant it.

"Jen." He came close enough to take her hand. "What happened? Nate wouldn't say. Joan won't say. Aunt Nina doesn't know for sure. She knows you were spooked by something."

"Doesn't matter." She turned from him and knelt again to pull more weeds. It felt awkward to have him there, in her space. He felt different to her there. Or maybe she hadn't forgiven him.

He knelt beside her and yanked a dandelion out by the root.

"Don't do that. You're not dressed for work and those stain..."

"I know they do. Think I've never played with dandelions?"

"I don't know. Have you?" She pulled at a root that decided to be stubborn and wrapped one of her gloves around it. It still didn't want to come out. Trevor wrapped his hand around hers and yanked the thing. A long strong weed. Getting rid of it would help...

He set his hands alongside her face and forced her to look at him. "What happened, Jenna?" He looked worried, upset.

"Not here. I can't talk here."

"Then call it a day and come with me. Alan says the job's nearly done. He doesn't need you here."

"Great. I'll have to thank him for saying so."

"Jen, please. I came all the way from Italy because you moved suddenly after telling me you'd stay until I got back, because something spooked you and no one would talk and I couldn't get you on the phone. I want to know..."

"Are you in love with her?"

He stared a second. "What?"

"The girl you were with. Do you? Are you still with her?"

"No. And no. And again, I'm sorry. More than I can say. But Jen, stop changing the subject. Either tell me here or come with me. I'll take you anywhere you want to go where you can talk."

"You left me."

"You pushed me away."

With a nod, she stood. She needed to move around, to dig a hole or ... or something more physical, more tiring. She knew he followed only a couple of steps behind as she went back to the main work area and asked what still needed to be done.

Alan glanced between them. "We're good here, Jen. Take off early. It'll help make up for the work you did on the pots on your own time." He fixed his gaze on Trevor. "Her car's at my place, and so are the kids."

"Yeah I was there. Thought I was going to have to bring them out here with me. Hope they aren't driving your wife nuts by now."

"I'm sure she's fine."

Jenna felt her head spin. All the control she'd built up for herself had just crashed as they planned things for her, as Alan sided with Trevor. She walked away in a near jog, but where would she go? She rode in with Alan since there was no sense taking two cars out to Pekin when she had to drop the kids off with Cheryl anyway.

Dave asked if she was all right as she walked past him. Did she look not all right? Did she dare ask him for a ride ... somewhere? Before she could think how to answer, or whether to answer, Trevor was at her side, then in front of her, making her stop.

"I can't do this here." She swallowed hard. "I'm at work. And you should have let me know you were coming. Nate has my number."

"Jenna, I am so sorry. Okay, I screwed up big time. I know. Please, let's go somewhere and talk."

"What is there to talk about? I'm not leaving. I have a house, the Taylor house. I'm renting it but they've offered to let me buy it and ... I think I'm going to buy it, put a studio in the basement, work with Alan part time and... I'm not leaving. And I know you won't move here to this *nowhere* city as you always call it, so what is there to talk about?"

"You're fully set on staying."

"Yes."

His chest rose fast and he whooshed the air back out through his lips as in a silent whistle, a slow silent signal whistle that sounded like a loud and deep foghorn. It echoed its bellow through her body.

Trevor asked her to at least walk with him, farther away from Alan's men. He didn't go far, only enough. "I have to know one thing. Do I still have a chance? Would you *want* me to move here? Or is this just done?"

Goosebumps spread up and down her arms. "It doesn't matter if I'd want you to stay here. You don't. And you know I would never want you to do what you don't want to do. I've always said that." She backed away. "I'm... The kids have missed you. I'll go with you, back to Alan's, so you can spend time with them."

"And then?"

"Then you go do what you need to do. And come visit us. Finish your year in Italy. Decide what you want afterward. And we'll be here. But we're staying here."

He moved in and dipped his head close. "And you'll be shacked up with that guy who was looking at your ass more than he was working and is now trying not to look like he's watching us?"

"Was he?" Her heart raced. Shacked up? Just for that, she decided to make it sound like more than it was. "He just asked me out."

Trevor nodded and looked over at Dave, studying him. "He's not so scrawny, is he?"

"No. And he's not an artist."

"Two strokes in his favor. What did you tell him?" He set his hands on her hips.

"And he likes to play in the dirt."

"Three." He nudged closer.

"He's pretty cute. And he's funny."

"Okay, I got it. I guess that means you agreed?"

Just because she was angry, and hurt, Jenna nearly said she had, and she would, and ... and she couldn't. "No. I said no."

"Why?"

"Good question."

"Jen, can we go somewhere?"

"I'm not ready to talk about it."

"Okay. Then ... lunch? We can talk about anything else."

"I ate."

"You're not going to make this easy."

"No. You hurt me. And I know I hurt you, but it's really not the same. I might have pushed you away at times, but I stayed. I never would have walked out. Never. I never would have cheated on you."

He gasped a quick breath and his eyes moistened. "I know. But hell, Jen, you called me by your ex husband's name. You don't think that hurt?"

"I'm sorry I did. I don't think it should be an excuse for you to turn to another woman since it was unintentional and you know it was, but I am sorry I did. And I know I messed up, too, more than just that. I know. But I don't know where to go from here."

"And I don't want to lose you."

Jenna pressed her lips together. They weren't alone enough for this. It felt like a break up and ... and she didn't want that.

"You have dirt on your face." Trevor reached up to brush it away and the touch spread down through her palpitating heart all the way to her toes.

"That's why." She whispered it and he didn't understand, but he didn't have to understand. "Come with me."

She knew what she wanted to do. At least right at this moment. He let her in the car, one of Nate's he'd borrowed which meant he had to go back to Chicago, and followed her directions. They didn't talk as she led him to the docks at Riverside. It was Friday. There would be a cruise leaving soon. The *Spirit of Peoria,* the beautiful not-so-old paddle wheel that replaced the *Julia Belle Swain* so long ago. He didn't hesitate when she asked him to go. They got tickets and he found a couple of hot dogs since he hadn't eaten all day and they sat and waited to be allowed passage.

He asked her about the work she'd done with Alan. She told him that he let her help plan, that he wanted her to be a partner of sorts, not just an employee, and use her artistic vision and whatever craft work she wanted to improve his landscape designs. She didn't think they needed to be improved, but she did have a flamboyant touch he didn't that would work well for some clients.

When she asked, he told her some of what he'd seen in Italy. Not the Uffizi yet, which surprised her, but he said he wanted to do that with her, not without her, although his fellow artists gave him plenty of grief about it since he was right there in Florence. He did go to the Acadamy Gallery to see the Statue of David, and to the Baptistry and Brunelleschi's Dome and the Palace of Bargello where he wandered among statues by Michelangelo, Donatello, and Verrocchio, among others. Everywhere he went, he found himself wishing she was there to see it, especially the architecture and the gardens. Jenna admitted she wished she'd agreed to go, that she should have and she was sorry she hadn't. Not only to see it, but to be with him.

Then it was time to board. As Trevor had during their architecture tour of Chicago, Jenna pointed out Peoria landmarks, places that meant something to her, and how she loved driving into or out of the city at night to see the sparkling lights along the Illinois River.

The river tour felt like starting over. Maybe they were. He'd asked if she wanted him to stay, to move there with her, and she tried hard not to let herself believe he might, that he would be happy there. But maybe he would.

He kissed her as the boat was docking and she allowed it, but only a light kiss. She didn't tell him why she left Chicago so suddenly. It was too soon. She wasn't ready. Since she was showing off her favorite things, though, they stopped at Emo's for a chocolate sundae with peanut butter and marshmallow sauce. Trevor hugged her and said it was his newest addiction.

She loved his hugs. Truly, she loved his hugs.

Alan was home by the time they pulled in and the kids flew out the door at Trevor as soon as he stepped out of the car. Jenna stood back and watched. She also loved seeing him with their babies.

"Coming in?" Alan took her side. She let herself be coerced to stay for dinner and she was glad to let the kids monopolize his time and attention. Alan and Cheryl talked to him like normal. Jenna couldn't. Trevor watched her all night but he didn't push.

He had a couple of weeks, he said, for emergency leave.

A couple of weeks. She wasn't sure it wouldn't have been easier if he'd just waited and come when could stay, at least in the same state.

Alan offered to let him stay. With the kids pouting about leaving his side, and Anna stuck to him like paper towel on a wet brush, Jenna said he could have Aaron's room and the kids could share Anna's. She would go that far, but not farther, not yet.

But it didn't quite work that way. The kids still wouldn't leave his side after they'd talked with the Taylors for a few minutes and their pajamas were on and they all gathered in Aaron's room, tucked onto his single bed.

Jenna stood at the door and shook her head. "Come on, guys. If you're having a slumber party, you might as well do it in the big bed so no one falls out." She meant she would take Aaron's room and let them have hers, but it didn't turn out that way, either. They pulled her along and insisted she stay.

With her on one side and Trevor on the other, the queen mattress was bulging with bodies and giggles and movement. Anna was next to Trevor and Jenna reminded him how much she moved when she slept. He grinned and cuddled her tightly against him.

They were all asleep before she was. Jenna watched them for the longest time. She studied Trevor's face. And his bare shoulder and top of his chest above where the sheet covered him. Finally, she drifted off with her arm around her son.

She woke with a start at a sudden noise. Trevor. He sounded in pain. "What's wrong?" When he didn't answer, Jenna pushed the sheet out of the way and crawled around the kids to get to him. "Are you okay? What's wrong?"

He grunted an answer. "Should have turned the other way. Damn her knee is hard for as little as it is."

Jenna snickered unintentionally. She'd warned him.

"Yeah, funny. Damn."

"Sorry. Should I move them back to their rooms?"

"No." He looked up into her eyes. "I think it might have been worth it for this. Nice to have you so close."

She was half-kneeling and half-lying over him, carefully, her weight on the side of his hip where she wouldn't add to the pain. He slid a hand up her bare arm.

"Trevor..."

"I know. You're not ready. But Jen, damn this feels right."

"The kids don't need to hear that..."

"They're asleep. They could sleep through anything. I've always found that amazing since we both wake up at the drop of a pin."

She looked over at them; their mouths were open and their soft breaths raised their little chests rhythmically. "We do make beautiful children."

"Children?"

"Oh." She put her gaze back on him. "Yes. Much of why Aaron is turning out so beautifully is because of you. I do know it is. I have to take him to work with me now and then recently, which is fine. He loves it and he's good, but he's... He needs you, Trevor. He's been so quiet. It worries me. And I'm not trying to make you feel guilty." His averted eyes moistened and she brushed them with her fingertips. "I'm sorry. I didn't mean to... It's okay. I just... I was an idiot for ever... He *is* yours. He is."

"I've missed them like crazy." He reached over to caress Aaron's head, and returned his attention, caressed her shoulder, met her eyes. "Let's try this again, Jen. Nothing could be more right than this."

She wanted to say yes, to believe he was right, but then why had he left? If it really was, he wouldn't have walked away.

"But don't do it for the kids. Or for me. This time, say yes only if you want it for yourself, if it's truly me you want. I can't settle for less than that. I'll be here for them anyway. Whatever you do, I'll be here as much as I can. I'll go to their activities. I'll teach them to throw a ball and... all of that stuff they need, that matters to you that they have in a dad. I'll be that, either way. Because yes, they are both mine and I can't tell you how much I want them, to be with them."

"I know. It is part of what makes me love you."

"I hope it's more than that." He pulled her gently in for a kiss and she allowed it to deepen, allowed her body to settle in against his. It did feel right. Absolutely right. It did.

"Yes." She whispered in his ear. "It is much more than that." With a quick breath to choke back her emotions, Jenna pulled back and returned to her side of the bed, faced the other direction. She couldn't give in so easily. She had to think.

She woke when the kids stirred but Trevor got up with them and told her to go back to sleep. She gladly agreed. It was his turn while he was there. The next time she woke, she smelled eggs and bacon and her stomach rumbled.

Laughter and voices hit her as she approached the kitchen. The Taylors had accepted him as well as Alan and Cheryl had. And he was helping Mrs. Taylor cook. The scene was too beautiful to interrupt so she stayed still and enjoyed it until Aaron saw her and hopped over like a bunny rabbit.

"What are you doing, silly boy?" She rubbed his head.

"We saw bunnies in the yard. Out that window." He pointed.

"Did you? Little bunnies?" He nodded and pulled her over but they weren't still there. "Maybe we'll see them later." She crouched to give him a hug and Anna came for one, nearly knocking Jenna over. "Wow you guys are bouncy already. Did Daddy put jumping jacks in your Wheaties?"

"They woke up that way." Trevor was giving her that look, the *I wouldn't be anywhere else at this moment if I could be* look, which is what he called it once when she asked. "Sit down, guys. Time to eat." He helped Anna up into her booster seat as Aaron climbed up on his chair. He wouldn't use his seat anymore. He sat on his knees instead.

When Trevor pulled out a chair for her, she gave him a quick hug. "This is nice. I've missed this."

"Yeah. So have I." He kissed the side of her head and helped push her chair in, with a quick touch of her shoulder.

She saw the Taylors glance at each other with grins. Obviously, they thought she should take him back, too. They let her know they'd be out of town for a few days, staying with Amber so they could more easily get their new place ready. Jenna knew it was an excuse to give her and Trevor time alone, and she was grateful.

They spent part of the day in yard, letting the kids use their energy under shade of the wide maples and tall oak while she showed him the various flower gardens and told him of her plans for them. She wanted a small pond and fountain in the one in the corner, to give the birds water and for the peacefulness of it, with maybe a little bench in front, and she wanted to turn another into an herb garden, just outside the back door.

When she sat in the grass under a tree, Anna came flying at her to play, the way she saw J.R. tackle anyone who dared sit in the grass. She took it as a sign. Jenna returned the tackle, tickling her just enough to make her laugh, and Aaron ran over to join them until she cried mercy and set them back to the swingset.

Trevor pulled grass out of her hair as he crouched beside her with a curious expression. "I've never seen you like this."

She shrugged. "I'm home." And safe, especially with her Trevor at her side. She wouldn't say that yet. "Just a warning, if you sit that cute little ass of yours in the grass, you're fair game."

"Am I?" With a spark in his eyes she hadn't seen in far too long, he lowered to the grass, knees up in front, looking every bit a city boy trying to fit in.

Jenna kissed him, pushing him down onto his back, running her hands through his hair as she lay against him ... until two little bodies jumped on top. She laughed. "I warned you. Get him, guys."

When they wrestled the kids back inside, Jenna sent them to wash their hands and took Trevor to the basement where she wanted a studio. Jenna found herself telling him of her thought that she might have kids in to draw, paint, model clay, and maybe add a throwing wheel. She'd been considering trying to learn to make her own pots. Of course firing them would be a problem.

"Wouldn't have to be. I could put a small kiln in the bare corner, away from the swingset and your pond, along with maybe an outdoor grill area? We'd have to put a small fence around it to be sure the kids didn't get close, but the yard's big enough."

"I don't cook on a grill."

"I do. Used to do it at Nina's plenty often. Of course that was just a little metal bucket thing and I'd want..."

"Are you staying?"

"Do you want me to stay?" He brushed fingers along her neck and back into her hair. When she didn't answer, because she wasn't sure how to answer his question to her question, he shrugged and looked out the glass-paned doors. "This could be addicting. We might have to work out a compromise. My work is in Chicago and it has a lot of potential there, but we could keep the apartment and I can go back and forth, or we all can..."

"Aaron starts school next year. He needs to be here on a regular basis. And I..."

"You just don't want to be there anymore."

She shook her head. "No. For an occasional visit, yes. Not more than that. But ... keep the apartment, Trevor. Come stay with us when you can. On weekends if you want. We have space." Jenna knew she was adding a separation line, but she could learn to be okay with it.

"Separate space?" He reached directly into her heart with his gaze, the question, the longing.

"I don't know yet. I have to be smart about this." She glanced over to see Aaron and Anna come back and grab their big bouncy ball to throw against the wall and chase after it. "My heart is saying full out yes I want you and I want whatever you can offer, but my head is saying to be careful. Until they agree one way or another, I can't say for sure. With Daniel, I listened to my head. With you, it was my heart. I just really would like them to agree. I have to have that."

"Okay. So we leave it at this for a while? You stay here where you need to be. Buy the house, Jen, so you can do what you want with it. I'll help you buy it if you want, or at least support the kids. I'll be here as much as I can. Maybe we can work back to where we were?"

"Yes. Maybe."

He took her hand. "So let's barge in on Alan and Cheryl so I can talk to him about building you a kiln. I'm guessing he'd know where to get what I need and maybe some help to do it."

"You don't have to..."

"I want to do that for you, Jen. Maybe Dave knows how to build a kiln since he's good with his hands. I can hire him for you."

"Don't be an ass."

He chuckled and kissed her head.

They accepted Cheryl's invitation to cook out since they were there anyway and the men were fully involved with talking building plans and codes and all that stuff Alan knew that she didn't. Alan also knew everyone on the township board so he didn't figure getting the permit would be too hard as long as they had professional supervision. And of course he knew who to suggest.

Jenna was starting to feel more at ease with having Trevor in the middle of her home life. She was a huge mix of settled and unsettled around him, which sometimes she loved and sometimes she didn't. She did feel more vivid, more colorful, more alive with him than with anyone else, and there was nothing about that she didn't love.

Taking the kids' plates, she went back inside, rinsed them and put them in the dishwasher – Cheryl never, ever used paper plates, even for cookouts – and stood looking at him through the window. Dusk was starting to descend. She would have to decide soon what to do for the night. The kids needed to get home and get their baths. She badly needed a shower. And her mind flashed to Trevor in the shower with her. One of his favorite things.

Alan brought more stuff in and came to her side. "What are you thinking about this by now? Sounds like he's making some permanent plans here."

"Yeah, maybe, and I don't know."

He leaned back against the counter. "There's nothing wrong with permanent, Jen. Life has plenty of adventures anyway. Trust me."

"You mean I should take him back." Jenna didn't take her eyes from her ... her children's father, as they both sat on his lap and talked in his ears, with Anna's arms around his neck.

"I wouldn't presume to tell you whether or not you should." He looked behind him out the window then back at her. "Tell me what you see when you look at him."

What did she see? "Love." She surprised herself by choosing that word first. But it was always the first thing she saw.

"What else?"

"Kindness. Laughter. He makes me laugh. A lot. Or he used to. Gentleness. Beauty. He sees things in such a beautiful way, different but beautiful. Patience. He'd have to have, right?" She pressed her lips together. She didn't want to do this anymore.

"Keep going, Jenna. Tell me."

She grabbed a deep breath. "Friendship. Respect." She shrugged. "Everything, really. Everything that matters. The way he loves to be with the kids. The way they matter to him so much. The way I matter to him..." She dropped her eyes. "Alan, I want him. I do. But what if it happens again? I don't know where it went so wrong and I don't know how to stop it and..."

"I think you jumped in too fast the first time and it was no more than that. You picked up and moved where you didn't want to be just to see if it would work and you never let yourself stop to really think about it."

"Yeah, I do that."

He chuckled. "One of the things I love about you."

She rolled her eyes.

"Maybe you both need the rest of his year in Italy apart to figure things out, but don't turn him away. Just my opinion, of course, but you should give yourself time to think."

"If he doesn't wait?"

"Then you have your answer. Once, I think you can get over, since by all rights, you were broken up and I'm not sure you can hold that against him. If he does it again, I would tell you flat out not to ever take him back. And if you don't wait... If someone else catches your eye in the meantime, then maybe..."

"I don't want anyone else."

"Then maybe you already have your answer."

"But it's not the same. After Daniel and I went through that bad time, it was never the same afterward and I don't know if I can do that again, if I can settle for almost as good as it was because I'll always know it was better before..."

"Jenna, Trevor is not Daniel. You have to stop doing that. It's not fair to him. He can only be who he is. He can't change what Daniel was. It's not fair to expect of him."

"I don't..."

"Don't you?" He pushed away from the counter and took her hands. "Besides, I think you're looking at it wrong. After you pulled through that rough patch, it wasn't the same; you're right. It was stronger. Deeper. I could see it. I could see how the young lust thing that drove you to him had changed to a more mature relationship, one you wanted, not one you needed. It made you strong enough to deal with his illness, to be what he needed, to let yourself grow, to adapt to being a single mom. You pulled through it and it's helped you be the amazing woman you are today, the one Trevor sees, and loves, and appreciates. If you let yourself, I think you'll feel a whole lot more with him and for him than you do so far."

He urged her to look at him instead of out the window. "You know that book you always read to the kids? That happens with a relationship, too. The more you go through together, the more the edges wear off, the deeper your feelings get, and the more real it is. At least if it's a good relationship down at the core, it will. It's taken a long time for Cheryl and me to get there but we're finally getting there. It's why I can get so close to you now and still resist you. Because I am finding that with her, as you said years ago I should. You were right."

The Velveteen Rabbit. One of her favorite books to read to her kids. The more something is loved, the more it appears worn out. She thought about all the times she caught her reflection in the mirror and noticed the lines, the fatigue. She thought about her kids surrounding her and spilling things on her and wearing on her nerves and crying when she left their sides. Mostly, she thought about the way Trevor's gaze had changed over the past three years they'd been together. There was less amusement and question in his eyes and more ... true feeling.

So this was their illness stage. He'd wandered off for the moment. Or she had. But this time, maybe she could have him back.

With a sigh, she went back outside and noticed Cheryl's wary look as Alan followed her. They still had a way to go, as far as Jenna could see. She hoped they would get there.

"You guys ready to go home? It's getting late." She went up to her little family and reached for Anna but the girl hugged his neck tighter. "He's coming with us, baby. You don't have to choke him."

Trevor stood with both kids in his arms, and he was so adorable, Jenna couldn't resist a light kiss.

"Careful. You'll make me drop the babies."

"No you won't. I know better. Come here, Anna." Her daughter wouldn't release him, but Aaron did. He got down and grasped her hand as they told their friends goodbye and headed home.

She showered as Trevor tucked the kids in, and while he showered, she went to a canvas she'd started that was set up in her room so she could work on it when she couldn't sleep. It was a distant lake scene. Hazy. Blurred. Too distant.

Adding brighter green next to the dark green and brown she already had, plus pink, purple, and white to her palette, Jenna started at the left corner and sketched in close up stalks of lavender. The background was a touch surreal but she tried to make the foreground as realistic as she could get it. The stalks came up over the forest green-blue field of grass and over the weeds at the lake edge to where the flowers floated in front of the water. But close to the viewer, as though she could reach out and pick them. They were Trevor. She knew they were. Her calming influence. Her uplifting, graceful, hardy artist boy.

She saw him pause at her door, freshly showered in shorts and an old T-shirt. Waiting for permission to enter. "Come here." She handed him the paintbrush and the palette. "Finish it for me."

"Oh, no, Jen. This is... really beautiful. I'm not messing it up..."

"Trevor." She took the palette back, pulled him to where he could reach the canvas, and cuddled into his left side. "You are my lavender. My creative, beautiful, tranquil inspiration. It can't be done if you don't help me finish it." Jenna wasn't entirely sure she was making sense, but she watched him study the painting and consider a moment.

"Can I add colors?"

"Do what you want." She kissed his neck and released him enough to let him find two shades of red and a deep yellow.

He added two twisted together tall sunflowers creeping in from the right side of the large canvas, their petals a gorgeous blend of reds and yellow, their stems more blue than green. They were a blend of realism and abstraction. He worked fast, much faster than she'd been able. But she didn't garden fast, either. She liked to take her time.

In the bottom right, not quite in the corner but not centered, where there was empty space in the field of grass between the flowers, a sketch of a couple emerged. Almost fully abstract. Tanned flesh colors angled and twisted together like the sunflowers, obvious in their act for anyone used to Trevor Dade's work. Not obvious for anyone who wasn't.

Jenna slid her hand up his back and into his hair as she determined that he was finished, and pulled him down to her for a long easy kiss. Then she reclaimed the brush, dipped it in red, and wrote along the side of the canvas, where she always titled her works if they got titles, *Complementary*. She signed the right bottom corner then gave it back to him to do the same.

Climbing on her bed to take the poster print of a Van Gogh beach scene down, she set it out of the way and hung their new canvas. Still on the bed, at the edge in front of him, she stroked his hair as Trevor set his head on her stomach and circled his arms around her hips.

"You need to know what happened in Chicago."

He raised his face, nodded, and helped her down.

She closed her door and told him everything about that night, in detail as much as she could manage. When she finished, Trevor pulled her in against him and held so tight she could hardly breathe. He didn't say I told you so. He didn't talk of revenge as Alan had. He held her, and he trembled. And he apologized for not being there.

The dampness under his eyes made her lose her own control that she'd been handling so well ever since she left the city. But she finally felt safe, inside-out safe, and it all hit her. The attack. The miscarriage. Her father. And she let it out, although she couldn't talk more. She couldn't tell him about the baby yet.

As she calmed and dried her face, she looked into his eyes and she knew. If he wouldn't stay, she would go back with him. After his year was up and he would be there. She would go. Or they would go back and forth together. She wanted to be with him. Where she was safe.

She kissed him and he responded like a brush fire until they pulled each other down onto the bed, entwined as the couple on the canvas, and again she could hardly breathe.

"Jenna." He leaned over her, his naked body against hers, and stroked hair away from her face. "Come to Italy with me."

"Trev…"

"Not now. Not for the rest of the year. Later. All those extra hours I was working at the bar were for that, saving to take you there. All four of us. For a good three or four weeks."

"You won't get tired of it by the time you finish your year?"

"I'm not going back." He kissed her neck. "Not without you."

"No, Trevor, I'll wait. I'll be here. Okay? Go finish…"

"I missed you. I missed our babies. And I'll never forgive myself for not being here for you when you were dealing with … everything. And I'm sorry…"

"Don't. It's just as much my fault. Maybe more my fault."

He met her lips, stroked her face. "My sweet Jenna, let me stay. I won't leave you again."

"Here?"

"Here. Where you want to be. I'll make do just fine in this little boonies town. There has to be something for an abstractionist slash bartender to do here. I can even learn to play in the dirt if I need. Just promise me we'll travel as we can. Not in twenty years when they're grown, but…"

"Why do you love me?"

He raised his eyebrows. "Are you serious?"

"I want to know. I need to know why you're willing to walk away from everything you have in Chicago."

With a light grin, he took her hand and kissed her fingers. "Jen, you are such an incredible mixture of so many things. You're gentle and open and yet you can be tough as nails and so inside yourself that I constantly wonder what's going on in your head. You're so giving and yet no matter what or how much you give, you always remain you. You're creative and humble and headstrong and you might not know where you want to go, but you know you won't let anyone change your mind when you decide. You're… How much do you want?" He paused and she stayed quiet until he continued. "Okay." He gave her a quick kiss. "You're mysterious and charming and elegant but still down to earth and very real. There's nothing fake about you. You are who you are. No fronts. No exhibition. Just you." He ran his fingers down her neck. "You're tender, and you're sensual and playful, and you can either lead or follow and be comfortable with either. You energize me.

You're independent and you're needy, both of which I truly love. You know what I need when I need it and never hold back. Well, you do to some extent and I hope in time that will change but I know that depends on me, too, and I know I'll have to re-earn your trust and that's okay because I will."

"Yes." She kissed him and ran her hand down his bare chest.

"Yes, you know I will, or yes I have to?"

"Yes to that question you asked so often. Yes, I want you to stay. Yes, I'll travel with you. Yes, I want to have another baby with you because three is a good number; it's artistic, and we already have a blue child and we have a red child. And a palette isn't complete without a yellow child, right? Think we might get that on the next try?"

He stared. Silent.

"I already feel like your wife. I have since you moved in with me. If you want to ask me again, and I'll understand if you need to wait to be sure you still want that, but if you do..."

"Yes." He sat up on his knees with the sheet only barely covering his hips and grasped her hand. "Hell yes, I'm asking again."

She stroked her fingers down his chest. "Let's make this official. Let's do this all the way. I want all the way with you."

Again, he held her so tight she could hardly breathe. "I won't let you down again." It was a whisper in her ear.

She laughed. "Yes, you probably will, and so will I. It happens. Just stay and we'll work it out. Just stay."

Twenty-three

"My fiancé wants to know if you'll go up to Chicago with us next weekend to finalize things and pick up the rest of the furniture we want to keep. Nate will help him carry stuff to the van, but I need to run to Elucidations while I'm there and he doesn't want me to go alone so..."

"Wait." Alan looked up from a sketch she'd given him, an idea for his next house landscape. "Fiancé?"

Trevor ran a hand over her back. "I finally wore her down."

"You're getting married?" Cheryl attacked her with a hug. "Oh Jenna, *congratulations*. You're doing it here, right? I'll help with anything you need."

Alan calmed his wife with a touch to her arm. "First things first. Are you actually getting married or are you just trying out the title?"

"Okay, I have that coming." She slid her arm around Trevor. "No, we're actually getting married. Soon. As soon as we can pull a small wedding together."

"But you're staying here?"

"Yes. I wore him down." She threw her fiancé a grin.

"Sounds like you have this marriage thing already in the bag." Alan gave her a hug and offered Trevor his hand. "You're sure about this? Because if you hurt her again, I won't help you out again."

"Not necessary." Jenna gave him the *back off* look. "Besides, this is just record keeping, really, since by all rights we already are. If he's that determined to call me his wife, I figure I should let him."

"So the town gossips won't talk behind your back?" Cheryl rolled her eyes.

Jenna wasn't sure she wasn't one of the town gossips, honestly, or wouldn't be if she lived in town instead of in Peoria. Probably wise on Alan's part to move to the city. "You know, I don't care about that. I really don't. I have better things to think about and I feel sorry for them if they don't. I guess it'll be easier on the kids, and that's good, but it's still not why I agreed."

"Can I ask why you did?" Alan studied them both. "Not that I should ask."

She looked up at Trevor. "Because it feels right. Head and Heart both agree this time." With a light kiss, she turned back to her friend. "What would you think about walking me down the aisle? You're the one who gave me the support I needed through the years to get here. And you seem to support this..."

"I would be honored, Jen. And yes, I fully support this. I think you're making the right decision."

"The first right decision?" She had to tease.

"Maybe not quite the first. But I can tell you it's quite the relief for me." He nudged Trevor. "You know how often in the past couple of weeks I stepped in to tell someone she was already attached?"

Trevor laughed and thanked him.

"You didn't need to. I can say no, as I did, and as I would have kept doing. Because I am already attached. Enough that I was wearing the ring you gave me here instead." She pulled it from her right hand to place on her wedding ring finger. "Guess I can again."

Trevor gripped her fingers. "But it's not a wedding ring."

She shrugged. "Rings are symbolic. It can mean what we want it to mean, right? It does to me. That's how I meant it. That's how I always meant it."

~~~

Jenna felt herself cringe when she stepped inside the apartment, and she stopped. She was glad Cheryl kept the kids in Peoria for their overnight run to Chicago to tie up loose ends.

"Jen?" Trevor turned back.

"I don't want to be here."

"Don't think about that. We've had a lot of awfully good times in this place. Yeah?" He kissed her head.

She nodded, but she'd also had horrendous times there, when he wasn't there. But he was now. And so was Alan.

"Especially in here." He half pulled her into the art room. Where they'd painted, alone or together, where she painted him.

Alan drew Trevor's attention to the mural-covered wall. When Jenna looked at it again, it looked to her like someone else's work. She picked up on the quality, the scale, the color use... It was quality work. And it was hers.

Trevor was silent a long while as he stared at it from a distance and then walked along the wall, looking it up and down. She watched him, noting which things he looked at the longest and his expressions as he moved along. The guy taking over the apartment rambled on and on
~~~

about it in Alan's ear but Trevor shut him out. Jenna could see he wasn't listening. He was inside his thoughts. Finally he came to her, slid a hand around the back of her head, the other against the small of her back, and kissed her deeply. Then he looked back at it. "I'm not sure I can leave now. Jen, wow, this is..." He shook his head, an arm still around her. "I have to tell you, I just fell head over heals with you all over again. This is amazing. How can you leave this?"

"I can't take it with me."

Alan held up the camera he brought. "You can in a way. I came prepared."

Trevor knew what she meant. She didn't mean just the painting. She meant all of the stuff inside it represented, things she had to let go.

As an impromptu going away party, The gallery was packed full of Trevor and Jenna's friends and coworkers, including Margaret and a couple others from Elucidations, Nina, who never went to bars, and Joan, who was pleasantly surprised at the upgrades and told Keisha she would be back now and then to entertain her artists.

Trevor wasn't back. Keisha had stolen Jenna away just after they got to Chicago and took her first to Elucidations where she picked up her personal things and invited a few people to the party, and then shopping in the Loop, then on to the bar. Nate and Alan stayed with Trevor to help pack things from the apartment and from his aunt's house. All three were still out somewhere and Jenna started to fidget. It shouldn't have taken them so long. They didn't have that much stuff to move.

"Don't fret, darling." Keisha set an arm around her shoulders. "My guess is they stopped for drinks and to play pool somewhere their women won't be watching. Men have to be men. No need to fear. Your little prince won't dare screw around again. Nate would turn him into a pretzel if he thought about it for even one iota of a second."

Jenna chuckled. "I could see Nate doing it, but I'm not worried about that. I know he won't. You're probably right. Alan doesn't get to go out with the guys much. I'm sure he's enjoying it, too." Maybe he would more often with Trevor there to encourage him.

Keisha hugged her. "Just be sure to come on back and see us now and again, and bring those babies so I can give them hugs."

"We will. And come stay any time you can. We have room."

Margaret bumped against her side. "You let me know when you're here, too. Even if I am upset about losing my best employee, I still want to see you when you're in town." With a grin, she nodded toward the door. "Your Musketeers are back."

Jenna smiled as she watched them get through the crowd slowly, talking on the way, with Trevor introducing Alan to almost everyone. She hugged his neck as he came to her. "Hey, I was getting worried." And it was so nice to be pressed against his warm, firm body.

"Come talk to me a minute." He told everyone to get the party going and they'd be right there, then he and Alan both took her into Nate's office and closed the door.

Trevor offered a large envelope but her eyes were pulled to his hand. His knuckles were covered in dried blood. "What happened?" She grabbed it to look closer.

"We had a little chat with Kent Graham today."

"Trevor..."

"Look in the envelope."

Her own hands were shaky as she undid the clasp and pulled out ... the sketches. Of her. That Daniel had done. The nude poses.

"He swears that's all of them. Is he right?"

"I ... I don't know." She flushed. "I hated to look at them so I don't know how many there were."

"Even if there are more, he won't dare let them surface. Along with what he did to you, Joan gave us enough ammunition that he won't dare. Seems she knows quite a lot about him and hated that she didn't know you were working with him."

Jenna was still looking at the sketches, more than she ever had before. Daniel's. Her hands shook more.

"Jen, he didn't sell them. I made the guy talk. Graham stole them out of his portfolio after he overheard the two of you talking about them at lunch somewhere. Had someone else do it, of course, while he pulled Daniel into an argument as a distraction. From what the guy said, Daniel threatened him good to stay far away from you." He set the non-injured hand against her face. "I don't think you were wrong. I think he loved you a hell of a lot. Even just looking at the sketches, it shows. They're nice. Respectful. Not what I expected. They're truly beautiful."

Her face warmed again and she glanced at Alan beside the door.

"I didn't see them. Nate and I were only there as support in case he needed it. Not that he did. He fights well for an artist." Humor reflected in Alan's voice and Trevor reminded him that he'd started out as a street artist at the edge of inner city Chicago. They had a nice camaraderie going that Jenna appreciated.

"I asked Joan about the child, too." Alan's voice lowered. "The girl came onto him, used him to get even with Graham for being with one of her friends, and walked away as soon as she got pregnant. They all went to school together and there was past history. She refused to let Daniel see the kid when he found out. He tried. She never allowed it. Joan said he had to just block it out. He didn't tell you because..."

"Because he had to block it out. And he married me when I got pregnant so it wouldn't happen again?"

Alan came to her. "No. Jen, he married you because he loved you. Trevor's right. He did. You know he did. And I was wrong to try to break you up. I am sorry. I was young and stupid and..."

"Just don't do it again."

Alan raised his eyebrows and glanced at Trevor. "With *him*? Not a chance. I have to teach him how to fly fish and he's going to get me away from work and the family now and then to go hang out and talk guy stuff. Been a while since I had that."

"Keisha was right; you were out having a good time without us women watching."

Trevor grinned. "Hanging with my friends didn't work for you, so thought I'd try it with yours. I'm not that picky."

"Good thing. He's not always easy to get along with. Not that I am, either." With a deep breath, she slid the sketches back inside the folder and set it on Nate's desk. "Okay. It's all in the past now. At least when I tell Aaron about his father, I don't have to be angry with him. Thank you for asking."

She gave Alan a quick hug, and set her hands on Trevor's chest. "I love you so. Thank you for getting them back for me. I would have worried forever." She met his lips and pressed hard against him, her arms circling his neck, holding tight. His firm delicate trained hands caressed her sides, her hips, drawing her in against his. She half heard Alan say he'd go on out to the party but Trevor was reacting far too much to her touch, her kiss, to let her pay attention to anything else.

"Mm, Jen..." He slid his hands up the middle of her back, under her blouse. "Careful or I'm going to lock the door and close the shades all the way. My adrenaline is already..."

"I had a miscarriage." She heard it come out and had no idea why she had to say it now.

His movement stopped. "With Daniel. I know..."

Her head shook. "Three months ago. A couple of weeks after you left. I couldn't tell you."

"A couple of weeks? Jenna..."

"I knew I was pregnant when you left. I should have said so, but ... if you had stayed only for that, you would have resented me and I was already having trouble. I knew it wouldn't... I hardly let myself accept it and you'd moved out already and... I'm sorry."

His face reflected shock and sorrow. And disappointment. She hoped it wasn't of her, that she hadn't just changed his mind. She felt strangely calm, or numb. She wasn't sure. Waiting. She was just waiting to see what he would do, if he would still stay.

"Guess I don't need to lock the door."

She swallowed hard. He wasn't even looking at her. He'd turned his head, staring ... at nothing. "I'm sorry. Trevor, I..."

He questioned her with a look and raised a hand to her face. "No. I'm sorry, Jen. I let you down."

"No..."

"Yes. I did. I should have been here. I should never have moved out. I should never have left you and the kids, including the one I didn't know about, for something I wanted to do with you just because you weren't ready yet. It was stupid and childish and I'm so sorry. Are you sure you can forgive me enough to really want this again?"

Jenna studied him, hard, thinking of the first time she'd seen him and how annoying she found him, but not only annoying: also curious, interesting, charming, funny, young ... he was so young when they met, only twenty-two, still a boy, single, carefree ... and she stuck him with herself, a widow, with a baby he gladly claimed and another who came unexpectedly. And still he was there. Her scrawny little artist boy. Not so much a boy anymore, but still a boy at twenty-five.

"I'm not sure I shouldn't be worried about how long it's taking you to answer that."

He was so cute. Sexy. Still charming. She ran a finger down his chest. "You know I'll be thirty in two years."

"Yeah." He gave her a light kiss. "And then I can tease you about being my old lady." He made the kiss stronger. "If you still want this, and I promise I'll do everything I can to make you keep wanting this."

Her eyes closed and she let her head fall back when he kissed her neck. "Careful." She lowered her hands to his jeans, to his luscious curves, and pulled him back in against her. "I'll have to lock the door and close the blinds better."

A chuckle came from deep in his throat and he kissed her hard.

She felt the news she gave him sink in only after they went back out to join the party. This time she knew why he got so quiet in the middle of all of the commotion he was usually fully a part of, and she stuck close to him and kept her hands on him because she knew when he was moody the best way to help was to stay very close.

"I'm okay, Jen." He whispered into her ear when she slid an arm up his chest to rest a hand on his neck.

"Are you? I shouldn't have told you tonight. I didn't want to keep hiding it, but I should have waited..."

"No. I'm just sick that I wasn't here for you. The more I think of you dealing with it by yourself, that I wasn't here, I... It had to be..."

"It's okay. I'm okay. I just don't think about it. I can't."

"Jenna, tell me you let yourself grieve."

"I... No. I went back to work sooner than I was supposed to because I had to and I just... I can't think about it."

He grasped her fingers to kiss them. "When it hits you, because I know it will, no matter how good you are at pushing things aside, I know one of these days it'll come back at you and make you face it, but I'll be here this time, so it's safe to let go. It is." His eyes watered. "I love you, Jenna. And I adore you. And I will be here."

"And you still want to marry me?"

With a light grin, he brushed a hand through her hair, walked over to the bar to grab something from Nate, then returned and dropped to one knee in front of her. The crowd hushed around them. The music lowered. He grasped her hand. "I know I've already asked you and you already accepted, but I've never had the chance to do this and I don't ever expect to have or want the chance again, so I'm doing it anyway. Jenna Elaine Rhodes, will you honor me by becoming my wife?"

"The honor is mine, Mr. Dade. Yes. Absolutely I want to be your wife. I want you to be stuck with me."

The crowd threw congratulations and wishes as he slipped the ring onto her finger and stood to take her in his arms. As he did, he told everyone they were invited to the ceremony and he'd have Nate let them know when.

"Soon." Jenna gave him a soft kiss. "Very soon, yes?"

His eyes sparkled. "In a hurry after all these years?"

"Yes. You know why?" She stroked the edge of his face down behind his ear. "Because all of those years I was married, I didn't really feel like a wife, like I was really *married.* It was more like ... someone else's life I got stuck in the middle of and I had to play the part I was given. This isn't the same. I already feel like your wife because I'm so connected to you in a way I never knew was possible. I want to give you a son. I want to try again, give him another chance. And maybe this time, we can do it in the right order."

He laughed and twirled her around. "My sweet Jenna, who cares about the order? I say we start planning and start trying both and see which one happens first."

She met his lips. He reacted hard and fast as his arms tightened around her waist and their friends whistled and threw comments and someone put their song on and she hardly left his side or his touch all the way through the night into the morning in their art room beneath her painted wall which she would take with her in many ways and leave there in other ways and she fell asleep on top of the sleeping bag against his bare warm skin, with the sketches, Daniel's sketches, on the floor beside them, spread out so Trevor could make her really look and see her own beauty that had nothing to do with the body parts but only the artistic quality of them, the captured meaning and intent.

Daniel had loved her as well as she had allowed. She would do better this time; she would allow Trevor to love her fully.

Twenty-four

Jenna gave Iris a hug as her family joined the Sunday afternoon housewarming. She and Trevor had signed the paperwork on Friday to buy the house and he insisted on meeting his new neighbors with an open invitation for anyone to come hang out. He even painted a sign to stick in the yard, and as people came over, he had them sign the back of it like a guest book.

"You're looking wonderful these days." Iris squeezed the top of Jenna's arm. "Look at those muscles and that tan. I'm so jealous."

"So am I." Trevor threw a grin. "I've been stuck inside working on the basement studio she wants while she's been out playing in the dirt under the sun."

"Playing? I'm not playing. Ask Alan. I work hard out there."

He kissed the side of her head. "Obviously. And she's right. You look incredible."

"Uh huh." Jenna was glad to know the skinny tank and shorts had his attention. She knew she was showing off and she was finally okay with that. She'd earned it. "Go help Nate with the hamburgers. He's supposed to be a guest."

"He doesn't want to be a guest and he's doing just fine." He grabbed a cookie from the plate Iris's husband held, handed the plate off to Denise as she went past toward the house since Daniel's sister was playing hostess of her own accord, and rubbed the top of Kaedin's head. "Kids are over there. Jenna's supposed to be watching them, but I guess I'll do that." With a wink, he led the kids and Jordy, Iris's husband, to where their more active guests were playing games. Jenna couldn't resist watching him leave. He had such a sexy walk.

"Hey *Trevor*." Iris waited until he turned back from halfway across the yard after the kids had run on ahead. "You know she's watching your back side as you leave. As usual. I think she does it every time."

"Does she? Glad to know it. Always a good thing when your fiancée's attracted to you, right?" He called over to tell Alan to be sure to grab one of the cookies Iris brought and continued his path. Alan didn't even react to their flirting. He was too used to it already. In the three weeks since their close-out trip to Chicago, Trevor often stopped in while she was working with Alan just to see how things were going, and he often talked more with her friend than with her. Jenna had a feeling he wanted Dave to know he was around and might stop by any time, although she assured him it wasn't a problem. The guy hadn't stopped flirting, but he did it in front of Alan and Trevor, also, more in front of them than alone, so she wasn't concerned. He was at the party, had already joked with Trevor and laughed at Iris's comment.

As Jenna introduced Iris to Joan, she caught movement from the house across the street. Her mother hesitated, and then headed her direction. Her stomach tightened. They'd said hello to each other from their separate yards but Jenna never expected her to come over into the crowd of people who were welcoming the wayward *embarrassing* daughter back to the neighborhood.

She excused herself to go meet her mother on the driveway, away from her friends, in case she only meant to complain about the noise or the cars parked up and down the cul-de-sac. Jenna had to wonder if Iris's comment had been loud enough to cross the street. That would make for a fun conversation.

"I supposed I'm invited to this thing, as well."

Caught off guard with the question, Jenna nodded.

"I did teach you to vocalize your answers. At least do it with me."

"Sorry. Yes. Of course. I'm just surprised..."

"It would look bad if I didn't since everyone else seems to have heartily welcomed you and your ... family."

"If that's your only concern, I'm not sure why you would bother. Everyone knows we haven't really spoken for years. No one will be surprised if you don't."

"Meaning you wish I wouldn't?"

"No. Meaning I don't want you to come only because it would *look bad*. If you're interested in welcoming my fiancé and my children, I'm glad to have you here. I can't care about appearances. Things are as they are and I have enough people who will accept me as I am. I'm not hurting anyone, so it's really no one's concern."

"Yes, well... Fiancé? That boy asked for your hand?"

"Trevor. And yes." She raised her hand to show off the beautiful too-big ring. "We're planning for November."

"Why wait? Get it done and over with as you did before."

Jenna refused to let it get to her. "I need time to plan the wedding we want, and we're doing it after landscaping season so we can go away for a month on an extended honeymoon. Trevor says it's a nice time to visit Italy, with fewer tourists, and not so hot. That's what we're doing."

"You're leaving your children for a month? What kind of a mother does that? And how can you afford..?"

"They're going with us. I would never leave them that long. And we can. My paintings ... the *little art thing* you always fussed about ... are selling well, and pretty high. Joan's doing well with them, and with Trevor's, which are doing even better since modern art is more in right now and he's been building his name longer. He's been saving for this for a couple of years and he has a job lined up for January..."

"A real job?"

She saw Trevor inch his way closer, keeping watch. "He'll be teaching art in East Peoria, mainly grade school, while he works on his master's. And we're setting up a studio here so we can have local kids come over and learn art more than they do at school for those who want more. I can do that and still be with my kids..."

"You're not certified to teach. Unless you've done that and didn't tell me."

"No, but Trevor is and he'll be there. My side will be more just talking to them, well, listening really, if they want to talk about what they're doing, or I'll just supervise as they create whatever they want. Using art as a kind of therapy is an idea that's just starting. I've read about it, and after Trevor is done with school, I may go and learn how to do that. But for now, with my kids here, it will be more of a play date. Instead of babysitters who put them in front of a television, parents can bring the kids here when they have date nights and such. So it's not every day and I'll still work with Alan three days a week."

Jenna paused for a breath and to let her head clear in the silence that told her she'd won, if not the war, at least a small battle. "We have everything set up and in place, so like you always wanted, I'll have structure and stability, and like I always needed, I'll have my art and plenty of people around to matter to and to make a difference with." Expecting to hear about the bad grammar, Jenna felt herself unwind at her mother's nod. "Do you want a hot dog or hamburger?"

Louise Givens pursed her lips at the idea of cookout food, which she detested, but she gave a little shrug. "I suppose I should say hello to the Taylors while I'm here."

"Of course." She hoped it didn't sound sarcastic. Heaven forbid her mother skip that propriety. She'd probably follow Jenna's father with her own heart attack if she even thought of doing so.

Slightly ashamed by the thought, she walked with her only long enough to be polite and left her with the Taylors to go find Trevor.

He wrapped her in a hug. "Everything okay?"

"Well, she's here. Should I find the kids and see if she'll speak to them this time or let it go so I don't set myself up again?"

"Let it go for the moment. It should be her move."

"I'm not sure she'll move that far if I don't push."

"Her loss, Jen, not yours. You remember that."

"But it is my loss. Mrs. Taylor told me once that you can miss something you didn't have far more than you can miss what you had and lost. And she's right. My father's gone and I ... I should have come back for the funeral as Alan tried to tell me but I kept thinking that I didn't know who he was, anyway, and it was right after the miscarriage and I couldn't deal with all of that, with not just the loss, but the fact that I have no idea who he was. I just don't think I'm okay with letting that happen again. At least Mom talked to me, not about anything important, but she did and ... I just really want to know *who* she is before I lose her. Does that make sense? She knows who I am. She might not *like* who I am or how I live but she does *know*. I don't even have that, so no, it's *not* more her loss. It's not."

"Okay, baby. Okay. How about we don't push it right now? You need to just kick back and have fun today, all right? There's time. We'll push it now and then when we catch her outside. She won't be able to keep seeing our babies playing in the yard and keep ignoring them. I don't believe she will. So let it go today while everyone's here..."

"Anna, no!"

Jenna shot her head around to find her daughter ... running to the street after the big beach ball. She flew into a run toward where a car was flying toward her baby. With the cars lining the side of the street, he would never see the two-year-old, but Jenna would never reach her in time. Voices screamed into her ears, calling the girl. Others were running toward her. Trevor passed her up in his sprint. They were too far away. The car was going too fast...

Her mother jumped out from where she'd been about to cross the road, to go back home, tires screeched, and Trevor helped pull them back off the road, her baby in her mother's arms. The beach ball made a loud *pop* as it was hit.

Jenna's heart pounded through her chest and head by the time she grabbed her baby and fell on the grass clinging to her.

"She's not hurt, Jen."

She heard Trevor's voice but checked her baby up and down, head to toe, as the girl cried.

"She's only scared. She's fine."

Everyone crowded around. Someone asked her mom if she was all right. Jenna heard her say she was through the waves of panic rushing through her head, through her ears, and the pounding of her heart.

"Come on, Jenna, let me take her. Let her calm down and I'll give her back. She's fine."

"No." She kissed her baby's face and held her tight. She wasn't hurt. Jenna told herself she wasn't hurt. It was all okay.

"Daddyyy..."

"Jen, let me have her."

Anna reached for him and she gave in and checked her again as the girl switched to Trevor's arms.

"Okay baby." He kissed Anna's cheek and smoothed her hair. "It's okay, but listen to me. Don't you ever go out in the road again. Do you understand me? Never *ever* go out there without an adult. You're little and that car doesn't see you. Promise me now."

Anna nodded and hugged him.

"Where's Aaron?" Jenna looked around the crowd.

"Inside." Alan knelt beside her. "Cheryl and Denise took the kids inside to find the popsicles. He's fine. I saw him go in. I'll take her in, too, so you can both unwind." He stroked her face and stood. "Come here, Anna. Let's go find a popsicle."

She watched her baby switch from crying to pouting to jumping into Alan's arms to go find a treat all in the matter of about a minute. She was obviously fine. Jenna's heart still pounded. Her hands shook. Trevor pulled her in and held her ... and she lost it.

"Okay Jenna, it's okay." He cradled her head against his chest, sheltering it with his hand, his head lowered against hers.

"I'm a horrible mom. It's ... it's why I lost them. It's a sign ... that I shouldn't..."

He released her and pulled her face up to his, his beautiful caring tender loving face. "No, it isn't."

"It is. I almost lost her, too. I was supposed to be..."

"Jenna, listen to me. You are an incredible mom. They love you and they absolutely adore you and it wasn't a sign of anything except that little ass was driving way too fast in a housing area and..."

"Which is what I just told him." Nate's voice pulled her attention. He had some teenage boy by the back of the collar. "Tell him again. I pulled him out of the car so you could tell him."

Jenna stood with Trevor's help. She thought of throttling the kid, but he was someone's kid, too, and she should have been watching her own better. With a shake of the head, she turned away from him and held onto her fiancé.

"She's too upset to yell at you, so I will." Her mother's voice scolded in the way that demanded attention. "I know your parents and you can be sure I will tell them you nearly ran down my granddaughter driving like a maniac, and if you *ever* pull a stunt like that on my road again, I will have your license yanked for at least a good *year*. Do you understand me?"

"Yes ma'am." The kid sounded almost as scared as Jenna was.

"You apologize to my daughter."

Jenna heard the apology but she couldn't answer, so Trevor did. He told the kid to be sure he calmed down before he took off so he wouldn't hurt himself, either. As everyone backed away, he stroked her hair and kissed her head. "Let it out, Jen. You need to let it out."

She was gulping at air, trying to calm herself. Her head shook.

"I knew it would catch up with you. Let it out now."

"I can't. Too many people..." She gulped for breath. She couldn't breathe.

"Your friends and family. No one else. It's okay. You can't keep holding it in. They'll understand that you need to grieve." He explained to someone that it brought back losing their child a few months ago, which some of them didn't know and she didn't care now if they did. He didn't care if they knew, so she didn't care if they knew.

And it hurt. It hurt all the way down to her soul, to the middle of her being. She gripped him tight and let him support her as it forced its way out and she apologized to him, said it was her own fault and she deserved it but he didn't and she was sorry and he cried with her and swore it was not her fault and he loved her, which only made her feel worse, and she couldn't breathe...

When she calmed, she found herself inside with no memory of how she got there, with tissues in her hand and a cold cloth running along her face.

Her mother. Her mom was running a cold cloth over her face, as she had ... when Jenna was little and too upset to calm herself. She'd done it often. She'd forgotten. The only way her mom could calm her was with a cool cloth.

"This always works if you need to know in the future." She was talking to Trevor. Her mother, the one who disapproved of him, was talking to her boyfriend, her fiancé. Jenna's fiancé. She was going to marry him. And have his baby. Again.

"Feeling better?" Louise Givens had pulled a chair up close to where Jenna clung to her anchor, her loving, sweet, cheerful, beautiful anchor. Her stability. She needed him to be stable, to entrench them. He'd understood that long ago, before she did. He'd been working for that since they met. It was so clear now. She always considered herself the one who was down to earth and centered and he was adventurous and flighty and ... it was opposite. Why hadn't she seen it?

Her mom repeated the question.

"Yes. I'm sorry." She sniffed hard. "Nice way to ruin a party, wasn't it? I'm sorry..."

"Don't be." Her mom took her hand. "And you listen to me. Even if you never listened to anything I've ever told you, and I'm sure much of that was justified, listen to me now. You are *not* a horrible mother. You are a very good mother. I know because I've watched you play with those babies and laugh with them and involve them in what you're doing. And I've seen the way they look at you, the way they hug you with everything in their little bodies. You are a wonderful mother, Jenna, despite your own, despite my lack of an example." She set a hand alongside her face. "I am sorry I wasn't. I didn't have much of an example, either, but I could have learned, and I'm sorry I didn't. My dear child, I wanted so much for you and I was always so busy trying to balance keeping your father happy and doing what I thought I had to do that I forgot to think of your wants. I was told my only job was to be a good wife and mother and to always put myself aside and that's such a terrible thing to teach a girl. I told myself I wouldn't do the same to you, that I would show you a woman could have her own career and still manage everything else by herself and raise a child with manners and good grades and respectability, but look what I did. I spent so much time thinking I wasn't teaching you well enough how to do things right and proper that I missed just enjoying you."

"Well, you did that." Trevor stroked fingers down Jenna's neck when she looked up at him, but he addressed her mother. "You did teach her manners and respectability. Really, you oughta come hang out where people know her and you'll see they very much respect her. They can see her upbringing. I've teased her about it plenty, but I appreciate it, too. Her dignity shows and people are attracted to that. They do respect her for it."

Jenna stared at him. He always called her uppity. He grinned when he said it, but he said it. He appreciated it?

"That is nice to know." Her mom squeezed her hand gently. "I am glad you learned how to be more than that on your own. Maybe you and your beautiful children could teach me how to be a grandmother. If it's not too late, I would like to know them, and enjoy them with you. I should be able to manage that since I don't have the worry of responsibility for their upbringing."

Jenna felt the tears come again and she let them come, and she let her mother hug her. She couldn't yet return it with everything in her. She needed time. There was too much distance.

Trevor called to the kids and they came running and jumped on top of him. Aaron tilted his head at her and crawled over to her lap to give her another hug. Her Aaron. Her Daniel's child. And Trevor's child. He was both. Mostly, he was her child through and through.

The party continued around them and with them until it was late and everyone gave her hugs and best wishes and promised to come for the wedding and Jenna felt fully entrenched in her home, in her life.

~~~

Jenna sipped her coffee at the table and looked out over the backyard garden as she let her head calm. Her mom invited her to go to church since many would be glad to see her again, but she wasn't ready for that. A good thing, as it turned out, since Alan dropped by without notice.

She was exhausted from the party and her mini breakdown the day before and was still in her robe, but if he was going to make himself that much at home, he'd have to deal with it. The kids, on the other hand, were wired from too much company and too many sweets. "Anna, *please* lower your voice. Mommy has a headache."

Trevor corraled her from where the girl crawled under the table and ran around it after the puppy Alan gave the kids. Why he thought she needed that right now, Jenna didn't know. Payback, she figured, for doing it to him when she left Peoria. He meant it to be Aaron's, but Aaron said she wasn't the *right* puppy, so Anna claimed her. Jenna knew where that would lead; she'd have to take him to pick out his own. Trevor laughed at the idea and shrugged as though it was fine.

Puppy whined and Jenna picked her up. "You're all right." She stroked the shiny black hair and cuddled the pudgy mutt against her chest. "Anna, she still needs a name."

She nodded from her daddy's arms. "Anna's puppy. Her name is
~~~

Anna's puppy."

Jenna rolled her eyes. At least the girl didn't have self esteem issues so far. Trevor teased and told her to try again. This time she suggested Alex, which made Alan laugh.

"You can't give him the same name as your friend. If you call one, how will they know who should answer? How about ... Lexi?"

"*Yes!*"

Jenna cringed at her yell.

"Okay, Lexi it is." Trevor hushed her. "Think I'll take the wild things to the park and give Lexi her first walk. Maybe it'll wear this one out, too." He rubbed Anna's head and told her to go find Aaron and get their shoes and jackets on. As she scampered away, Jenna let the wriggling puppy down to follow and Trevor came over to rub her neck and shoulders. "Kick back and relax. Leave the dishes; I'll get them. It's a beautiful day. If you feel better later, we can get that flower bed ready to plant your herbs in the spring."

"You don't like to play in dirt."

"I can learn. To an extent." He kissed her head and went to help the kids along.

As they left, got dressed and slipped into a sweatshirt and went out with her coffee to the front porch.

Alan propped himself against the white railing that needed paint. "What's eating at you?"

"You know Mom has suddenly decided to try to be a mom?"

"It's what you wanted, isn't it? It's nice that she's coming around."

"Maybe. I guess it is."

"It'll take adjustment."

"Yeah. And I know it's good." She got up again and pinched off drying flower heads she could reach without putting her shoes on and going down into the yard. It felt both normal and strange for her to live in the Taylor house again and have it be hers. Hers and Trevor's. It felt much like her new relationship with her mother. Normal, and strange. There were too many empty pieces she couldn't fit together. "I need you to do something with me."

"Okay."

"Will you drive?"

"Where?"

"I have to visit my father."

Alan nodded, pushed away from the railing, and gave her a light hug. "Of course."

She went without shoes, which she knew was a bit of a dig since her father always complained when she went outside without shoes until she stopped doing it just so she wouldn't have to listen to one more complaint. The ride was quiet, short. And her insides clenched when she held Alan's arm and approached the gray stone. It wasn't her father's name on it that got to her. It was her mother's, on the same stone, just waiting. Jenna found it alarmingly morbid.

"Your mom's idea. She thought she would feel closer to him that way, but from what I know, she hasn't been here. I think it only scares her to see her name on a headstone." Alan rubbed her back. "Maybe that's why she's softened lately?"

Jenna couldn't answer. She found it scary, too. In two ways. With that fact that it might not matter much and the fact that it might.

"Want me to leave you alone a while?"

She nodded. "Not too far. I don't know if I can do this."

"Of course you can." He gave her a soft hug and moved away.

Jenna sat cross-legged on the grass at the foot of where the dirt was still mounded and fresh. He never liked it when she sat in the grass, either. It wasn't feminine enough, so he said. She felt some little creature crawl up on one foot, an ant she guessed, and let it alone. She didn't mind little creatures. Generally, if she let them alone, they did her the same favor. They were far more fair than most people. Of course, she had been bitten by ants she'd left alone, and she'd been stung by a big burly bumblebee she also wasn't trying to bother, so maybe they weren't. Or maybe it was fair to get stung by those you didn't sting, or at least didn't mean to sting.

Maybe it was. Maybe people misunderstood the meaning of *fair*.

Maybe she'd been given the parents she'd been given for a reason, too. Even if it didn't make sense to her.

Jenna noted the two bunches of mini carnations at the edges of the stone. They were newly planted, as well, but they'd been there long enough they were well established. She had to wonder who put them there and why carnations? Why white on her dad's side and red on her mom's? Shouldn't it be the other way? Wouldn't the ones on her mom's side get messed up when... She sighed and tore herself from the thought. Yes, it would matter.

And it mattered that her father left her without so much as a goodbye, and without telling her what she'd done so wrong.

Jenna felt a sting on her foot and brushed the big black ant away. "Why did you do that? I wasn't bothering you." Though maybe she was. Maybe she was in his way, covering his hole. She felt bad to see it wriggle, injured. She hadn't meant to injure it. She only wanted it to not bite her again.

And she supposed her parents hadn't meant to injure her, either.

"Okay. I'm sorry." She looked back at the stone. "For whatever I did that wasn't right enough, I'm sorry that you took it as an insult. It wasn't meant to be. I never meant to insult you. I didn't. Really. I just wanted you to see me. To see *me*. As I am. I wanted that to be good enough." She sighed and pulled a knee up in front. The grass tickled her bare foot and she concentrated on the coolness of the dirt beneath.

"I know I was disappointing to you, but you were disappointing to me, too. You were. Because ... I'm your child. Your *child*. You were supposed to accept me, to love me, to *want* me, no matter what. No matter *what* I did, you were supposed to still want me, and you didn't. And I can't forgive that because it hurt so much, because I knew there had to be something deeply wrong with me that you didn't.

"I guess I was wrong about that. Alan kept trying to tell me and I wouldn't hear him. Trevor tried to tell me. I wouldn't listen to him, either, because I knew you couldn't be so horrible as to not want me for no reason, just because I wasn't exactly what you wanted. I knew you couldn't be, so I couldn't listen to them. I knew it had to be something inside me that was..." She sniffed and wiped at her eyes.

"Why? Did you not want me? Was I a mistake? Did I interfere? I didn't do it, you know. I didn't bring myself into your life. You did. And I used to try so hard to please you but it never worked. You either didn't notice me or you yelled about what I wasn't doing right enough and there was nothing at all in between and I tried but it never worked so I quit trying. I had to either quit trying or bend to exactly what you wanted and I just couldn't. And I'm not sorry I didn't, because really, I'm not sure I even know what that was. And I shouldn't have had to."

She picked up a ladybug from a strand of grass and let it crawl over her arm as she ignored her tears. They were too long coming. She had to let herself grieve, as Trevor said.

A wise little painter boy, her Trevor. She only had to let herself hear him. She had to let herself hear. So she stopped talking, watched the ladybug spread its pretty round red wings and fly, and lay her arms on her knees, her head on her arms.

She heard a mower in the distance, cars go by on the road too far away to see, birds calling to each other, a chipmunk prattling its bird-like chirp in a steady rhythm, the wind wooshing through cornfields that would soon be plowed down and harvested...

And she heard her father's voice.

"Now, now, Jenna. It's not all that bad. You take things too personally." She was eight again. Some girl made fun of her for something she didn't remember, but she was upset, sobbing. Silly to sob over something that didn't matter so much. It embarrassed her dad for her to cry so easily. But she didn't do it on purpose. He wouldn't appreciate her doing it now, either.

"But it is that bad. It *is*." She raised her head and wiped at her face. "And it was then, or at least it *felt* like it was. Couldn't you see that?"

You take things too personally.

Maybe she did. Maybe he had to give up trying to convince her not everything was so personal because she wouldn't listen enough. She'd started pulling away... She'd pulled away. She forgot she had. She had to. He didn't understand.

But maybe neither did she.

With a jagged deep breath, Jenna dried her face and sat still. The ladybug was now on one of the open white mini carnations. She would have to ask her mom why carnations, and why white and red. Maybe, when there were two mounds instead of one, Jenna would find a mini carnation with mixed white and red flowers to put in between.

"Okay. I guess Mom can fill me in, right? And don't worry, I'll come keep the place neat so it doesn't drive you crazy the way I did." She sniffed again, grabbed a deep breath. "I hope you can see me now. I hope if you can, you'll watch your grandchildren grow. Aaron is a lot like you, actually, though you may not care much for the thought, but he is. Anyway, Mom says he is. I guess she would know. Maybe he can help me know you." She chuckled at the thought. Her son, the one her father so objected to because of circumstances, was like him. Maybe things did turn out fair in an odd way, and Jenna was fine with odd. She liked odd. She'd nearly forgotten how much she liked odd.

With a light grin, she said goodbye, forced herself up, and headed back to Alan, to let him take her home to her family where she wanted to be more than anywhere else in the world.

~~~

"Kids are sound asleep. As exhausted as they are, they should sleep well." Trevor lifted her hand and kissed her fingers. "Coming to bed?"

"Mm, not yet. Come paint with me."

He raised his eyebrows. "Should I strip first?"
~~~

"Well you can." She kissed his neck. "But I meant on canvas."

"Darn. That's disappointing."

She chuckled. "We'll start on canvas and see where it goes from there." Enjoying his charming, boyish grin, she led him down to the studio and closed all of the blinds. Just in case. Setting up a freshly made canvas, Jenna dabbed several colors of her choice onto a palette and told him to choose his colors.

"What are we doing?"

"Painting. Get your colors."

"I generally know what I'm going to paint before I choose colors."

"Not this time. Just choose."

With a grin, he globbed five different paints in a row adjacent to her row. Complementary schemes. She had to smile.

"Come here." She held the palette in her left hand, gave him a brush, and picked up one of her own. "We need art for our walls."

"We both have quite a few..."

"Separate. We have separate paintings. I want them together. Paint with me. Anything that comes to mind."

He stood with his chest against her back and reached around her to the canvas. In between his geometric red orange yellow bright teal and vivid purple heavy-stroked fast dabs, he kissed her neck, her shoulder, and helped support the palette with his left hand under hers.

"Trevor."

"Hm." He trailed his lips down her neck to her shoulder.

"I think I'm doing more of this than you are."

"I'm preoccupied. Keep going. It looks great."

"That wasn't exactly my plan."

"We'll trade places on the next one and I'll do more painting while you get preoccupied. How's that sound?"

"Very tempting."

When she stopped and studied the odd work of art that did have nice motion and depth, he took the palette and brush from her hand and turned her to face him. "I think these are going to be my absolute favorite works of art. And I think we should do a lot of them."

"We don't have all that much wall space."

"When we get our fill, we can share."

"Our personal art?"

"All art is personal, Jen."

She looked back at their mesh of abstractionism and surrealism that somewhat formed a house and yard and children playing, or at least that's what she saw. Her blues and greens; his reds and oranges. Complementary, as they were to each other. All art was personal. Of course it was. But she could share. He'd made her realize that her problem with trying to sell her art wasn't so much that she didn't think it was good enough, but that she didn't feel she had enough inside to give part of it away. She was wrong. The paintings she'd sold, first to Alan and then to buyers she didn't know, didn't feel like a loss. They felt like a release, like she had more room to create, to expand, without bursting, without contracting.

It was like the way she loved him. She could afford to show him everything she felt, good and bad, inside out, and the way he accepted it and made it part of who they were together gave her more freedom to continue without fear. He let her expand enough that she saw bits of abstraction in her own work along with more bits of realism and it was all fine. It didn't matter how it came out.

Jenna ran her fingers through the wet paint, tracing an outline of a heart as the colors, his and hers, swirled and mixed. It was finished.

And it had just started.

Turning back, she slid her clean hand under his shirt to rest on his stomach. "I think it's time for my little artist boy to strip for me."

He pressed close. "You forgot the scrawny part."

"No. I didn't. I was wrong. There's nothing at all scrawny about you. I just felt too big in comparison, too bulky, too ... in the way of myself, of us. And I was only letting myself see part of you because I didn't think I could handle the rest."

"And you do now? Think you can?"

"I know I can." She gave his a soft kiss.

"Come here." Trevor took her hand, the one with her fingers painted, wiped them with a cloth and swirled them in the yellow paint. He did his in red and led her upstairs, to their front door, grabbed the stool the kids sat on to get in and out of their shoes, and helped her up on it. One arm around her, he painted a heart with a long tail onto the wall above the door frame. She grinned and entwined it with a yellow heart. They put their first initials in the middle: *TJ*.

"This is forever, Jen."

"Longer. This is going to be longer than forever." Like a work of art itself, it would fade, crack, eventually disappear into oblivion, but its effects would linger in their children, their grandchildren, and in everyone they touched with their work, with their love, in the passion, the memories. In every stroke they created.

Epilogue

Jenna leaned in against her husband to add a few more touches to their canvas and listened to the murmurs rippling through the Peoria Art Guild. Along with the exhibition, she and Trevor agreed to do a demonstration of how they painted the canvases together.

"What do you think?" Trevor tilted his head back to see her.

"Done. Yes?"

"I'd say so."

"Your turn to sign."

"Not this time. Do it with me." He dipped the small brush into the black paint and waited until she took his hand around the brush. In the bottom right-hand corner of the new painting, they inscribed it *TJ Dade* and stepped back to look.

"What do you think, buddy?" Trevor brushed his fingers over the soft wisps of his son's hair and kissed his tiny head.

Jenna grinned and took the baby's fingers. "I don't think he could care less about this painting. Just don't put him down and he's fine."

"Maybe he doesn't yet, but he will, and this one we're keeping."

She couldn't answer before they were overwhelmed by the crowd praising the work and their method. The baby fussed, so Jenna pulled him out of the front carrier Trevor often held him in as they painted. Their son was attention needy, as Jenna was, so Trevor always teased. She didn't bother to deny it. "Okay Avery Dean, you're fine. Let's go find your brother and sister." She cuddled her little guy against her shoulder and excused herself to let Trevor handle the crowd, which he did so well.

Alan and Cheryl were nearby with all of the kids behaving terribly well beside them and looking terribly adorable all dressed up. Her friends offered to take the baby so she could stay with her husband and talk with their audience and buyers, but her mom jumped in and insisted on taking him. She'd been a big help since he was born, and before, mainly entertaining Aaron and Anna while Trevor was at work.

Joan came over to rave about how well their sales were going. The Italy paintings based on memories of their honeymoon and on photos Jenna took while there were doing especially well, she said. Jenna had professional photos of all of the paintings in their portfolio, since it was the only way she could convince herself to part with them.

"I think my wife is free. Ask her yourself."

She turned to find Trevor heading to her and went to meet him to keep the crowd farther from her children. Not that they minded. Aaron already told everyone he was going to be an *arch'tect* and build *big, big buildings.* Jenna had no doubt he would. He always watched close when she doodled houses in order to plan flower beds and painted pots and such around them and was drawing them himself. His kindergarten teacher was impressed with both his drawings and his pre-math abilities. The kid was definitely smart. Trevor always told Aaron he got it from his first dad. They'd been talking to him about Daniel ever since Trevor adopted him. Aaron Rhodes Dade sounded like a good architect name to her. She legally left his middle name in but they didn't use it. She wanted him to always know who he was.

Her husband had fussed when Jenna suggested Dean as the baby's middle name so it would be the same as his, since Trevor Dean Dade was why others called him D-Day, but he chose Avery, so the middle name was her choice. Anna already called her six week old brother Adie and it was starting to stick.

She managed to smile at the well dressed art patrons and converse with them easily enough. She thanked them genuinely and said yes there could be another show of both of their work in the future, but many of the paintings would be their separate work since they were ready to get back to that. And yes she loved painting side-by-side with him, but she also loved her solo work and seeing his solo work and Trevor joined in to insist doing their own thing as well was absolutely necessary.

The whole time they answered questions, his hand was on her back or sliding up to rest on her shoulder. When he noticed she was tired, he walked her over to sit beside Alan and reclaim her son. They were talking with Nate and Keisha about Anna so often being covered head to toe in dirt or mud. The girl reveled in trailing Alan on the job site and putting her little hands in the rich earth to help make holes, so he kept her with him once Jenna had been relegated to a supervisory, and sitting and painting, position while Aaron was in school.

Keisha asked if she was about ready to get back to playing in the dirt. Jenna shrugged. "Yes and no. I think I'm happy enough just doodling with my free hand right now." She kissed her son's cheek.

"And you need to just enjoy that as long as you want. They grow up far too fast." Alan played with the baby's fingers and looked over at his own children. "Before you know it, they'll take over the business and kick us old folks out of the way."

She chuckled. "Well, they might not want anything to do with art or dirt, you know."

"Could be. Except Justin already plans to be an architect and bring Aaron into business with him, and Anna will have a very green thumb within a couple of years if she doesn't lose interest."

"And the twins?"

He grinned at his youngest two, who were already eight, which was terribly hard for Jenna to believe. "I have no idea about those two yet. They bounce from one thing to the next in a matter of minutes."

"Like someone you know?" Jenna smiled at him.

"A little bit. And it'll be interesting to see what this one does."

"Yes. Our yellow child. Either way, we have the full palette."

A hand on her shoulder told her Trevor had returned already. Her mom nodded to someone across the room and reached down to take the baby. "My turn to show off my grandbabies. Aaron, Anna, come on dears. Come say hello to Grandma's friends." As she waited for them to get up, she leaned down to set a kiss on Jenna's head. "I'm proud of you, my dear child. You've done well."

She stared after her a minute, then held her unscrawny little artist boy tight and whispered a reminder that her doctor had given her clearance to be with him again.

"I remember. Trust me. And there's something I want you to do."

She threw him a grin. "Should you tell me here?"

He chuckled and brushed his fingers along her face. "Next trip is your call. Think about where you want to go. Anywhere."

"Hm, no. My call was settling here. Your call is where we travel. Choose the place, Trevor. I'm sure we can find inspiration anywhere."

Finishing Touches was my first published book, although it was the second I started when I got serious about writing fiction back in 1996. June 1996, to be exact, was when the first scene of the Rehearsal series came into existence (for the second time). Three years later, I started this story of a young artist and her constant debate with herself about whether or not she was good enough at painting to try to do something with it. It took four years to write, in between working on Rehearsal and taking a writing course and studying fiction, the process and publication methods, genres, expert opinions and commentaries, reading avidly, and of course wondering if my writing was good enough to do something with it.

I released it in June 2003. To date, with 8 published novels, some of my readers say it's still their favorite. And yet, it didn't feel quite finished. Jenna had only jumped from wandering onto a new path. Would it work? Time would tell. So I had to give her time, 3 years, and myself time, which turned out to be 10 years. At this point, I think we can both say yes, it's working, not without its flaws, but it is working.

Finishing Touches has been re-edited since I have learned a lot in ten years. *Final Strokes* is new. *The gallery* is the story of an artist, and of art and life in all of its colors, highlights, and shadows. It is set in my hometown area with flashes of real scenery and memories of real events, but it is fiction. It's also a lot of fact. Realism, if you will, with a touch of the surreal and abstract.

All art is personal. All life is art.

Thank you to all of those who have stuck with me through this venture so far, who encourage me on a regular basis, who keep asking for the next to come. I have many canvases waiting, some part finished, some lightly sketched, and others still blank. Let's see just how many we can create together.

Thank you to my early art teachers: my uncle, artist and musician Les Whisler; my grandma, teacher and artist Joyce Whisler who always encouraged us to be creative; and high school art teacher Valerie Kruzan who taught technique well enough any of us could have become artists. To my English teacher Mrs. Peterson who constantly encouraged my writing interests. And to those teachers in non-art classes who put up with doodles all over my notes and homework and folders. Doodling while listening helped me actually hear. Also, thanks to Lowpoint-Washburn High School for allowing me to take Art IV when there was no such class in the syllabus. To Mike, my classmate and cousin, who asked several years ago what I was doing with my art: how's this?

Thank you to Duncan Faure who allowed use of his lyrics at the end of *Finishing Touches*. The lyrics in chapter twenty-two are from *Love Is Yours And Mine*. ©1981 Duncan Faure Music

Thank you also to Brynn Kanikula of the Peoria Art Guild for assistance with Peoria museum and exhibit information. Find them at www.PeoriaArtGuild.org.

Finally: to my beta readers and editors Liz Ferguson, Kathi Hawkins, Dorothy Murphy, and Annette McRoberts. Writing is never a solitary venture.
On to the next...

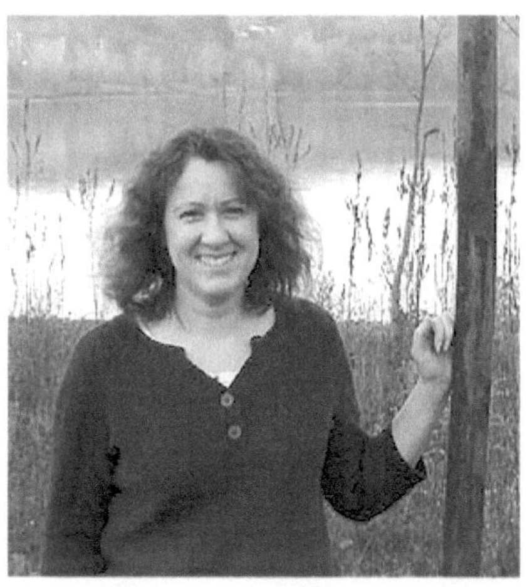

LK Hunsaker is the author of a string of novels centered around the arts and societal issues. Raised in Central Illinois in the midst of an artistic family and surrounded by cornfields, she married a career soldier and spent the next 20 years moving around the U.S. and abroad. During that time, she raised two children, worked a few odd jobs, finished her psychology degree, and embarked on a writing career. She and her husband are now settled in Western Pennsylvania surrounded by trees and lakes, but they still get restless feet and the urge to travel.

LKHunsaker.com
ElucidatePublishing.net